P9-DFQ-943

INVASION OF PRIVACY

By the same author:

MOTION TO SUPPRESS

INVASION OF PRIVACY

PERRI O'SHAUGHNESSY

Published by
Delacorte Press
Bantam Doubleday Dell Publishing Group, Inc.
1540 Broadway
New York, New York 10036

Library of Congress Cataloging in Publication Data

O'Shaughnessy, Perri.
Invasion of privacy / by Perri O'Shaughnessy.
p. cm.
ISBN 0-385-31413-2 (HC)
1. Women lawyers—United States—Fiction. I. Title.
PS3565.S542I58 1996 96-1251
CIP

Manufactured in the United States of America
Published simultaneously in Canada

August 1996

10 9 8 7 6 5 4 3 2 1
BVG

Dedicated to
Brad and Fritz

In memory of
Katherine G. Wright of Owego, New York
and
Rhoda Snedecor of Dallas, Texas

Once again, our grateful thanks to
Nancy Yost and Marjorie Braman.

INVASION OF PRIVACY

Through me you pass into the city of woe.

—*Commedia,* Dante

BOOK ONE

Twelve Years Ago: Tamara

On the other side of Tamara's locked bedroom door, her mother was pounding and yelling again. She yelled often, most often at Tamara, but when she was loaded she also yelled at Tam's father, who had an unpredictable, violent streak Tamara had learned to avoid. She guessed her mother used alcohol to stand up to her bully of a father, and also in the same way Tam did, to create a more tolerable reality, so she understood the attraction of being bombed. That didn't make finding her mother passed out on the kitchen floor after one of her periodic binges any easier to take, though.

Lately, things seemed worse around the old burg. Two weekends in a row now her mother had gone on a bender, and her father's response had been to tear through the house, breaking up most of the dining room one evening.

"Okay already, I'm putting it out right now." She took another long drag on her cigarette, and blew the smoke at the doorway. Her mother, temporarily placated by her words, retreated, probably to get another drink. Tam sat on her bed, trying to build her strength up for the battle to come, the one she thought of as her standard Friday night war. Her parents never wanted her to go out, but she was eighteen and had a right and they knew it. Still, she had to convince them, stormtrooping her way through a barrage of

questions, arguments, sometimes tears. Oh, God, it was hard living at home. She couldn't wait to have her own place.

Which brought up another depressing issue, her lack of money. She was flunking math and geology in school, something her parents didn't know yet, but they would soon. Maybe then they'd let her get a job. She knew they were holding on to this old college dream for her, one she'd given up a while back, along with her dreams of staying forever with the first man she'd ever really loved. Life had taken an unexpected turn for her, and she discovered right away that she liked not knowing what came next. She liked pissing into the wind like a man, and seeing which way it blew, without caring who or what it hit.

She took a deep breath, stuffed her last bills into her pants pocket, and unlocked her door. She grabbed her rabbit coat. That was a must. A storm was coming. The windchill made the temperature feel like zero degrees all around Tahoe tonight, the radio said. She really ought to wear her down jacket; that kept her warmer. But not tonight, no, that wouldn't do, would it? She needed her favorite coat tonight. . . . She put it on and smiled, ready for anything the evening had to offer, as she walked downstairs to confront her parents.

She nursed the old pickup slowly along the slick Pioneer Trail to Manny's, pulling into a parking spot right by the front door. She was still going over the evening's fight in her mind. No matter how nice she was, no matter how hard she tried, they hated everything about her. They wanted her chained to the old person she was a long time ago, their baby girl, forever. They hated the way she looked, the clothes she wore, that "ratty" coat. They hated her attitude. They hated everything she said, trying to talk over her, afraid to listen, afraid of what they might hear. She couldn't go on like this!

Shake it off, she told herself. Don't let them totally burn you out. She tried an old trick, rewriting the evening into a silent conversation with her parents that ended better, with everyone civilized and normal, and her like any other girl just going out for a few hours to have a little fun, but it didn't work tonight. Their words stung. Their anger hurt. She sat in the car, letting her own anger flare up and burn for a few minutes, until she started to feel the deep winter of the outside creeping into her car. She walked into Manny's without looking around and sat at the bar, ordering a gin for a quick, clean buzz. They didn't even bother to check her fake ID. She'd left the house a little early. The fun started later; meanwhile, she intended to kill an hour or so sitting in a dark corner, just her and Mr. Alcohol for company.

"Hey, Tam!" said a voice across the room.

Oh, no. She turned to look, spotting Michael and Doreen across the room. She gave them a wave and turned back to her drink. It would be Michael. He was like a black cat crossing her path, a curse on her. Maybe if she ignored him they'd leave her alone.

They approached, Michael eager as a racehorse after the starting shot, Doreen trailing miserably behind.

"Mind if we join you?" he asked, sliding his jeans onto a stool beside her and ordering a beer. He winked at her, and sat as close as he could without touching. Doreen stood near them both, looking unsure about where to put herself. Tam ordered another drink and put it away as fast as she could.

Michael launched into a monologue about what he'd been doing lately. When he noticed she wasn't listening, he switched gears and started pebbling her with questions. He'd heard about her troubles in school. She'd always been smarter than any of them, and was certainly the best looking of them all. What was going on? And what was the story with this new dude she was seeing, huh? Was it true this was the man to see if you had it in mind to get wasted?

She didn't feel like getting involved in his song and dance, and she told him so. She didn't know what it was with him, but any attention from her just made things worse. He seemed to think she was bored, so he talked faster and more vehemently, probably just trying to get her interested in what he was saying, but he made her nervous and jumpy, and she didn't need that. He kept after her, picking and picking, jealous of the mystery boy he thought she might be meeting tonight, and unable to lose the topic, like a parakeet that knows only one word and shows it off day and night until you go bonkers.

Sick of him, she tossed her beer in his face. He closed his mouth, looking hurt, his lip trembling like a baby's.

While Doreen mopped him up, she went to make a phone call. It was late enough.

She went to pay for her drink and had one more brief fracas with Michael while Doreen stood by, looking disgusted. He apologized. He wanted them to be friends. He insisted on paying.

Fine, let him. She was down to her last few bucks. She left without saying good-bye.

The truck balked at first, but finally started. She headed up the highway toward the turnoff, then tackled the unplowed road in four-wheel drive. A bright moon cast shadows over the road, lighting the way. She pulled off the road and checked her watch. It was time.

Glad to have her warmest boots on, she slipped and slid up the trail to their rock. Her friend would meet her there.

But he was late and there was nothing there, except the moon and the shadows that moved in the wind. Nothing there, she told herself. But as the minutes ticked by, and the darkness settled around her like a freezing shroud, she thought there might be something. She felt eyes, even though she couldn't see them. She felt afraid. She thought about leaving, but that would wreck everything. She needed something from him to keep her going, just this once. This would be the last time.

She would give him one more minute.

1

Blue mountain air, the crunch of boots on snow, a deep breath, and one long last look at the snow-laden evergreen forest around her—Nina Reilly walked into the court building with lips as cold and blue as the Tahoe winter, entering the Superior Court arena for the first time since she had left the hospital.

She had a nice, peaceful preliminary injunction hearing, with some interesting legal issues, a civil case, the kind that gets decided on the paperwork, on the intellectual arguments she had thought, way back in law school, that practicing law was all about.

No more criminal law, she had promised herself. No more contact with physical violence and murderous emotions. She'd had enough to last a lifetime. She had made simple resolutions in the hospital—to practice a kinder, gentler law, and to leave the office at five o'clock.

Today she would keep her resolutions, if she could avoid sparring with her opposing counsel, the pugnacious Jeffrey Riesner, and keep Terry London, her headstrong client, away from the people who were suing her.

As she started up the stairs to the main Superior Court courtroom, she heard Terry's voice behind her. "Can't go wrong with navy blue."

"Thanks." Nina chose to hear the comment as a compliment. "You look good too. Are you ready for the fight?" She turned to let her client join her.

Terry London was a tall, slender woman. Today the icy wind outside had tangled a mass of long, curly chestnut hair. Her face had become sculpted over forty years into hard beauty with a large, full mouth and pale, flawless skin.

But darkness circled her eyes, and her mouth bore a slash of red lipstick too dramatic and citified for Tahoe. A white wool pantsuit with an ocher scarf amplified the intensity of her yellowish-brown eyes. She held a full-length fur coat, silvery and thick enough to disappear inside.

"Sure, why not. I've got the current champ on my side," Terry said. The two women climbed up the stairs. At the landing Terry stopped Nina and said, "I expect you to maul them."

"Our chances are good, as I told you."

"It's not your job to take chances," Terry said as they stepped into the second-floor hallway. "Not with my business, anyway."

"I'll do my best."

"Yeah," said Terry. "Win."

Jeffrey Riesner waited for Nina on the second floor. One glance at him and she could feel her hackles, whatever those were, begin to rise. Remember, she said to herself, a kinder, gentler Nina. . . .

"May I have a moment with you, counselor?" he said, the polite words asked with unmistakable mockery.

"See you inside, Terry," Nina said, unable to avoid noticing as Riesner's eyes followed Terry's gently swaying ass. He kept at it long enough to make sure she noticed. The rest of the crowd had gone inside, leaving them in the dim hall.

Nina forced herself to turn and acknowledge him, telling herself again to stay calm. Even in her high heels she had to tilt her head up sharply to make eye contact. She could smell the acrid, musky scent of his aftershave, mixed with his sour coffee breath. From a foot above her, the opaque eyes looking down from his long, mean face glittered with suppressed rage.

Her entry onto the Tahoe legal scene the year before as defense counsel in a murder case had angered him. He had made it clear from the start he didn't like competitors, especially women, and he didn't let manners deter the open expression of his feelings.

Worst of all was the fixed way he watched her, like a snake before it struck. . . . Jeffrey Riesner was an ugly guy, and he was about to get uglier, she could tell.

"Couldn't wait to see me again, could you?" he asked, adjusting the immaculate Hermès tie he wore to accent his thousand-dollar suit and offensive grin.

"I managed to pass the time somehow." Her voice sounded good, strong and confident.

"I've been looking forward to a moment alone with you, Nina." Somehow he had cornered her.

She had avoided being alone with this particular lawyer ever since she first met him. Did it have to be today? Mentally she sighed, put her resolution on the shelf, climbed into her armor, unsheathed her battle sword, and held her shield over her heart.

"We're not on a first-name basis," she said. "It's Ms. Reilly to you—"

"What I am trying to say is," he interrupted, ignoring her, "that I have again consulted my clients, and they have again asked me to try to settle this matter. Persuade your client to can the psycho-killer stuff, and the aspersions of parental drunkenness, and we can go somewhere with this thing."

"My client isn't willing to let them censor her film. She won't edit it to suit their sense of propriety. I've presented your proposal, and she says no, absolutely not."

"You could try exerting a little control over her."

"Don't tell me how to deal with my clients," Nina said. "This lady has her mind made up, and she's within her rights. Now, do you have any practical suggestions about how this matter could be settled?"

Riesner shrugged. "I told them it was useless to try to talk to you. You've got your rent to pay, don't you? I hear you stopped taking criminal cases. Those bad ol' crooks are too scary. And if you settle this case, you won't make enough of the do-re-mi. I told them all that. They understand."

"You're going to lose this case and you know it, but you push your clients in deeper just because you're itching for a fight with little old me." Her voice shook a little. She was so mad, she could feel her throat choking on the words.

"There, there," Riesner said, smiling widely, making a motion as if to pat her head, and withdrawing his hand without actually touching her. "Why don't you ladies agree to the injunction? Then you can go have tea and talk about your hair and nails."

"We'll have a nice time totting up the court costs your clients will owe my client. Meanwhile, I have work to do, even if you don't." She turned to leave, but he blocked her way.

"Wait. I just want to show you something," he said. "See this?" Her eyes drew automatically down to his white, big-knuckled right hand. On his ring finger, embedded in thick gold, a ruby gleamed. "Stanford Law School. Class of '72."

What was he going to do with it, slug her? She braced herself, looking past him in the empty hall for help, but she saw only Terry London peering around the door, her face avid, as if she were feeding on the encounter.

"I've been around a little longer than you, Nina, quite a bit longer actually. And I want you to know, your intransigent attitude in this case is exactly what I would have expected. Because all you lady lawyers, and I use both of those terms loosely, have to rely on bravado, having lost—"

"Move it," Nina said, putting all her weight into slamming against his shoulder, pushing her way past.

"—all vestiges of feminine charm," he said, regaining his balance. "My, my. Here we stand chatting, and our clients are waiting for us inside. Shall we?" He strode ahead to open the door for her.

Deputy Kimura stood just inside the main doors to the courtroom, his heavy key ring jingling as he hung it back on his belt next to the holster. He smiled at Nina as she walked inside. He had been the bailiff on duty in the main courtroom on that day three months before when Nina was shot. "Don't worry," he said to her as she walked past, patting the holster. His words, meant to be reassuring, brought it all back. He went to the front of the court, and Nina tagged along after him, carrying her heavy briefcase up the aisle.

Sweet v. London was the only case on the eleven o'clock docket, but the room seemed jammed.

Along with the strangers in back row, Nina recognized a news reporter for the *Tahoe Mirror*. She would bet some of the spectators came merely to luxuriate in the warmth of the overheated court. She wondered if they realized they probably paid more for this comfort through their taxes than they paid on monthly furnace fees.

Jessica and Jonathan Sweet, two of Riesner's clients, sat near the middle. They turned and watched her approach. "Hello," she said pleasantly. She would not blame them for Jeffrey Riesner.

Today Jonathan Sweet wore a black sweater and baggy khakis, which with his boyish face made him look about thirty instead of fifty-two. He was a real estate investor, with several precious, undeveloped lots on the Nevada side of Lake Tahoe. He sat in his wheelchair, partially blocking the aisle, next to his wife. Mrs. Sweet, whose gray hair was cropped short, looked much older than her husband, but tanned and healthy from her work at a local ski resort. She fidgeted in her seat. They nodded at Nina's greeting.

Next to them, Riesner's other clients in the case, Doreen and Michael Ordway, ignored her greeting. These two looked to be in their middle thirties. Ordway wore a windbreaker and cowboy boots, as if he had just ridden in from the range. His wife wore her long, gold-streaked hair down her back, and a purple leather miniskirt that cried, hey, look at me!

Nina stopped at the gate that separated the audience's seats from the lawyers' area, taking it all in again. A large room lit to brutal brightness, its center formed by the counsel tables and the high judge's bench, a little *circus maximus* where the gladiators fought each day. The empty jury box on the right, where a couple of lawyers lounged. The scribes toiling at their tiny desks below the judge's bench. The bailiff at his desk on the side, behind a new transparent bulletproof shield, answering the phone. And behind her, Romans in the rows of seats, bloodthirsty, spoiling for the fight.

Really, the adversarial system was one hell of a primitive way to settle a dispute.

⋆ ⋆ ⋆

The clock on the wall said eleven-fifteen. Judge Milne was late. Nina had thought everything was ready, but she began feeling unsteady as she sat down at the defendant's counsel table next to Terry and took out her files, too aware of the attentive eyes behind her.

The scene in the hall with Riesner had been business as usual, and she'd stayed cool—well, as cool as she could. As for Terry, all clients had their drawbacks. She preferred an intelligent client, and Terry was certainly intelligent, though she was also on the hostile side.

She was perfectly fine, she told herself, perfectly safe. And . . .

This was the chair she had been sitting in right before . . . She had been standing in front of that witness box. . . . She had turned and seen the gun suddenly swing toward her, watched the finger pull the trigger from less than twenty feet away. . . . She should be dead. . . .

She squared her shoulders, fighting off the emotional overload, dragging her eyes away from the spot a few feet away where she had fallen. That case was over.

Terry sat at her left at the counsel table, quietly wary. On her right, Jeffrey Riesner set his briefcase down on the plaintiff's table and began pulling out his files.

Deputy Kimura said, "All rise. The Superior Court of the County of El Dorado is now in session, the Honorable Curtis E. Milne presiding." You could almost hear the trumpets. Judge Milne appeared on the bench, flipping open his own file. Nina couldn't help a quick nod to the emperor who would do a thumbs-up or a thumbs-down in his ceremonial robes.

The court reporter flexed her hands and crouched over her machine, and Edith Dillon, the henna-haired clerk at the desk under the judge's dais, began to wield her pen over a fresh pink form.

"Be seated," the bailiff said. Everyone sat down except the two lawyers. Nina stood up straight, as tall as five feet three inches plus Italian pumps allowed.

"*Sweet v. London,*" Milne said, opening a thick file. "A hearing on a preliminary injunction, is that right, Mr. Riesner? All parties and counsel of record are present?"

"Yes, Your Honor," Riesner said.

"Welcome back, Ms. Reilly. We've missed you," the judge said, giving her a small smile.

"Thank you, Your Honor. I'm glad to be back," Nina said.

She watched Milne carefully, but his face was a model of judicial decorum. He gave no clue about his mood, the effects of his breakfast, or his reaction to the briefs he had read. He pooched out his lower lip and tapped it thoughtfully with a finger. "Proceed," he said.

Riesner threw his papers down on the table, leaned on it, and said, "The court has on file our complaint for invasion of privacy, declaratory relief, and breach of contract. The relief sought in the complaint is an injunction providing that the defendant, Theresa London, be permanently prohibited from showing, publishing in any manner, distributing for sale, licensing, promoting or otherwise publicizing the existence of, copying, or otherwise disseminating in any manner a film of approximately one hour in length known as *Where Is Tamara Sweet?*

"I will summarize the basic facts briefly.

"Tamara Sweet disappeared in 1984 at the age of eighteen from South Lake Tahoe. Because she had talked about leaving for some time, and had some problems at home, and because there was no evidence of foul play, the authorities chose not to consider her disappearance a criminal matter.

"Over the years, Mr. and Mrs. Sweet have worked with missing persons organizations and hired private investigators in an attempt to locate their daughter. To no avail—"

"Counsel," the judge interrupted, "you've covered all this in your Points and Authorities. Let's move along to the film."

"Certainly, Judge." Riesner picked up his brief, flipped a few pages, and said, "Twelve years have gone by, distressing, sorrowful years for her parents. Then, on January tenth last year, the defendant, Terry London, contacted the parents and asked them if they would be interested in having a film made about their daughter's disappearance, a film that might help them find out what happened to her. Naturally, they agreed.

"The defendant has filmed and produced several video documentaries and appeared well qualified to undertake the project. The Sweets opened their records and their hearts to Ms. London. They authorized Ms. London to review Tamara's school records, talk to her old friends, do whatever was possible to help make the film.

"And make the film she did. But rather than a well-intentioned film that might prove helpful in ascertaining the facts about a lost young woman, Terry London exploited access to private materials to make a film that depicts Jonathan Sweet as a self-absorbed and selfish father, Jessica Sweet as an alcoholic mother, and Tamara Sweet as a promiscuous, drug-abusing woman of questionable morality." Riesner paused for effect.

"The other two plaintiffs in this lawsuit, Michael and Doreen Ordway, who were close friends of Tamara Sweet and who saw her on the night of her disappearance, have similarly been depicted as immoral, semi-alcoholic, selfish, and uncaring.

"In creating each of these depictions, the defendant has very carefully chosen only those facts that support the depiction. In other words, technically she hasn't libeled the plaintiffs, because the facts chosen were true. But she has emphasized private facts in a way that has caused them great emotional distress.

"And there is one instance in which she has ventured into an area of wild speculation. She has attempted to link Tamara Sweet's disappearance to several other disappearances of young women in this area over the last twelve years. Her 'theory' that Tamara Sweet was murdered along with these other women is completely without foundation, and you can imagine how it makes the parents feel, Judge.

"They met with the defendant after she invited them to preview the film, and tried to explain their feelings about the distortions of truth they perceived, but she has repeatedly refused to discuss any kind of compromise. The defendant has already negotiated an agreement to have the film shown on a major television network. The declarations of the defendants, Your Honor, can only give the slightest indication of the mental anguish viewing the film and anticipating its national exhibition is causing the plaintiffs—"

"You have five minutes, counsel."

As Riesner sped up, his deep voice stepped up slightly in volume, giving his final words added power. "Distraught, the plaintiffs turned to me, Your Honor. Today we ask the court for a preliminary injunction that will last until such time as the court's calendar permits a full hearing on the issue of a permanent injunction. Since that could be a year or two down the line, Your Honor, and the temporary restraining order expires today, we need this interim order to prevent the irreparable harm to these good people that would come of finishing and distributing this film."

Milne's pen scratched over a pad. Nina turned to gauge the reactions of Riesner's clients to his statement. He turned his head to the side. For an instant their eyes met.

Terry elbowed Nina. "How's he doing?" she whispered, indicating Riesner.

"Fair to middling. We're up soon," Nina muttered back as Riesner began again, his tone now soft, intimate.

"To rush on to the applicable law, Your Honor. It is the plaintiffs' burden to show that there is a substantial likelihood they will prevail at the time of the hearing on the permanent injunction. The other legal requirements are briefed in our points and authorities. At this time I would like to discuss the tort of invasion of privacy.

"The law provides that the plaintiffs may prevent the public disclosure of private facts which are offensive and objectionable to a reasonable person. The court has declarations affirming that the plaintiffs in this case are deeply offended. They object strongly enough to have entered into this lawsuit and to have retained the best possible counsel." He cleared his throat so that the words had time to register with the judge. "It is not necessary to show these matters are false, Your Honor, only that they are private.

"Second, plaintiffs' privacy rights are violated by publicity that places a person in a false light in the public eye. It is easy in editing hours and hours of raw film footage to twist true facts into a false picture, Your Honor, and that is what the defendant has done.

"As Justice Stanley Mosk stated in his concurring opinion in the Lugosi case, cited in our brief, quoting Prosser, 'The gist of the cause of action in a privacy case is . . . a direct wrong of a personal character resulting in injury to the feelings. . . . The injury is mental and subjective. It impairs the mental peace and comfort of the person and may cause suffering much more acute than that caused by bodily injury.' "

Milne heaved a restive sigh to let Riesner know his patience had worn away.

"The film in question, *Where Is Tamara Sweet?,* is going to have just such an effect on the plaintiffs, Your Honor. Private facts are cavalierly and callously disclosed. A false, indeed, a coarse light is cast over their lives. The facts have been twisted and will be passed on to the public so the defendant can profit from my clients' misery. . . ."

Riesner's gestures had become wide and expansive, his voice louder and louder as he upped the drama. Listeners anticipated the grand finale, and sat up straight to see better. Nina waited for him to go over the top, as he always did, usually to the delight of juries.

"The defendant's perverted take on the story of Tamara Sweet is designed to play down to a similarly voyeuristic and prurient audience. She's a sick opportunist with a crude goal: to make big bucks at other people's expense.

"Do the right thing, Your Honor. Tell Peeping Terry she's looked through the wrong window.

"Tell her it's curtains for her and her sick little film."

Silence in the court. The only smiles came from the middle of the room where the Sweets sat, holding hands. Milne wiped his glasses on his robe, rubbing his eyes before putting them back on. Nina knew he had a criminal trial resuming at eleven-thirty. He had no time for wordplay. She felt the weight of the crushing time pressure caused by too many cases and too few judges, which made attorneys forget their best points and judges miss the ones they remembered to say.

"Ms. Reilly? Would you care to respond?" Milne was saying. She picked up her notes, gulping the dry air, as the courtroom waited for the first words to issue forth from her empty mind. Up you go. . . .

"Just a few brief points, Your Honor. Let me first introduce my client, Theresa London." The judge gravely inclined his head. Terry also nodded, as Nina had coached her to do, and sat back down gracefully.

"Opposing counsel's bombast aside, Your Honor, Terry London has been working on this film for over a year. She has put countless hours and a lot of her own money into it. It's a work of art, based on truth. The world will be able to judge its merit. The plaintiffs, Tamara Sweet's parents and friends, encouraged Ms. London to make this film because they thought it might help them to locate her. And now they want to destroy it. Why?"

Nina caught Milne's eye, held it, and made him listen.

"Our expert, Monty Glasser, producer of the television series

Real-Life Riddles, says this film has considerable artistic merit. As a documentary, it takes a point of view. The plaintiffs are offended by the filmmaker's point of view, because the film portrays them without masks, as they are, no more and no less.

"That's what this lawsuit is all about.

"But the film doesn't belong to the plaintiffs. They did not finance it; they did not labor over it; it is not their artistic effort.

"The United State Supreme Court doesn't look kindly on muzzling artistic expression in this country. Plaintiffs don't know what the reaction of the public to this film is going to be, Your Honor, so there has been no harm to them. There may be no harm. To prevent a book or film from even being made public is prior restraint. It's the kind of First Amendment censorship our courts are least likely to order."

Milne looked at the clock. Even the United States Constitution didn't sing for him today. Nina decided to finish quickly, with her best ammo.

"And, of course, the plaintiffs can't win this case on the merits," Nina said. "One of our affirmative defenses makes it a lost cause. Consent, Your Honor."

Milne stopped writing and gave her his full attention.

"This is really just a simple contract matter. Let's assume for the sake of argument that the film does invade the privacy of the plaintiffs under the usual definitions," Nina said. That woke everybody up.

"The contracts my client made with the plaintiffs said that she was going to make a documentary about the circumstances surrounding the disappearance of Tamara Sweet based on film footage she gathered, and that she reserved the sole right to edit the footage. It's all here in the exhibits, signed, dated, and notarized. Consent was given in the broadest possible terms.

"There's no invasion of privacy if there was consent. It's as simple as that. The plaintiffs had the right to say no, I don't think I want to participate. But no one ever said that, Your Honor. These people gave their consent to be filmed, so there's no case, and we should all go home."

Nina turned and looked at Jonathan and Jessica Sweet, as if challenging them to rise meekly and file out the door, but they just sat there, looking shaken. She quelled a stray pang of compassion. They were suing her client. They were the enemy.

"In short, Your Honor, this case meets none of the requirements for issuance of a preliminary injunction. There's no proof the plaintiffs will be harmed by this film. There's no tort, because there was consent to the filming and no agreement the plaintiffs could take part in editing the film. The equities are in favor of the defendant. And there's a strong constitutional reason for not issuing the injunction—namely, that this film is protected free speech."

Milne nodded. Riesner scowled. Nina allowed herself a slight smile.

"Last of all, Mr. Riesner has called my client a voyeur, and a sick opportunist, and asks this court to tell her, quote, she's looked through the wrong window. . . ."

Nobody was breathing. Nina smiled.

"She only recorded what was already there, the dirt, cobwebs, and cockroaches. I suggest to the court that she was invited in, and it's bad law to try to make her pretend the house was clean."

Nina sat down. Terry gave her a thumbs-up under the counsel table.

"Thank you," Milne said. "The Court will take this matter under submission." He went through his private door, chuckling.

A few minutes later, Nina and her client stood just outside the courtroom doors, alone. The first snowflakes swirled past them at a forty-five-degree angle from a steely sky. Terry's fur coat brushed sensuously against Nina's hand just as she was pulling on her glove.

"Lynx," Terry said. "Just the thing to wear on a freezing day like today. Women want to bury their faces in it. Men want to bury their pricks in it. So, did we win?"

"It went fine. We'll know in a few days, when the Minute Order comes out. I'll call you right away." Nina said. Unwritten rule of legal practice number 678: Never promise a client she'll win, particularly Terry, who had now buried her own hard nose in her fur.

"You never know, though," Nina went on, tucking her long brown hair under her upturned coat collar. "Sometimes judges make the wrong decisions, and then you have to appeal. I still don't understand why you won't make a few changes to the film, Terry, delete the part about Jessica Sweet being a regular barfly, and the bit about Jonathan Sweet being unemployed for two years around then. And your theory that she was murdered by some psycho lurking around Tahoe. Even if we win today, the trial itself could be lengthy and costly."

Terry's face, white as milk against the soft gray of the lynx, looked sly. She stepped closer to Nina, and Nina felt the lush fur brush her again. "Did you see the woman from the *Tahoe Mirror* in back?" Terry asked.

"Yes."

"Controversy. Lawsuits. Publicity. Worth every dime. This is my chance. No more chamber of commerce propaganda films. No more PBS shit that pays close enough to nothing. After this is shown, I'll be able to get the backing for a full-length feature film. It's already in the planning stages. And it'll blow everyone away. I'll be rich and famous. Riesner got it right. He's an asshole, but he reads me right."

"That's not what you told me at my office. You said you had put your heart and soul into this work of art—"

"And a hundred fifty grand, mostly borrowed."

Nina realized then that she disliked Terry. The First Amendment was America's most shining statement of liberty. She had taken this case because it presented a constitutional issue, but Terry mocked it while she hid behind it.

Terry said, "Come on, don't give me that high-minded crap you gave the judge. You're not that naive. You look like one thing, but you're really something else, hmm? Soft on the outside, doe-eyed. Curvy little female body. Inside overloaded with that big bulldoggy brain. I saw you push Riesner away. That was gutsy. He must outweigh you by a hundred pounds."

Nina said, "Well. Call you next week, as soon as we get the judge's decision." And when I get it, I'm outta this case, she said to herself.

"Don't you want to know how Riesner's right?" Terry said. "I mean, between you and me, confidentially of course?"

"Okay. How's he right?"

Terry leaned close, pushed Nina's hair away from her ear. The snow had begun falling. The lynx coat pressed against her, deep and warm and sensual, but made after all from carnivores. "I am a pervert," she whispered. "Maybe someday you'll find out some of the things I've seen and done. I gave up on conventional standards a long time ago, and I'm not just talking art here."

Nina cleared her throat, moving away, thinking that no one knew what lawyers had to put up with on a daily basis. "I see."

"Wait," Terry said, taking her by the arm to stop her. "I want to ask you something—you lived in Monterey before coming to Tahoe, right? I mean, you've been up here less than a year."

"That's right, except for a few years in San Francisco. Of course, I spent almost all my summers up here."

Terry stared at her. "I'll just bet you did," she said, nodding, her initial astonishment slowly giving way to a more calculating expression. "How is it I never made the connection before? I saw you with Riesner, and it started me thinking. . . . Here I am going through life congratulating myself on how damn smart I am. Well, is my face red. I thought I'd hire the new local hotshot woman lawyer, do my bit for the females of the world. And look what I got!" she said. "You, of all people."

"What are you talking about?"

Terry let go of Nina's arm and stood a few feet away, seeming to study or memorize her features. Then, in a burst, as if she couldn't help herself, she began to laugh, and the laugh built until tears ran down her cheeks. "Gotcha!" she said suddenly, stepping toward Nina, then back. "Gotcha!"

Nina moved far enough away to feel she had an adequate safety zone between her and her client. People passed in the hallway, some noticing Terry's crazy laughter, some ignoring everything. Some time passed before the torrent spent itself, and Terry's face spasmed back into focus, reorganizing into the person Nina had thought she knew.

"Are you all right?" Nina finally ventured to ask.

"Me?" Terry said, her voice miraculously restored to normal. "If I were you," she said slowly, "I'd worry more about myself." She turned, her heels clacking on the hard floor and out the door into the snow, enveloped in her dead skin, looking like a strange thing, an animal walking upright with a human head.

2

AT NINA'S OFFICE, IN THE OUTER ROOM BY THE DOOR TO THE HALL OF the Starlake Building, an elderly man in a tan parka and slacks waited for his free half-hour consultation, leafing through one of her state bar journals, his eyes uncomprehending. The only other magazines out on the rack beside the client chairs were a Native American monthly and the Greenpeace newsletter. A new basket in the corner held unidentifiable dried plants. Sandy Whitefeather, her secretary, had been at it again, trying to remake the office into a style Nina privately thought of as nouveau tribal.

Sandy was a Washoe Native American, one of the tribes of people who had lived at Tahoe for ten thousand years before the prospectors and millionaire vacationers and gamblers came, and she let no one forget it. The Oriental rug Nina had started out with, the black-and-white photographs, the ferns—all had disappeared, item by item, over the months, to be replaced by bright hangings and striped woolen rugs and baskets.

Sandy had once been Jeffrey Riesner's file clerk and she still resented being treated as his firm's token minority employee. Although she had been Nina's legal secretary for only a few months, she was now the solid backbone of Nina's solo practice. Since the beginning, when Nina opened up at Tahoe after a sudden flight from San Francisco and her five-year marriage to Jack McIntyre, Sandy had brought in clients, whipped off the paperwork, and, after the shooting, kept things going while Nina convalesced.

Today she wore a new skirt, a bold black-and-white print, with a long black overblouse and heavy silver jewelry, and black boots. She was stapling the appellate brief Nina had dictated the day before, while keeping a vigilant eye on the new client.

"Hi, I'm Nina Reilly," Nina said to him, walking over and shaking his hand. "I'll be with you in five minutes. Sandy, would you come into my office?"

She stood by the door as Sandy walked in, her slow and dignified tread a protest against being diverted from her task. Nina went to her lakeside window and looked for her favorite sight—the goliath Mount Tallac, almost ten thousand feet of snow and ice on the western horizon, jutting into the sky, soaring above the infinite blue of Lake Tahoe, which she could glimpse through the trees. The mountain put her puny troubles with Riesner and Terry into perspective.

Sandy had chosen the more comfortable of the two orange client chairs. "Did you win?" she said, right to the point.

"Milne took it under submission. We'll hear in a few days."

"How did it go?"

"Fine, I guess. Riesner collared me in the hallway and tried to bully me, and Terry dropped all pretense of being a suffering artist who can't deal with these small minds attacking her. She's in this for the money. I wrapped her in the flag, talked about the Constitution, but after talking with her afterward, I wondered why I even took the case."

"It's how you cover my paycheck each month," Sandy said. "How did you feel, being back in that courtroom?"

"I had a couple of bad minutes. I found myself examining the floor for bloodstains. I felt eyes on my back. I was hunching my shoulders, waiting for the blast. Then Milne came in, and I forgot all about it."

"That's good," Sandy said, nodding.

"I'm taking only civil cases, Sandy. I mean it. I don't want that kind of fear haunting me ever again. But I'm starting to wonder if civil cases are any different. I had to fight just as hard, and we were all splashing around in a sea full of bad feeling, as usual."

"Admit it. You enjoy the fight," Sandy said.

"Yeah. I haven't lost that."

"My nephew got shot two years ago, cleaning his gun. It left a circular scar on his foot; looks a lot like the one on your chest. Know what he did?"

"I can't wait to hear."

"He got a tattoo on top of it. A rose."

"Why a rose?"

"He doesn't have much imagination. What I'm sayin' is, his foot looks like an art object instead of a—"

"I'm not going to get a tattoo, Sandy. You're not going to decorate me too."

"I was thinking for you, maybe, a smoking gun," Sandy said.

"Which reminds me of why I asked you to come in here. I want you to put *Time* back in the magazine rack, and *Ladies' Home Journal,* and *Sports Illustrated.* Nobody wants to read the stuff you have out there."

"Reactionary drivel," Sandy said. "We have an obligation to bring people politically up to speed."

"That's not my business here. The magazines are to keep stressed-out people in a good mood until I can get to them. And reading about the evils of French nuclear testing is not going to relax them."

Sandy considered, and saw Nina wasn't going to back down. "Could we keep *Native American Life*?"

"If we must."

"Okay. Here's Mr. Powell's Client Interview Sheet. Divorce."

"Send him in." The rest of the day began.

Matt opened the door and grabbed the grocery bag from her arms. Nina's brother wore his baseball cap and a 49ers sweatshirt, though the living room was warm from the fireplace. "Drop everything! Plan B!" was all he said as he made for the kitchen. He was two years younger than Nina, and, she usually thought, much wiser.

He had straightened out early, married, fathered two kids, built himself a home, and stayed here. He'd grown up gracefully.

When she and her son had moved to Tahoe last spring, Matt and his wife, Andrea, had invited them to stay with them. The partnership worked out well, so far. Nina had a home and backup for her son and herself, and she offered in return occasional child care along with some financial relief.

"Where's Bobby?" she called after him. "What's going on?"

She went to the door of the boys' bedroom and looked in. Lying on the floor in the gloom of winter's early darkness, her son pushed the buttons of his control unit with utter concentration, a video game on the TV, while his cousins Troy and Brianna watched, enthralled. "Hey, guys," she said. "Bobby, come say hi."

"In a minute," Bob said, never taking his eyes from the screen. She backed away and went into the big extra room Matt had built, with its pine chest and yellow spread, and hung up her blazer, changing into jeans and an old flannel shirt.

In the kitchen, Nina surprised Andrea and Matt in an embrace, their eyes closed and arms tight around each other. Andrea was the same height as Matt, and his face was buried in her curly hair. At the sight, a wave of longing washed over Nina.

They broke apart as she came in. Matt looked sorry to see her, but Andrea smiled and said, "How'd your day go?" Two big rattan baskets sat on the table covered with red-and-white gingham cloths.

"It's improving," Nina said. "Aren't we making dinner?" Matt put a beer in her hand, which she popped standing at the counter.

"New plan," he said mysteriously. "I'll go rustle up the kids."

Andrea sat down at the table, pushing her red hair out of her eyes. "I'm beat. End of the week," she said. "Two new women in today." In addition to her extraordinary efforts at keeping things going at home, she managed the local women's shelter. "To tell you the truth," she said, "I'm delighted to let Matt cope with dinner for a change. I didn't know what he was up to until I got home, and you had already gone to the store. He made stew. And coffee, and hot chocolate."

"He's usually on call on Friday night, isn't he?"

"His buddy Hal is answering the pager and taking the tow truck out for him tonight. I think Matt's sick of hauling cars out of ditches, and he wants to do something different tonight."

"But where are we going? It's dark out there and, what, twenty degrees?"

"All he said was 'dress warm.' Down coats, boots, the works."

At the Lakeside Park beach, Matt scraped snow off a redwood picnic table and bench, and threw first plastic, then cloths over them. He placed an oil lantern on the tablecloth, lighting and adjusting it to low. "See? Better than those ultrabright gas ones," he said. "The moon's out. The kids can build a snowman." The three kids had started one already, over by the lake's edge, where the snow was thinner. "And I brought wood and charcoal for the pit. I'll get that going."

"I don't suppose we brought any moonshine, Andrea," said Nina. "I'm in the mood." Lake Tahoe slapped a few feet away. The mountains surrounding it glowed in the dark off in the far distance. Silver light cast tree shadows across the wide beach.

"Hot toddies," Matt said, his breath making clouds in the still, cold air. "Red thermos, basket number two." He put four big mugs on the table, then walked over to the nearby pit.

"Which of the kids reached twenty-one while I wasn't looking?" Nina asked, looking at the four mugs.

"Oh, we have a guest tonight, one who will require liberal hot libation after his long journey." She poured Nina a steaming cupful. "Your favorite private investigator."

"Paul? But how?" He lived in Monterey, over two hundred miles away.

"Well, he called and asked for you, and I said you were at the store, and he said he was in Sacramento on a job and could he stop by, pretty please. What are you going to do with a guy who asks to stop by a hundred miles and six thousand feet up the mountains from Sacramento? He's coming to dinner."

"Here?"

"Any minute now."

A few feet away, Matt busied himself with building the largest bonfire a concrete stove could hold.

Andrea and Nina stuck to the table and the red thermos. "He keeps calling me at work, but I haven't been calling back," said Nina.

"And why is that?"

"A good question, one well deserving of an answer."

"Which is . . . ?"

"I'm not sure why." Nina finished her first cup and offered it up for a refill. The hot liquid traveled in a fiery stream down into her chest. Despite the frigid air, she felt cozier by the minute. "Because he knocks things over," she added. "He's too big and he's unpredictable."

"He's got a house in Carmel."

"He's pushing too hard. And all he's after is a fling."

"That's right, just keep coming up with excuses to keep him away," Andrea said. Nina had more to say but Andrea's comment squelched her.

"He has one hell of a set of shoulders on him," Andrea went on, grinning. "He's a prime specimen of the male persuasion."

"He's an ex-cop. He has that attitude, you know. 'Spread 'em.' And he hates babies and children."

"He's willing to sit down with three kids tonight, just for the honor of sharing supper with you. He's brave enough to try to get close to you, which I suspect not too many men are."

"Why do you say that, Andrea?"

"Who are you saving yourself for?" Andrea said. "Isn't it about time you got over being shot and let the world back in?"

"You're really on my case tonight," Nina said. "Too many people have already been on my case today. If you don't mind, I'd like to just sit peacefully on this bench for a few minutes, get my strength back up."

"Sorry," Andrea said, reaching across the table to give her hand a pat. "I just hate seeing you all alone. It's in my genes. My little old grandmother was a matchmaker in a little old ghetto in Lithuania."

Bob materialized inside the golden circle of lamplight. "Would you like something?" his aunt asked him.

"I'm cold." He was holding his black No Fear baseball cap, which had fallen off and was covered with snow. Andrea took it from him and brushed the snow off.

"I'll warm you up, kiddo." Nina held her arms out.

He came to her, letting her hold him and kiss him on the cheek. Eleven years old, in the middle of a growth spurt, his frame was still childish and narrow, his shining dark hair was getting longer by the day, and his skin remained soft and unblemished. But male hormones marshaled invisibly behind that little-boy face. His feet were already bigger than hers. At some point soon his voice would darken and lower. More and more he looked like . . . but she didn't want to follow that thought on this cold night, with Paul coming to keep her warm, in good company. Banish old ghosts to the closet, where they belonged.

Andrea handed him a mug of hot chocolate, which he drank in one gulp, wiping his hand over his mouth when he finished.

"How was school today?" Nina asked.

"Okay." And he was gone. She watched him running to his cousins, wondering why he wasn't talking to her. "Back in a minute, Andrea," she said. "Bobby, wait up! Let's take a little walk."

They had gone a few hundred feet from Matt's warm fire when Bob stopped.

"Mom . . ." He hesitated, standing with his hands in his pockets. The last time he wore that expression, he had accidentally dumped Sandy's word processing files on the work computer. "I have to tell you something. You're going to be mad."

"I figured," Nina said. "What is it?"

Silence for a long moment. Then he said, "I punched a kid out at school. Taylor Nordholm. I had to go talk to the principal. Mrs. Polk's gonna call you."

"Are you hurt?"

"Not me. But I knocked him against the wall of the gym. He was bleeding and he had to go to the doctor."

"Bobby," Nina said. "Why were you fighting? Look at me; don't look the other way."

"How should I know?" her son said. "Sometimes you just have to hit something. And he's such a jerk—he was laughing at me and trying to knock my hat off. . . ."

"He started it, then?"

"Yeah, it was him. Trust me, it was. So they can't sue us, can they?"

"That's not what I'm worried about. We have to call his parents, find out how he's doing."

"Mrs. Polk said they might suspend me."

"Oh, sh—"

"Let 'em. I don't care," Bob said. "I hate school."

She took his cold face in her hands, saying, "How long have you been feeling this way?"

"I got my reasons. You know. You almost died when you got shot."

She looked at him in the moonlight, such a beautiful, healthy kid, except now she was seeing he wasn't all right, finally seeing what she had been trying not to see in the months since the hospital. The shooting had affected him. He wasn't over it.

"What if you had died?" he cried. "Who would have taken care of me? Jack? He doesn't care about me anymore. He's not my real dad anyway."

"Uncle Matt, Grandpa in Monterey . . . but I didn't die. I'm right here, and I'm going to be fine."

"What about my real father? Would they have called him, and would he have come and got me?"

She pulled him to her, saying again, "I'm here."

But he wrenched himself out of her arms, jumped up and ran over to a pine tree and started hitting it, yelling, "I'll kill him next time! Messing with my hat!" Snow sifted down from the branches, turning him into a comical snowman. But she did not laugh. She let him spend his fury. Finally, he came back and sat with her on an icy patch of sand right at the water's edge.

They talked for a long time, looking out across Lake Tahoe and into a night so clear, Nina could see the lights of Incline Village and King's Beach on the northwest shores, twenty-six miles away. A huge inland sea, deep, impersonal, full of secrets, the lake showed its personality in colors and moods, exerting invisible influences on its neighbors. Now black and impenetrable, its still surface slicked like wet tar, it called like a dangerous road to those outside on a winter's night like this. A few foolhardy adventurers bobbed in distant boats. A few stayed safe, their yellow lights close in, beaming out of the boat harbor at the Tahoe Keys.

Paul arrived as Matt had begun unpacking his goodies. Nina got up to greet him and let herself be enveloped. Bigger than ever in his overcoat, his breath warmed her frosty cheek. He shook snowflakes off his sand-colored hair, kissed her, and held out a large shopping bag bunched at the top and tied with a red ribbon.

"For me?"

"Found it today in a store window. I thought of you," Paul said.

"Should I open it now?"

"Let's wait until we get back to Matt's."

They all sat down and demolished big bowls of hot stew in about five minutes. The kids ate everything, without picking out onions or carrots for a change, starved and flushed from all the running around. Later, when the red thermos was empty, Matt got up to make camper's coffee, boiling water in a pan over the flaming stove, and tossing grounds in to steep and settle. He filled the adults' mugs and refreshed the kids' hot chocolates.

"So how was court today?" Paul said.

"He lunged. I parried, and attacked from the side. He stepped back, and I thought I had him, but then his henchmen poured boiling oil over my head. I released the lions, and they made short work of him," Nina said. "My head is bloody, but unbowed."

"I feel that way sometimes after a day home with the kids," Andrea said.

"What kind of case is it?"

"My client made a film about a girl who's been missing from the Tahoe area for a long time. The parents and friends didn't like the way she portrayed them in the film, and decided they wanted to stop her from distributing it. They couldn't sue her for libel, because she didn't lie about anything, so they sued her for invasion of privacy."

"That's a quaint notion," Paul said. "As if anybody has any of that in this day and age."

"The trouble is, I think I'm on the wrong side, Paul. She couldn't care less about the feelings of the people involved. Plus, there's the way she looked at me today."

"How did she look at you?" he asked.

"Like . . . she hates me. I'm used to looking for hidden motivations, you know, figuring people out as quickly as possible. Most people are pretty simple. But she's buried deep. She's an angry woman, and I definitely got the impression she's turning some of that anger my way for some reason I can't figure out. Suddenly, it's not business between us. It's personal."

"Creepy," said Andrea. "Why the sudden interest?"

Nina shrugged, and sipped from her mug.

"What happened to the missing girl?" Paul asked. "The one in her film. Does she say?"

"No. Tamara Sweet had some problems at home. The Tahoe police listed her as a missing person, because there's never been any sign of an abduction or anything criminal."

"How long since anyone has heard from her?"

"Twelve years."

"That's a long time," Paul said. He was an ex–homicide detective. Nina knew what he was thinking.

"I think that what really led to this lawsuit is my client's idea that the girl was murdered. Not only that, she tries to link up her disappearance with three other disappearances of young women around the lake over the past decade."

"Does she have any hard evidence?"

"No. She insinuates, you know, Paul? And it's hard on the parents."

"She'll get more exposure that way," Andrea said. "She's just sensationalizing it so she can cash in."

Nina said, "I'm afraid you're right."

Matt had been tossing wood on the fire, listening. He turned and said, "Paul, can't you talk some sense into my sister? She's just out of the hospital, and she's getting mixed up in a bunch of unsolved killings—"

"I am not, Matt! It's just a civil case."

"Here we go again," Matt said.

"Matt, I've already decided I'm getting out of the case," said Nina.

"We ought to be getting back," Andrea said.

But Matt wasn't ready to leave. "Nina, I moved up here to be left alone to raise my family," he went on. "That's all I want out of life. Peace for my family. You and Andrea both have jobs that invite all the weirdos of the world to your doorsteps. Fine. Maybe you can't avoid what's out there, and maybe you shouldn't," he said, "even if it's a choice that makes me very uncomfortable. But I can live with it if I know that, having decided on a risky business, you use common sense. If you see trouble coming, you run."

"I do what I can to stay safe, Matt, short of stopping the world," said Nina.

"If that woman looks like she hates you, she probably does," Matt said.

"I'll be careful," Nina said.

"When are you going to get rid of her?"

"As soon as I can," said Nina. "I promise."

Matt flipped the blackened logs with tongs, setting loose searing heat and loud crackles as the wood split into pieces.

"I guess none of us are really over the shooting, Nina," Andrea said a little apologetically, to fill the conversational void that followed Matt's speech. She held out a stick. "So, Paul, you want the last marshmallow?"

Back at the house, the kids were tossed into hot baths, and came out flushed pink and bundled in pajamas. In the living room, by a cozy fire, Nina opened up her present from Paul, a stuffed bear with brown glassy eyes and a soft round head, a black nose and a tiny sewn-on mouth. She held it up, and Brianna made a rush for it, but Paul said, "Press on his chest."

Oh, no. A talking bear. She pressed her thumbs into the bear's chest. In a slow, plaintive, strangely familiar-sounding voice, it said, "Waiting . . . waiting . . . I'm just sitting over here in the corner waiting for you. . . ."

They all burst into laughter. The bear's expression was so lonely yet expectant, and its tone was so lugubrious. Nina let Brianna press it a few more times, then she sat down on the couch with it.

"Do you like it?" Paul said. He was standing, looking down at her. She nodded.

"The voice is so . . . unusual. They did a great job."

"It's a recording bear," Paul said. "You get to put your own voice on it."

"You mean it's you?" Andrea said. She headed for the kitchen, holding her hand over her mouth, her shoulders shaking with laughter.

"I'm just trying to open up a dialogue," Paul said. "Press the bear whenever you want to know what's on my mind."

"Well. Thanks, Paul," Nina said. She walked him out to the porch.

"Let's go skiing tomorrow," he said. "I'm staying at Caesars until tomorrow night."

"Skiing?"

"You have a clean bill of health. I'll make sure you don't go off any cliffs."

"Sometime soon. I have too much to do this weekend."

"And tonight?"

"I'm sorry," she said. "I can't come tonight."

He leaned in for a long kiss, closing his eyes and holding her close. "Call me," he said.

"I will."

3

UNWRITTEN RULES OF LEGAL PRACTICE:

Rule 1: It's always worse than you ever dreamed possible.
Rule 2: The other guy lies and takes advantage.
Rule 3: You never get a break.

Taylor Nordholm's mother, on the other end of the phone early Monday morning, was a reminder that there is another world outside law.

"No concussion, not even a headache. We made him stay in bed, but he didn't really need to. He said he tried to take Bob's baseball cap. I hope Bob isn't in trouble."

"I'll be talking with the principal this morning," Nina said, relieved.

"Boys start getting a little crazy, testing each other and all that. The end of the latency period, and look out, adolescence is just around the corner. I'm a marriage counselor, and I can tell you, unless it gets to be a habit, your son's not turning into a delinquent.

Tell you what—I'll talk to Taylor about inviting Bob over. Make 'em smoke the peace pipe, figuratively of course."

"You are really being nice about this."

"Taylor says you're new in Tahoe. We ought to get together, have coffee or something. Sometimes the mornings really drag. Are you working?"

"I'm a lawyer in town. That sounds good."

A short silence on the other end suggested Mrs. Nordholm had met with the likes of her before. Nina couldn't blame her for being a little nervous. She had already been turning over arguments to make to the principal that centered on the dastardly attack on Bobby by Mrs. Nordholm's son.

"Well, good luck with Mrs. Polk," Mrs. Nordholm said, apparently deciding to forgive Nina for her profession. And to repay her kindness, Nina decided to rethink her approach to the principal.

She took two minutes for a hot shower, clean hair, pants, and a green blazer. In the kitchen she fed Bobby soft-boiled eggs and lingered with the kids over a favorite comic.

Outside she had to wear sunglasses to prevent being blinded by the bright, fresh snow. Sports utility vehicles loaded with skis crowded the streets, filled with the beaming faces of those who had not yet broken a limb.

Starting at nine o'clock sharp, sitting on a very small chair at the John Muir Elementary School, Nina waited. Thirty minutes later she was invited into the principal's office, feeling naked without her briefcase.

Mrs. Polk, a large, dark-haired woman with expensively chic tortoiseshell glasses, pointed to a chair. She didn't go around behind her desk, but sat down with Nina at a small table stacked with Central American artifacts and toys.

"I talked to Bob's teacher on Friday," said Mrs. Polk. "He's a bright child."

"Mrs. Nordholm said Taylor was not hurt badly."

"Taylor's back at school. It was just a scratch. I talked to him this morning. He and Bob came into my office and apologized to each other."

"It's the first time Bobby's ever been involved in an incident like this. I don't see a major problem."

Mrs. Polk removed her glasses and set them on the table. She wore no makeup, but her eyes had a piercing, tell-the-truth quality that must have served her well. "Oh, but he does have a problem," she said. "He's alternately depressed and angry. He's been acting out in the classroom. He's had three notes sent home in the past two months."

"Three notes?"

The principal walked over to her desk, picked up some papers, and handed them to Nina. "Haven't you seen these?"

Whistling in class, must stop disruptive behavior. Shouting on playground, got in a pushing match. Failure to make up homework after absences. She had seen none of the notes, though her initials had been scrawled boldly at the bottom.

"Oh, sure, those notes," Nina said carefully.

"And six absences since Christmas. Does he have any health problems we should know about, Mrs. Reilly?"

"Ms," Nina corrected automatically. "No, just the normal stuff. Minor colds and so forth." Six absences! As far as she knew, Bobby hadn't missed a day.

"You did sign the absence slips?" It was just the same as twenty-five years ago, when Nina had been sent to the principal, who beneath her genteel manner was the executioner, and she'd better make up a story fast. . . .

"Naturally. What do you think, Bobby forged them?" she said, looking Mrs. Polk right in the eye.

"You'll forgive me for asking, Ms. Reilly. But are there any problems at home that could be upsetting your son? For example, marital problems. A child of eleven knows more than you might think, and does tend to hear things, sometimes misinterpret things—"

"Bobby's had his share of changes. I've just been through a divorce," Nina said. "And we moved to Tahoe only last spring. And my work does take time away from him. And I was injured recently and ended up in the hospital. But he's such a little trooper about everything—"

"Does Bob see his father regularly?"

"Bobby doesn't have a father," Nina said.

Mrs. Polk didn't seem put off by Nina's tone. She was a lot tougher than Nina had first thought.

"Even though the parents don't get along, the child still has a father," she said.

"My ex-husband was not Bobby's father," Nina said.

"An earlier relationship? Bob knows this?"

"He knows Jack—my ex-husband—is not his father. The previous relationship did not work out, and all contact with the father was cut off before Bobby was born."

"You have never talked with him about his father?"

"That's a part of my life I don't discuss with anyone."

Mrs. Polk shook her head, opening her mouth to say something Nina did not want to hear, some sympathetic-sounding observation that would haunt Nina at night. Nina leaned forward to cut her off. "Look, Mrs. Polk. I can see your concern about Bobby's welfare. I'll talk to him, keep closer watch. I'm sure he'll shape up."

"He knows his father is a taboo subject. That's probably difficult for a boy his age."

Damn, she had got to Nina after all. Her words cut deep.

"Think about opening up with your son."

"I'll deal with it as I see fit," Nina said, getting up, letting Mrs. Polk know the meeting was over. "Are you going to take any further action against Bobby?"

"Not if you are willing to try to help, and his behavior improves."

"Then thank you very much. I'm sorry, but I have an appointment and I have to go."

Mrs. Polk stood up, shook her hand. "It's good to meet you, Ms. Reilly. I'm sorry you are in such a hurry."

"Mrs. Polk . . ."

"Yes, Ms. Reilly?"

"I'm doing the best I can. My son is by far the most important thing in the world to me." Having said that, she hurried out, past the secretary, out the doors, and onto the empty schoolgrounds. Somewhere around here Bobby had a science class. She really should get more involved with the school. She would make it a point. And she would have a talk with Bobby, tonight.

Right now, she was late to a deposition.

* * *

That evening she had to go to a city council meeting to protest on behalf of a client whose home building plans had been rejected. When she finally arrived back at the house, the lights were out and everyone had gone to bed.

The next day she drove Bobby to school and said she would talk to him when she got home. She stayed in the Bronco, watching him, until he was inside his classroom.

Then she went on to her court appearance, a motion to compel discovery of information from a large accounting firm she was suing. The hearing examiner waffled; opposing counsel made fine points in that long-winded, obsequious, slightly grating style that made judges cranky; Nina waxed indignant. She won the right to some answers and lost the right to others. They would be back in court in two more months, squabbling again. The insurance company for the business had adopted a tried-and-true strategy: paper her into babbling idiocy and her client into bankruptcy.

Her chance to talk to her son finally came at six-thirty. Under a darkening late-winter sky she picked Bobby up at home and took him to a coffee shop by the Greyhound station, just across from the Stateline movie theater. They ordered burgers and fries.

He sat across from her, fiddling with the straws he had taken from the dispenser, wearing a dark blue sweatshirt with a skateboard logo on the back. At Christmas this year he had asked for a skateboard, a hockey stick, and clothes, and had known just what brands he wanted.

"Remember, we always take our hat off inside," she said. "And quit shooting the paper off the straws. I need to talk to you."

He took off his baseball cap, laying it carefully on the table. Now she could see him better. The bulky clothes and black cap he wore protected him from unwelcome scrutiny. He had no room of his own and no place to himself. Maybe his hat furnished his only privacy.

"It's about school. I talked to Mrs. Polk. She showed me some notes from school that you never brought to me."

He hung his head, hands still playing with the straws.

"I couldn't believe it, Bobby. You put my initials on the bottom and turned the notes in, didn't you?"

No answer.

The cross-examiner in her was roused. She would get to the bottom of this. "Answer me."

His face tightened in a way she had never seen before. It was as though the adult he could become, an unhappy adult trying to hold himself together, peered out at her. Suddenly overcome by compassion, she wanted to comfort him. Why had she brought him to this public place?

Because they had no place of their own. The waitress brought them plates of food, and Nina handed Bobby the ketchup. "Go on," she said. "Speak up now. Tell me where you went."

"I went . . ."

She sat still, tense.

"Up to the ski lodge at Heavenly."

"The big lodge by the parking lot?"

He wouldn't look at her. "Yes."

"You went all by yourself?"

"Yeah. Except once . . . I took Troy."

Nina groaned. "Why?"

"What do you care, Mom? You're so busy."

"Come on. I'm really worried about you." She put her hand out and held his, gently touching the top of it with her fingers, trying to make a connection.

"I can take care of myself."

"I want to take care of you too," Nina said. "If anything ever happened to you, Bobby—"

"I was safe. I sat on the bench close to adults, you know, so the waiters thought I was with my father." He said the word *father* so formally.

Nina bought herself a few seconds by biting into her cold burger and sipping her milk shake.

"Of course, I don't have a father, right?"

"Stop that. You have a father just like anyone else. You were born at Community Hospital in Monterey—"

"I'm a bastard, aren't I? Just like Taylor Nordholm and everybody says."

"What? He doesn't know a thing about it. And neither do you. Plenty of the kids at your school have different kinds of families, just like us. Let's leave it at that. Now why don't you finish that burger so we can go home."

"We don't have a home."

"Matt's is your home."

"That's not the same, Mom, and you know it."

She felt the life she had built crumbling. "I can't do anything about that right now, Bobby. It's a good place to live and most of the time we both like it there, don't we?"

"Is my dad dead?" Bobby moved back into radioactive territory. "Where is he, anyway? Why don't you want to talk about him? You always get mad whenever I ask anything."

"It's just . . ." Words failed her.

"When are you going to tell me?"

"Someday I will."

"I want to know now."

"I know you do."

"When will you tell me?"

"I don't know when!" She tried to keep her voice loving but firm, but heard it shifting into anger.

"Promise."

"I'll think about it. Now you promise me you'll never do that again—cutting school. School's important. But most of all, you are important. I need to know you're safe, and where you are supposed to be."

"Okay." The word came too easily; she doubted his sincerity.

"Shake?" She held out her hand and he took it, automatically, as he used to when he was little. She would dangle an open hand by her side, and his hand would rise to clasp it, as if drawn up by a magnet. But now his hand took up more space in hers, and could break free easily. This larger hand was strong and wiry, and didn't settle for long in hers.

He was growing up and away, and she would have to find a way to accept it.

Her morning appointment the next day didn't show.

It was impossible to concentrate. Milne's Minute Order in the London case would be coming in today or tomorrow. She would be through with the troubles of Terry London.

"What's the afternoon look like?" she asked, strolling into the outer office. Sandy was proofing some forms that had to be filed by the end of the day.

"You're due at the DMV to try to save Mrs. Audray's driver's license," Sandy said.

"I better read the file, then."

"This is one you won't win," Sandy said. "She's had too many speeding tickets in the past year. Why do you bother?"

"Ah, Sandy, Sandy. It's all in the wrist. You have to approach the DMV the right way."

"Which is?"

"To grovel. Cries, complaints, explanations, sincere protestations, promises to reform: worthless, all worthless. You have to get down on your knees."

"She can do that without you."

"She's an amateur. She needs an expert. A lawyer must grovel. It's DMV policy."

Sandy, who never laughed, almost cracked a smile.

The DMV hearing went well. Nina begged for mercy, and her client got it. Feeling pleased with this small victory, she returned to the office and dug into the endless pile of trouble on her desk.

The phone buzzed. Sandy said, "Bella called from the county clerk's office. They just finished filing the Minute Order in the London case."

"That was quick. What's it say?"

"She said you can come get it or they'll put it in the mail."

"Could you go, Sandy?"

"Hmph," Sandy said, but she put on her coat.

At three-fifteen Bobby showed up, homework-laden, dropped off by Matt after a little disagreement with Troy. Nina set him up in the conference room with a short lecture, sharp pencils, and strict orders to stay out of the reception area.

A half hour later Nina had a new client in the office when Sandy came in with the court's order in the London case.

She had won. Milne had declined to issue a preliminary injunction, on grounds that the plaintiffs were unlikely to win when the issue was finally litigated on the merits. The argument about consent had carried the day—not the argument about the Constitution, but they had prevailed.

"Terry London's here to see you," Sandy said. A few minutes later Nina finished with her client and poked her head into the conference room.

Bobby, whose books lay scattered and disregarded on the oak table in front of him, looked out the window, his expression unreadable. His black hair had gone too long without a barber's attention. The line of his jaw, the most remarkable physical change in a boy just eleven years old, had firmed into a triangular suggestion of the impending adolescent. Shaking herself out of a stare, Nina noticed Terry at the other end of the long table, her eyes moving back and forth between the two of them.

"Terry, have you met my son?" Nina asked.

"I can see the resemblance," she said, opening her lips into a wide, toothy smile. "Though he doesn't look much like you, does he? We've had such a good chat. He tells me he just turned eleven."

Everything she said felt wrong somehow, as if the words she spoke had nothing to do with the meaning she intended. All Nina's uneasiness flooded back.

After Terry left and Matt picked up Bobby, Nina realized she had forgotten to give her client a copy of the Minute Order, something Terry had specifically requested. She decided to drop it off on the way home to keep Terry happy until Nina could gracefully bow out of the rest of the case.

"Do me a favor, Sandy."

"What?"

"Please don't put Bobby into the conference room with clients anymore. It makes me nervous."

"Now that you mention it, he did look a little upset coming out of there," said Sandy. "Guess it makes him nervous too. I wonder why?"

4

TERRY LONDON LIVED IN A MID-SIZE A-FRAME IN A BOULDER-STREWN neighborhood off Pioneer, at the end of a road called Coyote Trail. The house sat right at the top of a hill that was almost entirely enclosed with crisscrossed ranch fencing, protected street-side by a locked gate.

Through the gate, deep in the pines on the left, Nina could barely see a small stucco bungalow, half-buried in old snow, that must be the studio where Terry worked. A steep, narrow trail connected this building to the house above. Even though the curtains to the studio were closed, a light from inside faintly illuminated the windows. She parked at the gate, looking for an intercom or some other way to signal either building.

When she got out of the car, a black dog almost as large as a St. Bernard appeared out of nowhere, drooling silently from a mouth fixed into a permanent grin. He gave her a little thrill, licking her cold hand with his warm, wet tongue.

A small sign nailed to the gatepost said DON'T WORRY ABOUT THE DOG. BEWARE OF OWNER. The outline of a handgun had been scratched next to this welcome. Nina could locate no bell or intercom.

Nina had changed her mind anyway. She didn't like the place and she didn't want to see Terry. The wind blew at the envelope in her hand. She couldn't just spear it on a twig and stick it on the fence, to flap away at the next gust. She would hop back in the truck, and Sandy could mail it out tomorrow—

"Looking for Terry?" a bass voice said behind her, and she whirled around.

A man stood about three feet away with a rifle in his hand. He had white hair, a white beard, a red face and white eyelashes, and wore a wool shirt and a dirty down vest. His pants hung low under a puff of belly. As Nina turned to answer, the wind gusted and his hair flew around his head.

"Hope you're not selling anything," he said. He held the rifle negligently by the stock, barrel pointed toward the ground.

"I'm just leaving."

"That envelope for her?"

She hesitated, and he went on. "She's here. She just locks the gate when she's not expecting anyone. She expecting you?"

"No."

"I'll make sure she gets it, if you want. I'm her neighbor. Jerry." Noticing that her eyes stayed stuck on the rifle, he said, "Rabbits are bad this year. The hunters don't pay no attention to the 'no trespassing' warnings. They take down anything that moves. Don't wander around in the woods. Bunch of bad shots out here. The hill's private property, hers and mine. They got no right."

"Thanks. But—"

"Jerry! Get outta here!" a woman's voice said loudly from the studio, at a moment between the bursts of wind. The silhouette of a head had appeared behind a drawn-back curtain.

"She doesn't like me," Jerry said.

"I guess she doesn't like me either," Nina said.

"She don't like nobody," the man said. Without another word he turned and walked down the hill, giving the Bronco an appraising glance as he passed.

"It's me, Terry. Nina Reilly," Nina called after he made his hasty exit. Several minutes later the door opened. An uncombed mop of chestnut hair covered most of the face that looked out.

"What are you doing here?"

Wondering more each second that very thing, Nina opened her briefcase. "Just the Minute Order," she called. "You forgot to take your copy."

"Why didn't you call first?"

"You know, I'm getting frostbite standing out here in this wind. If you don't want to let me in, fine. I'll leave the envelope here with a rock on it."

Terry came out, pushing her arms through a down parka. "Hang on, hang on," she said. She strode down the path, unlocking the gate while Nina waited.

"Come in," Terry ordered, pushing her hair back. She led the way, her long legs pumping quickly up the studio path. Inside, she threw off the parka. She wore a bulky, rust-colored sweater that reached halfway down her thighs over black tights. Without makeup her face was older, paler, and more masculine.

She gestured Nina toward a couch with mussed pillows that still bore the imprint of her head, tossing a chenille throw to the floor. "Have a seat."

"I really don't have much time, Terry," said Nina, sitting primly on a corner of the couch. Terry watched her from a swivel chair in the middle of the room, a tiny glimmer of amusement in her eyes telling Nina that she knew Nina was squeamish about sitting where Terry had lain. "I'm running late." Nina rummaged in her case and found the papers. She laid them neatly on a small glass table in front of her.

"Coffee?" said Terry.

"No, really—"

"No trouble." Terry's peremptory tone made it clear it would be rude to leave. She was already moving as she spoke, crossing to a counter near the doorway where a small refrigerator and coffeemaker sat, giving Nina a chance to look around the studio.

The single, long room had white walls and picture windows covering one long side, interrupted only by the doorway and counter. On the other side a long counter held a clutter of built-in tape decks, a laser disc player, a double cassette deck, a CD player, a computer, a video player and large monitor, and, among other machinery, some film editing equipment Nina couldn't name. Wires, neatly labeled, were plugged into rows of surge protectors built along the back edge of the counter.

"What is all this equipment here? Do you really need so many speakers?" Nina said, seeking a neutral topic until she could make her escape.

"Well, let's see," Terry said, slapping the coffeepot in place and punching the on button. "Two custom VIFA speakers, two custom subwoofers, two custom UIFA speakers," she said. "All necessary if you want to keep your slander audible. Then there's the three-quarter-inch video equipment for making easy rough cuts from film I've dubbed to video.

"The tape decks I use for sound editing and creating a track. Some smaller format, to play rental movies and help me plan shots in advance. Oh, and things like dubbing the Tamara Sweet film down to VHS so that her folks can have a nervous breakdown watching on home equipment.

"That's a bad way to see a film. Video's a poor cousin to film, even if you've got an eighty-inch screen and the best possible quality dub. Two hundred watt per channel power amp for the subwoofer. The Steenbeck, of course—"

Nina put up a hand. "Enough. I'm assuming you have a decent alarm system."

"I don't worry too much. I have a solid storage closet to lock cameras in when I'm gone. I leave only the big equipment out. The portable stuff goes in there if it's valuable. So Jerry and his bonehead son, Ralph, don't get any ideas."

"Quite a setup."

"I've been doing this for a long time. You accumulate equipment, and you always need more. And you always need something newer. Naturally, that takes cash." She took a chamois cloth and polished the lens on a video camera. "You know I went into debt to make this thing. I just couldn't resist. What a topic. It spoke to me. Plus, of course, I plan to make my money back, and more."

"Listen, Terry—"

"Bob should come see it sometime. He likes movies. He wishes you had a video camera. He told me when we talked in the conference room."

"I wanted to ask you about that. . . ." Nina started, and then changed her mind. She would talk to Bobby.

Enough coffee had dripped into the pot. Terry poured two cups, and Nina drank hers swiftly, intending to leave at her first opportunity. She didn't like the feeling being on Terry's territory gave her, of being ensnared, trapped and out of control of the situation. She gave a series of uninformative answers to what eventually became a heavy barrage of questions about her and about Bobby. What a strange mix the woman was, with her expensive equipment and her notions and her nosiness!

Then Terry picked up a camcorder and pointed it at Nina.

"Don't do that!"

"You're very photogenic," Terry remarked from behind the black box. "Small people look bigger onscreen. The camera gives them presence they lack in real life."

"I don't like this," said Nina. "Please, turn it off."

"Where's his father?" Terry asked, the camera in front of her implacably humming. "He doesn't seem to know."

"What?" Nina, struck by the question, forgot the camera.

"He said he doesn't even know who his father is. How about it? Tell Terry. Was his daddy a bad man? Did he leave you or did you leave him?" Her voice had a cajoling, teasing tone.

"You talked with my son about his father?"

"He brought it up, I think."

"What did he say?"

"I don't really remember."

"What did you say?"

"I forget. Maybe I told him it was high time he found out."

Nina stood up, putting her hand in front of the camera lens. "Keep out of my business," she said.

Terry jumped to one side, continuing to shoot. "Talk to me," she said. "I won't tell."

"You don't have my permission to film me." Nina walked to the door, the camera in pursuit.

"I don't need permission to film, just to show it in public. I'm going to watch this film later, in private, Nina, and learn all about you. I'm going to figure out a few things. And then I'm going to shake your world."

"Don't you ever talk to my son again. And I can't represent you any longer. If you need further legal work, call my office and we'll refer you," Nina said. Why wait? This woman was impossible. Walking rapidly down the path, she half-turned so that she could see the camera and the dark figure behind it, blown by the wind, backdropped by the dark forest and the small, half-buried building.

"You fought for me in court, my right to plant myself in other people's lives," Terry called loudly from the doorway, putting the camera down far enough that Nina could see her white face back there, but keeping it pointed her way. "What's the matter, Nina? Why should your precious privacy be so different?"

Nina hurried to the car and drove away, heedless of the joyously slavering dog that chased her all the way down the hill.

Bob lay in his bed Wednesday night long after his mother left the room. He waited until everyone had fallen asleep, listening to the forest sounds. His thoughts traveled to where they usually did lately, circling around his father. When he tried to picture him, television characters came to mind. He knew that wasn't right. He'd give anything just to know who he was and what he really looked like. And maybe where he was now, where he lived.

He held his breath for a minute, deciding. Okay, he'd break the rules. He'd go to hell if he had to, like Huck Finn. This was worth it.

On Thursday morning Nina rose early to grab the first precious moments with her hot steaming coffee and newspaper. Within a few minutes the rest of the household erupted. Andrea came in with her kids, helping them arrange cereal, running to dress herself, answering the phone, snatching coffee. Matt presided over breakfast, his usual angelic look replaced by a haggard stranger until he'd drunk a few cups.

Nina finished two sections of the paper before she realized she hadn't seen her son. He had overslept. That's what happened when you read comics late into the night.

"Bobby awake?" she asked Troy.

"I didn't see him. He got up before me. He's probably in the bathroom."

She went to track him down. She looked first in both bathrooms, but saw no sign of him. Then she looked in his bedroom.

"Where's Bobby?" she asked next, in the kitchen, to Matt's assembled family, who looked up, momentarily diverted from their breakfasts. "I can't find him."

"Did you check the pantry? Maybe he went down there to get cereal or something," Andrea suggested, taking Nina by the arm and leading her toward the pantry door. "How about the garage?"

When Nina gave up and sat down at the kitchen table, unable to move or think, Andrea called the police.

5

By midmorning the police had issued a statewide alert with Bobby's description. They didn't hold back on missing children's cases anymore; they hit the tarmac running. Andrea got in touch with missing children organizations. Matt hounded neighbors and friends. Sandy told everyone Nina had been called away on some important business.

Nina called her father in Monterey. Harlan Reilly said he'd be on the lookout and distribute the flyers she was making. Then she called Paul at his office in Carmel.

"Van Wagoner Investigations," said his voice, gruffer and deeper than she remembered. She took a breath to speak. "We're unavailable at the moment. Please leave your message after the tone."

What could Paul do from so far away anyway? Bobby would turn up any minute. Feeling unable to leave a message, she hung up.

"Community Hospital," the bus driver said. Bob stood in front of the long white building shaded by Monterey pines. People bustled in and out, some dressed all in white, some with red coats.

He had slept most of the way from Tahoe to Monterey, and, up early, stopped for breakfast at the McDonald's near Fisherman's Wharf. Then he returned to the bus station and found out how to get to the hospital.

He turned right after going through the automatic doors, heading for the volunteer information desk. A lady with stiff white hair and a peach-colored dress sat behind bunches of flowers. These ladies didn't get paid, so they were always very cheerful, really cheerful, not fake-o cheerful like people who were paid for it.

"I need my birth certificate. I was born here," he said to the lady. In a quavering voice she said, "Oh. Well. Let's see what we can find out. Alma? Alma!" A girl came over, maybe even a teenager, wearing a uniform just like the girls at Boulder Hospital at Tahoe, where his mom had been.

"This young man wants a birth certificate," she said to the girl, who looked at Bob with a lot of doubt in her eyes.

Lots of gray-speckled, shiny floors later, they turned into a room with a tall counter that he had trouble seeing over. Alma left him there. The man behind the counter didn't notice Bob. "Excuse me," Bob said. About a century later, after some other people came and went, Bob said "Excuse me" again. No reaction. Was he deaf?

"Hey!" Bob said loudly. The man turned. Bob had never seen anyone so bald, but he had a dark tan all over his head and the neck coming out of his shirt looked as thick as a boxer's. "Sir," he added.

"What do you want, kid?" he said.

"My birth certificate. I was born here."

"That's a legal record. We don't have it here." He looked at a list for a minute, saying, "You have to go over to the Salinas courthouse. West wing, third floor. County health department. Unless you want an original. Then you have to write to Sacramento."

"Where's Salinas?"

"You trying to be funny?"

"No, sir," Bob said. He could see the man liked that. "I just meant, how do we get there?" He used "we" to keep the man from getting too interested in a kid all alone.

He looked at Bob and shrugged. "Take the Highway 68 bus outside. That takes you to the Salinas Transit Plaza, and you get a transfer, or walk from there. It's just a few blocks."

"Do you know if birth certificates have the father's names on them?"

"Usually."

"Do they *have* to have the father's name?"

"No. But they usually do."

At dinnertime, an exhausted Nina suggested dinner out for Matt's family. At first they refused. They would sit with her. They would wait together. "Please, go," she insisted. "I'll stay here." Matt tried and failed to convince Nina to come along. She didn't want to leave the house. He wanted to bring food home, but she said she'd make some soup.

"Go to a movie," she suggested at the door in a low voice. "This is just awful for the kids."

"Are you sure you'll be all right?"

"I'm fine. I expect to hear from someone any minute."

"We won't be late." Matt and Andrea hugged her, and even the kids each gave her a kiss on the way out. "They'll find him, Nina," Andrea whispered. "I know he's all right."

"Want to grab your keys and move your car? Andrea and I parked in the garage," Matt asked.

She reached into her pocket and tossed him her keys. "Take the Bronco, Matt. Everybody fits better in there anyway."

After they left she went into the kitchen to make herself some soup. She hadn't eaten all day, and the aggravating needs of the body called to her according to their own clock. Dinner, they said. Eat. She ate the tomato soup with the morning newspaper in front of her.

From the living room she watched the evening cast its shadow over the snow outside the picture window, then stoked the fire, ready to leap to the phone or the door, whichever rang first. She sat on the round hooked rug by the hearth, looking into the orange and blue flames, thinking about what Mrs. Polk had said.

By late afternoon Bob had found the county buildings. He had gone with his mom once to watch her argue an appeal in the San Francisco courthouse, so once they arrived in Salinas he knew how to find the particular office he wanted. You looked at the directory, and stood by the elevator looking alert. He took the elevator to the third floor, going up with a redheaded lady with a heavy briefcase just like his mom's. At the county health department office he put his things on a plastic chair, then waited in line for his birth certificate. The clerk told him it cost thirteen dollars, and Bob gave her a twenty from his birthday money. He told her his birthdate. She came back a few minutes later with a sheet of paper. He didn't look at it until he got outside.

Behind the courthouse, a large grassy yard held no people to bother him. He sat down and took off the pack. He held the paper, smoothing it, not opening it until he felt ready.

A crow landed a few feet away and eyed him. He dug down in the pack for some bits of cheese. Soon many crows pecked around him. He examined a colony of ants wending their way into a clump of dirt near his feet. A sharp pang of fear made his hands shake. He felt like a chick scratching on the inside of its egg, about to pop into someplace completely new.

He opened the paper and began puzzling it out.

CERTIFICATE OF LIVE BIRTH, STATE OF CALIFORNIA, he read at the top. ROBERT BRENDAN REILLY, he read, shivering a little, though the sun shone. The crows flew up together, cawing. Waving his hand and squinting, he read on.

Under *Father of Child* it said KURT GEOFFREY SCOTT. Blinking, he read it again.

He wanted to tell somebody, jump up and say this is my father, look here, Kurt Geoffrey Scott. He did jump up, and ran around for a minute on the grass, kicking at the ants.

His father was real and that made him real. Strange, half-formed ideas and doubts flew away, off into the cloudless sky.

Mother of Child, Nina Fox Reilly. Father of Child, Kurt Geoffrey Scott.

Nina was lying down, her head propped on a pillow on the floor. The fire, down to glowing embers, made the only light in the house. She had been sleeping. Something had awakened her. Bobby?

Not Bobby. The sounds, at first just soft, shuffling sounds, made her train her ear to make sure she was not mistaking branches of trees scraping the roof in the wind. No, the floorboards were creaking somewhere in the house. What she heard was the sound of footsteps, stealthy and deliberate, moving across the floor.

She sat up slowly, still maintaining a small emotional distance born of disbelief. Could she trust herself to recognize reality in the dark like this? Could she be dreaming? But her bare toes felt cold. Her fingers, clenching and unclenching the blanket, responded to the texture of the fabric. Heat emanated from the embers at the bottom of the fireplace.

A loud thump, the sound of something large crashing to the floor, convinced her. She jumped up, looking for a weapon. She found the shovel and brush among the fireplace tools, but no poker. Matt hid the poker from the children.

Looking around the dark room, she spotted the ax. Wasn't that just like Matt to leave his ax out and the poker hidden, she thought stupidly, her teeth chattering as she picked up the ax and made her way slowly through the room, trying not to run into furniture.

She wanted to get to the kitchen, with an aim toward getting to the phone, but before she could, the atmosphere had subtly changed. The sounds stopped.

Irresolute, she stood at the door to the hallway, looking around. Was it possible whoever was here was waiting for her?

The house, still and expectant as a waiting room, breathed along with her in response to the sighs of wind outside. She heard no other sound.

Standing in the doorway, completely rattled by now, Nina reconsidered. She did not want to go down the hall. The hall had a public feel to it suddenly, like a room with eyes. But what alternatives did she have? The living room opened only onto this hall and the entry foyer.

Should she try to open a window and climb out? That made her think of the storm windows. She could not get out that way. Not quickly enough.

Moments passed. The Bavarian cuckoo clock ticked in the kitchen. She didn't know how long she had been standing there, but she couldn't remain still another minute. Her nose itched; she needed to sneeze. To top it off, she heard the mushy sound of tires easing up the road, approaching the driveway.

She ducked back into the living room to think about what to do.

At the same moment, a thump near the hallway told her that someone was there. She hadn't imagined anything. Someone was out there.

Raising the ax in her right hand, she bolted toward the hall, her fear and rage exploding into one earsplitting, gut-spilling shriek.

"What in holy hell happened?" Matt asked, once he had looked her over and reheated some coffee in the microwave, and Nina had assured him a number of times that she felt fine, aside from the large bump forming on the back of her head. "We go to the movies and come back to find you, lying on the floor, bleeding."

She told him about her evening, starting at the beginning. "I guess somebody broke in while I was asleep. I heard your car coming up the driveway and I was scared—for everybody. I wanted to chase him off with the ax, I think. At the time, it seemed like the right thing to do."

"Could be he was just trying to get you out of the way so that he could escape," said Matt, his voice unusually hard-sounding. "Could be he intended to hurt you, but I interrupted. Why in God's name did you have the ax? He could've used it on you."

"I had to do something."

"Anything missing?" Matt asked, working latches on the windows and doors.

"Nothing I could see," said Andrea. "The police are on the way. Nina, when you feel up to it, you should check your room. Check your jewelry."

"I'm really okay. I just wish I'd killed the bastard."

She walked down the hall to her room. She let herself in, and stood gaping in the doorway at a scene of utter devastation.

Her bedding lay strewn around the room. Something had slashed into the bed, dribbling her shampoos, creams, and makeup over the mattress. The contents of her room, her shoes, her clothing, her treasures, had all been shredded, cut, defaced.

She moved slowly inside, toeing the remnants of her belongings, making a path for herself to the closet. Her clothes had been torn off hangers and flung to the floor. She checked her jewelry, which she kept in a silk bag on a shelf, now lying on the floor, one or two earrings smashed, but the full collection remained, as far as she could tell.

Checking the dresser drawers didn't take long, since they were empty—her bras and other underwear in blue, red, black, and beige ripped into confetti and thrown around the room as if in celebration.

She backed into the hallway, slamming the door to her room, just as the front doorbell rang.

The same two officers from the morning stood in the doorway. She invited them in to take a look.

"Anything missing?" they asked, after picking their way around the room, making notes.

"Nothing I can see except an old box full of souvenirs. The lid was pretty tight. He's going to be disappointed when he gets a chance to check out his booty."

"You keep saying 'he.' Why?" the woman cop asked Nina. "Are you sure it was a man?"

"Well, no, I guess I'm not. I guess I don't know that."

Back down the brightly lit street, back down to the wharf Bob walked, wearing his parka, his sweatshirt hood up. Fog had rolled in from the ocean, blurring the restaurant signs.

He'd taken the bus back to Monterey, and found a public phone on a busy street near the waterfront. Because there was no listing for a Kurt Scott in the phone book, he'd spent an hour and several dollars in change phoning any Scotts that looked promising.

He didn't know what he'd say if he had found his father anyway.

Still, he didn't feel ready to give up, so instead of calling his grandfather in Monterey, he prepared to spend the night somewhere. He tried the post office, but a bum had already staked out that territory. He had lunged at Bob, laughing at his fear. Bob didn't think it was funny at all.

At the end of the wharf, about ready to fall over from sleepiness, he stepped down some ramshackle stairs off the main pier, to a landing that smelled like old fish, only a foot or so above the water. Some rusty sinks stood near him, but he found a spot that was only slightly damp. He slipped into his sleeping bag, put his other stuff in there with him, and curled up.

Through the fence slats the ocean floated in the fog. His wooden floor creaked and swayed. Warm and comfortable, the watery scenery obliterated by fog, he swayed with the waves, cradled by the ocean.

"Kurt Geoffrey Scott," he said to himself. Before long, he fell asleep.

Late in the night, he woke up.

He saw a face in the fog.

It was looking curiously at him, a face that seemed to roll back into the mist without any shoulders. And its nose was black, with a whiskered smile below, chinless, and its black eyes were not human eyes.

Bob sat up too quickly, thumping his head against the rail, and the seal jerked his head back, remaining a few feet away on the landing. Now Bob could see where its flippers made puddles on the deck.

Neither moved for a while. The harbor seal seemed to be trying to decide whether to slide back off the deck into the ocean. Bob was wondering if he should jiggle up and down and holler, chasing the seal off. He must look like a seal himself, in his long black sleeping bag. The animal twitched his nose, but made no other move.

Bob wasn't afraid. He had never heard of a seal biting anyone, though if it rolled over on him it would certainly hurt. He felt like he was the one out of place. He was sleeping in the seal's spot.

The mists drifted overhead; the deck moved. Green water lapped at the pilings.

The seal began backing up, using its flippers to push itself. Leaving a wet trail, it retreated to the far edge of the deck. Its mouth opened in a huge yawn. It sighed just like a human, put its head down, and rolled over, so Bob could see only its roly-poly, long gray back.

Bob joined it in another yawn, pulling the edge of the bag over his head, lodging himself a little farther into his cubbyhole, and fell back to sleep.

6

SITTING IN HER CAR AT TERRY'S GATE THE DAY AFTER BOBBY DISAPpeared, Nina put the heel of her hand on the horn and let it stay there.

Terry threw open the door of the house at the top of the hill and stood on the porch, her hair flying out from her head like something alive in the wild March wind. She'd thrown the lynx coat on. "What do you want?" she called.

"Come on down here and I'll tell you."

Terry picked her way down. Already taller than Nina, she looked larger than usual in her baggy clothing, with the effect of an animal bunching up its fur to look menacing to an enemy. When she got to the gate, she stood there, arms folded, and said, "So?"

"Just returning the visit."

A small smile curled around Terry's lips. "I don't know what you mean."

"I want to talk to you."

"I'm busy."

"If you don't let me in, I'm going to talk to the police. They'll get a search warrant. You broke into my house. And my son's missing. I'm not here to play around."

Terry looked surprised, but Nina didn't know whether or not to credit the raised eyebrows or slightly open mouth. "Have it your way," she said.

Once again she opened the gate and Nina followed her up the hill, but this time they took the main trail to the house. Rivulets of melting snow ran down it, making the walking harder.

Up close, the A-frame needed a paint job, and the porch needed new supports.

A man sat at the oak table near the window, smoking. Young, blond, and strapping, wearing a blue baseball cap, a dirty plaid jacket, and muddy boots, he looked a lot like the man Nina had met on her last trip here, Jerry but with a stubble instead of a beard. This must be his son.

"Go home, Ralphie," Terry said. "I'm busy now."

"I got here first," the young man said. "You promised."

"Get lost."

"Is she the lawyer lady?" He talked deliberately, with slight pauses between words, as if the language made sluggish progress from his mind, only to get stuck in his throat.

"None of your business," Terry said, but he got up to stand by her, reeking of gasoline and oil. He reached a hand out absentmindedly to pat Terry's arm. She pulled her coat away, making a face. "You're filthy."

"Pleased to meet you," he said to Nina. "I like your coat collar. Is it mink?"

"It's fake," Nina said. "I don't wear real fur."

"But you wear leather shoes, I bet," he said with a laugh.

Terry, who had had enough, said loudly, "Ralphie, I said get going!" She herded him to the door, opened it, and invited him out.

"I'm going, I'm going." He stubbed out the cigarette on the hardwood floor and stomped out in his heavy boots.

"Jerk-off," Terry said contemptuously, watching his retreat down the path. If Ralph was her lover, the relationship was definitely doomed. She made sure the door closed behind him, then turned to Nina, who was wondering at the heavy furniture, the Early American oils on the walls.

"My parents' stuff. I never bothered to take any of it down. I basically live in my studio," Terry said. "Let's get this over with quickly. I know nothing about your kid being missing."

"You broke into the house and trashed my room," Nina said, "I saw you."

"Really? Prove it."

"Where is he?"

"Read my lips. I don't know."

"Okay," Nina said. "I think I can make a report to the police that's going to guarantee you get picked up on a seventy-two-hour psychiatric hold. Maybe they'll let you go at that point, maybe they won't. You familiar with the inside of a mental hospital, Terry? Oh, I see you are."

Terry's face had paled. "You can't do that. I'm your friggin' client!" she cried.

"Not anymore."

"I don't have your kid. Look around. He's not here."

She wouldn't tell Nina to look if Bobby was there. Her heart sank. "You trashed my room last night, didn't you?"

"What if I did?" Terry asked, with genuine curiosity. "You going to get me arrested for reading your love letters?"

"You hit me on the head," Nina said. "You tried to hurt me."

"Looks like you've survived," Terry said, "so far."

Nina said, "Don't bullshit me anymore. And don't come around trying to bully me or scare my family. I've got a gun and I will use it if I have to." She didn't, but Terry didn't have to know that. "I won't be off guard next time."

As soon as she said it, she wished she hadn't mentioned a gun. That could magnify the seriousness of Terry's vandalism and incite her. There were already too many nuts with guns running around.

Because she still hoped to find Bobby, she searched the small untidy house thoroughly. Terry didn't try to stop her. There was no sign of him. In the bedroom Terry took off her coat and tossed it onto the bed, where it lay in a furry heap, like an exotic pet. Under the kitchen sink Nina found her letters, out of order, some of them torn.

Terry had followed her around, saying nothing. She eyed the box, her expression, for once, blank.

"You've got it back. I just borrowed it. So let's forget the whole thing," she said.

"Why do you care about my personal business?"

"Just checking something."

"Checking what?"

"To see if you are who I thought you might be."

"And who is that?"

Terry wore a look as cold as the landscape outside the windows, and didn't answer.

"What's this all about?"

Terry opened the front door, and said, "If you know what's good for you, you'll get out of here right now."

"What did I do?"

"Only ruined my life."

"Is this about the case? Maybe I can fix it."

"It's too late," Terry said calmly, neatly guiding her out. "You're not getting out of this." A mountain of hate rose behind her yellow eyes. She shut the door in Nina's face.

For the last two years, Paul had worked out of a small office on the third and top floor of a building just off Ocean Avenue in Carmel. Big Sur, to the south, and Monterey, just over the Carmel Hill, added to his client base.

The office had one thing to recommend it. The main window overlooked the neighboring courtyard of the Hog's Breath Inn, a restaurant and bar where he spent much of his free time.

Paul kept the shade up at the window above his desk while he punched numbers and letters onto his keyboard and skimmed the information on his video monitor, even though it made it a little harder to read. He didn't like desk work much, but this project had to be done on the computer.

His client, a biotechnology firm in San Jose, needed to find someone, a reported computer nerd who had recently set up a home page of his own on the World Wide Web. The nerd called himself der Fliegel, the Fly, and had loads of info to share on a certain proprietary formula. Paul went searching for tiny bug-tracks in cyberspace.

While he searched, Paul looked down at the Hog's Breath courtyard, where tourists in shorts mixed with local business types. He checked his watch and dreamed of lunch, a thick steak with home fries, coleslaw maybe—no, how about a Caesar salad, crunchy and tart. . . . There were some attractive women down there. One dark-haired girl with pale white skin, wearing a halter thing that showed off her magnificent breasts, sat cross-legged, disconsolate, alone. Should he quit now and go down early?

A guy in a white T-shirt with tattoos up to his armpits sat down next to her and put his hand on her delicate white knee. A shame, but now he gazed upon a tall, golden Californian who had just walked in, swinging her purse, her narrow ass swinging along in rhythm. . . . The Hog's Breath was a great place to unwind after work and meet women, and, of course, it was owned by his favorite steely-eyed movie actor.

Now and then Clint did show up at his restaurant, soft-spoken and mellow, shaking hands with the locals, asking how the steak was tonight, if there was anything they needed. Once, about a year before, when Paul was working late in his office, Clint came in with a few friends and opened up the place just for them, lit the fireplace in the middle, and they all settled down to talk and laugh.

Paul had met him once, while Clint was still the mayor of Carmel, at a chamber of commerce reception. Clint had an inch or two on him, but he slouched a lot, and he was getting downright elderly. He had the dignity of a senior statesman, the big hands of a wrestler. He said, "How are ya, Paul?" in that soft, almost sinister voice of his, and Paul said, "I really liked that scene in *The Dead Pool* where you—" but Clint was being pushed gently forward to meet his next well-wisher.

Paul didn't really envy Clint. He liked his freedom, and Clint didn't seem to have much of that—but he would have liked to sit down with him some night over a couple of bourbons and talk with him about the Dirty Harry movies, how much he loved them but how full of crap they were, the police procedures a joke.

At one time Paul had worked in San Francisco as a homicide detective, and he'd always wanted to tell Clint that Inspector Callahan would have been out on his ass in about twelve seconds with that attitude, like Paul had been.

The computer beeped, pulling Paul back into the present. "You have been idle too long," the screen said. He took one more longing look out the real window before he turned back to his virtual window to redial the on-line service.

A kid that looked just like Nina's kid came strolling through the courtyard, down there in the crowd. Paul got up, looking hard.

About eleven, shaggy black hair, tall for his age, carrying his No Fear hat, a backpack on his back, looking around from under Nina's exact eyebrows—yes, Nina's kid.

The kid walked up to a waiter and asked him something. The waiter shrugged his shoulders, moving on.

Where was Nina? Paul jogged down the hall, down the stairs, opened the back door of the building, and crashed right into the boy, and the kid staggered back. Paul held out his hand to steady him, saying, "Whoa! Take it easy!"

Upstairs again, the boy set down his bags and plopped down on Paul's black Italian leather couch. Paul gave him a soda, which he guzzled, eyeing him warily.

"I was coming up here anyway," said the kid.

"Why don't you start by telling me where your mother is," Paul said. For the life of him he couldn't remember the kid's name, even though he'd seen him with Nina many times.

"She didn't call you?"

"Nobody called me to say you'd be dropping by two hundred and eighty miles from Tahoe, no. What's going on?"

"Not much," the kid said jauntily, dirty face smiling above muddy pants. "I'm visiting my grandpa. He lives in Monterey."

"Is he here in town with you? Or are you alone?"

"I took the bus. I wanted to have an appointment with you."

"Sorry. But your name escapes me," Paul said.

"Bob."

"Right. Your grandpa forgot to wash your face this morning, Bob."

The boy's hand almost made it to his cheek before he checked himself, and lowered it. "So, you got a minute for an appointment?"

"I guess so," Paul said. He sat down opposite the couch, put his hands on his knees, said, "What can I do for you?"

"I need to hire you to look for someone for me."

"I see."

"This would be me hiring you, not my mom. She says you're good."

"I'm very good at some things. Who are you looking for?"

"My father."

Uh-oh. "Your mother know what you're doing, Bob?"

"Not exactly." He bunched up his grungy sweatshirt, producing some bills. "I can pay you thirty dollars today, and I'll give you three dollars a week for as long as it takes." He put the bills on the table, giving Paul a challenging look.

Paul didn't pick them up. "I think I'd like to hear some more about the case first," he said. "I'm picky."

"My mother won't tell me anything about my father, so I'm going to find him without her help."

"Nothing?"

"Nothing," the kid said. "She won't talk about him. But," he said, riffling through pockets on the outside of his backpack, "I have my birth certificate with his name on it." Triumphantly he produced a folded-up sheet of paper, which Paul examined carefully.

"How about your grandpa?" Paul had met Harlan Reilly several years before. He still remembered him, a golfer with a wide, ruddy face, and a new wife named Angie-baby. "Doesn't he know anything?"

"He's no use. My mom won't let him tell me anything."

"I'll have to think this over for a few minutes, Bob," Paul said. "Meanwhile, let's walk back over to the Hog's Breath and have some lunch, okay? If you don't have to be getting right back. Then I'll drop you off at your grandpa's."

"I could use a sandwich," the kid said. "But you don't have to drop me off, I'm meeting a friend here."

"Right," Paul said. "You go on down to the bathroom at the end of the hall and wash your face and hands. I'll get my wallet, then we'll go." The kid nodded and went out the door, leaving his backpack and sleeping bag on the rug.

Paul shut the door behind him and called Nina's office.

Sandy put him through to Nina right away and he heard her voice, clear and close as if she was in the next room.

"I thought you might like to know your son is down the hall washing up for lunch," he told her.

"Bobby?"

"Only son you've got I know about." He gave her a minute to collect herself. Her voice had been shaky. She must have put the phone down for a second. When he heard her breathing on the line again he said, "How long has he been gone?"

"Since Wednesday night. We've got the police up here combing the town, looking all over. I never dreamed he'd go so far." A distant nose blew. "Is he all right?"

"Fine. Not upset, no sign of any physical trauma. He ran away?"

"In the middle of the night. He didn't leave a note, but he took some food and his sleeping bag. Oh God, Paul, I've been so worried. Is he back? Let me talk to him."

"Wait a minute," Paul said. "Your son disappears and you don't call me?"

"I tried once. But . . . we've been concentrating up here, Paul. Nobody saw him at the bus station or the train station. Who would ever dream an eleven-year-old boy would go so far on his own? Hang on." He could hear her call out, "Sandy, Paul's got him! Call Matt and Andrea." She got back on the line and said, "Is he there?"

"No, he was pretty dirty. Don't worry. He'll be back. We are discussing some business. And he doesn't know I called you yet."

"Promise you won't let him go."

"Don't worry."

Neither of them spoke for a minute. Then Nina said, "Paul, why did he come to you?"

"He offered me a job."

"What?"

"Seems he's looking for someone. Smart kid. Hires the best."

"He's hunting for his father," said Nina flatly.

"That's right. Kurt Geoffrey Scott."

If Nina was surprised he knew the name, he couldn't tell from her voice.

"Tell him whatever you want, but keep him with you. Take him to my father's. I'm coming down right away, but it's going to be five hours—"

"Can't you fly?"

"It's snowing again, poor visibility, the airport's closed. . . ."

"I'll take care of him."

"Thanks. Thanks so much! I was so scared!"

"And you wonder I don't want kids," Paul said. He kicked himself for saying it after she hung up the phone.

Paul explained to the boy that he was still thinking about whether he could take the case, but that Bob had taken it as far as he could, and his mother needed him. Then he fed him a big lunch, which the boy paid for with an abbreviated story of his past couple of days.

As they drove, Paul sneaked looks at the kid. Only eleven years old, and he had traveled across the state, done some investigating, slept out one full night and part of another, sauntered into restaurants and ordered meals, traveled around the Monterey Peninsula on the bus.

He didn't want to think what the kid would be like at fifteen.

He'd never talked to an obsessed eleven-year-old before. What would Nina do with him? Whup him good? No, that went out in the fifties. You didn't hit kids anymore. Counseling, that's what she would do, keeping her toes on the politically correct line. He thought about what he would have done if Bob had been his kid.

Whup him good, tell him all about his father, and dispel the cloud Nina had put over the guy's name.

He could sympathize with Bob on at least one point: Nina kept too much to herself, things she had no business hiding.

Dropping the boy at his grandfather Harlan Reilly's house, he stood in the doorway attempting to pick the man's brain about Nina's former lover.

Harlan insisted he come in for a little coffee. Round as his beloved golf balls, with powerful arms and a perfect tan, Nina's father led Paul out to a backyard patio that overlooked hills dotted with gnarled Monterey pines.

All around the yard, yellow and red flowers were sprouting in the early spring. There was a late afternoon sparkle in the air, and the day's weather had settled into a temperate seventy degrees. Paul couldn't help picturing Nina braving the storms, coming over the pass from the mountains. Didn't she get tired of living up there, with all those months of cold weather? Tahoe was one of those amenities for Californians who craved winter snow, a place to visit and then have the pleasure of leaving for sunnier climes. She would love living back down here again, if he could only convince her. . . .

Pouring a lot of whiskey into the cups and a little coffee, they each drank one cup and most of a second before Harlan had satisfied himself that he trusted Paul enough to tell him anything.

"Naturally, she never told me a thing about Bob's father. Once the bum took off, she had too much pride to go after him."

"You don't know anything?" Paul asked, disappointed.

"I know plenty," he said. "I'm her father, aren't I?"

7

NINA ARRIVED AT HARLAN'S HOUSE AT SEVEN. SHE HAD DRIVEN UP THE mountains, down the mountains, and through the Central Valley at a speed completely incompatible with snow, rain, narrow roads, and poor visibility. By the time she reached Monterey Bay, she had decided to make Bobby stay in his room after school for the rest of the school year. Without TV or video games.

But when she saw him at the door, looking shamefaced and shabby, she drew him to her and held him. He said, "I'm sorry, Mom."

"We'll talk about all this, honey, until I really understand what happened."

"I had to go."

"Shhh. Lots of time to talk on the way back home. Are you really all right? Nothing bad happened?"

"Of course not. I had my knife. I wasn't scared."

"But . . . where did you sleep?"

"Down at the wharf. It was pretty cold."

"Supper!" Harlan called.

They all rushed through dinner. Paul sat next to her, joining cheerfully into conversation with Harlan and his wife Angie, quizzing Nina's dad on his par. Bobby ate three servings of the chicken, but Nina could hardly eat. Food choked her. She sat next to her son, touching him frequently.

As soon as she had carried the dishes back to the kitchen, she said, "We have to get back."

"You could stay over," Paul said. "It's too far to drive back now."

"No," Nina said. "I had two cups of coffee. I want this boy home in his own bed."

Paul walked them out. While Bobby settled himself in the passenger seat, Nina took Paul aside and said, "I'm so grateful."

"I didn't do anything."

"Did you tell him you aren't going to help him?"

"Not yet. I'll call him tomorrow after school. I thought you should talk with him first. And maybe you should tell me what's going on."

"There's nothing to tell. I haven't seen Bob's father for twelve years." She looked into Paul's inquisitive eyes.

"Bob's not going to let you coast too much farther on this one," he said.

"We'll see. Thanks for everything, Paul."

"My timing is rotten, but every time I see you, my mind tends to run in the same tracks."

She smiled.

"When can I spend time with you? Let's ski, soak in the spa at Caesars, maybe more. . . . I like you, Nina. I'm getting attached."

"Don't get attached. I'm—"

"Involved with someone else?"

"No."

"Love can't always wait," Paul said. He put his arms around her. She could feel his desire as he stroked her back, pressing against her. "And as you know, in both our lines of work, control's a luxury. Chaos is the norm."

"I've got to go," she said, pulling gently away from him and climbing up into the driver's seat of the Bronco. "I promise, I'll call you soon."

She reversed herself driving back, over the valley, up the mountains and down the mountains, never exceeding the speed limit, while Bob lay in the backseat, the seatbelt fastened firmly around his sleeping form. They didn't get back until two in the morning. Dragging him to his bed, she left the car packed with his dirty bags and jumped into her own bed, trying hard to sleep, images of Bob and Paul and Terry popping like balloons in and out of the courtroom of her mind.

Paul called Bob the next afternoon, telling him as kindly as he could that he would see what he could do. For one thing, that would keep the kid from running off again. For another, he didn't want to refuse outright and get on Bob's bad side. He was Nina's kid, after all. Of course, Paul couldn't do much. Poking his nose into Nina's business might net him a black eye.

All morning he cruised cyberspace. At noon he finally caught up with and swatted der Fliegel on-line. He called his client, ate lunch at the Hog's Breath, played racketball, and watched *The Good, the Bad and the Ugly* for about the forty-seventh time on his office TV.

He drifted into a lonesome mood. At four o'clock on this balmy March afternoon, a certain brown-haired pixie was far away. It was St. Patrick's Day, and he didn't have a date for the evening. One of the lawyers he worked for in Salinas had invited him to a party, but he couldn't let loose among the stuffed shirts and potential employers he might encounter there.

Come to think of it, he hadn't let loose for a long time. What had happened to all those parties he remembered in hot, squalid apartments lit by firelight and candles, loud crashing music and cheap wine stripping away clothes and inhibitions, bodies packed together, everyone available at least for the night, heavy anarchic conversations in the kitchen, clouds of marijuana smoke out on the back porch—what had the world come to, when he couldn't find a decent party on St. Patrick's?

Down below, in the Hog's Breath courtyard, extremely young people caressed each other, argued, made up, smoked, drank too much, and did all the self-destructive things he had sworn off since receiving the results of his latest cholesterol test. A big sandy-haired kid down there reminded him of himself at nineteen, jock turned nihilist. His long hair struck Paul now as sloppy; did indulgent parents pay for the espressos and the sky blue Miata he figured was parked down the street?

He went to the mirror behind the office door and examined the four gray hairs up there, just above his hairline. There was a new one, number five. He plucked all five.

At least he had a hairline. He shouldn't complain. He still had the shoulders, the 'ceps, from his football days. Where *was* his football? He scrounged around, finding it in a neglected corner, and drew back his arm in a couple of imaginary passes. A terrible thought came to him. Perhaps such parties were in full swing at this very moment, and he wasn't invited.

He suddenly realized how lonely he felt. He saw Nina's face the night before, as she had talked about Bob's father, the way her brown eyes looked away from him toward a whole history that still propelled her life. She had made it plain that the subject of Kurt Scott was off limits.

He should respect that. He had no right to invade her privacy. This was between Nina and Bob.

He was just . . . a friend. He didn't like thinking of himself like that. He wanted to get closer. That made Scott his problem now too. A strong sensation of inner turbulence moiled and boiled in his gut, saying, "Do something!"

Apologizing mentally to Nina, he sat down at his computer, dialing up CompuServe. These days, you couldn't disappear. Nobody escaped the clutches of cyberdick.

His fingers typed KURT GEOFFREY SCOTT.

He had decided to find the son of a bitch.

"Sandy? Can you come in for a second?"

Sandy, who had been passing Nina's door, said, "Okay. Just let me get the frozen coffee out of the freezer. Then I'll measure it carefully and put it through the grinder. Then I'll get out the gold filter. And all."

A few minutes later she returned to Nina's office, carrying two cups of fresh brew.

"Thanks," said Nina, breathing in the smell. "I'm waking up already."

Sandy looked at her watch. "Four o'clock in the afternoon. Right on schedule."

"You don't like it that I freeze my coffee," Nina said. "You think it's a waste of time."

"It's a white middle-class ritual," Sandy said. "You don't mess with my rituals; I don't mess with yours."

Sipping at the fresh, strong liquid, Nina asked, "Have we received our final payment on the London case?"

"There's no balance outstanding." Sandy returned to her desk, looked it up on the computer. "The retainer covered everything," she said.

"Excellent," Nina said. She picked up her microphone and began to dictate. "On letterhead. To Theresa London."

When Sandy brought letters in for Nina to sign at the end of the day, she remarked that Nina sounded remarkably pleasant in the letter. "You stone her and then just say 'good luck.' "

"That's standard insurance. Give her nothing to object to. Cross your fingers. And pray she'll sign the substitution form and let me out of the case."

"What did she do to get on your list?"

"Plenty. Don't forget to mark the calendar to send her another one in a week with a follow-up letter. If she doesn't return it, I'll get a motion ready."

"What do I do if she calls?"

"Field my calls for the next couple of days, will you? I'm not available to Terry London."

"Will do."

Paul's fingers twitched. In couple of hours of hunting on-line, he had established that Kurt Scott didn't live in Monterey, Pacific Grove, Carmel, Big Sur, Seaside, Marina, Salinas, or Carmel Valley. He had no California record of felony convictions, at least in the major counties that had such information computerized. TRW had no credit records on him. And he did not possess a California driver's license.

Poking through Harlan's mind for irrelevant bits of information that he'd gathered or come by over the years had helped more. Harlan knew some potentially useful things. He knew Scott had been working for the U.S. Forest Service when he'd met Nina, and he was some kind of musician. Harlan couldn't remember what instrument he'd played. Not rock and roll though. In fact, Harlan even remembered that Scott's favorite musician was Van Cliburn, a pianist, so maybe he'd played the piano too. His family was from Tahoe, but he'd lived for a bit in Germany as a child.

And Scott had met Nina while she was vacationing in the Tahoe area twelve years before.

Paul had always wondered, why had Nina fled her divorce only to settle in South Lake Tahoe? Now he knew she had one reason, and he didn't much like it.

He decided to call Harlan, who answered on the second ring. Retirement probably made every phone call a treat. Harlan told a couple of jokes in honor of St. Patrick and Paul laughed. Then he said, "I just wanted to clear up something you said when we spoke yesterday. You said you thought Scott had finished college. Any idea what college he attended?"

Silence for a moment. When Harlan spoke again, he had dropped his usual bantering tone. "You intend to find Bob's father, don't you?" he asked.

"Yes."

"Why?"

"Gotta do it. He's in the way."

"Have you considered how Nina's going to feel when she finds out?"

"No."

" 'Love has pitched his mansion,' hasn't he?"

"In a mess, as always," said Paul.

"I like a man who knows his Yeats. But you realize she won't like you digging up old dirt."

"I'm not doing this for her."

"Will you tell her what you find out?"

"I don't know."

Harlan thought about that, then apparently bestowing his tacit approval on the endeavor said, "Try UNR. The University of Nevada at Reno. That's the four-year college closest to Tahoe. And I seem to remember something about it."

Once upon a time Paul had married a robust cross-country skier from Reno, Nevada. He consulted his watch, a gold Rolex, his one and only treasure. Six o'clock. She would be home from work.

On impulse, he called her.

Her new husband, Ronald something or other, answered, and Paul explained in a slightly affected tone that his wife had ordered *Vogue* and *InStyle* recently, or was it *Vogue* and *Vanity Fair*? He hoped his company hadn't inadvertently erred.

"Just a minute," Ronald said, putting his hand over the phone. "Some asshole says you ordered *Vogue*," he said in an only slightly muffled voice.

"I never," a woman's voice protested.

"Like the vacuum cleaner you bought last week from that jerk at the door."

"That was different, Ronnie, I'm telling you. . . . Never mind, hand me the phone." The volume of the TV in the background went back up. His ex-wife, Tricia, said stridently, "You better talk fast, 'cuz I have diarrhea and I've got to go." Laughter exploded in the background.

"That's disgusting, Trish. Why did I ever marry you, anyway?" Paul said.

"Oh, right, those magazines," Tricia said. "Hang on, I'm going to get on the phone in the other room." A minute later she picked up an extension in a quieter place and said, "No, I won't come back to you. You can beg and plead all you want."

"I've matured a lot since then."

"So have I. That's why you don't have a chance."

"How are you?"

"I have three kids, that's how I am, and I haven't heard word one from you for about a decade."

"I have no excuse."

"You used to be great at thinking those up. So why are you calling me? Ronnie gets all cranky when your name comes up. I guess it's a boy thing, so I'm glad you used an alias." She sounded friendly and curious.

Paul suddenly had a vivid memory of her in bed, on her hands and knees as he approached her from the rear, her round pink-and-white behind presented so invitingly. It was funny, the images you remembered most from your marriages.

"Are you still a cop?" she said.

"No. I moved on. I'm a detective agency now."

"Well, I hope you're making better money."

"Better than Ronnie," Paul said.

"Hunh! I doubt it. Ronnie's a gynecologist."

He decided to let that one pass.

"Listen, Trish, I need a favor. A little favor, tiny, minuscule in fact."

"Like what?"

"I'm looking for a man."

"You *have* changed. I never would have guessed."

Paul ignored her. "This man might have gone to the University of Nevada at Reno, maybe even while you were there, sometime in the early to middle eighties. I thought maybe you had some old school annuals—"

"Why are you looking for him?"

"His great-grandpa wants to leave him his fortune," Paul said. "Who knows, he might be very grateful to know you helped find him."

"You're such a liar, Paul," Tricia said, but she was amused enough to go and drag out her old yearbooks and look for Kurt Scott.

The fog had thickened outside Paul's window. He was getting antsy, dredging up the past in pursuit of a guy he had no business looking for. Long shots like this never paid off. He'd do better buying a Lotto ticket. At least then he'd have one chance in a trillion.

"Aren't you the lucky boy," Tricia said. "I found him in one of Ronnie's yearbooks. Kurt G. Scott, class of 1981. He was a couple of years before my time."

Jackpot! "What would I have to do to get you to fax me the photo?"

"Promise never to call me again. Or call more often."

"For that, you have to fax me everything in there about him," Paul said. "Teams, clubs, whatever he was involved in."

"I'd have to cut out some pages. I could do that. Ronnie bought me a fax for Christmas."

"Now? You'd do that now? That would be wonderful, Trish. You always were a good girl."

"No, I always was a bad girl, Paul," Trish said. "That was why you fell for me. I'll help you for old times' sake, though. For the sake of the way you cussed at the climax of passion."

"That's what you remember about me?" Paul said.

"That was so cute."

Bob had to stay late at school to finish some makeup work from the days he had missed. His Uncle Matt was supposed to be picking him up, but he had a tow job—someone had crashed into a tree over by Emerald Bay. He'd get there as soon as he could. He wanted Bob to wait in front of the office if the teacher kicked him out.

Sure enough, at four-thirty Mrs. Yeager slammed her lesson book shut and sent him and the other kids out.

One by one, moms and dads pulled up in cars to cart off their kids, while he sat on a bench in front of the office, wondering if anyone was left inside behind the blinds. Although there were still a few cars in the parking lot, the school had a deserted, lifeless feeling without all the kids, almost spooky.

He decided to go into the office to wait. He tried the door and found it locked. He pulled a quarter out of his backpack and called his mom's office. Her machine answered. It must be after five. He looked for another quarter to call his aunt at home, but remembered loaning it to Jasper at lunch for milk. So he would just wait.

Only one car remained in the parking lot. The door opened. A big black dog jumped out and ran straight for him.

"Hey," Bob yelled. "Stay back!" He jumped onto the bench and got his foot ready to kick. The dog stopped short, wagged his tail, and licked Bob's shoe.

"Hitchcock!" a woman called. "C'mere, boy." She came running up behind the dog with her hand on a dangling leash. "Oh, hi," she said. "Bob, right?"

8

UNCLE MATT DROVE UP IN THE BIG YELLOW TOW TRUCK A FEW minutes after the lady and her dog had gone.

"Sorry to be so late, Bob. You okay?"

"Fine, Uncle Matt."

"Boy, it got dark fast, didn't it? Just sneaked up on me."

"No problem, Uncle Matt. I just sat here on the bench. Mostly."

"Finish your work up?"

"Yep."

Matt turned the radio on.

"I almost got a ride with that lady Mom knows. She didn't like me being alone in the dark."

"What lady?"

"She has this black dog who slobbers all over the place. He's a real bruiser. She lets him run out on the field after everyone leaves. Don't worry. She cleans up his messes."

"Who was it, Bob?"

"Terry somebody. Like I said, she's a friend of Mom's."

"You were right not to take a ride with anyone, even if it's your mom's friend. You did the right thing."

"I ran with her and the dog for a while, though."

"You should have just waited for me. What if I couldn't find you?"

"We stayed right on the field!" he said, although Terry had wanted him to join them on a walk up the street. He'd refused and she told him she understood that he sure wouldn't want to make his mom mad.

She'd been nice, and wanted to hear about his trip to Monterey. She'd even said that name, Kurt Scott, sounded familiar, and she might be able to help him look.

He told her how he had promised his mom not to look for him himself while she was thinking things over, but Terry had said, well, Bob, that doesn't apply to me, does it?

Maybe the look on his face made his uncle soften. "Really, it's okay," he said. "Here you are, no harm done. Now, you leave it to me to tell your mom it's my fault you're late tonight. I hate to worry her with this."

"We don't have to tell her you were late. That would be fine with me."

"I guess she's less likely to get upset if she doesn't know I left you to fend for yourself for a few minutes."

Bob felt relieved. Uncle Matt hadn't made a big deal out of him talking to Terry, so he didn't need to feel guilty.

Anyway, he'd probably never see her again.

As it turned out, Paul did find a St. Patrick's Day party, and he paid his respects to Dionysus, who repaid him with a skull-splitting headache on Saturday morning. When he stopped by the office on Sunday, wearing shades to keep the fog from hurting his eyes, he found several curled sheets of fax paper on the floor, where his machine always filed them.

The faxed photo of Scott showed a large young man with longish dark hair swept back from his forehead, wearing a polo shirt, solemnly facing the camera. The features were all normal size, no awesome forehead or jutting nose or geeky neck and Adam's apple; no facial hair.

You could tell a lot about how a guy looked into the camera for a class picture, even if the picture quality was poor. From the polo shirt, Paul deduced that he wasn't a flaming radical. He could even be a science student. His expression meant he wasn't a fun-type guy either, took himself seriously. Longish hair? Youth, that was all, could go on to become a corporate banker. Normal weight, neither a runner nor a linebacker.

So . . . studious type, too big to be a nerd, though. Paul pondered the young Scott's face for another minute or two. Well-defined lips, deep-set eyes, very light, could be green or blue. Some character there.

He had Scott memorized. Under the picture a heading said, *Kurt G. Scott. Major, Music. Minor, German.* Well, that fit with everything Harlan had told him.

As expected, the next page presented the University of Nevada's orchestra. The dark-haired fellow at the grand piano, face shown in profile, was identified as Scott. Yes, the piano. The Chopin type, Paul thought. Sensitive, intellectual, attracted women like a goldfish attracts cats. Probably wouldn't have the slightest idea how to go out for a pass. . . .

Next page. Track and field. Kurt G. Scott, javelin. Well, that took shoulders. Scott stood on the college track, his javelin poised for a throw, his eyes whited out by glare. He wore a sleeveless T-shirt and shorts, showing off a medium-size, rangy body with good muscle definition. Behind him a few others worked the long-jump pit and bleachers. Scott had picked up a distance-throwing record in his junior year.

Sissy stuff. Real men played real sports: football, baseball, and basketball, in that order. Hockey had the requisite vicious spirit, but unfortunately fell to the indignity of men wearing skates. And no self-respecting American man bounced a ball off his head to play soccer.

Javelin throwing was in the category of activities for guys that couldn't cut it on any team at all.

Last page. The German Club consisted mostly of girls. Kurt G. Scott sat in the back row. And well he might. The club's adviser, Frau Ingrid Sheets, a gray-haired lady in long skirts, stood to the right.

Paul tried to think charitably about the guy. Not all men could measure up to his standards of excellence. Not all men were all-man. Musicians, except jazz musicians, and language students were excluded by definition. Why did women fall in love with them so regularly? It was another mystery, like where he'd put his favorite comb, that he might never solve.

He didn't like it, but he could see Bob in Scott. Black hair, the same. Chiseled chin, the same. Build, similar, if scaled up from age eleven. A complicated expression, maybe guile, maybe repressed feelings, played over the father's face in the same way he'd seen it in the boy's.

He called Frau Sheets at the University of Nevada. She had retired years ago, but someone in admissions dug around and found her number once Paul mentioned the large win she'd mistakenly left behind at Harrah's.

When he got her on the phone, he explained about the inheritance Scott had coming to him from his distant Uncle Dieter.

He had to talk at top volume. The lady was quite elderly, although still compos mentis. She didn't remember Kurt very well, she told him, but Paul kept her on the line, unwilling to let go of what might be his only direct link to Kurt Scott. A more impatient person would never have put up with Frau Sheets's rambling, but he'd discovered that a small investment of his time often paid large dividends, and this time was no exception.

After reminiscing at some length about her years at the university and lingering conversationally over some favorite students, she recalled Scott's mother, who had worked as a teaching assistant in the German program for years until the commuting from Tahoe proved too much. "She always wanted to go back to Germany. You know, they lived there briefly when Kurt was young."

"Do you remember where they lived?"

"Hmm. Kurt's father was in the military at the time, so they must have lived on a base."

"Frankfurt?"

"Wiesbaden," she said. "That's it. Yes, I'm sure it was Wiesbaden."

"You've been a great help," said Paul.

"*Auf Flügeln des Gesanges,*" she said. " 'On the wings of song.'

That was his motto, from Heine. All my students had to read the greats and select words to live by. Pretty good memory for an old biddy going on seventy-six," she said briskly, "wouldn't you say?"

"Pretty good," he agreed, "though I wouldn't use the word *biddy* to describe you."

"That's what that other woman who wanted to know about Kurt called me. Her story was even more specious than yours. She said he'd won the lottery. I didn't tell her anything."

While Sandy was at lunch on Monday, a middle-aged woman messenger in jeans and a sweatshirt with metal clips around the ankles of her pant legs brought a thick yellow envelope to Nina. FAST WOMEN her red sweatshirt said. The silhouette of a bicycle and rider zoomed across her chest.

The envelope bore Riesner's firm's return address. Jeffrey Riesner had disagreed with the wording on her proposed order. A further hearing was set on *Sweet v. London* on March thirtieth, ten days away.

Damn it! She'd won the case. She had drafted the language for the formal order. Ordinarily, if the opposing counsel didn't sign the order in ten days, it was submitted and accepted by the court unchanged. In cases where the draft gave somebody trouble, the two lawyers would put their heads together and work out wording they could both accept. Apparently, Riesner did not want to put his head that close to hers at the moment.

The new hearing on Terry's case put to rest any hopes Nina had of getting off the hook easily. She could seek a delay, further holding up the film, dragging out the relationship, fueling the fire of her client's anger. Or she could put this with all the other necessary evils of the job, on the calendar, to be skulked through and finished.

Sandy returned, swinging a voluminous purple coat through the door behind her.

"Did we send the letter off to Terry London, the one where we fired her?" asked Nina.

"Went out last night."

"Grrr. Can you send another letter today with a copy of this, saying I'll appear with her on March thirtieth, but that will be my last work in the case."

Sandy was taking off her coat with such phlegmatic indifference to how long she took at the job that Nina said, "Sandy?"

"Did we fire her or not?" asked Sandy, picking off a bit of lint.

"I can't fire a client, if by doing so her interests are negatively affected. It's not ethical. Now she's got a cleanup hearing in ten days. I'm stuck."

"If you say so. If it was me, I just wouldn't show up."

"It's much more complicated than that. If I don't show up, and have no legitimate reason for my failure to appear, Judge Milne will sanction me seven hundred fifty dollars. If I file a motion to withdraw as attorney now, he won't grant it, because it's only one more hearing and Terry'd have to hire another lawyer with another retainer. If I postpone the hearing with some excuse, her film is held up longer, and I'm acting unethically because she's been prejudiced."

Sandy pointed her finger at her ear, drawing little circles. "Wacko," she said. "Problem is, you lawyers think too much. Things get too complicated. And you make all the rules, so your clients have to pay you to tell them how to follow the rules you made. And now—"

"Back to work, okay, Sandy?"

"You're slaves to all these rules," Sandy said, undeterred, and settled her large personage into the creaking chair.

"You're right," Nina said.

Sandy inclined her head, accepting this homage.

"I still have to do it, though."

"Is she dangerous?"

"Maybe."

"And to think I was actually bored at my last job."

"I hate to have to say this to you on such an exquisitely beautiful day, Sandy. But keep your eyes open wider than usual."

"Expect an Uzi poking through the door any day, check."

9

THAT NIGHT PAUL DREAMED HE WAS THE GREAT PIANIST VAN CLIBURN, in black tie and tails, sitting at the piano in an enormous recital hall filled with surly private detectives who spoke only Hungarian. He pressed his fingers to the keys to begin, but then a kid came up and tapped him on the shoulder from behind. He woke up smiling.

Early the next morning, he contacted the city orchestra in Wiesbaden, asking for Kurt Scott. They had never heard of him. Well, then, how about Van Cliburn? The efficient lady who spoke to him in perfect English said, "Oh! Could it be Mr. Scott Cliburn you are looking for?"

Incredible, thought Paul. I'm one brilliant effing SOB. This would make a good story to tell Nina . . . someday. "Yes, yes, that's right, Scott Cliburn," Paul answered.

"I believe Herr Cliburn is performing in a series of spring concerts at the Hessische Staatstheater." He would be playing a special Bach program this coming Saturday. An extraordinary interpreter of the fugues, he would also be playing the two Saturday nights after that. She gave him a number, although she couldn't provide an address. Paul sat up straight in his rumpled bed. He was just an old hound dog. He had hardly slept with the scent of prey tickling his nostrils. He punched the number.

"Ja?" said a deep voice.

"Is this Scott Cliburn?"

"Speaking," said the unmistakably American voice. "Who's calling, please?"

Paul hung up. He didn't want to scare the man off.

He had to go one way or the other. Oh, he could stick to the good old status quo and let the qualms and doubts and compunctions take over. He could sit on his hands, acting like a gentleman, respecting Nina's privacy while she drifted away from him.

But he wanted to shake things up. He wanted to jostle Nina out from under the bones of an old relationship that was stifling her and him both. How much damage had the ghost of Bob's father already done to her, haunting her every move?

If he blew it, if he made things worse, at least he wouldn't have to look in the mirror later at a face that said, you idiot, you lost her because you chickened out. Why the hell didn't you do something?

He gave himself another day or two to brood about Nina, sinking into a state of irresolution he found unbearably frustrating. He needed to get on with his life. This limbo was driving him crazy.

He phoned a former Peace Corps colleague who was now working as a policeman in Munich, who had nagged him about visiting for years. He would stay with Hermann for a couple of days after a weekend stop in Wiesbaden, do a quick tour of the local law enforcement facilities, and write most of the trip off as business. Anyway, what was life for, if not to satisfy curiosity? At the least, it would remind him of what a fugue was.

On Thursday he called Nina and told her he'd be gone for a week. She didn't seem to mind. He found her casual attitude about his absence from her life damned galling.

Late Friday morning he flew on a twelve-seater from Monterey to San Francisco, then took a nonstop flight on American Airlines to Frankfurt. He would arrive Saturday morning, in plenty of time to catch a show that night.

* * *

Frankfurt airport, endless green tunnels, sickly yellow lighting, rain—he caught a cab out on the Kaiserstrasse. Wiesbaden was only about twenty miles west, but for the cab fare he could have been driven from New York to Florida.

Following a long morning nap at the hotel and a hefty lunch of sausage and beer, Paul explored the little city of Wiesbaden. The sky darkened and drizzle began again about four, so he retreated into a smoky stube for a couple of hours. There he stumbled upon a number of new beers that had somehow escaped previous notice. The time passed all too quickly.

At seven, back at the hotel, he showered off the tobacco fumes. A taxi got him to the State Theater, barely on time after all his efforts. Ducking his head into his jacket, he ran up the long walkway of the theater. Cloudy light and the sound of laughter drifted out into the entryway with its tall Greek pillars and empty urns.

Inside, he realized he was seriously underdressed. The women flashed jewelry, perfume, decolletage; the men all wore sober black suits. They would have to put up with his American tielessness. He took his seat at the back.

Kurt Scott came out, took a bow, and sat down at a tall, carved wood organ amid thunderous applause, wearing long dark hair and a tux. He took a deep breath, placing long fingers precisely on the keys.

Quiet fell.

A long, rich note seemed to grow out of the organ, soft gold hovering in the air. It was chased by other dark, somehow brutal notes. Slowly, then with a rapid, even pace, the notes uncurled, physical things that pushed you back into your chair gasping, then grasped you and buried you in swirling undercurrents until you felt you were drowning. The fugue was dizzying, harsh, unsparing, yet somehow dispassionate.

Paul had never thought of music as powerful. The rafters of the theater shook with it.

He looked around him. The audience leaned forward, rapt. The man at the organ slowed, moving into a stately air. Expelling a sigh, his devotees rested upon the notes. But soon trouble entered, an emotion like evil began to struggle with the sounds, until the two melodies rolled over on each other and fought, until it seemed neither could win. The result would be chaos. At the height of this monumental struggle Paul, too, clenched the red velvet armrest, caught up in the dark, thrilling battle.

And gradually the two strands moved toward each other, unwillingly at first, then faster and faster until they merged into a crescendo of love and triumph. . . .

The fugue was complete. The man at the organ bowed, accepting the applause of his audience.

The orchestra came out after the intermission, and Scott moved back to the piano. When the concert finally ended, Paul was sorry.

Scott left the stage. Paul went backstage to find him. Holding a large white lily one of the girls had just pressed upon him, Scott relaxed in the middle of a circle of well-wishers, the focus, looking like any man with the world at his fingertips.

Paul hung back, waiting for his chance, not knowing what he would say to him. He had no rehearsed speech. He had enjoyed the hunt, but found himself amazed that it had actually paid off. Now he would have to step up to the plate and do something.

The crowd thinned, and Scott turned away. "Excuse me!" Paul called out in English. He hurried after Scott, who had paused at the top of the stairs leading off the backstage and ending at an exit from the building.

Scott was almost as tall as Paul, but weighed twenty or thirty pounds less. He still brushed his hair straight back. Under the cocked eyebrows were green eyes and an amiable smile. He was extremely good-looking. Years younger than Paul, an athletic-looking type, he even played piano.

Paul felt an unwelcome emotion. Okay. Let it come: he was jealous of the guy Nina had loved so much, once, that she gave him a son. This made him a tad less circumspect and polite than he might ordinarily be in greeting a new person. "Kurt Scott, right? We need to talk."

His words had an unanticipated result. Scott turned and rushed down the stairs, flinging open the door and disappearing into the night. Paul ran after him, pissed off at his own lack of restraint, wondering if he should tackle the musician.

The rain had stopped again. They ran into a small park with iron chairs and pseudoclassical statues, moonlight creating shadows that brought them alive. But a quick jog through muddy grass was nothing compared to the workout sand usually gave him. Paul caught up swiftly and dove for Scott's legs, bringing him down, gasping, onto the wet grass. Paul sat on him until he stopped struggling, then slowly gave him room to breathe.

"I just want to talk to you."

Scott sat up, rubbing his jaw where it had hit the ground. "Who are you?"

"I'm a private detective, out of California."

"Oh, God. Have you told her yet?"

"Nobody knows I'm here," Paul said. "I'm a private investigator."

"She sent you to find me?"

"Not exactly."

"At least she didn't come herself," Scott muttered into his hands. He took a deep breath and looked up. "Let me see your license." Paul pulled it out, and he said, "Okay, you're legitimate. How did you find me?"

"It was easy."

"Shit!"

"Look. I'm just here to obtain some information."

"She didn't tell you a thing, did she?"

"Not much."

"You're just supposed to report back?"

"You got it."

"She'll never let go," Scott said, mostly to himself. "It's been years." His face drooped into some old familiar suffering.

"Yeah, a long time," Paul said. "What do you say—you don't treat me like your worst enemy, we get up like gentlemen and go and have a drink? I'll buy." He took the unresisting man by the arm and marched him the few blocks to his hotel, taking him down the stairs to the weinkeller. They sat down at a small table in the corner.

The place had the ambience of a dungeon, its damp air soaked with the vinegary tang of wine. There were only a half dozen tables, with white cloths and candles. Behind the chair where Scott sat, another room with rough stone walls held rack after rack of horizontal bottles. A waiter in a tux something like Scott's wandered out of the gloom and handed them a long wine list.

"How about you order for me," Paul said. "Something white."

Scott ordered a bottle of 1987 Schloss Biebrich Gewürztraminer. The waiter brought the bottle, displaying the label to silent fanfare, making further ceremony out of pouring an ounce for Scott to taste. The pleasant atmosphere and good wine had a salutary effect on them both. Scott had calmed down and now appeared to be studying Paul. He'd lost the desperate air and moved into survival mode.

He was looking for an angle or a way out.

"To Bach," Paul said. They drank. The wine was spicy, light-bodied, and flowery. "You sure can play that organ."

"I try to do a few concerts each year. During the day I have a different job."

"Where?"

He didn't answer. "I'll pay you double to tell her you can't find me."

"Convince me with information," Paul said. "That's what I'm after, not money. See, I took the job on because I was curious about you."

"What do you want to know?"

"Why you left. Here, have some more."

"You don't want to know. You might get her looking at you. And that would be dangerous for you, just like you finding me is dangerous for me. She's completely crazy, you know."

"Wait a minute," Paul said, shaking his head. "That's a little hard. She's—"

"Of course you don't believe me. She's spent her whole life perfecting an act. She knows how to hide who she really is."

"Nina's got her flaws, no doubt about it, but I've never heard anyone describe her as crazy. Unless you know something I don't?"

"What did you say?" Scott's face grayed. "Who?"

"Calm down, Mr. Scott," Paul said. These sensitive musician types, you had to go easy on them.

Scott stood up and stuck his face in Paul's face.

"Nina Reilly sent you?" he whispered.

"I'm here in connection with her, yes." From ten inches away, Paul watched relief flood up into Scott's eyes, until he covered them with his lids and sat down.

"I'll be damned," he said, as if to himself. He picked up his glass and drained it. His face rapidly returned to a healthier color.

"Isn't she the lady in question here?" Paul said.

"Nina? No. Forget everything I just said. I made a mistake." His guard slightly relaxed now, looking more cocky, he sprawled gracefully in his chair. The sprawl disguised a taut readiness of position. A toughness settled itself around him. He was more man than his cowardly flight had suggested, his body told Paul. His eyes were narrower than his pictures had shown, cagier. The face held the promise of a fight, if it proved absolutely necessary. "Tell me, how is Nina?"

"It surprises me you'd want to know. After all, you ran out on her."

"Why did she want to find me? Is she all right?"

"Hunky-dory. Of course, lawyering ages a woman, toughens her up. She smokes cigars, wears a buzz cut. You wouldn't be interested, believe me."

"Is she still living on the Monterey Peninsula?"

"No, she's moved," Paul said shortly.

"So she became an attorney after all."

"I can see you haven't kept in close touch." Paul found the knowledge soothing. "Yeah, she's a lawyer, has been for a while." He had suspected Nina may not have told Scott he had a son. Now he was sure of it. Better tread lightly.

"I'm glad. I can't believe what you said, that she's gotten hard—"

Paul said, "Don't mind if I do," and poured out the last of the bottle. "Don't help me. Hey, Herr Kellner! *Noch eine Flasche, bitte*!"

"Very good," Scott said as the waiter arrived with another bottle.

"High school German I. How could I ever forget?"

"Tell me, why is Nina looking for me after so long?"

"I'll make you a deal, Mr. Scott. I'll tell you what brings me here. And you tell me why you and Nina called it quits."

"You start," Scott said.

Paul nodded, thinking quickly about what not to say. "Nina and I are involved, but she's been hanging back. It's obvious this old . . . friendship with you meant something to her. I thought you might be the problem, but she won't talk about it. So I came here to ask you."

"Whew," Scott said. He drank more wine.

"I tracked you down without telling her about it."

"You're in love with her?"

"We're engaged," Paul said, fibbing a little, in case the guy was getting any bright ideas. Let him know straight out whose territory they were talking about.

"I loved her so much I never wanted to leave her."

What was this guy? Italian? He had been living in Europe too long. You didn't just come out with something like that, not to another guy. Not to Paul, Nina's fiancé. "But you did," he said in his friendliest voice. If you couldn't kill them, kill them with kindness.

"I had to. It's complicated, and I can't go into it."

"You might as well, Mr. Scott. We've got plenty of time."

Scott took a long time to think it over, until Paul's patience wore out. "Let me get you started. You ran for years. You're still scared of someone, some female someone, who you think is crazy. The law fits in here somewhere, doesn't it? You in trouble?"

"Not in the sense you mean."

"Maybe you could use some help getting this thing cleared up," Paul said. "It's a hell of a life."

Scott rubbed his forehead, looking doubtful.

"Did you find somebody else here in Germany? Get married, buy a place, have kids?" Paul said.

"No. Nina was my last chance," he said. "I suppose it was ridiculous for me to hold on to a fantasy that someday I could return to her."

"Not gonna happen," Paul agreed. "She's with me now."

"Yes, of course."

"So you don't intend to return to Tahoe to try to see her?" He felt slightly guilty. The poor guy obviously had no idea about Bob. The tip of his tongue was adding, You've got a son, man, he needs you, go see him, but he couldn't say the words. Nina would never forgive him. And that self-seeking bastard part of himself didn't want Scott to go to Tahoe, at least until he had Nina in the bag.

"She's moved to Tahoe?"

So much for being discreet. "Yeah," Paul said, kicking himself mentally, "as of last spring."

"This is horrible news."

"What is? What's the problem here?"

"Stop," Scott said. He held his hand up to stop Paul's questions. "I have to think."

"For chrissake . . ."

Scott got up. "Give me a minute. I'll be right back," he said, gesturing toward the rest room.

Paul drank his wine and waited for Nina's old lover to take a leak, with one eye on the exits. Distracted by the waiter, he caught only a glimpse of Scott's broad tuxedoed back heading out. He was one second too late getting out the door, where the cobbled streets and the half-timbered old houses told many a story, but not the one about where the freaked-out musician had run.

10

THE FOLLOWING WEEK, EXACTLY TEN DAYS AFTER NINA RECEIVED Riesner's Notice of Motion, Tahoe was digging itself out after a three-day avalanche of sticky, late March snow. Nina left the house early, shovel in hand, to free her tires and hit the dangerous roads at a stately pace. Terry she greeted quickly, taking her own place in the courtroom, feeling cold and out of sorts, but quite matter-of-fact. Familiarity had done its usual job of breeding contempt. She no longer heard imaginary guns going off in court. The imaginary bloodstains had disappeared once and for all. After several months the room had returned to the bland setting of yore.

Nobody wanted to go to court again on this matter, including her. She couldn't wait to be through. She wanted to win, but she didn't feel optimistic. Riesner had set her up for this, dodging her phone calls and intentionally picking a fight when he called so that they couldn't resolve things simply.

"*Sweet v. London,*" Milne said, adjusting his glasses and opening the file the clerk handed him, "again."

★ ★ ★

After the hearing, out in the hall, Nina moved Terry to a quiet spot, sat her down in a chair, and stood over her. Terry's hair had fallen across one of her eyes, but she didn't brush it away. Something sly slid through her eyes.

"We pushed too hard," Nina said. "The judge might have accepted a compromise."

"Screw them all. And screw you," Terry said. "You blew it."

"I know you're disappointed. Riesner's making a determined effort to delay the showing of your film on orders from Tam's parents."

"You did a shitty job in there."

"I'm sorry you think so. But realistically we're talking an additional delay of only one month. We get the wording on the order approved by all parties, and everyone leaves you in peace to show your film."

"You fucking loser."

"Terry, I urge you to sign that substitution of attorney form I sent you right away. I really can't continue to represent you."

"You dump me, I'll sue you for malpractice!" She stood up to face Nina, raising her voice. A number of people in the hallway cocked their heads to listen.

"I'm filing a motion to withdraw as your lawyer today," Nina said firmly, trying not to look into the yellow eyes, aware of the quiet in the hallway, and the eavesdroppers. Her ears burned. "I've done nothing wrong."

"Oh, that's rich! Nothing wrong?" said Terry. She balled her hand into a fist and pulled back, taking aim at Nina, but Nina saw it coming. She ducked and ran as fast as she could for the exit, the clumping of Terry's boots close on her heels.

A man in brown tweed came straight at her. He stopped, caught her eyes in his green ones, and held them. Nina, intent on her flight, glanced at him, continuing on her way.

She looked harder. She slowed down.

The man began to move toward her again. He stepped once, twice. And as suddenly as the moment began, it ended. Disgust or fear—Nina couldn't tell what—swelled up to muddy the clear gaze of his eyes. For a moment he stood about fifteen feet away from her. In the next moment, he was gone.

★ ★ ★

Terry didn't follow her into the parking lot. She had veered off in another direction.

Nina got into the Bronco, then got out. She had left her briefcase in the hall. She walked slowly back, looking anxiously around, trying to convince herself that she hadn't seen what she saw.

"Did you happen to see a guy come out of here a couple of minutes ago? He was moving fast, almost running," she said to Deputy Kimura.

"Yeah. Not the first one I ever saw needing to run from the law," he cracked.

"Did you see where he went?"

"Out the main door is all I know."

She needed to give herself time to think, and even more, to explore this event, the look on his face when he saw her, the man before her older, but the same.

She could have sworn the man she had seen was Kurt Scott.

Back at the office, a letter in the bunch Sandy handed her caught her eye. Intrigued by the handwritten address and big red *Personal* marked across its face, she slit the envelope open with her finger.

"Dear Nina," the letter began. "I've thought of you many times." His firm, vertical script hadn't changed. He wanted to meet her at seven the next morning on Pope Beach, where they could talk privately.

"Be careful," the note warned. "I'll explain when I see you, but I'm afraid my arrival here may mean some real trouble for you."

A familiar signature at the bottom said "Kurt."

"Some guy dropped it off," Sandy said.

She went home early, thinking about the note. Before she had a chance to tackle the clean laundry awaiting folding on her bed, Paul called from Carmel. She was glad to hear his voice. "How was your trip? You took off so suddenly. Where did you go, anyway?"

"Oh, I visited with an old buddy for a couple of days and did a little business. I won't bore you with the details. So how about it?" he asked. "I just happen to be in town."

"You're here? Why?"

"I thought you might join me for supper and a spa."

She didn't know what to say. She felt pleasantly surprised, and pressured at the same moment. He had come a long way. . . .

"Everything okay?" Paul asked. "How's Bob?"

"He's trying hard to behave himself, though I don't think he's a real happy camper at the moment. Okay," she said. "What time?"

Right before Nina left to meet Paul, the phone rang again. Nina asked Bobby to get it. He and his cousins had the afternoon off from school. They were happily squandering their time planted in front of the tube. He talked for a few minutes in the kitchen and returned to his cartoon show.

"Who was that on the phone, honey? Paul?"

"Nobody."

"Well, it had to be somebody."

"They hung up. It was nobody."

Paul picked her up at seven and they had a quiet dinner at the main Caesars restaurant. She knew she seemed distracted, but the past kept snapping back up into her consciousness. Paul watched her, made silly jokes, and touched her hair. He was sweet, he really was. She put the note out of her mind, laughing and trying to relax and enjoy the flesh-and-blood man beside her. After dinner they changed into swimsuits in Paul's room and took the elevator to the pool area, sliding into the luscious heat of the spa with a group of handsome young revelers.

"Just in time to avoid becoming one huge cramp." Nina breathed in the steaming air, leaning back against the smooth tub. She had tied her hair up in a rubber band.

"It's almost as good as a back rub. Though there's no substitute for a really good back rub."

On cue, the three other men in the tub heaved themselves up and out. Nina and Paul luxuriated in the silence and each other.

"Aren't you going to say you know how to give really good back rubs?" Nina asked. The heated water covered them up to the neck; steam clouded their eyes. Nina was getting downright rosy. Her breasts floated in the bubbles. Paul was noticing.

He caught her by the wrist. He was sitting so close, he could rub thighs with her. He did. Then he took her hand and gently ran it into the line where their legs touched, so she could feel them both at the same time, up and down, while she remained riveted, unable to remove her hand.

Breaking a long silence, he said, "I want to show you how lovely you are, how much you mean to me. Come upstairs with me." He turned her to face him, lifting her onto his lap, and smoothed his slippery fingers along the line of her backbone. She wrapped her legs around his waist and put her arms around his neck, giving in to the silkiness of the water and this muscular person who had magnets in his skin.

He closed his eyes, and put his cheek next to hers, the only sound the bubbling of the water against the sides of the tub, and his soft breathing in her ear. He began on the side of her neck, low, below the hairline, and patiently worked his way around to her lips, kissing her gently, finally pulling away to take her by the hand and lead her out of the tub.

"Stand right there," he said. He took a white towel from the chair and rubbed her, caressing and fondling her as he went until she was reaching for him too, and a mist was coming up over her eyes. . . .

They took the elevator up to his room.

She stood at the window to look at the dark, serrated outlines of pine boughs against the red neon sign below. He put his arms around her from behind, lifting her straps, kissing her neck, lowering her suit, scooping her butt up with his hands and pressing himself against her.

"Paul, I don't—"

"Nina, you don't have to be in love with me. Just love me."

"There are things I haven't told you. . . ."

"Shut up, woman. . . ." He put a finger over her lips and she let it slip into her mouth, where she began to work on it. She let go of the doubts. She let the worries about him fade away. His damp hair smelled of chlorine and his kisses fell like a gentle waterfall all over her body, until she was moving with them, letting herself be urged down onto the fresh bed. She put her arms around his neck and held on for dear life.

* * *

Nina came from the bathroom into the dark early morning of Paul's room dressed only in her long slacks.

"You're going?" Paul pushed the covers down, sitting up against the pillows, and smoothed the blond hair that stuck out from his head in all directions.

"Why, Paul, where are your jammies?"

He hopped out of bed, swaggering into the bathroom. "Can I order up some coffee? Aren't you hungry for some breakfast? It's still really early," he called above the sound of water in the sink.

"I'll get something later." She put on her shirt and sweater. "I want to get home before Bobby gets up." It was an excuse, but this was not the moment to open a discussion about Kurt with Paul. Maybe she never would. She would see Kurt this once if only to satisfy her curiosity, and then decide where to take things from there. Maybe seeing him would help her to decide if she wanted more from Paul.

"I was hoping . . ." Paul began.

Hunting for a sock, she picked up his baggy blue trunks from the floor and twirled them around one finger before tossing them onto a chair. "What?"

He came out of the bathroom and pulled them on. "Sit here for a minute," he said, patting the bed beside him.

"Oh, no. I fell for that once already."

"I promise I will not ravish you."

"I fell for that once already."

"This time I really mean it."

"I fell for that once already." She laughed, plopping down on the bed beside him to put on her socks.

"And here you go again," Paul said, grabbing her and rolling her over. "God, women are so gullible."

"I've really got to go." He was locked to her, every piece of him touching her somewhere, but she said weakly, "Really . . ."

"Promise me something first."

"What?"

"That you'll stay with me."

"Paul, you have to let me go."

"I'll let you go in a minute. Maybe longer, if you stop wiggling so much."

* * *

She kept her appointment to meet Kurt on Pope Beach. She waited for a long time, watching the sun play with the color blue over the glassy surface of Lake Tahoe.

He never came.

Standing on the sand, she remembered another endless time waiting for him to come.

He had gone again, amorphous as fog.

Put him back where he belonged. He was the past. Erase him.

11

By nine A.M. Nina had come dragging back to Matt's, just in time to hear a yelp and a whomp coming from the backyard. She ran to the gate and threw it open.

"Are you okay?" Nina asked.

Andrea was sitting in the dirt, her face streaked with mud. "There's still all this snow melting. Even though this yard gets pretty good sun." She stood up, making dusting motions with her hands, spreading muck around on her denim pants. "It's a minor boo-boo." She resumed her work with a hoe.

"Looks like very satisfying work. Need a hand?"

"Thanks, but we only have one hoe. I'm aerating the dirt. By June, this yard will be a thick green carpet."

"I never could understand why you'd want a lawn up here. Rocks, pine needles, chaparral . . . the natural scene is so marvelous, and your yard will only last through the summer—"

"You haven't lived here long enough to understand," Andrea said, puffing. Half the lawn area was already hoed into damp, pungent earth. "A lawn is a sign of human civilization. That's why the locals work so hard to have one. We live in these grand natural landscapes, and it makes us feel pitiful after a while. So we fence in a little piece around our cabins and plant flowers and grass, and feel safer."

"It'll be warm today," Nina said.

"How was last night?" Andrea leaned on the hoe, looking at Nina.

"Thanks for taking care of Bob last night. Paul and I had a great time."

"I'm really glad, Nina. You've been alone for too long. Why didn't you ask him to breakfast?"

"I . . . guess you could say I had another early date."

Andrea stared at her. "Really? Well, shut my mouth. Who is he?"

"Just come right out and ask."

"Well?" Andrea said, unmoved.

"A ghost."

"Very mysterious. What ghost?"

Nina sat down in the dirt, picked up a damp clump, and smelled it. Andrea sat down beside her.

"I saw someone I haven't seen in twelve years, after court yesterday morning," Nina said. She squeezed the clump and dirt sifted down. "His name is Kurt Scott."

"A man you knew twelve years ago. Hmm. Maybe you can guess what I'm guessing."

"Right. Bobby's father."

Andrea was silent. Then she said, "Oh, boy. Did Bob find him after all?"

"He said he didn't. But Thursday, there he was standing in the hall. I came toward him, and he seemed to recognize me. He looked thrilled, and he opened his arms. I knew it was Kurt, but at the same time I couldn't process it. Now I know what people mean when they say they can't believe their eyes."

"What did you do? I think I might scream if my ex-husband surprised me like that. I prefer these things court-ordered."

"I just felt flooded, floored. I don't know how to explain it. Overcome with feeling. I couldn't move. Our eyes met for one instant. Then—and this is the strange part of the story—I had just recognized him, just recognized his existence, that it wasn't someone else who looked like him. That it might really be Kurt. His expression changed. I never saw a look filled with such . . . loathing. Then he disappeared. Ran out the door to the parking lot."

Andrea laid her hand on Nina's arm, and said, "Listen, Nina. Something's rotten in the state of California. First Bob goes looking for his father. Bingo, after twelve years, the guy shows up. What's going on?"

"I don't know. I had to work the rest of the morning. Later on, I had some time to think. Maybe he didn't expect to see me there and it was just an awful shock."

"Please. This can't be coincidence. Why would he be in Tahoe?"

"We met here. He must still have some roots. When I moved up from San Francisco last April I thought I might see him. I thought he might still be here."

"Did you try to find him?"

"I looked in the phone book, that kind of thing. But nothing came of it, so I tried to forget about it. Then Bob started obsessing about who his dad was, which is why I thought I might be imagining it when I saw him yesterday. But Kurt dropped off a note at the office saying he wanted to warn me about something and he wanted to meet me at seven this morning."

"Wow."

"I was pretty nervous, but I went. And he never showed. I feel so angry and . . . tricked again. Brings back some old bad feelings."

Andrea put her arm around her. "You going to fill me in? You've never said a word about him before."

"I was too ashamed to tell you," Nina said.

"He was married."

"Yes. Separated. But yes, married."

"He left you when he found out you were pregnant."

"Worse. I never told him. He has no idea Bobby exists."

"Oh, Nina. Jesus. But how . . . ?"

"I was up here in the summer the year I started law school, staying at a friend's cabin near Fallen Leaf Lake. You know how they have trouble with bubonic plague from the fleas on the squirrels up there once in a while? Well, the Forest Service wanted us evacuated, but I wouldn't go because I was young and didn't give a damn and that kind of terrible disease could never happen to me. I was determined to stay up there. I'd never had a month in Tahoe in my life and I would not go."

"You got bubonic plague. He was a doctor with experience in Africa who saved your life. . . ."

That made Nina laugh. "Not at all. I didn't catch the plague. I had that whole part of the lake to myself. No, he was a summer employee for the Forest Service who took it upon himself to hassle me unmercifully. I'd get up and find him sitting on my porch steps, making sure no squirrels came up on the porch. If anyone was going to catch the plague, it would have been him."

"Must have been lonely up there, with no one else around," said Andrea. She got up, her eye caught on a clump of invading weeds, which she attacked with a forked hand tool.

"Not for long. There was an old out-of-tune piano in the cabin, which he offered to fix. I invited him in to tune it."

"I'll bet you did. What do you know about his wife?"

"Nothing. He wouldn't talk about her. He was in the early stages of getting divorced. Or so he told me. She was down in L.A. the whole time I knew him. The whole six weeks."

"I take it things didn't work out," Andrea said dryly.

"We all have unpredictable things that happen in our lives, people who change toward us for no reason we know, lotteries won and stocks busted, relatives who suddenly die. . . ." said Nina. "It was like that. We fell madly in love, Andrea."

"This doesn't sound like the solitary lady we've seen recently," Andrea said, but her smile softened her words.

"Madly, passionately, in love. I trusted him totally. I would have done anything for him, made any sacrifice. . . . My life had changed utterly. We decided to get married as soon as he had the divorce."

"He must be quite a guy."

The words rushed out. "We made a plan to meet at the end of the summer. I had to go back to Monterey to get some things and he needed to get things finished up with his wife. I didn't tell him when I found out I was pregnant. I was saving it for a surprise. He wanted to meet my dad and Matt. But he never came."

"Oh, Nina. How sad."

"I was going to pass on law school. Kurt was a fine musician, and he was going to join a symphony orchestra in Europe. . . . We planned a whole different life than the one I ended up with. But I did know he was keeping something from me, something important. I always knew that, but I convinced myself he'd tell me when he could. And then . . . nothing. He never called, never wrote. He disappeared, just like yesterday."

"Why come back now?"

Nina shook her head. "No idea. He's gone again, though, it seems." Her voice hardened. "Thanks for listening to my pathetic tale of romance and betrayal."

Having given up all pretense of gardening, Andrea opened the garden shed door and started putting her tools away. "Was it so easy," she asked, the clattering of hoes, rakes, and shovels making it hard to hear her, "to give up the idea of becoming a lawyer when you decided to get married?"

"I wasn't sure I could do both things. You know, Andrea, to do this work I have to put on one hell of a thick hide every morning. I knew it would be a hard business for a woman with a family."

"But when he left, you went ahead."

Nina thought back. "That's what made me realize how vulnerable I was. I knew being a trial lawyer would toughen me up, give me what I needed to deal with . . . anything."

"Nobody messes with you and gets off lightly."

"Not anymore."

"You still got shot," Andrea said, almost casually, shutting the door to the garden shed and clicking the combination lock shut.

"Dammit, Andrea. What are you driving at?"

Andrea turned around, her small freckled face and pointed chin smudged and glowing from her work. "Maybe you're ready to try a different approach, and drop the thick hide. I think you have already started."

"What do you mean?"

Andrea smiled. "You're strong on the inside now. You're opening up and showing a little more of that big-hearted and generous person I know."

"I'll get eaten up alive by people like Terry London and Riesner if I drop my protections. The work I do—"

Andrea plopped down beside her again. "You can't be ruled by fear. You go to the grocery store, right? Well, so do the lunatics. You can't escape. They spit on your dang armor. Besides, most of these so-called crazies you're so worried about aren't violent."

"Okay, I'll give you 'most.' And remain alert."

The warm sun slanted through the trees onto the upturned dirt. From the house came the shouts, bangs, and thumping of children.

"I'd better go in and see what's going on," Nina said.

"Wait a minute. I just had a thought. Who else was in court with you when Kurt skipped out? Is it possible he saw someone else he knew and didn't want to see?"

"There were several people in the hall. And my client, of course. She's been in Tahoe all her life. She might know him." Nina filed away this intriguing thought.

"What do you plan to do? Try to find him?"

"Don't worry. He adiosed, and I'm not going after him."

"If you saw him again—would you tell him about Bob?"

"I never will."

The phone rang in the house.

"Will Matt get that?"

"He's still in bed. Something's bothering him, Nina."

"Let's talk later," Nina said, making a run for the phone.

Collier Hallowell, brusque and businesslike, asked her to meet him as soon as possible at Terry London's house. He hung up before she had a chance to ask why.

This time the way up the hill on Coyote Road was clear and dry, though pocked with mud holes. Rushing water from under the dirty piles of snow along the road ran in gullies down both sides. Two teenaged girls trudged up the road, talking excitedly. Nina wondered where they were going.

She had missed breakfast. She needed a cup of coffee. What could Collier want?

She followed the row of trees lining the drive to the gate and almost ran into an ambulance. The gate hung open.

The ambulance, rear doors gaping and waiting for someone; several squad cars, lights turning and flashing; and a firetruck with a couple of big men in yellow sitting on the back had all crammed into the small curve in front of the studio. Terry's blue minivan looked lost amid the emergency vehicles.

Down the short path to the left of the house, half-hidden in the pines, several people hung around outside the white bungalow where Terry worked. Nina drew up away from the other cars and jumped out, leaving her briefcase, walking quickly toward the group.

The spectators made way, but Nina was stopped at the door by a young South Lake Tahoe police officer who held his hand up and said, "No entry."

"Is Terry London here?" Nina said. "She's my client. I'm an attorney."

He cocked his head to the side, said, "Nina Reilly?"

"Yes. What's going on? Where's Ms. London?" The cop nodded toward the inside, and Nina's heart sank. "Sorry," he said. "You can't go in there right now. It's a crime scene."

"A crime?"

"The victim's still in there," the cop said. "They're getting ready to take the body away." Nina tried to push past him. "Hey!" he said.

"Let me in!"

Collier Hallowell, a deputy district attorney for the County of El Dorado, walked out onto the porch. She hadn't seen him in months. His gray eyes looked bloodshot, as if he had been up as long as she had.

"What's happening? What's going on? Is it Terry?" Nina said, as Collier took her elbow and guided her to the side of the studio.

"I'm afraid so."

"What's happened?"

"Gunshot," Collier said. He wore heavy beige rubber gloves, an old unpressed shirt, jeans. Plastic booties covered his deck shoes. No socks, she thought automatically. He looked like he had been rousted from his bed. The gloves and booties frightened her. He had lost his usual friendly and kind expression and looked unapproachable and fierce. "We've been here all morning. We're ready to wind things down. Where've you been?"

"She did it, didn't she?" She tore her eyes from him and closed them, trying to collect her senses. "She was awfully worked up about everything, somewhat unstable . . . but it was just a short delay, we won the case. . . ."

"She didn't kill herself, Nina," Collier said. The gloves, stained on the fingers with something dark, transformed his hands into something terrible.

"Somebody came in last night and blew her away. You have any ideas about that?"

"Me?"

"Sure you do," he said, watching her closely. "You come over to my office first thing tomorrow morning. Do you have the film with you?"

"You mean *Where Is Tamara Sweet?* No, but I have a copy at the office."

"I want to have a look at it right away."

"I'll see what I can do—"

"Where were you last night?"

"Me? Home in bed."

"Alone in your bedroom?"

"Of course. Why? You think I killed my client?"

"It's happened," Collier said. "You had a scene with her at the courthouse yesterday. You were filing a motion to get out of the case. I'll need to know all about that."

"Okay, sure."

A white van drove up, with KTHO-TV painted on its side. "Shit," Collier said, watching the van. "I have to go back inside."

"I want to see her," Nina said.

"No. There's no reason."

"She's my client, and she's been killed. I want to see her." She said it calmly, professionally, so Collier would understand. She would not make a scene unless he turned her down. He tried once more to move her along, but she crossed her arms, saying, "I'm not leaving." She didn't have time to make him understand. She had to see Terry for herself.

Casting one more unhappy look at the news crew unloading the van and beginning to make their approach, he said, "Come on." To the officer at the door, he said, "Hey, Mike, don't let the press in, whatever you do. Let me know as soon as the medical examiner arrives." He kept a hard grip on her arm, pulling her along with him, then drew her inside and closed the door.

She was back again in the long white room where Terry had

shown off her equipment collection so proudly. But this time two homicide detectives and a fireman leaned against the wall, waiting for the photographer to finish.

Terry lay on her back on the carpet, close to an extended wing shelf, her right arm crumpled under her, her left arm flung out.

Nina noted the black pants and the billowing white cotton shirt bibbed with blood.

Starting with thick clots at the neck, a reddish-brown river had flowed down the side of her body, onto the slightly uneven floor, into streams several feet long.

The fireman left, and the remaining detectives watched Nina, keeping their feet carefully out of the evidence.

Terry's dark yellow eyes gazed up toward the ceiling, emptied of personality. Another gusher of dried blood had flowed from the right side of her mouth, the direction in which her head, resting on a bloody pillow, tilted. Between her legs, a videocamera was propped.

A photographer in a khaki vest loaded with pockets moved slowly around Terry, dropping to her knees, leaning forward, documenting every feature of this final indignity, in close-up, in wide angle. With and without flash. Camera cases, a jacket, and a black baseball cap were stacked near the door, away from the mayhem, presumably hers.

The wall behind the counter, too, had been splattered with blood and tissue, seemed to have a hole in it. . . .

The lights were so bright, and something smelled bad in here with the door closed, wet and hot and . . .

Collier's hand appeared in the confusion of talk and light, reaching out and taking hers, leading her to the door and opening it. She was outside, dazed. Neighbors and newspeople were asking questions, their faces ugly with curiosity.

"When can I see you?" Collier said, the suggestion sounding as incongruous to her after what she had seen as the rustle of the wind through the pines outside Terry's studio.

"What?" Nina asked, startled out of her reverie by the question.

"I need to know everything you know," said Collier. "How about first thing Monday morning?"

12

Two uniformed officers came out of Collier Hallowell's office, too intent on their instructions to notice Nina. "You can go in now," the woman receptionist said. Nina waited for the buzzer and walked back into the joyless world of criminal justice, which she had never wanted to enter again.

In the large front room the secretaries hung on the phones, fighting to keep the frantic scheduling of witnesses and court under control, taking messages for the deputy district attorneys who were usually in court, soothing victims and processing paperwork. On the right side, the attorneys worked in cubicles in a line from front to back, forming an obscure status system she couldn't fathom. Collier's office was second from the back. He stepped out, arguing vigorously into the phone he held to his ear, and beckoned her in.

The office hadn't changed since the last time she'd seen it: twice as much paper littering an office half as large as hers; nondescript paint flaking here and there; desk buried under teetering files; stuffed bookshelves; bare, scratched flooring; no paintings, plants, or curios; a phone, a computer, a fax, and one prosecutor conducting the state's business from a swivel chair—disheveled, genial or grave as the circumstances demanded, perceptive, overcaffeinated, and potent.

"Tell them we don't have the money to do that sort of thing anymore," Collier said to the phone. "Tell 'em not to fuck around. If they insist, I'll talk to them directly." On that softly threatening note, he hung up.

Before Nina sat down, she spotted the only personal item in the office, the photograph that he looked at all day long, the one of his dead wife. A dark-haired girl, athletic, straight-backed, seated on a horse with High Sierra peaks in the background. He must have taken the picture, so the smile was for him.

"Are those the same papers that were here last time I saw you here, last summer? Or do you freshen them up once in a while?" asked Nina, tapping the side of one stack, unable to budge it. "Solid as a brick fence."

"Oh, they change weekly. There'll never be enough room until I get the corner office I covet."

"Which leads me to ask, did you ever decide to run for D.A.?"

"I announced last week. I guess you missed it."

"Good luck. I mean that."

"I appreciate it. Before we start, I wanted to tell you I'm sorry about your client."

How should she respond to that? I'm not? Or Thanks, like a grieving relative?

She nodded and said nothing.

"Thanks for coming." His gray eyes drifted over the paperwork on his desk. He held a pen in his mouth, which hung like an exotic black cigarette, and chewed on its plastic tip.

"You told me to."

He opened a file folder with her name on it and said, "Mind if I record this?" Though she should have expected it, this question irritated her, bringing her back into her role of prickly defense attorney.

"Do I have a choice?"

This time he came around the desk and sat on it, facing her, catching her eye. "I've never gotten used to going out to murder scenes. Fragile, is how it makes me feel. All those people out there working at that house on Coyote Road may have looked callous to you, but they all felt the same—fragile. How did you feel?"

"Shocked. Angry."

"You want to tell me about it?"

She thought for a long time before saying anything. "I got shot in that courtroom last year. I saw people shot. So I said, never again. I'll arrange my life so I never see that again. And Terry came to me with a problem that spiraled back down toward a place I tried to escape. Before I could pull out, she died. I suppose this will sound selfish, but I can't grieve for her. I hardly knew her, and what I knew I didn't like."

"I understand," Collier said. "You're over the physical effects of the shooting? I mean—"

"You mean when I got shot? Yes."

"But there are other effects. I don't mean to insult you—I really don't. But you don't look like yourself."

"*Fragile*'s one word for it. How about *expendable*? How about *targeted*?"

"And now you've been yanked back to that moment of terror like you're hooked to a bungee cord."

She nodded again, feeling relieved to talk about it. Collier inspired confessions. That was his job. She should keep that in mind. "My family gets yanked back too. It's as though we're walking on narrow planks above an abyss—but it's not empty like an abyss, it's fulminating with violence and insanity. Have you ever been to Lassen and walked that trail into Bumpass Hell?"

"Yes, I have. Bumpass is the guy who fell in and got boiled, right?"

"I think so. Anyway, for the first mile or so of the trail you've got these spectacular views of Lassen, Diller, and Diamond Peaks. On a clear day you can see all the way to the Sierra, almost to Tahoe. It's all the deceptively benevolent world on display for your viewing pleasure. Then you reach a summit. You drop into a hydrothermal area. Steam billows out of the ground. You get hotter and hotter. Pits of mud bubble and spit at you. They warn you not to step off the trail because the earth's crust is so thin there, you would sink in and be scalded.

"There's a volcano under you all the time. Whether you feel it or see it, it's there, alive and waiting. Terry's death reminded me of that place, where it's hot and potentially lethal, waiting to get you if you step off the trail, or if the planks you're walking on break through. That kind of sudden disaster is always out there."

Collier said, "I see it in my work every day."

"Yet . . . you stay."

"I do."

"Why?"

"For the same reason you do."

"I get sucked in!"

"You may not want to admit it to yourself, but you make a decision about it, just as I do."

"I'd much rather move to a South Seas island and live on piña coladas. Be a bartender at a thatched-roof bar."

"Then why don't you? Because hiding doesn't work. Already been tried. Marlon Brando bought himself an island, but trouble found him anyway."

"Well," Nina said. "Here's a short bounce of the bungee. I brought my copy of the film, and I'll answer any questions you have. Then I'm going to go back to my office and draft the dullest trust instrument you ever saw, and forget all about Terry London." She leaned over and laid the film canister on his desk.

"Tell me about the last time you saw her," Collier said. He was still sitting on his desk, and she had to crane her head up to see him. She got up and moved toward the bookcases, closer to the books on homicide investigation, criminology, criminal law, evidence . . . fascinating books in the abstract. He worked in Bumpass Hell, all day, every day.

"The last time? That would be on March thirtieth, at the regular law and motion session of the Superior Court. Jeff Riesner had filed a motion to clarify the language of the proposed order I had drafted. Milne ordered us to meet again and submit a joint order."

"Terry was present throughout?"

"She was there, but we hardly spoke until the hearing was over. She became very irate in the hall, irrational, I would say. I couldn't calm her down. I walked away from her and she followed behind me. Then . . ."

"Then . . . ?"

"She ran out to the parking lot and pushed past me. I didn't see her drive off. I'd forgotten some papers and had to go back inside."

The phone buzzed. Collier ignored it. "Why was she angry?"

"Her case . . . the delay . . ."

"Was she going to lose money? How serious was the delay?"

"Not serious. She had sold the film to a TV show, but the date for airing it hadn't been set. The producers were working with her on it."

"Then why? What was the source of her anger?"

"She was angry at me." Nina explained as well as she could the disintegration of that particular lawyer-client relationship. When she told him about the burglary, Collier closed his eyes, leaning back as though trying to comprehend.

His eyes still closed, he said, "How did you know Terry was the burglar?"

"I knew right away it was personal when I saw the condition of my room. She was the one who was mad at me at the moment."

"Why didn't you tell the police who it was?"

"No proof. But my son was missing, so I went to her house. This was about two weeks before the hearing. I think I frightened her. If she'd hurt Bobby . . . but as it turned out, he'd run off to Monterey. She returned my letters. I had what I'd come for. I left."

"Was anyone else there?"

"No . . . oh, at first, when I came in. A neighbor. Ralph Kettrick, I think it was. He lives next door with his father."

"Jerry Kettrick," Collier said for the tape's benefit, and Nina thought, maybe one of them saw something. The cops must have talked to them, because Collier already knew all about them.

"I'd like to see the letters you took back from her. I may have to see them."

"They're gone, Collier. I burned them."

He didn't believe her. She didn't care. She had put them into a safe-deposit box and intended to leave them there for herself, till she had a home of her own someday. He would need a court order to go after them even if he knew they existed, and nobody was going to know except her and the bank.

"This may surprise you, Nina, but you may have been Terry London's main contact with the human race during her last weeks.

She handled her business by phone and fax. She doesn't seem to have had any close friends. Her parents and her older sister were killed in a plane crash in the early seventies."

"You mean to tell me she had no men friends? She was attractive. We never talked about her past."

"No boyfriends that we've found. We're looking into her past now. I need to know who you think might have killed her. Your speculations could be important. I'm sure you've thought about it—"

"Not really. But there are four people who were fighting to suppress that film. The plaintiffs—Jessica and Jon Sweet, Tamara Sweet's parents, and Michael Ordway and his wife, Doreen. They must have spent a ton of money on this case, and they had essentially lost it. The thing is . . ."

"Go ahead, I'm interested in your thoughts."

"Well, in the same way that Terry's motives for making and distributing the film seemed obscure to me, their motives for suing her seemed obscure. I mean, they had stated surface motives. It's just that I felt undercurrents from both sides. Maybe one of them . . ."

"Killed Tamara Sweet," Collier said. "I look forward to seeing what kind of evidence she'd gathered."

"You won't see much hard evidence, although everything in the film is based on fact. It's impressionistic, moody, an art piece as well as an investigative piece. And the stuff about the other three girls who disappeared seems tacked on. I guess what I'm saying is, the film's not that threatening to any of them. You figure it out."

"Oh, I will. At the very least, we'll be looking again at all four of the disappearances."

He was rubbing his cheek, as if he had realized he needed a shave. When he didn't speak again, Nina said, "Anything else?"

"One thing. Did you notice anything missing at Terry's?"

"No, but I was so shocked."

"Okay. That's it for now." Loud knocks at the door. Collier's next customer had come calling.

"Oh, no you don't," Nina said. "Before I go, I want you to give me one honest-to-God straight and sincere answer."

"What other kind have I ever given you?"

"I want to know if there is any danger at all to me or my family, based on everything you know to this point."

"No," Collier said. "I believe not. We have a suspect in custody, seen running from the house after the shots were fired."

"Great. Who is it?"

"Can't give that out yet. But this person will be locked up. So you can relax."

"Okay."

"Drop by sometime after court. We'll talk."

"It could happen." He let her out and a frizzly-haired policewoman in. As the door closed, Nina heard her say, "You're not going to believe this, Collier," so naturally she stopped and leaned up close to the door.

Faintly, through the door, she heard the policewoman say, "The London case? Do you believe this? The victim turned on her video camera after she was shot."

"She was still conscious?"

"Still conscious—and she made a fuckin' tape."

"Can I help you?" said the secretary at her elbow. Nina let herself be led to the door, full of unanswered questions.

Out in the courtyard between the county offices and the courthouse, Nina saw Riesner heading her way. He didn't extend his hand. She hadn't planned to shake it anyway.

"Provocative, your client getting knocked off like that," he said.

"In what way?"

"Because the police have made an arrest in the murder, and I have been contacted regarding representation. So, if you learn anything new regarding the murder, I expect to be contacted immediately."

"It's more likely I'd be contacting Collier Hallowell," Nina said. "Sorry, but anybody you represent is probably guilty, and I have an interest in assuring that the person who killed my client is put away. Who has been arrested, anyway?"

"I don't know why I even do you the courtesy of telling you. However, his name is Kurt Scott. I will be talking with him later on today. And stay out of it. You're on notice." Without another word, he walked past her. She saw him beep open the lock on his red BMW, get in, and roar off.

Her breathing had stopped. She leaned against the courthouse wall for a minute or two, looking blankly after him. She looked at her watch. Eleven-fifteen. She went inside to the bank of phones and called her office. "Sandy, I'm going to go over to the jail for a while," she said. "I'm not sure when I'll be back."

"You've got a deposition here at three. The doc in your malpractice case."

"I'll be back."

"You better."

13

THE DEPUTY OPENED THE DOOR TO A LONG CORRIDOR AND A SERIES of open cubicles facing glass windows. Similar cubicles on the other side of the windows held inmates. Nina sat down, pulled out her yellow pad, and waited to see Kurt Scott for the second time in nearly twelve years.

She picked up the phone, licking her lips to quell the dryness caused by her agitation. She had brought herself to the jail quickly, before she could feel anything. Now the emotions growing in her were entirely personal, not professional. She wondered how much she had changed or if he would notice, then shushed herself, thinking, why should he care? He's had other things on his mind, such as a life in prison.

She replayed what she knew in her mind: He had killed Terry. He knew Terry, and Terry knew her, hated her. Why? What was going on?

She would ask him. Meantime, another narrow plank fell into the darkness. She looked at her own past.

She had waited for him on the day they were to meet at the

Tinnery, the restaurant overlooking Lovers' Point in Pacific Grove, dressed up for once, excited about her news. He had said he wanted to come straight to the house to meet her father, but she put him off. He should hear about their child first. She wanted to tell him, to toast their new life together in this beautiful place looking out at the ocean and the sunset. They would be leaving for Europe soon. She wanted him to know her favorite spot, and love it like she did. She had arranged for a room for the night at the Seven Gables Inn, with a view and fireplace.

As the hours ticked by and he didn't come she was worried, then frantic, then dumbfounded. From a pay phone she had called Kurt's Forest Service work number in California, but no one there knew anything. She had called his apartment without getting an answer.

When night came, bringing with it a heavy drizzle, she walked to the hotel alone, checked in, and sat in her soaked dress on a flowered armchair by the window until she fell asleep there. In the morning, nauseated and faint from the pregnancy, she had gone back to the restaurant, asked for messages, and called again, all for nothing.

She waited all that morning on a bench at the cliff edge, watching the happy people enter and exit the doors to the restaurant. By afternoon she had started to shake.

She had gone home to bed.

The next day she unpacked her bags, filed her passport in a box, and called the Monterey School of Law, saying she hoped there still was a place for her in the fall. There was.

For three or four months, she felt nothing when she thought about Kurt. She was working, pregnant, going to school, trying to stay together. Her pride had come up strong, like iron walls in her heart.

Then, one fine Saturday, she woke up in her aunt's small Victorian house and looked out the front window. Six blocks down the hill, Monterey Bay floated, emerald and turquoise in a sapphire sky. The view was so heartbreaking that she cried for three days. At first she didn't know what she was crying about, but when his name came wrenching out of her mouth over and over, she knew. And when the crying finished, she put him away very deep where he wouldn't ever hurt her again.

Twelve years passed.

* * *

Through the glass he suddenly appeared, a man in the orange jumpsuit issued to the guests of El Dorado County. The man who now sat down heavily in the chair opposite her and picked up the phone was not the boy she had loved. The uniform, pushed up on the left arm to reveal a gauze bandage; his long, lank, uncombed hair; the downcast look; the spiritlessness of him made him a stranger. When he sat down, though, he put his hands on the table in front of the window, and she saw that his hands were the musician's hands she knew, large and long-fingered, with clean, square nails.

He raised his head, and his face still compelled her: the eyes, greenish-blue, darkly fringed; the strong nose and finely cut lips; the narrow jaw. But the hope had left him: this man was marked by experiences that had knitted his brows and hollowed his cheeks.

She heard the unforgettable voice. "Hi," he said. "A blast from the past."

"Hello, Kurt."

"You shouldn't have come."

"It was the only way I was ever going to see you again."

"I don't know why you would want to. You don't owe me anything."

"This was something I owed myself. Besides, you seem to have murdered a client of mine. I was curious." So an oily reservoir of anger still existed to fuel her words. His presence through the glass disturbed the old sorrow, resurrecting it. She didn't want to feel it again. She had to remember, this was a different person, shaped by unknown forces. "Why did you come back?"

"To find you." He smiled a little, and said, "You look great. But you swore you were going to get through life in jeans. Look at you now. You're a lawyer."

"And you're a cold-blooded killer. I never would have predicted that for your future."

Something like pain moved through his eyes and quickly retreated. "Hmm. I guess I shouldn't be surprised you bought the party line."

"Contrary to movie wisdom, the person in custody is almost always the person who ought to be in custody."

"You even talk differently, more authoritatively. And you wear lipstick. But under all that I see you," he said, smiling and nodding a little as if with melancholy pleasure. "And you still doodle what you're thinking."

With a start, she looked down at the yellow pad she had brought out from habit. She had sketched a few lines, a stick woman in the left margin, a stick man in the right, with a wide expanse of paper between the two.

"Do you still look for the secret of life in your psychology books, with your philosophers? Is your bedside table still stacked high with books?"

"No," Nina said.

"Did you wait a long time at the restaurant, all those years ago?"

"No." Through days of hell and weeks of misery, she had waited. "Not long."

"That's good. You won't believe me right now, but I loved you—I never have loved anyone but you. I'm sorry, Nina."

"It doesn't matter anymore," Nina said. "I moved on."

He dropped the hypnotic gaze that had held her. Suddenly he looked older than he was. "Congratulations," he said. "Mr. van Wagoner told me about your engagement."

Nina dropped her pencil. She took a long minute to find it. When she straightened up again she said, "When did you talk to Paul?"

"He hasn't told you? You should talk to him."

"Oh, I will."

He had cocked his head to the side, as if to see her from this angle. Every expression on his face reminded her of something long buried.

"You kept up your music?" she said unwillingly.

"I've been living in Germany. I worked most of the time in the Taunus Forest in Hessen, not too far from Frankfurt, as a kind of naturalist. I labeled trees, caught poachers, cleared brush. I had decided to give up music, along with everything else, but after a few years I discovered I couldn't do it. I bought a used spinet piano from an old lady in Wiesbaden. Every night I came home to my apartment on Moritzstrasse and played. There were no distractions. The walls are thick in those nineteenth-century buildings. I entered a local Bach competition, and won."

"The fugues."

"Yes. And so, occasionally, I played concerts here and there under an assumed name. And that became my life, until now, when everything has changed again."

As he spoke, she too was remembering so much happiness, followed by so much anguish.

"How did it go with you?" Kurt's accent sounded slightly foreign. He had spent twelve years in exile. Why?

"Pretty simple. I finished law school, got married to another lawyer, became an associate in a firm in San Francisco. After five years, I left the firm and divorced. That was last year. My brother had moved to Tahoe. I moved here, too, and started a solo practice."

"If only you hadn't come here," he said after a minute. "If only Mr. van Wagoner hadn't found me—"

"Paul went to Germany?" She would have to have a long talk with Mr. van Wagoner.

"He mentioned that you were in South Lake Tahoe. I knew she was here. I decided to come here to warn you."

"About what?" But she already knew, she was only waiting for him to say it.

"About your client. Terry London."

Nina waited.

"She was my wife, when I met you."

"Your wife!"

"I didn't lie. I had filed for divorce. But I . . . omitted some things. That she opposed the divorce. That she and I had a child."

Nina made a sound, a choked-off moan. "It was all based on lies," she said. "You came back here and you killed her. I should go."

"Go. Good idea."

"Why should I stay here!"

"You shouldn't."

"You killed her!"

"I didn't kill her. I hated her, but I didn't kill her. One reason I stayed away for all those years was because of those feelings. I didn't want to be tested. I never wanted to see her again. Then, when I saw her behind you at the courthouse, I panicked. I thought she was going to hurt you because of me. She had followed me to my hotel, but she didn't come in, maybe worried about how I might react. So she called me. At first I wouldn't even talk to her."

"But you did see her. You went to the studio that night, didn't you? Why did you go? To threaten her?"

"I was throwing my clothes in my bag while I was on the phone, I was so anxious to get out of there. But she was smarter than I was. She came up with a story, the one lie guaranteed to keep me here, and make me think maybe I didn't waste all those years running. She told me you had my child, a son. She said she met him at your office and learned from him that I'd probably never been told about him. She was so persuasive! All these details! She said she made friends with the boy, told him about me, and arranged for him to come to her house that night."

"A son?" Nina whispered. "She told you you had a son?"

"She'd say anything, Nina. But, of course, it made me think. I knew what you must have felt when I never came for you. I know, it was stupid, but I thought, what if? What if you had decided never to tell me? Is there . . . is it possible? Is there a child?"

The mixture of wistfulness and hope in his eyes almost pierced her armor. Almost. "No," she said. The lie sat heavily on her heart.

"That lying—! Goddamn her!" He slammed the table with his hand. The glass shook.

"You went there that night," Nina said.

He took a deep breath and tried to calm himself. "Of course I did. I had to. If she was telling the truth, if I had a—child, she could do anything. Hurt him. You didn't know her. Nobody knew what she was capable of doing better than I knew.

"So I went, but she was alone. It was a trap. I think she wanted to kill me.

"I tried to leave, but she wanted to rehash some old, old business. We argued. She grabbed my old rifle, and before I could get away she took a shot at me.

"Jesus. Nobody tells you how much it hurts to get shot. I ran like hell out the front door while she was screaming at me."

"Your gun?" Nina asked.

"A Remington. I recognized it. She must have kept it all these years. Everyone up here keeps a rifle."

"Oh, my God, Kurt. This is hard to believe. You didn't take the gun there?"

"I swear I didn't."

He shouldn't tell her any of this; there was no lawyer-client privilege between them, but she didn't stop him. She had to know.

"She fired a single shot at you?" Nina asked.

"It's funny you should mention that. I got to my car. I thought I might have heard another one when I was about a block away, but I'm not sure. My windows were up, and I don't know if I trust anything I heard or saw right then. Then I drove around a long time. I parked on Jicarilla in the bushes. My arm bled for a while, but then it stopped. I knew it was nothing serious. I wasn't going to die that second.

"Then . . . I guess the shock or something got me. I sat there for a long time, maybe even dozed off. Next thing I knew it was light. I needed to see a doctor, but I was more concerned that this thing had to stop, so I headed for the police station. You know the rest, probably. I was weaving on the road because of my injury, so a patrolman stopped me."

She had one question, the only one that really mattered. She wanted to be absolutely sure. "Think back. Are you positive there was no one else at Terry's? On the porch, somewhere around?"

"You mean did I see the real killer?"

Actually, she had been thinking more along the lines of possible witnesses.

"I didn't see anyone, not that I searched every corner. It was dark, and I didn't see anyone."

Nina looked down at her yellow pad to hide her relief. She didn't want to hear anything else. "I have to go, Kurt," she said.

"Sure you do."

"I understand you've retained Jeffrey Riesner to represent you."

"He was recommended by the deputy here."

"You never thought of calling me?"

"I've done enough to you, Nina," Kurt said. "Go home."

BOOK TWO

Eight Years Ago: Susana

Dangling high above the snow, the weight of her skis tugging on her legs, her face stiffening in a cold wind, Susana stuffed mittened hands into the tight pockets of her fur-lined parka, deciding to make this her last run of the day. Her legs ached, and she could think of a better way to spend the afternoon, a woozy, dreamy, fun thing to do that didn't involve cold wind and athletics. Her brother, Tom, wouldn't approve, so she wouldn't tell Tom. She'd just meet him at home later, and take the flak then. It was worth it.

Beside her on the ski lift, Tom adjusted himself, acting nervous. She knew he was only coming up here to keep an eye on her. They'd skied all the resorts around Lake Tahoe for years, but he didn't get anything like the kick she got. He was born gutless. Mom and Dad's good kid, that was Tommy. After a whole day of his vigilant baby-sitting yesterday, and no end in sight, she was sick of it and cooked up this plan to ditch him. To the right, now far below, on a simple, wide plain of white, they could see other people in colored hats and down jackets wobbling down the bunny slope, legs rigidly positioned in the snowplow V *of the beginner. Beyond them, the big blue lake spread out like an ocean.*

"Susana, this is only your second day skiing this season. Besides, you're

not good enough to hit a black diamond run yet,'' Tom said, starting in on her. ''This guy I talked to said this is the worst run at Heavenly. It's really narrow, with bumps and turns like you've never seen before. Come on, be reasonable. Mom and Dad will kill me if you pop a mogul and crack your skull open today. We can take the lift back down, or an intermediate run.''

They were passing over the sunlit tops of tall evergreens where marshmallows of new snow weighed the limbs down, making them droop. Her glasses had fogged over. She took a cotton kerchief out of her pocket and cleaned them. ''I don't want to take an easy run. You don't have to go with me. You can meet me at the lodge.''

''Why do you have to be so damn stubborn!''

''I'm sixteen years old. A hundred years ago, I'd be married with kids by now, so quit telling me what to do, Tommy. I'll be careful.''

Her brother punched her arm, hard. ''Yeah, sure. You ski like a locomotive on speed.''

She fitted her glasses back over her eyes, slowly. She was surprised to hear her brother say something like that. Even though he was two years older than her, Tom always talked so straight. He probably suspected a few things about her, but was this some kind of nasty little hint that he knew something he shouldn't?

Before she could frame an innocent-sounding question to find out more, they had reached the end of the ride. They pushed themselves off the moving chair, sliding easily down the small slope from the lift. Susana quickly located the black diamond marker, and skied to the slight hump at the top, looking down at the narrow, winding way full of potholes and rocky moguls, the almost unmarked snow that suggested even the best skiers avoided this run. Tom looked down the run with her, shaking his head. ''Jesus. You take too many risks.''

''Hey, I just know how to have fun.''

''Don't go, Susie,'' he said, but too late. ''You don't even have goggles.''

She waved at him with one of her poles, saying, ''See you later!'' and started down the run.

She took the first moguls cautiously, wending her way around, forging a fresh path through the snow, her excitement growing by the minute. She had found her ski legs, and the careful, slow rhythm of traversing quickly bored her. Halting momentarily beside a wicked pile of snow-covered boulders in the middle of the pathway, she saw a straight shot down a white ribbon of pathway in front of her. Even though the trail intimidated her, it was inspiring, awesome. Partway down, the trail disappeared over a hill. Who knew what horrible obstacles lurked beyond?

She could make it, she told herself. She could do anything and get away with it. She always plunged right into the hottest water, and always got herself out again, right? Today would be no exception. Pointing her skis straight down the mountain, she took off, sliding faster and faster, her arms tucked beside her, her head down, her glasses freezing over, the landscape whizzing by in a blur of green and white. Throw caution to the wind and live, she thought joyfully. Fly!

She beat Tom to the lodge with ease, turned her boots and skis in at the rental counter, and made a quick phone call.

Her ride came swiftly.

14

FOR SEVERAL WEEKS NINA DID NOTHING FURTHER ABOUT KURT SCOTT. She appeared in court, went to Bobby's softball games, and stayed out of it. She owed him nothing, as he had said. The gnawing curiosity she kept in check, though talking to him had only brought new questions.

April turned to May, and the snow retreated upward to the high mountains. Most of the ski resorts finally closed, defeated by the harsh mountain sun. Occasional news came to her. Bail had been denied because of the seriousness of the charge. Riesner had agreed to a fast preliminary hearing, and Kurt had been bound over for trial. She heard nothing about either the videotape she had learned of at Collier's office or the progress of the police investigation. Even the *Tahoe Mirror,* inhibited by the lack of new information, limited itself to minor updates on the case.

Presumably, Riesner was working late nights, reviewing the police reports with experts he consulted, filing pretrial motions, hearing Kurt's story until he could recite it by heart. She told herself to presume these things, presume Riesner would help Kurt just as she would have helped him. Even if Kurt had killed Terry, and she assumed he had, there would be extenuating circumstances. Riesner would call her eventually, and she would appear as a witness if it would help. That was all she could do. She only hoped Collier would not decide her testimony would somehow be useful to convict Kurt.

Many times at home she noticed how movements of Bobby's, like the way he rubbed his forehead when he was tired, now reminded her of Kurt. She saw him from a new perspective, as a boy who belonged in definable ways to the man who was his father. He became a constant reminder of the man in jail.

Bobby didn't try to talk to her anymore about Kurt. He had heard things, she knew, but he held his feelings inside. She felt the chill of separation from him, from the remote way he answered her questions to the way he shrugged off her hand on his shoulder on their walks up the hill behind the house. She knew she needed to talk to him, but she didn't know how.

Matt and Andrea, too, seemed preoccupied. They knew who Kurt was, but they avoided the subject, giving her room to think, or maybe, in Matt's case, just hoping the problem would go away.

The usually boisterous and open household seemed quieter than usual as Nina mulled over Kurt in private, as if they had all picked up the habit of secrecy from her, as if they all had things to hide. And wasn't that a ridiculous thought on Nina's part? What secrets would any of them have from her?

Angry at his brash thrusting into her affairs, Nina didn't return Paul's calls. If she told him now what his snooping around had caused, he'd come crashing up, shattering the already fragile situation. News of a homicide in Tahoe would not necessarily be reported in Monterey, so he probably had no idea. If he had stayed out of her private affairs, Terry would still be alive and Kurt would be . . . safe, somewhere.

One morning Nina stopped at the bank and pulled the papers from her safe-deposit box. She pulled out her old journal, a small, spiral-bound book of black cardboard wrapped in rubber bands. During the summer with Kurt, alone in her cabin at Fallen Leaf, she had recorded snatches of their conversations and details of their meetings. She had meditated endlessly on him. Reading the journal after so long, she relived the night she had allowed herself to fall in love with him.

She had been at Fallen Leaf Lake almost two weeks, and had seen Kurt almost every day. They had sat on the rickety porch of the cabin that endless evening, watching shadows lengthen over the lake and talking until the mosquitoes drove them inside.

Kurt sat down at the old stand-up piano and began to play, his hands light and gentle at first, the music light, then deepening. She knew little about classical music; she had always thought it too forbidding and highbrow for her. She couldn't make personal contact; she imagined men in powdered wigs and dirty satin playing to lords and ladies in castles. It had nothing to do with her.

This was different. She leaned against the piano, watching Kurt. Now and then he looked up and smiled, his eyes half-closed. For a long time the music made a background to the picture of him, his fingers rippling over the keys like water in wind. After a time the music worked on her. She joined him in its tides, letting him lead her through it. She heard him play the languor of the evening, the coolness of the lake, the breezes springing up. He was courting her now, embracing and caressing her with the notes. . . .

She lit candles beside the bed, and left him there to wait for her. The water in the shower fell on her skin as softly as his music had fallen. Finally, pink from the heat, she put on his gift, a yellow silk robe that felt soft as talcum, and walked barefoot across the pine floorboards toward the flickering light.

He waited on the bed, naked, hands behind his head. He glowed there, the dark night all around them, magical, attractive, hungry, as alone as she was, with nothing but the dark night and forest for miles around.

She sat down beside him, saying nothing, bending over him, letting her damp hair fall around them like a curtain to enclose their kisses. She felt the connection formed in those minutes would always exist invisibly, that they created one being, a new person, not him or her, someone better than them both.

He took her by the shoulders, laying her gently down, opening the robe. She saw how he looked at her body with amazed pleasure. She bent up toward him, like a lily bending toward moonlight.

His skin like velvet, and the hardness of his muscles underneath . . . she let him lead her through it.

Her utter trust in him made nothing forbidden. In that way, she expressed her love.

All this she had written in her journal, the journal of a young woman in love. All this she had forgotten. All this she had felt.

And never felt since.

"I wanted to talk to you about your client," Nina said in Riesner's office the next afternoon.

"I'm feeling very benevolent and helpful today," Riesner said. "Witness my rearranging my schedule to accommodate you. So plunge right in. Amuse me." He arranged a red Japanese vase full of pussy willows on his desk.

His office reeked of success. There were pictures on the walls she couldn't afford the frames for; oil portraits next to cherrywood bookcases with leaded glass doors displaying backlit artifacts from Asia and Africa, and leather volumes. Even the pen he wrote with was valuable and beautiful.

She could easily visualize the television ad: Jeffrey Riesner surrounded by the fetishes of his success, his low-end baritone hovering artificially in that masculine bastion, the bass zone. With this man, you are safe. You, too, can own a suit like this. Call today.

She should have picked up the phone.

"I'd like to know how the London murder case is going," Nina said.

"Why?"

"You know why."

"I thought you wanted to have a civil conversation. Why should I be civil when you seem to be incapable of it?" Riesner unwrapped a large, fragrant cigar, lighting it with a large silver lighter. "Oh. Excuse me. Would you like one? Cuban, rather rare." He blew a gamy cloud of smoke her way.

"No. Thank you," Nina said.

"That's better. You were saying?"

"I'd appreciate your discussing the Scott case with me. I'd like to know what your general strategy will be. I understand there is some damaging eyewitness testimony. And that the police have some sort of videotape. Is there any direct physical evidence? Have they found the gun, for instance?"

"The attorney-client privilege prevents me from telling you much," Riesner said thoughtfully, gazing down at the cigar between his thumb and forefinger as if for advice.

"How strong is the eyewitness? Have you interviewed him yet?"

"In due course," Riesner said. "I have his statement to the police."

"May I see it?" Nina said.

"No."

"You won't let me have a look at any of the reports?"

"Why should I? It's not your case. I don't want any interference."

"What do you think are his chances of acquittal based on the preliminary hearing?" Nina said. Riesner was enjoying her visit, her need to approach him, but she knew him too well to think he would say anything at all he didn't specifically intend to say.

"The D.A. established that there was a body, that it was a homicide, and that there was probable cause to believe my client did it. Three cops and criminologists, one medical examiner, one eyewitness, and a partridge in a pear tree. Three days and he's bound over to the Superior Court for trial."

"You chose not to present any defense?" Nina said.

"I never waste my time with that sort of thing at a prelim," Riesner said. "With the standard of proof being probable cause, he's going to go to trial no matter what I might have said. It's a bad idea to let the D.A. see what you've got. I learned a few things on the cross-exam."

"Do you think he's guilty?"

"Let's put it this way," Riesner said. "He was seen running from the studio. The rifle used in the shooting was originally registered to him years ago. There's no record of a sale or transfer of ownership. He left his blood on the rug, and he admitted to the cops he was there that night. Hallowell has a dying declaration from Terry London on video, where she says my client popped her. The D.A. didn't even bother to use it at the prelim. He had enough without it.

"So you can draw your own conclusions. I don't ask myself that particular question. It might hinder me in the zealous performance of my duties."

"Has he admitted to it?" Nina asked.

"Do any of them ever admit to it?"

"So he says he didn't do it?"

"It doesn't matter what he says. Self-defense or involuntary manslaughter are his only possible defenses. Innocence is not an option."

"I know Kurt told you about me. You probably know by now that—"

"About the love nest at Fallen Leaf Lake? He told me all about it. Funny how it didn't come as a total surprise. You have a way of insinuating yourself into unsavory situations."

"It was a long time ago."

"Even so," he said, examining the fine ash on the tip of the cigar. Nina would have to wash her hair after she left. "You'll probably have to testify."

"I didn't see anything. I knew nothing then about Kurt's relationship with his ex-wife. I didn't even know who she was. I'd never met her until she called me about this case last fall, and she certainly never told me about her prior marriage."

"What about the fact that my client returned to Tahoe solely to protect you? Don't you think the jury ought to hear about that?" Riesner said.

"Terry never really hurt me."

"Apparently he knew her better than you did. He had good reason to believe that, had she lived, you would have become some kind of target."

"Let me see if I'm following you," Nina said. "You're going to tell the jury that he came here from Germany because he wanted to tell Terry to lay off me, and he killed her when she refused? You're putting me right in the middle of some harebrained scheme?"

"Why not? You adore the spotlight, we both know that. Enjoy the notoriety."

Nina gritted her teeth, trying not to show her reaction to his words. She took a deep breath before she spoke. "You're going to have to try the case," she said. "He's never going to agree to a plea bargain, no matter how you pressure him."

"I'll try the case, if his assets hold out. Why wouldn't I? I want him to get his money's worth." Riesner tapped the edge of the cigar against an onyx ashtray. White ash fell neatly in.

"Have you thought about whether you might have a conflict of interest? You still represent the plaintiffs in the *Sweet v. London* case. It seems to me one defense consideration might be, did one of them kill her? Or did someone else do it, someone depicted in that film?"

"Why should anyone do that?" Riesner said. "We were still litigating whether the film could be distributed. With all the money Tamara Sweet's parents were spending in court, it seems to me everyone would wait to see how the case came out before they started shooting."

"You have to look at those people as possible suspects."

"I'll handle the case as I see fit."

Nina felt Riesner was more interested in analyzing his bank account than his defense strategy. "I want to work with you. I could help."

"What?" He was well and truly amazed. She could tell by the way he dropped the cigar he had been twirling between his fingers, glared at it, and took a long time to recover it, roll it around in his fingers, move his mouth on it when he had it inserted back between his lips. With Riesner, she would take her pleasures where she found them.

"I'll help you line up experts, prepare for trial. I can associate in. We don't get along, okay. We'll divvy up the work so we don't have to see each other much. I'll work for free."

The man behind the desk smiled benevolently, back in the driver's seat where he belonged. "If I want help, I go to competent experts." He chuckled. "Turns out you can be funny. I can see how this might work. You would help me by taking away my clients and you would help me right out the door of my office. You would help me right out of town, if I let you." He puffed on the cigar. The tip glowed and dulled as he sucked vigorously, his face suffused with pleasure.

"Why don't you just head back to that game of cowboys and Indians you like to play with that dimwit secretary of yours?" he said finally, leaning back in his chair.

"You know, you look just like you're giving that cigar a blow job,'' Nina said, getting up swiftly, writing the whole thing off and not caring what she said anymore. ''Think about it next time the mayor offers you one after dinner.'' She left before he could kick her out.

15

BAREFOOT, HER BRIEFCASE AND HEELS LYING ON THE FLOOR TILES, Nina called Sandy from the kitchen at home to let her know where to reach her.

Bobby got home at three-thirty. He was now old enough to ride his bike when a friend was available to ride with him. Like every other jump forward in his life, this one made her nervous, but what good was life without freedom? Relieved, as she always was, at the sight of him pushing his bike up the driveway, she gave him something to eat, chatting with him about his day.

While he ate, he told her that he had stopped off with some friends at the shopping center on the way home, making a saga out of the short story, as his grandfather Harlan often did. He held out a small toy harbor seal for her to examine. They both played with the soft gray toy, squeezing its stomach for a squeak. Bobby was getting old for stuffed animals, but ever since his trip down to Monterey he'd shown unusual interest in the topic of seals, even writing an essay for school about them.

Matt dropped the two younger children off a few minutes later.

Troy joined Bobby at the homework table upstairs, and Brianna turned on her favorite kids' show in the living room.

"Cup of coffee?" Nina asked her brother, still in her work clothes, unable to get herself up from the comfortable padded vinyl kitchen chair.

"Can't," Matt said. "I've got work to do while it's still light. I'm getting things in order for the summer season. I need to get some equipment out of the shed and order some materials."

"You've been avoiding me and stomping all over here like a man with something on his mind. Even Andrea has mentioned it."

He lingered uncertainly in the doorway.

"You're the one who's always after me to slow down and smell the coffee. Come smell the Antiguan blend."

"Okay." He let the door swing shut, watching as if he was sorry to see it close. "One quick cup." He got a mug and filled it, turned a chair around and straddled it, leaning against its back.

"Where's the paper?" Nina asked. "I can't even find the recycling."

"I've been hiding it," he said. Getting up and walking over to the wall by the window, he tore paper towels off the roll, wet them under running water in the sink, and proceeded to lift the plants on the windowsill, wiping assiduously under each.

"Oh," said Nina.

"Because of Kurt Scott." Tossing a dirty wad at the trash can, he put cleanser on a sponge, squeezed and rinsed it, and wiped the table, motioning Nina to move her arms when he wiped her side.

"Matt, stop fiddling. Andrea told you about him and me, didn't she?"

"And Bob told me the name when he got back from Monterey. Also, remember, I helped get Bob registered at the school last spring? You needed a birth certificate. I looked."

"So you know all about it."

He stopped the kitchen cleaning long enough to say, "Mom taught us well, didn't she, Nina? Taught us all about keeping secrets. It's sad, all this energy put toward hiding things." He sounded more resigned than upset at the thought.

"We all have things in our lives that we don't want to talk about."

"Not Andrea." He dumped coffee grinds from the pot into the

sink, then turned on the water and ran the garbage disposal. "That's one thing I love about her. She blabs everything."

"Well, let's talk."

"You went to see him."

"Yes."

"What's he like? What kind of a man is he?"

"I really don't know. It's been a long time."

"After all this time . . . do you still have feelings for him?"

She considered this, finally saying, "I don't know."

"This is a helluva thing." Matt began to unload clean dinnerware from the dishwasher, stacking plates into steep piles and hurling silverware from the basket unsorted into the drawer, raising a racket that made Nina shudder.

"Matt, please stop! Sit down! I can't hear myself think!"

He sat back down at the table, tossing the towel down in front of her.

"Tell me what's bothering you."

"Who's bothered? Bob's father's back! I'm delighted for both of you! Oh, except—there's a minor problem. He's in jail on a murder charge."

"That's not your problem, is it, Matt?"

He looked at her, his expression unreadable, shaking his head. "Right. There I go again, thinking what happens to you and Bob has something to do with me and my family." He fell into a long silence, broken only by the thrumming of his fingers on the table. When he spoke again, he caught her eyes in his own, and held them, demanding an answer. "Did you think you could keep Scott's arrest from Bob, like you did everything else?"

"I plan to speak with him."

"Do all of us a favor. Don't tell him what he doesn't have to know. Maybe he won't find out until the guy's been shipped off to some penitentiary far away."

"I don't know—"

"I hate this."

Her heart sank. With her and Bobby living at his house, he'd never have the peace he had come so far to find. "I'm sorry, Matt."

"Just keep *us* out of it," Matt said.

"I'll probably be called as a witness."

"Most cases don't go to trial, right? That's what you said."

"Well, this one won't, if Riesner stays on as the defense attorney."

"And just what do you mean by that?" All Matt's restraint evaporated. "You're not thinking about getting involved, are you?" he said in disbelief.

"He's Bobby's father, Matt," Nina said. "I might be able to help him."

"Don't you dare. Don't you dare drag us into this," Matt said. "I'm warning you."

"How can I live with myself if Kurt's convicted for something he didn't do? Riesner won't give him the kind of defense he deserves—"

Matt slammed the screen door behind him.

That night, brushing her teeth on her way in to bed, Nina admitted it to herself: She was feeling out the degree of opposition she'd get if she took over Kurt's defense—if he wanted her to, if his story seemed credible, and if she could wrest it away from Riesner.

She couldn't go any farther without Paul's help. Crawling into bed, pulling the yellow cover up around her, she punched his number, saying "Howdy, stranger!" when he answered.

"Can't talk now, I'm smack dab in the middle of a ménage à trois," he said, but there was no real anger.

"Just keep your ear free. Really. Are you . . . busy? Because I can call back."

"In another month? No, the girls are already putting their clothes on. You've ruined everything. They're leaving now. Whoops! Hey, Eva, you'll need this out there! This better be good."

The joke had a hard edge to it. "You're still mad at me?"

"I can take only so much rejection before I take a breather. First we make love, then you won't take my calls."

"It's me that should be mad at you."

"What'd I do?"

"No idea, huh? How about that little trip to Germany, digging into my past?"

"Oh, that."

"And how about the fact that you said something that brought my son's father flying back here for a showdown with Terry London, and now he's in jail on a first-degree murder charge?"

For once, Paul had nothing to say.

"Well?"

"Well, I'll be an egg-suckin' dog."

"Go on. Bark."

"What does he have to do with Terry London?"

"He was married to her when he met me." Nina listened closely for his reaction, a mistake, as he whistled into the phone.

"He killed her? I knew she was your client. Now I can guess where she fit into his life. She must have been the crazy one that he was so scared of. I had no idea they'd arrested him for her murder. Uh, I owe you an apology, don't I?"

"It's too late for that. Paul, did you say anything at all about Bobby?"

Paul said, "You think I'm stupid?"

"Well, thanks for that. You stomped through my past, invaded my privacy, tracked down my old lover. But at least you left my son out of it."

"It's like an instinct or a bad habit. I got carried away. I thought I could find out what was keeping you away from me."

"You told Kurt we were getting married. You're an arrogant, high-handed, macho—"

"I have my bad points too."

She had to laugh.

"Thank God," Paul said. "Will you forgive me?"

"I already have."

"Will you marry me?"

"All right, Paul, quit teasing me."

"I'm not teasing. Let's get married."

"You're serious!" She laughed again.

"Will you?" Paul said. His tone had changed. He meant what he said.

"I can't marry you," she blurted out, but he didn't seem bothered by her graceless response to his proposal. Not that the proposal had been the most suave one she'd ever had.

"Why not?" he said.

"You're not supposed to ask that, are you?"

"Why not?" he repeated.

She felt compelled to be honest. "I went to the jail to see Kurt, but I haven't talked to Bobby yet about what's happening. I'm bewildered and unsure about this whole situation. Marrying is the last thing on my mind."

"You sure?"

For the first time it hit her. Paul might give up on her and move on. Why did he have to pin her down now? Why couldn't they just stay friends and colleagues? But she knew better than to say those things to him. Instead she said, in her softest, most soothing voice, "I need time, Paul."

An inarticulate grunt emanated from the other end of the phone line. She imagined him at his apartment, silently cursing the female gender, its indecision, ambivalence, and ability to make a man spiral like a kite on a string. She felt embarrassed and thrilled by this power, a strictly female one she rarely allowed herself to experience.

"I can't believe my own stupidity," he finally said. "I mentioned you were in Tahoe, and Scott left me holding hands with the waiter."

"I want to hear all about that trip. Soon."

"So not yes, but not no, either," he said, and fell into silence. After a few moments he said, "You're afraid of my love." This sentence came out in the doleful tone she associated with the talking bear he had given her. Down where it counted, he was as romantic as she had ever been, but, as with everything else about him, his love was bigger, stronger, and more formidable. He wanted to take over for both of them. She wondered whether she could stand up to him as his wife. She barely stood up to him now. This thought, which should have been unpleasant, made her smile.

"Maybe so," she said. "But I sure do feel flattered at the offer." Paul didn't press her further. She congratulated herself, thinking, I got past that one for the moment. Now back to the real subject of my call.

"Er, Paul. I wondered, if by some event it should shake down that way—if I took over Kurt's defense—not that he's asked me, or I've made up my mind or anything—would you be willing to help?"

A few seconds passed while her question registered with him. Through the next long silence she waited, sensing an immense volcanic pressure building up down there in Carmel, the man glowing hotter and hotter. . . .

"So," Paul said, his voice suspiciously soft. "It is him. It's always been him."

"I just can't leave him to Jeffrey Riesner. He says he came back here to warn me that Terry had reasons to want to hurt me or my family. I owe him something for that—"

"I can't help. Find a guy who doesn't give a damn about you to help with this one."

"I don't think I can do it without you."

"Good thinkin'. Now you listen to me, Nina. We've been friends for a long time. Above and beyond everything else, right?"

"I'm really glad to hear you say that, Paul."

"Well, as your old pal, I'm begging you. Don't take this case. It's going to screw up everything. Your life. Bob's. Matt's." He waited for her to say something. When she didn't, he exploded. "For God's sake, woman, what perverse character flaw is it that drives you to take the good life you've earned and pound it into hammered dog shit?"

"Could we leave it that your answer is not yes, but not no, either?"

"No! My answer is no!" Paul shouted.

She couldn't sleep after talking to Paul. She spent the night trying to decide what to do. Doing nothing would be as decisive as doing something, it seemed to her. Either way led to a cataclysm for them.

Matt and Paul had made their wishes known. Without their support, she would really be on her own. And did she really believe Kurt enough to go against her family and friends? She wanted to believe him, which didn't amount to the same thing.

"Mom?" Bobby stood in the doorway wearing his red plaid flannel pajamas, backlit by the hall light and striped in front by the golden light of dawn creeping through her blinds.

"What's up, honey? Can't sleep?"

He came over and sat on the edge of her bed. "I heard you."

"What do you mean?"

"I heard you and Uncle Matt shouting yesterday."

So he knew. She had not been able to protect him. Putting her arm around his narrow shoulders, she told him how Paul had found his father, feeling her words travel through him like voltage as his breath came faster and he pulled away from her to jump out of bed.

Hitting his fist into his palm, he said, "I knew he'd find him! I knew it! Where is he, Mom? Can we see him? What did you tell him about me?" He had a million questions, and in his elation he knocked an elbow into her nightstand hard enough to bruise himself without seeming to put the slightest dent in his spirits.

She had never seen him so agitated. "Sit down here." She patted the bed beside her. Instantly receptive to her serious tone, he settled back down on the bed, jiggling a foot but otherwise calm.

"He's here in Tahoe, Bobby." She didn't know how to say this, so she dove in, unable to see a way around the brutal truth. "He's in jail, charged with a serious crime."

"Murder, right? They're saying he killed someone. Who, Mom?"

She'd already said more than she ever wanted to have to say about Kurt. "I promise, we'll talk more later."

"Don't say that. You always say that."

He was right, she did.

Apparently realizing she would add nothing further, he asked, "When can I visit him?"

"You can't." Because she wouldn't allow it, not until she knew, incontrovertibly, that Kurt Scott was an innocent man. Even as she had the thought, she knew that moment might never come.

"You didn't tell him about me at all, did you, Mom?" She watched with sadness as the realization hit him, the slight hunching of his shoulders as he absorbed the blow. "He doesn't even know who I am, does he?"

"Bobby, you have to trust me on this. I have to protect you."

"From my own father? Didn't you love him at all?"

"Of course I did. But that was a long time ago."

"He is a good man, if you loved him."

"People change."

"Are you his lawyer?"

"He already has another lawyer. I went to see him, though." She led the way back into his bedroom, where Troy's even breath steadily inflated and deflated the covers on the bed across the room. Bobby groped under his pillow and squeaked his new toy seal in his hand.

Nina tucked him in. Just before she left, he put both arms around her, reaching up for a kiss.

"Mom, he needs us," he whispered into her ear. "You have to help him."

His words took hold of her and lodged inside her heart.

16

"Tell me why you left me, Kurt," Nina said into her telephone in the visitor cubicle.

She had gone back out of curiosity; that was all.

They didn't talk about the case but had tried to make small talk about jail and the weather. You couldn't have a casual conversation with a man in jail. You couldn't say, so, how's it feel to be back? Soon enough all that was left was to say what was between them.

"The story begins before I even knew you," Kurt said. "It's an ugly story. I suppose I was afraid you'd leave me if I told you everything. After I left I thought of finding you, but I couldn't. Terry was after me, and I might lead her to you."

Nina waited. She could hear him breathing over the line. Was he thinking up a story, or would he tell her the truth? She would judge that later. "I was twenty-three," Kurt began. . . .

He was twenty-three, and she was eighteen. Her name was not Terry. Her name was Tamara.

Dragged along by an old friend to a hoedown hosted by the local high school, he'd found her tipsy and pretty as a wildflower, swaying to music. Because he didn't like crowd scenes, he'd taken her outside. And one thing led to another.

That was all that happened at first.

Her parents would have disapproved, if they had known about the relationship. They didn't know him by name. They only knew what she told them, that he was five years older, out of college, a musician, nothing about what they did together.

Tam's father hadn't worked for some time. Any little thing would set her father off, Tam complained to Kurt. Her wearing a leather jacket. Her dating a boy who wore an earring or didn't like sports. Anyone who might take her seriously. Anyone who might tempt her from the academic goals they had set for her. The family was religious, but not hard-core, according to Tamara. Her father's obsessive protectiveness drove Tam up the wall. Against all Tam's angry protestations, her mother stood by her husband, and therefore firmly against her daughter. Tam said her mother drank secretly.

At first Kurt had believed what Tam told him about her parents. It wasn't until later that he realized her parents had good reasons for pulling in the reins on their wayward daughter. Tam had problems, big ones, too big for her parents, and eventually too big for him.

He agreed when she insisted on seeing him on the sly, although it made him uncomfortable. But meeting parents was not his favorite thing. He was happy to put it off, figuring that, as things got more serious, they would come around.

Months of secret dates had followed, arranged by Tamara, at her whim. She had other friends that she saw occasionally. He met them once, Doreen and Michael, but had decided years before that he had nothing to gain by being stoned, and getting loaded was their primary form of entertainment. Music sent him to a better place, and he needed to keep his wits about him to play. They found him boring. He found them boring.

But sex with Tam was never boring. As time went on, they settled into a routine of meeting once or twice a week and going to bed. They enjoyed each other, and they could have gone on for a long time that way. He liked her energy, her bright eyes and cheerful manner. She was a rebel.

One night in early winter they parked on a knoll above Emerald

Bay with Lake Tahoe below them, broken by the wind into crushed diamonds.

"Kurt, stop," she said, extricating herself gently from his touch, moving to her own side of the red Toyota, smoothing her hair. "I've got to tell you something." A faint bleariness in her eyes revealed to him that she had smoked at least one joint before meeting him that night. He was disappointed, but not surprised. She wasn't ready to quit, but she would. He just had to show her a better time than those clods Doreen and Michael ever could, take her traveling, show her what was out there in the world. "Someone's been watching me."

"Who?" He couldn't entirely stifle his skeptical tone. Grass made you paranoid, everybody knew it. She smoked too much grass. Lately, she had been high every time he saw her.

"I don't know, but someone's watching my window at night."

"Have you told your father?"

"I thought maybe you could do something."

"Such as?"

"After you drop me off tonight? Stick around. See if you see anyone."

To please her, he spent the rest of that evening skulking in her neighbor's scrawny oleander bushes. He loitered behind bushes and trees on several other nights. He never saw anyone. Tam got madder and madder at him, insisting someone was out there. But she wouldn't give him any details. He thought it might have to do with drugs, and she didn't want him to know about that part of her life. Or she was just using way too much.

And then, one day, she told him it was over, just like that. He knew she'd changed and found somebody else, and he found he didn't mind too much. They agreed to be friends, and stay in touch.

A few weeks later, when the local paper carried a story on her disappearance, he didn't worry. She had talked often about leaving. Naturally, her parents didn't know her whereabouts. However well-intentioned, they didn't get along. She would make them wait a long time, he guessed, wreaking this vengeance on them for their expectations and interference.

The days went by. Then the months. He began to wonder. Should he have done more to deal with her fears? Had someone really been after her? Who? He considered and rejected the notion of telling her parents. They couldn't do any more than the police were already doing. Had Tam run off? He didn't believe she could resist the urge to call or write him. She wouldn't treat him that way, would she? He was uneasy for months, but his concern changed nothing. He never heard from Tamara Sweet again.

Terry had been someone Kurt and Tam didn't know very well. He remembered running into her several times around town while he was seeing Tam. An artistic type, she had very long chestnut hair and liked to dress in bright colors. Tam said Terry had a crush on him, but he laughed it off.

He was living at his parents' cabin at the time, alone while they finished out the winter on the coast, near San Luis Obispo, their final winter, as things turned out. A month or so after Tam disappeared, Terry showed up one day out of the blue, on his doorstep, with a homemade lasagna.

"I heard you were back," she said. A sky blue wool sweater with reindeer running around the border topped her tight jeans. She wore a muffler wrapped around her neck, and her nose poked out, red in the biting wind.

"I never went away," Kurt said.

"I mean, in circulation," she said.

She looked like she was freezing. "Come on in," he had said, showing her in. He made a cup of coffee for her, which she drank greedily, her fingers clutching the mug, thin and white as bone. And then she had gone.

A week later he had run into her at a coffee shop. And then a few days later, at the movies, he ran into her again, alone, like he was. He invited himself to sit beside her. Alone at home, with no one to talk to, sending out résumés and driving the local librarians crazy with his requests for information about symphony orchestras in his search for a real job, he had gotten tired to the sound of his own voice singing off-key in the shower.

A few weeks later, plotzed from a heavy meal and the red wine, they had stumbled out of a local theater in the middle of the play they had gone to see, and kissed for the first time.

January. A month of wind, snow, and cold that froze blood in Tahoe.

Kurt still thought often about Tamara. He felt guilty that he hadn't taken her concerns seriously enough. He worried as the time went by and she never called. But Terry kept him busy and his thoughts well occupied, and, wearing the fabulous lynx coat that had once been her mother's, kept him tucked closely beside her.

They spent more and more time together and at some point he realized she was in love with him. He knew he should break it off, but he enjoyed her wit and her great ambitions. He let things slide. Within five months from the day she appeared at his door, Terry and Kurt were married.

It was a whole different level of the oldest story in the world. Terry had gotten pregnant.

He found out by accident. They were scheduled to go to a party, but had spent the afternoon in bed together. As had happened repeatedly since their first encounter, Kurt got the distinct impression that Terry was faking her excitement. He didn't have a lot of experience, but he could tell when a woman responded, and she just didn't, although she made quite a show of hard breathing. Her heart remained steady. Her cheeks stayed pale. She never sweated. She was like chiseled stone to touch—smooth, perfect, and cold. Kurt got up first, picking his jeans and shirt up off the floor. Having washed his face and checked his armpits for stink, he reappeared in the bedroom door, thinking they needed to have it out.

"Terry . . ." he started to say, but stopped at the sight of her.

Terry stood in front of a full-length mirror with a sheet covering nothing but the round of her stomach.

"What are you doing?" he said.

She pulled the sheet up over her breasts and turned to look at him. The swoop of her back and hips filled the mirror behind her. "Nothing."

"You're pregnant," he said.

"It doesn't matter," she said. "It doesn't change anything." The look on her face should have told him something, but it didn't. He took the tightness of her mouth and the furrow of her forehead as expressions of the same anxiety, hope, and awe that filled him.

"Oh, Terry. Of course it does."

"I don't want to talk about it," she said. "I'm getting dressed." Her clothes hung on a wooden chair beside the bed. The chair, which she had painted vermilion one day while he played the piano in the next room, had two high points edging the ladderback, onto which she had draped various items of her colorful clothing, a scarf in pinks and blues, a royal blue sweater. Changing her mind, she sat down on the chair, completely nude, her eyes as wide and bright as a child's, fixed on his own, examining his reaction.

He knelt in front of the chair, then on impulse, put a hand up to the curve in her belly.

"I'm having an abortion," she said, matter-of-factly.

Stunned, he sat back on the rug. "Don't do that," he said. "There's no reason to. You're healthy, aren't you?"

"Yeah, and I've got business in the world. I'm not about to have a kid. Don't make me laugh."

"You're twenty-eight. It's the right time. I'll help you."

"You have it then. Nine months looking like a pachyderm, followed by years of slavery to some little brat. Not me."

He couldn't believe it. They had made a child. He was going to be a father. She couldn't destroy his child.

"Terry, please—"

"You don't love me," she said. "One always loves more than the other. I hate loving you so much. I'm like a beggar with you. And you're just waiting for someone else to come along, and then you'll leave me."

"I do love you." It was a lie. He didn't love her, he never would, but they were in this together, something wonderful had happened, and he had to prevent her from making a dreadful mistake.

As if reading his mind, she said, "Liar."

"Don't," he said. "Marry me."

"So I won't get rid of the kid?"

"No. Because I love you. I've just been waiting for the right time to tell you." He'd cemented the lie, made her believe it and almost convinced himself.

He got used to the idea over the next few days, convincing himself that this child would bring them together in a way nothing had so far. The relationship between him and Terry hadn't gone much beyond the roll-in-the-hay phase. The disappointments could be fixed, he told himself, pushing his worries away.

He had many other doubts. She kept so much hidden. She told little lies that had no purpose. He might say, "Did you go to

Safeway?" and she would correct him, saying she had gone to another supermarket. Later, he'd unload the groceries from bags clearly labeled Safeway. Without any close friends or relatives, this strange and needy woman had no one except him, and soon, their child.

He could see nothing but a vague cloudiness where his feelings were concerned. A baby would make things clear. Priorities got straight when a baby cried, his mom said. "Pick 'em up real quick or suffer the consequences."

Was he more unprepared than most people for the reality of a child? It was about then, when he would talk about their baby and how great it would be for them both, that she would get quiet and thoughtful and sometimes, he had to admit it, downright sullen.

They had a quick ceremony in Incline Village. His parents came. Terry's parents had died in an airplane crash a few years before he had met her. The same crash had killed her only sister. She had nobody to invite. The lunch afterward, in an empty restaurant, had been a bad idea. Terry drank too much champagne and Kurt, whose early warning about alcohol had been followed by a nasty public rebuttal, didn't stop her. "Let's drink a toast to the goddamn baby!" she said, spilling a little from her raised glass. "Baby got Kurt to the altar when he didn't want to go, and took over Terry's body just when she was beginning to have some fun with it!"

Kurt's elderly father, who had also gone the excessive champagne route, cast a befuddled eye around and raised his glass. He was the only one who drank with her that time.

They honeymooned at a hotel overlooking the lake in South Tahoe. Terry spent the night hanging over the toilet, throwing up.

The last good times together turned out to be before the baby, before the wedding, before he really knew her.

The morning after their wedding, she sprang her first surprise on him.

Sitting on the balcony in a heavy white robe, she drooped over a cup of coffee and a congealing egg. "You didn't want to marry me, Kurt. So why did you?" she said.

"Eat the egg," he said. "You're just feeling low this morning. Something in your stomach will help." He had not criticized her, even though he had spent the whole night listening to her activities in the bathroom, wondering how much damage she had done to their baby.

"You married me because I'm pregnant." Despite her dirty hair and unpleasant mood, she looked fresh in the morning sun. And he had no reason to believe this ugliness of spirit would continue. There was no precedent to make him think she would change in ways he could never before have imagined.

"No, honey. I married you because you're Terry."

She lowered her lids until they covered half of her eyes. "If I hadn't been pregnant, would you have asked me to marry you?"

"You look pretty in that red chair in the sunshine."

She refused to be placated. "I mean it. Answer me, Kurt."

"Maybe not that minute. But we were heading that way, Terry." He took one of her hands when he said the words, as if touching might convince them both.

"Really?"

"Really."

"Because I've been thinking . . ."

"Hmm." He had grown tired of the conversation and wanted to get back to the newspaper. On the other hand, they were newlyweds. He left the paper on the table.

"I'm not ready for a child."

"Well, of course you aren't," he said. "Luckily you've got several months to prepare. It's natural to worry about it. This is something entirely new, but we can take a class or something. It's scary, but there are two of us and we're going to do great. We'll still outnumber the little guy."

"Please, Kurt. Spare us both the lower-middle-class fantasy. Let's set our heights a little higher, hmm?"

He withdrew his hand.

"You'll be around long enough to change exactly one of each type of diaper. Then you'll finally land a real job in music, just like you've dreamed of. You'll take off for months to travel with some orchestra while I sacrifice all my own dreams to stay at home mopping up puke. I've thought this over. I'm telling you, I'm not ready."

"What are you saying?"

"It's not too late. I checked." She rushed along. "I've got about a week or two to do an early procedure."

"You want to abort our baby?"

"It's not a baby yet, Kurt. It's a bundle of cells about this big." She pressed her thumb and forefinger close together in front of his face. "We can have a child later. We need more time together, just the two of us."

"No," he said.

"I don't need your permission."

"Of course you don't. It's your decision, not mine. Your body, not mine. But you're carrying my child and I've made a commitment to that unborn baby—"

"By marrying me? That's what it comes down to. You never wanted to marry me."

"Don't start on that."

"Didn't you just say we were heading that way anyway? Didn't you say you married Terry? Not Terry and a bunch of cells that are just nothing. Not Terry, a woman who stays home all day with a screaming infant and yells at her husband when he gets home because she's used up before her time!"

"Why didn't you tell me this before?"

"Before we got married? Why do you think? I knew you wouldn't marry me!"

"You weren't fair to me. You weren't honest."

"Have you been honest with me, Kurt? Have you? Haven't you wished things were better than they are? Haven't you, once in a while, when you're holding me, wished I was someone else?"

"Don't try to distract me. You married me yesterday knowing full well you had made up your mind about not having this child."

"Yes, I did!"

Cold and hard as metal in the shade, she put cold fingers on his, trying to take the hand back he had taken away, but he would not allow it. "Having a child now is a mistake, Kurt. I'm not saying we should never have one."

"Terry, I'm going to tell you the truth now, because you want to hear it. Correct?"

She nodded.

"I don't know what would have happened with us in the future. I only know, I married you yesterday because of our baby. Whatever I thought about it in the beginning doesn't matter, because now I have pictures of it toddling around in my mind that I can't just forget. If you decide to get rid of it, I'm out of your life."

"This is so wrong, Kurt. You shouldn't make me have this child."

"I can't make you! You have to decide. But I'm not going to pretend it's okay with me for you to have an abortion. It's not."

"So that's the choice. You and baby or nothing."

"Your decision."

"You bastard!" She stood up, so he stood up. Making fists hard as stone, she beat on his chest and shoulders. "God damn you for making this so hard!"

"Terry, please, stop. Don't cry."

"You don't love me."

"I love you both. I'll do my best to love you both forever, if you give me the chance."

Thanks to his parents, Kurt and Terry were able to stay in the small cabin on the fringes of Tahoe City, up a steep hill on the side of a mountain. They moved in after a disastrous honeymoon in which they did nothing but fight.

Almost immediately after speaking the words, Kurt realized he had made what might be an irrevocable error in telling Terry he would leave her if she didn't have the child. He had put things wrong, he knew that, but he found it impossible to put them right. No matter what he said or did, no matter how concerned and caring he was, she rejected the feelings he offered her. She never let him forget that he was forcing her to do something she didn't want to do.

He could never see it her way. Soon after their marriage, his father died, followed closely by his mother, and Terry attended the funerals with him. She stood by him. He would do the same. The baby would make up for everything wrong between them, he told himself.

As time passed, and her pregnancy progressed, he did everything he could to make it easy on her. He took over the majority of the chores, which was easy, since he had an undemanding part-time job with the U.S. Forest Service that held them together financially while he searched for something in his field. He cleaned, cooked, shopped, and did the laundry while Terry sank into an exhausted stupor.

She had the child in November, at home, which had been her wish, with a midwife in attendance. She screamed and cried for a full day.

Kurt named the child, a girl, Lianna, after his mother.

Lianna and Kurt developed a deep relationship from the start. Terry refused to breastfeed, so it was Kurt who got up to rock and change the crying baby, and Kurt who, at four months, was favored with Lianna's first real smile, a smile of great regard and charm that made him into her willing slave.

Terry never took to her. During the day, while Kurt worked, they hired sitters. At night, Kurt kept the baby propped on his knees while they watched television, or played with her on the floor, endlessly amused at her antics. Terry watched them.

He and Terry quit having sex during her pregnancy. After the baby was born, they tried a few times, but everything had soured between them, including sex.

In the spring following Lianna's birth, Kurt quit trying with Terry. He harbored resentments that had grown over the months. All conversations about sex ended with them blaming each other. Yet she was so possessive, she had to know where he was every minute, and constantly accused him of being with other women.

And, most disturbing, he couldn't stand the neglect of Lianna. What kind of a person could ignore her child so utterly? He had caught the fleeting glimpses of repugnance on her face, when, forced to touch her own child, she would hold the curly-haired baby in her arms, squeezing too tight, pinching or prodding, laughing when Lianna cried.

He knew he had to leave her.

He took her to the Christiania Inn for dinner.

"Isn't this wonderful?" she said, looking around happily at the white tablecloths and bustling waiters. "Just us. It's like it was before." She put a hand up to his cheek. "Maybe there is life after baby. Let's drink a toast." She raised her glass. "I've signed up for a summer course at UCLA film school," Terry said. "I'm leaving next week."

"What?" Kurt said, unable to believe what he had heard.

"Only for six weeks," she said. "This is just too good an opportunity to pass up."

"You never said a word about it."

"I didn't know I'd get in. I filled out the forms months ago."

"It's a good idea, Terry," he said, adding quickly, because he could sense her wariness, "it's what you've always wanted."

"I arranged for the sitter and a backup, so it shouldn't disrupt your working routine too much."

"Thanks."

"We'll talk every day. You won't even notice I'm gone."

Guilt at the relief he was feeling washed over him. Maybe this was his way out. Where her career ambitions were concerned, he and Lianna did not fit in. If she got going in that direction, found a substitute for him in her work, found him useless and peripheral to what she really wanted out of life, he would be free.

"Terry, we need to talk. Things aren't working."

"I warned you that having a kid wasn't going to be easy," she said, sipping her wine, looking out at the lake in the distance, smiling. "Just don't expect me to pick up the slack. Now it's my turn again."

What was she talking about? "This isn't about the baby." He intentionally didn't use Lianna's name. He found that, with Terry, just mentioning the child by name, lending her human being status, could degrade an ordinary conversation into a painful scene. "This is about the fact that we have no sex life—"

"Oh, Kurt, is that what you're all worked up about? I told you, that's not a problem. We just need to give ourselves plenty of time, plenty of opportunities, get to know what we both want."

"You don't understand, Terry. I don't want to try anymore. Our relationship is over."

"Jesus, you men. Such a catastrophe! You can't get it up a couple of times. Big deal. Why don't you grow up and get over it."

"Our marriage is over." He took the time to make her understand, using the exact words he intended, saying them slowly and solemnly enough to penetrate the defensive walls of her fortress.

The idea got through. She had a look he'd seen a few times over the past year, a look that worried and unnerved him on more than one occasion. Her face collapsed onto itself, the whole thing vacuum-sucked, the skin stretched over her cheekbones, her eyes protruding unnaturally, as if she had to implode, preparatory to exploding.

"Over my dead body!" she said, throwing her glass to the floor.

A couple passing by their table turned to eye them, but when they maintained a silence punctuated only by Terry's ragged breaths, they went on without comment.

"Can you cool it with the hysterics? This can't be a surprise to you."

"We have a fabulous marriage. The best!"

"Terry, we don't sleep together. We don't laugh anymore. There's no there there."

"Ha! Gertrude Stein, turn in your grave! Here's a man using your words to dump his wife!"

"I'm not dumping you, Terry. This is not a situation that demands blame. I'm just stating the obvious. We have no marriage."

"Well, let's see. Maybe if you were more than half a man. Maybe if you hadn't insisted on having a child when I never wanted one. Maybe if you could just love me like you love that damned kid—"

"Don't bring her into this," he warned. "This is about you and me. Let's concentrate on that."

"How can we have a conversation that doesn't include the third party who intrudes on everything? Every evening we deal with her needs, her hunger, her dirty butt, her wheezing, her sniffles. Every evening I wait for you to turn to me, to need me, to need something from me—"

"This is not another lover you're talking about! This is our child! She needs both of us. Maybe if you had some attention to spare for her instead of some obsessive love story spooling around inside your head all the time—"

"I spend plenty of time on her! What the hell do you know about it? What about all the times the sitter is late? Or sick? Who's gonna be there when the school calls a few years along the line because she's skinned her knee or gotten into trouble?"

"Me. That's what I'm trying to tell you." Her words, her demeanor, everything conspired to tell him what he didn't want to know about his wife—how much she hated their child.

"You? An excuse for a man who can't even keep his wife happy in bed? You're going to be both mother and father to our child?"

"Right. Why would you want a man like that, Terry? What use am I to you now? If you really let yourself think about it, you deserve better."

"I deserve a man who loves only me! And that's the way it was with you and me, remember? Whole days in bed together. I can satisfy you better than anyone, if you'll only let me!"

"Why would you want to? Even if the sex was good, Terry, that wouldn't be enough." He wondered how Lianna was doing with the sitter. He wondered if she was still awake. He felt tired and unhappy. He wanted to go home to his daughter. "This is not an argument, you know. This is not a situation where you can win a debate and persuade me that I'm wrong."

"You don't even want to give me the common courtesy of dealing with my pain."

"I don't want to hurt you. I don't believe I am hurting you. The circumstances are painful. Our marriage is over. Now we need to move forward and past a lot of broken-up hope."

"What a weasel. That's so irresponsible. 'The circumstances are painful,' ha!"

"I have plenty of responsibility here. This has been a mistake since the beginning."

"He admits it! We never should have had a child!"

"That's the only thing we've done I'm proud of."

"What about how much we've meant to each other?"

"Terry, it's not real. There's never been much more than sex between us, and now that's not working out either."

"Don't deny you love me. Don't you dare."

He got up to leave. She followed him outside.

"I want a separation. This trip to L.A. is a good time to try one," Kurt said.

"Don't leave me, Kurt, please." She tried to kiss him, but he turned from her, hurrying around to the driver's side of the car. "I can be a better mother, if that's what you want."

"You're a good mother," he said, unwilling to kick her while she was down, as if his faith could make it so. "I'll never say you didn't try your best."

"But you insist that we separate."

"Yes."

On the ride home she leaned her head on her arm, resting it across the open window of the car door. "Wait until I get back before you do anything drastic, okay? Don't move out. We'll see how you feel when I come back," she said. "Six weeks is a long time. You'll see then how much you need me."

He helped her pack her car. At first, he could hardly believe Terry was gone. He could breathe again. The house settled and calmed, the baby slept through the night, and he and the sitter cleaned the place thoroughly, exorcising the last of her frantic, disturbing presence.

Thank God she had gone. He realized how sick he felt, how afraid he was of her, how lonely and isolated he had become.

He began looking for another place for him and Lianna.

A week later, he met Nina over at Fallen Leaf Lake.

Terry returned on a weekend in August. Kurt waited for her in the cabin. She brought her bags in and threw them on the floor, opening her arms for a welcome home, which he made an effort to deliver. Then he sat her down on the couch.

"While you were gone, I moved out, Terry."

"What?"

"I rented an apartment in Incline Village."

"Wait a goddamned minute. My leaving you was supposed to be temporary, and I had time to think. I decided to come back. We can have it all, Kurt. Work, baby. Everything you and I both want."

"I don't see it that way." Let her think she had left him. He didn't care how much she lied to herself anymore.

She shook her head, frowning. "This is a very bad thing you've done."

"I've got a room set up for the baby over there. I mean, she's here today. She's sleeping at the moment. I thought you'd want to see her. But she'll be better off with me. I know you must agree with that."

"Who is she?"

"Who?"

"Who's the bitch you ran off with?"

When he didn't answer, she continued. "You're not the type to make it on your own. You've gone from one woman to another without Terry to keep you warm at night, but sweetie, you forgot one thing. Nobody breaks a promise to Terry. You're not going anywhere."

He stood up. "I established residence in Nevada while you were gone. I'm getting a divorce. Now, you can take this well, and continue to see your child, or you can blow it, and get hurt."

"Kurt, why are you doing this?"

"We've said everything. I'm going to get the baby. You can have a little visit, and tell her good-bye for now. We'll work out some kind of deal so you can see her, when you know better what you'll be doing."

After a pause Terry said, "I would like to see Lianna."

"You're taking this well," he said. "I can't tell you how much I appreciate it." He had played the scene a dozen times in his mind, and it had always been much more dramatic. He walked with her toward the hall, feeling reluctant to turn Lianna over to Terry, but unable to think of what he could do about it.

"Let me get her, Kurt. I want to see her face when I wake her up."

He agreed, holding back the instinct to say no. She was Lianna's mother.

He sat on the couch in the living room waiting for them to return. He waited longer than he wanted to, trying to be fair, giving her the time she needed to be alone with her child, to make her peace with what might be a long good-bye.

"Terry!" he called finally, but there was no answer.

He peered down the hallway, giving her another few seconds to come out. She hadn't left. She couldn't get past him to the door. A minute, then two minutes ticked by. He knocked on the bedroom door. "Everything okay in there?"

"Well, I don't know," Terry's voice said, sounding annoyed. "She just . . ."

Why couldn't he hear his daughter? "Let me in, Terry. Unlock the door."

"I don't understand it," Terry said, coming out at last to stand in the doorway. She moved her shoulders in a funny half shrug. "She just won't get up."

He flew into the room. Lianna lay in her crib, facedown, a light knit blanket floating over her tiny body. He watched her for a moment. He touched her back. Still. Still as his heart.

The paramedics came, and then the coroner. He fell apart. Between his sobs he told them that Terry had killed their daughter. They listened to his story, and Terry's story. Before long, he knew she had won. He had witnessed nothing. They had no evidence. They patted his shoulder, and comforted his grieving wife, who sat so pale and quiet on the couch that they gave her a shot to prevent a shock reaction. Nobody knew the cause of sudden infant death syndrome. Nobody could have done anything to prevent it.

Kurt Scott died that day, along with his daughter.

That pillow in the corner . . . He knew she had done it.

The next day, at his new apartment, while he sat in the living room engulfed by rage and sorrow, someone had knocked at the door until he could ignore it no longer. He opened the door. Vivid in a bright red dress, her face twisted with possessiveness and hate, Terry pushed her way in.

"Now, let's talk about this bitch you're seeing," she said.

He had turned his back on her and walked out. He ran away from Tahoe. He ran away from Nina, who was in danger because of him.

And Terry began looking for him, as he had known she would.

17

NINA SAT ON A ROCK UNDER A SHADY SPRUCE TREE, LOOKING OUT over Emerald Bay, waiting for the horror of what Kurt had just told her to diminish so she could think.

Farther down the rocks, a young Japanese man took a picture of his friend. Her black hair blown back by the breeze, she smiled into the sun, leaning with one hand on the warm granite. Behind her, Lake Tahoe, miles of cold, deep water, glittered in the afternoon sun. They saw only the beauty of it, not the awful, unknown depths.

She knew she had to make a choice. Believe him, or not believe him. If she believed him, the responsibilities that would follow were so heavy, she wasn't sure she could bear the weight.

If she believed Kurt, he had suffered a blow from which few people could recover. He had tried to escape, but like some harpy Terry had sought him, her revengeful hunger still unsatiated. Over the years, he had made himself a sort of life in exile, which Terry had again shattered with her death. Terry had murdered their child, and tormented him almost to insanity. He ran, not just to protect himself, but also to protect Nina. And she had been ignorant of his sacrifice. She had despised him.

While Nina had continued her own life all these years, changed by knowing him and the suddenness of losing him, he had been out there living too. She had only a few years on this earth, and her time and Kurt's time ran parallel. How could she ever have thought she wouldn't see him again!

She thought of his fingers—graceful, long fingers—and his large hands, which spread so far across the keys. He played the fugues of Bach, those complex point and counterpoint melodies in which one series of notes fled from another . . . *fugue,* from the Latin word that meant "to flee." . . .

If she believed him, she would have to try to help him. At least she was clear about that.

She slipped her trembling hand inside her blouse, touched the smooth scar. She wasn't sure she had the strength.

If she believed him, she would have to fight Riesner before she could even begin to help Kurt, and he would make sure she got hurt. Matt had reacted badly to the thought. He might even ask her to move. Paul . . . she might lose Paul. Her legal practice would suffer. She would look foolish. Woman defends love-child's father! What would it do to Bobby, who had reached such a vulnerable place in his development?

The tourists climbed back up the rocks, moved on. She was alone for the moment, facing the great body of water. The lake looked like a cauldron of blue energy, its emanations blurring the air above it, the mountains its protecting walls.

Could she even see the case clearly? If Kurt didn't kill Terry, then someone else had, someone who might be connected with the film. . . . Funny, she'd never thought about the film this way, but Terry had essentially said in the film that a mass murderer haunted Tahoe. The notion had seemed half-baked—until now.

There might be danger. She wasn't an Amazon, dagger in her belt, striding through the forest in search of a man-eating tiger. She was a mother.

What about her resolution to stay away from criminal cases?

And . . . what if she believed him, and lost the case? How could she live with that?

Could he be lying, his story a clever and self-serving appeal to her sympathy? What if she won, and he had lied? What about Bobby? Would he be safe? Was he safe now only because Kurt didn't know about him, and was imprisoned? If Kurt learned about his son, what would happen then?

If he was lying, and had killed Terry, and Nina found out later . . . she would be destroyed emotionally. He still had the power to do that to her.

The reasons against taking over the defense were so strong—how could anything outweigh them?

The reasons to help him were so small, lost in the din of warnings in her mind. Maybe—just maybe—he was innocent and she could save Bobby's father. Then, one day, they could meet, Bobby and his father, Bobby complete at last, Kurt given an amazing gift that would make up for so much. . . .

Really, the reasons for fighting for Kurt came down to a boy saying, please, Mom, you have to help him . . . small reasons. A tiny chance for the three of them to be . . . happy? Could they go back twelve years and start over, even if Kurt was free? Did she really dare to think that thought?

Strange how that thought of the three of them together spread like cool water across her mind, filled the gaps of doubt, moistened and soothed the dust of her dread. It tugged gently in the corners where her strengths lurked, the intelligence, the courage, the obstinate will to find the truth. It drew these strengths out, cleared the muddiness from her mind.

This was the challenge, affecting her life so intimately, that she had been preparing for all these years, without even knowing it. She couldn't walk away from this.

Over an hour had gone by. She was stiff. Her foot had gone to sleep. She moved it gingerly, enduring the prickles, eyes still fastened on the lake.

She had come clear. She would fight.

First, Jeffrey Riesner.

Several of Riesner's clients had switched to her, probably because she was cheaper, hopefully because she was better. Riesner charged two hundred dollars an hour plus costs, very stiff for the working community here in the mountains. Nina often agreed to a flat fee for her services, which made the clients happy, as they could call her with questions without having to worry about the clock ticking. Of course, after office and other expenses, she sometimes found herself working for a few bucks an hour.

Nevertheless, Riesner had lost several clients to her and that was only adding fuel to his antagonism.

And now she had decided to give Riesner a doozy to complain about. She couldn't help Kurt unless she took control of his defense.

Wasn't it unethical to blatantly steal a client? And who'd ever heard of a lawyer taking a case in which she was likely to be a witness?

This lawyer needed a lawyer, one who specialized in that jumble of ambiguous rules and regulations known as legal ethics.

Back at the office, she talked to a potential new client and turned him down. She had remembered that there was a hotline to the California State Bar, where a lawyer could call anonymously and receive advice on legal ethics.

Ordinarily, Nina stayed away from the California State Bar. Its official function was to support the legal community in California. But it seemed to her, as to many other lawyers, that ninety percent of its activities involved punishing lawyers, and the other ten percent involved reporting the public reprovals, suspensions, disciplines, and disbarments in the State Bar newspaper. Each month she read the details of the downfalls of dozens of her colleagues, hoping she wouldn't recognize any of the names. The State Bar was like the tax man: capricious, confiscatory, and unavoidable.

Yet there was this one service from which she could receive the help of anonymous, free advice from the people who ought to know. And she faithfully paid the State Bar four hundred seventy-five dollars a year in dues. Now was a good time to see if her professional organization would put its mouth where its money was.

Closing the door, she looked up the number in San Francisco. The phone rang a long time, and then she was put on hold. Finally, a cordial male voice said, "Hi, State Bar."

"I'd like to be transferred to your professional responsibility hotline." It ought to be called the deep-shit hotline, the place lawyers called when they were sued by disgruntled clients, arrested for drunken driving, or under investigation for dipping into the client trust fund.

"Are you an attorney with us?"

"Yes."

"Certainly, counselor." She deeply distrusted the cheer in the operator's voice.

A new voice came on, this one exactly what she had expected: impatient, world-weary, suspicious. A woman.

"Hotline."

"I'd, uh, like to ask a couple of questions regarding professional ethics. If that's possible."

"You'll have to leave your name and number, and someone will call you back."

Leave her name and number? What about anonymity? But such was the authority in the telephone voice, that Nina meekly stated her identity, then said, "When, uh, may I expect a return call?"

"Today," the voice said, and hung up. She hung up, too, wishing she had never called.

She stood at her lakeside window, looking out at Mount Tallac, some granite showing through the melting snow at its lower elevations. A few miles farther around the lake, in the northwesterly direction she was looking, was Emerald Bay, out of sight around a curve, and behind it, Fallen Leaf Lake. She hadn't been out to the summer rental cabin where she had been staying when she met Kurt since she moved to Tahoe.

Sandy came in with a pile of papers. "For you to proof and get back to me by four-thirty, so I can make copies and send them out."

Sandy rescheduled her late-afternoon appointment in Carson City. Nina imagined troubled lawyers all across California, waiting all afternoon for their special phone call, missing court appearances, house closings, settlement meetings. She thought about the State Bar calling everyone back long distance. She thought about her bar dues.

But when Sandy's buzz came at four forty-five she had a moment of panic. She had voluntarily brought her otherwise obscure self to the attention of the regulator of 150,000 California lawyers, the mysterious powerful presence that meted out justice and punishment to those who feared nothing else, That Which Disbars. "Thank you for returning my call," she said in a humble tone.

"My pleasure, Ms. Reilly. How can I help you?" said a confident young female voice, serene and unsettling. Why was it so placid? What calamitous news did it regularly report in that soothing tone?

"I have a couple of minor little, er, hypothetical questions for you," Nina said.

"Certainly."

"Okay, let's assume I want to represent somebody in a criminal case, but it's possible I may be a witness in the case. I don't really think I should be called, I have no direct knowledge, but the prosecutor might think I know something relating to motive or, uh, the res gestae. You know, the stuff that happened the day before, the defendant's movements and so forth. Am I making myself clear? You could maybe look up for me—"

"Lawyer as witness," the inhumanly confident voice said. "Ms. Reilly, I would refer you to Rule 5–210 of the Rules of Professional Conduct. Generally, a lawyer may not represent a client if it is likely that the lawyer would be called as a witness in the same matter."

"Oh." Shot down already . . .

"However, the third exception to the Rule may be of interest to you, Ms. Reilly. A lawyer may represent a client and also serve as a witness, so long as the client has given informed prior written consent."

"Oh!"

"Your second question?"

"Uh, yes, this is all hypothetical, you understand, of course—"

"Of course, Ms. Reilly. Your second question?" Nina felt the sense of a tremendous time pressure, as if the voice was so superbly valuable, not a moment nor a syllable could be wasted. Perhaps her clients felt a little of that sometimes, dealing with her.

"Well, let's say I want to represent this same client, but he's already represented by counsel. The client wants to switch. I know there's some kind of rule about soliciting the other guy's client—"

"Indeed. Rule 5–2100. You are prohibited from communicating with a person already represented by counsel upon the subject of representation."

Nina waited. She was learning. Bad news, then good news.

"However, you might wish to consult the exception at paragraph C, subparagraph 2. Communications initiated by a represented party seeking advice regarding representation from another independent attorney are not prohibited."

"So long as the client initiates the discussion about changing lawyers," Nina said. "I understand."

"You should be aware that the State Bar does not give legal advice, it merely provides information as to the content of the Rules referred to," the voice said. "Would you like me to cite some cases on the points mentioned?"

"No, thank you," Nina said. "You've been most helpful."

"The State Bar is here to serve you," said the State Bar. Nina guiltily enjoyed for a moment the feeling of power that all those dues multiplied by all those lawyers brought. With so much money, the lawyers could all move to their own litigious little island and leave the rest of the world alone.

She made a note or two beside the doodle she had drawn of a nervous little man stretching out his hands toward a fat, complacent, dangerous gorilla. Her stomach was growling. She was wondering if the State Bar had taped the phone call. She was in some computer data file now. Her questions had been duly noted and could be recalled.

The flip side of the coin was that she could prove she'd called the State Bar before she did what she was going to do. She had covered her rear, and the State Bar's attempt to cover its own rear there at the end of the call, with its disclaimer that it was providing legal information only, was patently absurd. Or so she would argue if it ever came up.

Of such paranoid reflections are the thoughts of lawyers made.

18

She called the jail. They had evening visiting hours.

After dinner she went to see Kurt again. Time to set the wheel in motion. "Nina Reilly to see Kurt Scott," she said to the intercom.

A pause. "It says here that Jeff Riesner's his lawyer."

"I'm just visiting again."

"If you say so, Ms. Reilly." He buzzed her in. She wondered if Jeff Riesner knew she had been to see Kurt.

A few minutes later, in the visitors' cubicle once again, she looked through the glass at Kurt Scott. He looked as apprehensive as she felt.

"How are you?" he said.

"Thinking hard."

"I didn't expect you back, matter of fact."

"I had to decide if I believed you or not."

"My lawyer doesn't, so why should you?"

"Your lawyer doesn't know you."

His whole body relaxed slightly, and she could see how tightly he controlled himself, and how little slack he allowed.

"I tried to find you before, you know, a few years after I left Tahoe, during a time when I felt relatively safe. Those were years Terry was traveling in her work and didn't have much time to devote to her hobby of hunting me and harassing everyone I knew. You were living in San Francisco, and I learned you were married."

"That's nice, that you tried to keep track of me."

"But now I'm an interference in your life, one you'd just as soon had never arrived. Isn't that true?"

"Absolutely," she said. "But here you are."

"Like mud on your shoe."

"Like a thunderstorm. If lightning doesn't burn my house down, I'll have an interesting garden."

So much remained unspoken between them. He knew her better than anyone, though their time together had been so short. Seeing that curvy-lipped smile again and his eyes lit up as they now were, she remembered acutely what he had been to her.

"How are they treating you?" Nina asked as casually as she could.

"I asked if I could bring in an electronic keyboard with headphones so I could practice. They're afraid I'd make the keys into weapons."

"Oh, no."

"My hands miss the exercise. But I probably couldn't make music here even if I tried."

"What about your life in Germany?"

"My job is gone. My landlord rented my apartment and put everything in storage. My other responsibilities are taken care of for the moment. I had only come out of hiding two years ago to play music again. Terry was fading from my mind. I thought she might have finally forgotten me, too, but I used another name, just in case."

"What's the trial date?"

"July fifteenth. Mr. Riesner doesn't think it'll last more than two weeks."

"That's only a couple of months away. Will you have enough time to get ready?"

"He says it's a simple case. We haven't really talked about it much. Is it a simple case, Nina?"

It was the opening she had been waiting for, an unsolicited expression that Kurt didn't have full confidence in Riesner. "I can't communicate with you on the subject of your representation, since you're represented by Mr. Riesner," she said deliberately.

"Huh? What are you talking about?"

"If you were to initiate a conversation with me about the subject of your representation, I could talk with you about it, but I can't initiate such a discussion."

"You're hinting at something," Kurt said, "but I'm damned if I can figure out what."

"Sure you can."

He was thinking. "Okay, I'm initiating a discussion," he said, "about what you said."

"And if you are thinking Riesner might not be a good lawyer for you, if you would like to seek other representation, and if you say so, we can discuss it."

"I don't want him. I don't trust him. But it seems like I'm stuck with him." Nina analyzed the words for legal content and decided they would have to do.

"Now that you bring it up," she said, "no, you're not stuck with him."

"He's got all my money."

"He'd be obligated to return the unused portion."

"Do you know this guy?"

"Regrettably," she wanted to say, but she couldn't criticize Riesner without influencing Kurt unfairly, so she said, "Yes."

"Then you know he's not going to let me replace him."

"Eventually, he'd have to. As for the money, I would represent you without a large advance retainer," Nina said, and then hurried to add, "Of course, you could pay me as soon as the balance of Riesner's retainer is repaid to you." Over a waterfall in a barrel was how that statement made her feel.

Kurt's face flickered through many emotions.

"I have to tell you there are some possible drawbacks to changing counsel now. There might be some ups and downs coordinating with Mr. Riesner to get your case file and your retainer. In fact, there might be hand-to-hand combat. You'd have to file a motion to substitute me in as your attorney. I might be a witness in your case. You'd have to give me written acknowledgment that you understand that, and still want me as your lawyer."

"I don't know if I do."

Something in her said, okay, I did my best. "I understand. He's had a lot more experience. I'm sure he'll do a great job for you. Forget I mentioned it," she said at once, her pride shooting sparks.

"You think it's because I don't think you'd be any good, Nina?"

"Well . . ."

"I've talked about you with some of the other prisoners. You're respected in Tahoe as a result of your last case, at least with some of these guys. I know you're good enough. But don't you see? I've done enough to you."

"Don't worry about me. I can handle it."

"Don't get involved with me. I'm—"

"Doomed? Not with me on your side, buddy."

He shook his head, but she saw a glimmer of hope in his eyes.

"You believe I'm innocent?"

Nina couldn't look him in the eye on that one. "I want to believe you. I can say it seems to me you might be telling the truth and you deserve a good defense."

As she spoke, Terry's bloody corpse on the floor of the studio rose like a specter on the glass in front of her, superimposed over his face like the grisly red mask of a warrior. He could be lying. He could be maligning Terry's memory. A hard place in her mind still said, if you did it, Kurt, I'll—

"You've changed, too, Nina. I have to ask myself why you're offering to do this."

"I want to help you, and I have a personal stake in this." She kicked herself mentally. What would he make of a statement like that? She couldn't provoke any questions. What if he saw through her to their son? Bobby was off-limits. Kurt could never know about Bobby unless he was acquitted.

"Thank you for wanting to help me. I'm not sure it's the right thing—but how do I tell that fathead Riesner he's fired?"

Kurt must have mailed out the substitution of attorneys form he'd signed, along with his cover letter requesting a refund of any unused retainer, the next day. Just before five o'clock the following Monday, when Nina and Sandy were washing the coffeepot and putting away books in the library, the fax burped and began a transmission. First came a letter, then came another letter.

The first letter, from Jeffrey A. Riesner, Attorney-at-Law, said with admirable succinctness:

Dear Attorney Reilly:

I have reported your disgraceful breaches of professional ethics to the State Bar of California. I trust you will be hearing from it soon. A copy of the State Bar letter is enclosed.

The so-called "Substitution of Attorney" that you prepared and manipulated my client into signing is also returned, unsigned by me. I advise you to cease and desist immediately from making any more attempts to contact my client or otherwise disturbing his working relationship with me. For your information, I am considering filing suit against you for tortious interference with a contractual relation.

Very truly yours,
Jeffrey Riesner

She read the attached letter, addressed to the California State Bar. Riesner had drawn, quartered, and beheaded her in impeccable legalese.

Sandy read along in silence. When they were both finished, Sandy said, "You do get him to frothing at the mouth."

"I expected it," Nina said. "The motion to substitute attorneys and supporting declaration is already dictated, Sandy. Type it up first thing in the morning and file the papers to have it heard as soon as possible."

"Another murder case," Sandy said, her lips pursed. Nina waited for the negative reaction.

All Sandy said was, "Bring on the clowns."

A couple of days later, a letter from the State Bar arrived. Nina was told that she was under investigation based on Riesner's complaint. She was told that the matter was serious. She was given ten days to respond in writing, enclosing all pertinent evidentiary support in her possession. Riesner was right on schedule.

She took out the lengthy declaration she had filed with the

Superior Court in preparation for the hearing the next day and read it again. Milne would not take testimony. His ruling would be based entirely on the paperwork and the arguments mustered by Riesner and herself.

It was damn good.

She wore extremely high heels and her stiffest suit, a black number from Nordstrom's with shoulder pads solid as blocks, for the occasion. "Rip his lungs out," Sandy said as she grabbed an umbrella from the rack on her way out off the office into a heavy downpour.

With all the pugnacity she had stored up, the hearing was an anticlimax. Milne didn't even want to hear her.

"Mr. Riesner," Milne said, "I think you'll just have to face the fact that you've been fired. Ms. Reilly seems to have covered her, ah, flanks quite well in her declaration. There are no legal ethics violations. Clients do occasionally change attorneys, you know."

"Only when they're manipulated by money-hungry ambulance chasers—"

"That's enough."

"She can't go over to the jail and whore her way into a job—"

"Mr. Riesner," Milne said. "I'm going to sanction you in the amount of five hundred dollars, payable to Ms. Reilly, for the frivolous opposition you've made. I'm going to order that you pay the legal fees and costs, if any, incurred by Mr. Scott in being compelled to file this motion. I also order you to immediately refund all remaining retainer money, along with a detailed accounting of moneys already spent. And I'm going to ask you, as a fellow member of the Bar, to apologize to Ms. Reilly for the ungrounded accusations you've made."

"In a pig's eye!"

"What did you say, Mr. Riesner?"

"I said, in a pig's eye, Your Honor."

"The sanction amount is hereby increased to one thousand dollars, payable within five days," Milne said. "Clerk, please ensure a transcript of this hearing and the Minute Order is forwarded to the State Bar of California. Next case."

* * *

"Oh, Mr. Riesner," Nina said from under her umbrella, out in the parking lot as the other lawyer unlocked his BMW.

His turned to face her, livid with fury, his carefully coiffed hair now dribbling like wet noodles onto his forehead. "What the fuck do you want?"

She thought of Riesner and his cigar, sitting behind his cherrywood desk not long before, insulting her and Sandy both, and she said, "I just don't want you to worry. I'm not holding this against you. You're entirely forgiven. And if you can't scrape up the sanction money right away, I'm willing to give you a short extension." Riesner jammed his car into reverse, sending up a stream of rainwater. Nina stepped neatly out of the way, giving him a pleasant wave as his tires burned out into the street.

At the main door to her office building the next morning, she passed her landlord, a spry, elderly man named Mr. Gant who had kept the two biggest offices across the hall for his real estate office. "Hi," she said brightly.

"Howdy there," Mr. Gant said. "Sorry about that article. You just stare down anyone who gives you a hard time about it. Damn reporters." He went on out, giving her a pat on the shoulder.

"Hey, Sandy. What's this about an article? Something in the paper?" Nina said as she came in and tossed her briefcase onto a client chair.

The *Tahoe Mirror* lay on Sandy's desk. Sandy jabbed her finger toward it, as if she didn't want to have to touch it. "You'll be wanting to hire a hit man," she said. "I know a good one."

"Your brother or your nephew?" Nina said. "I hope you're kidding."

"I never kid," Sandy said.

She grabbed some coffee and sat down to the usual pile of pink messages and papers to be signed. Ignoring them, she opened up the paper.

She had made the front page.

SCOTT ATTORNEY CONFLICTS RAISED IN STATE BAR COMPLAINT, the headline said. The byline was Barbet Cain, a reporter who had left several messages on the office voice mail the previous night.

"The California State Bar is investigating complaints of attorney misconduct against Nina Reilly, a local attorney who made headlines last year in the Patterson case," the paper said. Nina read on, her coffee forgotten.

According to the complaint, filed by Jeffrey Riesner, a well-known criminal lawyer and partner in the prominent local firm of Caplan, Stamp, Powell, and Riesner, Reilly has violated numerous ethical rules of the Bar, which regulates attorney conduct in California. If after investigation the charges are found to be valid, Reilly may be subject to court sanctions and disciplinary action, including possible disbarment.

The complaint alleges that Reilly convinced Judge Curtis Milne of the El Dorado Superior Court to allow her to substitute in as the attorney for Kurt Scott, who is currently awaiting trial on murder charges.

Reilly had no business taking on the Scott case, the complaint says, because she used undue influence to cause Scott to fire the competent counsel he already had. Apparently, Scott and Reilly have been involved in a common-law relationship for years and they have an eleven-year-old child.

Additionally, it is alleged that Reilly is a witness who will be testifying at the trial. Assistant District Attorney Collier Hallowell, the prosecutor assigned to the case, refused to comment, stating that the witness list has not been finalized. Although State Bar rules don't completely bar attorney-witnesses from representing a party in a case, according to Riesner, it is both highly unusual and likely to affect the ability of an attorney to competently represent the client.

In a bizarre turn of events, Reilly was representing the murder victim, Theresa London, on an apparently unrelated matter at the time of her death.

London was found shot to death on March 30, and Scott was charged with the killing based on eyewitness testimony.

The news that Reilly is the mother of Scott's son has caused consternation among courtroom insiders. "I don't think I'd go to a criminal lawyer who is the lover of an accused murderer," one source said. Questions have also been raised regarding what Reilly herself may know about the murders.

"It's the most appalling conflict of interest," Jeffrey Riesner stated. "It makes me ashamed to be an attorney."

Reilly did not return repeated phone calls to her office.

"Delightful," Nina said between her teeth. So Riesner had surprised her with one trick after all.

The office phone buzzed, and she picked it up. "Mrs. Salazar on line two," Sandy told her, a warning in her voice. Nina punched the button and her client came on.

"Is that you?" Mrs. Salazar said. Nina had just finished drawing up a will for Mrs. Salazar, who had struck it rich with her three husbands and wanted to leave all her money to the local animal shelter.

"Hi, Mrs. Salazar. How are you?"

"I'm surprised you're still showing your face around here," her client said. "If I had known more about you, I certainly wouldn't have hired you. Consider yourself fired, and don't bother sending me a bill—I won't pay it."

"But, Mrs. Salazar, your will—"

Mrs. Salazar had already hung up.

"—is ready for signing," Nina said into the dead phone. "Okay, fine."

The phone buzzed again. Nina looked at it, then answered. "Do you want to talk to the *Sacramento Bee*?" Sandy said.

"Are you kidding?"

"You also have a call waiting from Judge Milne's office."

"I'll call back soon. I'm tied up."

"Did you see the pile of messages?"

"I'm looking through them now. It's Riesner's revenge," Nina said. "I meant to tell you about all this, Sandy."

"Don't worry about me. Worry about your outraged public," Sandy said.

Nina filed the newspaper in her wastebasket. She had worked hard for the respect that had just been stripped away with that article.

Riesner had humiliated her, but she had to remember—she had won the first skirmish.

19

SANDY BUZZED. "MR. HALLOWELL IS OUT HERE. HE DOESN'T HAVE AN appointment, but you do, in fifteen minutes."

"I'll be right out." She opened her door to Collier's back. Studying one of the Washoe hangings, he wore his usual rumpled gray suit, which blended with the silver in his hair, more silver than last year. Running for office could do that to you.

He turned a friendly smile on her. His eyes were old in his compact, middle-aged body. He looked unguarded, a little uncared-for. He was the kind of man who needed to be married.

He carried a heavy file box under his arm.

"It's very fine," he said to Sandy. "It looks old. Nineteenth century? Hi, Nina."

"It is old," Sandy said. "My great-grandmother made it. How'd you know that?"

"My wife collected Washoe baskets," he said. "I still have them on a shelf in my kitchen."

"I know where you could get some more."

"No, thanks. I just want her baskets, the way she set them up."

"Sure," Sandy said, and for once Nina thought her irrepressible secretary seemed abashed.

"Come on in," Nina said. He followed her in and dropped into one of the client chairs.

"I apologize for showing up like this. I worked Sunday, and came in about seven this morning. I was sitting there in my office on about my fifth cup of coffee and the messenger came in to pick up this box of reports to take to you. I decided to go outside into actual sunlight and come here."

"It's good to see you. We're not at each other's throats yet, are we?"

"Not yet. You haven't insisted that your client is being railroaded. I haven't said the needle is the only way to protect society from the likes of him," Collier said.

"It takes you a while to work up to that rigid, condemnatory mood," Nina said.

"And I have noticed you stay rational far longer than most defense attorneys." He looked at her with interest. He'd never seen her without her suit jacket. He seemed mesmerized by her pale orange sweater.

"You caught me," she said. "Sleeves rolled up, formality out the window."

"You look smaller," he said. "Like a girl who has somehow been forced into playing war with the boys."

Automatically, she reached for her jacket. "We may not enjoy it like the guys," she said. "We prefer not to judge and punish. But when we have to fight, we tend to annihilate the opposition quickly, so you won't suffer for long."

"I see. I didn't mean to offend you."

"Well," she said, forgiving him.

"Well. Why don't we try to talk like pals this morning? I get tired of the gamesmanship. Here." He took off his own jacket, exposing a wrinkled white dress shirt, and hung it on the chair back. "Now we're even."

"All right, let's give it a whirl. Thanks for bringing over the reports."

Collier laid his file box on the desk and looked around the inner office. She saw it through his eyes, her oak bookcases, her brown leather couch, her certificates from the Monterey School of Law and various courts, and her prized fiddle-leaf ficus in its brass pot, taking a sunbath in the corner. "Very nice. You know, it's too bad we can't be friends. I like you."

Somewhat startled, Nina said, "I like you too. But at the moment I happen to be on one side of a war and you're on the other. You attack, I defend, and if I'm lucky, I counterattack. We're only human. We have to mobilize our emotions in line with the fight, or we're weakened."

"I used to see it like that. I don't anymore. I try to represent the victim in seeking justice. I try to prevent further harm. There's nothing personal about it."

She had heard that old D.A. standby, "I represent the victim," before, but Collier had an earnest sincerity she believed. Unfortunately, so did most of his juries. "You're light-years ahead of me," she said. "For me it's often personal."

Collier said, "I guess that means you won't have a drink with me after work."

"What?"

"Why not? Agree not to talk law at all. Talk about you, and how you like it up here in the mountains. Talk about the Washoe. Talk about . . . I don't know, just talk."

"I don't think so. I wouldn't feel right. I mean . . ." The sentence she didn't finish would have sounded something like this: It's complicated enough, without having to worry about how a friend on the other side is doing.

Collier may have mastered the difficult art of staying both disinterested and committed in his courtroom work, but she hadn't.

You're an admirable opponent, she thought, a worthy challenge; and perhaps he caught some of that thought in her eyes.

"Forget it," he said gently. "No problem. Let's talk about the Terry London case. First of all, congratulations on wresting it away from Jeff. But watch out for him. He never forgives, and he never forgets. He'll find a way to express his unhappiness."

"It's too bad it turned out that way. With someone else I might apologize, but he'd bite my head off and feed it to his . . . exotic statuary."

He laughed at the characterization, a long-drawn-out growl ending in soft, friendly barks. "Now to business," he said. "Somewhere in that pile of papers on your desk you have Judge Milne's Order substituting you in as defense counsel of record. I guess you know Scott's already been arraigned in the Superior Court."

"I've just started reading the transcript of the preliminary hearing. This big package here is Jeff Riesner's file on my client. After I've skimmed through everything, I'll call you and we'll set up a pretrial conference with Milne," Nina said.

"Okay."

Sandy buzzed again. "Your eleven-thirty is here."

"I'll be a few more minutes," Nina said. She put down the phone. She walked over beside Collier, who was exploring her view of Mount Tallac. The eastern sun washed its jagged and tremendous flanks with golden light.

She looked at him, while he looked at the mountain. In spite of herself, she was seeing him outside his role. What she saw was a reflective, complex, somewhat sad and lonely man.

"The snow's melting fast," Collier said. "I hiked up there with my wife one summer. We spent the night on top during the Perseid meteor shower on a warm, windless night. We watched them shoot across the sky."

"I'm sorry," Nina said, picturing him snuggling inside a sleeping bag with the woman he loved, watching the night sky spraying silver. "About your wife."

"So am I," he said. "She was only a little older than you. I can't understand how it could happen. I lie awake at night, wondering how it could happen."

"How did she die?"

"She was a probation officer. Anna Meade. You may have heard the story."

She had heard the story from another defense lawyer a few weeks after her arrival at Tahoe. His wife had been killed by one of her case clients. She had suffered. . . .

"Do you have children?" Nina said, inadequately.

"Nope. No luck in that direction. No luck at all." He ran a hand over his eyes, walking back to the chair. "Sorry, Nina. It's been three years, but now and then I still lose it."

"Don't worry," Nina said, handing him a tissue. "I have an unlimited supply."

"Anyway, Jeff was really after me to stop you from taking over. I decided not to become involved. Then I saw the news article, and realized you do have very close ties to Scott. . . ."

"Old ties, yes."

"To be blunt, I think you've made a mistake." He tossed the tissue into her wastebasket, missing, and bending down to pick it up and heave it again. "I speak as one who wishes you well, no matter what I try to do to you in court."

"I know how to take care of myself."

"We have some camcorder tape that we are still working with," Collier said. "Terry London made it just before her death. The copy still isn't ready, but it's part of the discovery you're entitled to. I think you may want to come over to my office and see it right away."

So she had heard correctly, that day in Collier's office. Terry had filmed herself dying.

"It's only about ten minutes long," Collier said. "Come over this afternoon, if you can. I have a break from court around one o'clock."

"I'll be there."

"We consider it a dying declaration. She says your guy pulled the trigger."

"I might not accept that idea as easily as you. No matter what she says. But I'd like to see it. I'll be there this afternoon."

"Fine. You may change your mind. All I'm saying is, don't let him bamboozle you. Whatever hold he has on you, fight it. We're looking into the possibility that he was involved in the Sweet girl's disappearance. This case has a slippery, nasty quality to it that I don't like. He's a very dangerous, unpredictable man, Nina. I'm glad there's glass between you and him at the jail."

"The situation's under control," Nina said. "Don't be such a worrier, Collier."

He moved to the door, his hand on the knob for what seemed like minutes. Then he turned back to face her. "My wife used to say that," he said, twisting the knob and leaving without saying good-bye.

* * *

She found Paul sprawled in a chair in the outer office, hands in the pockets of his beige chinos, his blond hair ruffled up like a rooster's, dark rectangles shading his eyes.

"My eleven-thirty?" she said to Sandy.

"He was hoping you could fit him in." Sandy continued her stapling, her broad brown face as stoic as an Easter Island statue. She might have been making a joke. It was impossible to tell, because she didn't give out the usual helper cue, a smile. Nina couldn't recall ever seeing her laugh.

"I'm so happy to see you, I'll even buy you lunch. Come on in," she said. "What are you doing here?" He followed her in and closed the door firmly.

"A birdie summoned me," he said. "I'm here to work for you, if you haven't already made other arrangements."

"You're going to help me with Kurt?" How off-balance she must have been feeling. In an instant she felt steadier. "Thank goodness."

"Not that you couldn't handle it without me."

"Goes without saying." He bestowed a crooked smile on her, acknowledging the slight tone of reproof in her voice.

"Where do we start?"

"You sounded so definite. I didn't let myself hope. What changed your mind, Paul?"

"Like I said. A birdie. A large birdie in tennis shoes, with a sharp tongue. Called yesterday and said she was coming down to Carmel to beat the crap out of me. Either that, or I help you. Actually, she didn't use exactly those words, but the intent was clear."

"Sandy."

"Sandy."

"I had nothing to do with it. I'll talk to her—"

"Don't bother. Talking to her is like talking to a lava flow. Besides, she was right. It didn't take long to shame me into agreeing to come up."

"Wonderful! You're staying at Caesars?"

"As usual."

Nina reached into her briefcase and handed him the police reports on Kurt's arrest. "Read these. That is, if you can start right away?"

"I'm all yours. I just finished a job for Solly Lazar. He owns a Mexican restaurant in Monterey. Took exactly two days."

"That's fast."

"His employee was perfectly happy to tell me his recipe for cooking books. A five-minute job. Then we worked on just desserts."

She laughed. She would not inquire further. Sometimes, she didn't want to know. "You can get people to open up. It's one of your strong points."

"Doesn't work so well with you."

Giving in to impulse, she put her arms around him in a heartfelt hug. "You're a good guy, Mr. van Wagoner. With you on our side, we can win."

"It's for you, Nina. Not him." Paul was so wonderfully uncomplicated. He said what he felt.

"I know."

"I'll go outside to read these. Then what?"

"Then we have an appointment to watch a tape."

Paul drove his van, and Nina the Bronco. Nina arrived at the courthouse complex first. "I'm not looking forward to this," she said, rising from her bench as he came bounding up the steps.

He took her by the arm, and they walked heavily, like an old couple who had been married forever, through the thick glass doors.

By the time they reached Collier's office, Nina and Paul weren't touching each other. Paul's sunglasses had gone into his jacket pocket. Nina, lost in her thoughts, hadn't said much, and Paul didn't seem to mind.

Collier came out to meet them. He gave Nina a touch on the shoulder, shook hands with Paul, and sat them down in two chairs squeezed between file cabinets in his office.

Nina found herself quite interested in watching Paul and Collier measure each other. Paul, too big for the little chair, moved it back to give himself legroom, instigating a polite invasion of the other man's territory. His body looked relaxed but ready for anything. His eyes moved curiously around, frank in his physical appraisal of the setting and the other man.

Collier, standing in front of his desk rather than sitting down, maintained a position of superiority, using the moment to make more circumspect but, Nina knew, no less acute observations about Paul.

She was drawing. She looked down at her yellow pad. Two toucans, beak to beak. Hastily she folded the sheet up so they wouldn't see it.

"Thanks for setting this up, Collier. You could have made us wait. And I know it's not easy for you to take the time," she said.

"As I mentioned, Nina, the certified copy hasn't been prepared yet. I'm showing you the original."

"Isn't that a little risky?" asked Paul. "I mean, video can be easily damaged."

"I'll take that risk in order to dispose of this case promptly."

His words, his whole manner, sympathetic yet so very self-assured, stepped up Nina's anxiety.

"I won't make you wait long to make up your own mind," he said. His face assumed a look of unpleasant expectation, as if preparing for a bitter drink. "There are a couple of things I should tell you before we watch it. Nina, I know the victim was your client for a while there . . ."

"I'm as prepared as I'll ever be, Collier. I know from the police report that the camera caught her dying."

"It's bad, Nina."

"Fill me in here," said Paul. "This film shows her death, that I get. But who filmed her?"

"The video camera, really just a camcorder, must have been knocked to the floor during a struggle. Looks like she managed to press the button somehow to record. No fingerprints, just smears. Like she used her toes."

Nina steeled herself against the nerves she felt quivering beneath her skin. She was remembering Terry on her studio floor. Yes, the camera had been close, trained on her. Her yellow eyes, and her head lying so peacefully on the bloody pillow . . . It had taken time for her to die.

In the same dispassionate tone Collier had adopted, Paul asked, "Was there sound?"

"That's what I wanted to mention," said Collier. "There's a soundtrack. But the bullet damaged her vocal cords."

"You mean she doesn't say anything about Kurt?"

"I mean, she tries to speak."

The words hung heavily in the stuffy air. They were using the present tense, she noticed with shock. Terry lived on in her video.

"What I'm asking is, you want me to keep the sound off while I run the tape this time? You can play it another time, when you get your copy."

Paul said, "Nina?"

She ought to receive the full impact, the way a jury would. After she had seen and heard it a thousand times, it would be just another piece of physical evidence.

And Collier wouldn't talk to a male defense attorney this way, would he? Trying to spare his feelings? "Let's hear it," she said.

"Up to you," Collier said. "She raises her head and tries to talk, but she can't. So she forms words. We got help from a mostly retired guy who used to work for the county health department, Willie Evans. He's deaf, and considered an expert lip-reader. He's helped us before. He gave us a transcript of what she's trying to say." He handed Nina and Paul separate copies of a one-page typewritten document. "You can follow her on the video. She's trying hard to communicate."

"How long is it?" Nina asked. "The tape?" She remembered staring at the clock above the teacher's head in school. Sometimes it helped to know.

"She gives up after eleven minutes or so." He motioned toward his office door. "Shall we?"

In the dark of a conference room, blinds down, Nina and Collier sat on one side of the long table, Paul on the other. A sheriff's deputy struggled with a rolling cart, plugged in some wires, punched some controls, nodded to Collier, and departed the room, softly pulling the door shut behind him.

From a speaker in the corner, silence preceded a loud hiss, which abruptly cut out as the picture came in.

The autofocus mechanism on the camera seemed unable to decide what to focus on. It shifted out to the patterned floor, threads of clothing, a hand, a foot.

Sounds like a potato sack being dragged across a floor and bumping into things accompanied the abstract visuals, which slowly resolved themselves into one horrible shot.

Terry London, her long, wavy reddish hair matted with blood, stared into the camera's eye. Propped along the cabinets that lined her studio, her legs extending beyond the camera, she looked straight at Nina. And blinked.

Her legs, spread-eagled in front of her to accommodate the camera, took up the bottom part of the frame. Her body, heaving in breaths with mighty effort, made up the midsection. Her head absorbed the top third of the frame, defiled by a bold red necklace of blood. Looking down toward the camera on the floor, she opened her mouth.

A woman's scream, loud and harrowing, choking and wretched, tore through the room. Collier leaped up, stepping around Nina. "Let me just get the volume . . ." he murmured, scrambling for the controller on the table near the machine. He pushed a button, lowering the level slightly, blocking Nina's path to the screen for a moment, jolting her away from its searing image. "Sorry about that," he said, his voice apologetic as he made his way back to his chair, controller firmly in hand.

Rhythm, a mechanical wheezing, started up as Terry continued to look directly into the camera. Sucking and wet, the sounds pulsed from the speaker. For a moment Nina thought there was something else wrong, and glanced behind to Collier to see if he needed to fix anything. His eyes were glued to the screen. She realized there would be no further reprieve and turned back to Terry.

Terry opened her mouth with a pop, to break the bubble of blood that formed when she separated her lips. She closed and opened it once again, her mouth twisting and horrible, as she attempted something she had always done before and would never do again.

Drowning in her own blood, she looked down at the red that increasingly filled the middle of the screen, that had grown and spread as blood from the wound in her neck flowed out of her, pooling on the floor below.

"This is where the transcript starts," Collier said quietly in the Boschian darkness.

"It doesn't hurt." Paul read the words from the transcript laid out on the table, a small penlight illuminating them. The sounds Terry made, carefully mouthed, were unintelligible.

"I'm dying," she said next, and her lips trembled with the enormity of understanding that must have flooded her then. The words, read by Paul with no more emphasis than "Good morning," or "Hello," spoke so neutrally of her ending. Nina felt her feet pushing her chair back, as if reacting to acceleration, braking, trying to slow things down, keep her alive.

Terry's face rose toward the camera. Blood streamed out of her neck, obscuring the bullet hole. No one could help her now, her face said. Help.

Then:

"It's your fault, Kurt."

Gasping and rattling.

"Oh, oh. I'm dying."

Paul's voice followed Terry out loud, like a singer lip-synching a song.

Mouthing each syllable while the rest of her face twisted with pained grimaces, she wove her head slightly back and forth, as if she were rocking to soothe herself, like a child rocking itself to sleep, long past the time for a cradle.

The red of her blood, the blue of her clothing, and the checks on the floor combined with lamplight from a gooseneck lamp on the counter above to give the scene a fantastic, lurid artfulness. Staged, aesthetically sensational, Nina thought. Video lacked the distance of film, the framing, the soft faraway beauty of it. She could be lying right here in this conference room, in real time, breathing. Dying.

Terry hiccuped blood. Her head fell. For a long spell, maybe minutes, all they could see was her head, the neat parting of her hair along the top of her skull. But they could still hear the breathing. Nina looked away for a moment toward Paul, who sat across the table from her. He leaned an elbow on his knee. His chin rested on his fist. She couldn't see his face. From the back, he had the uncomfortably restive air of a man watching the strike count rise on a pro baseball game, or an action movie seconds before the bomb blast he knew was coming.

Nina turned back. Terry struggled to raise her face higher.

"You . . . pulled the trigger."

She nodded several times. How could her body produce those tears at such a time?

She seemed to shake her wobbly head. She strained to turn her face, now mottled with blood, to one side, toward the doorway Nina knew was there, as if she saw a ghost there, outside the camera range. Turning back, she showed her teeth in a caricature of a smile.

"What a . . . surprise . . . the Angel of Death."

Then . . .

"I'll see you in hell. . . ."

Her mouth closed. An indescribable, strangled cough took up a long breath. Tears mixed with blood on her face. She shaped her lips, her head still straining to the side, her eyes staring. "Oh," she said. "Oh, oh . . ."

Her head fell, as if in surrender. Her body stilled. The screen blinked off.

"That's all," said Collier. "She's dead at this point."

"Poor woman," Nina said. She was thinking about Collier's wife, wondering how Collier privately felt when he watched the video. "She really seemed to see the Angel of Death coming toward her."

"Maybe that's why she turned off the film at the end, with a kind of modesty," Collier said.

Paul said, "Some say you can see the soul come out from between the eyebrows at the precise moment. I've never seen it. Now, that would be the ultimate invasion of privacy."

"I need some fresh air," Nina said. They all got up quickly and left the dark room, where Terry could still move and speak, back from that lonely place to the throngs of the living.

20

"DYING DECLARATIONS," NINA SAID, THUMBING THROUGH THE EVIdence code. "Exception to the hearsay rule. Here it is, section 1242:

" 'Evidence of a statement made by a dying person respecting the cause and circumstances of his death is not made inadmissible by the hearsay rule if the statement was made upon his personal knowledge and under a sense of immediately impending death.' "

Two file boxes of discovery materials cluttered up Nina's desk.

"So the video of her dying is admissible as evidence," Paul said. "I guess you could argue that they doctored it somehow."

"Chain of custody is pretty tight in this case. Collier's very careful, and keeps a close eye on his troops."

"Collier? Getting a bit cozy with the deputy D.A., are we?"

Sandy harrumphed from the other side of Nina's door. Paul opened it, and she sailed in bearing burritos from the Mexican restaurant across the street and two cans of soda. Taking in the atmosphere, she said simply, "Lunch."

"Mmm," Paul said, picking up a plastic spoon. "Chile Colorado."

"You'd eat through a nuclear bomb."

"If you put a touch of pepper on it, I'll take care of that for you too," said Paul.

"A nuclear bomb?"

"I think he's talking about this." Sandy held out a gooey quesadilla on a plate.

Paul unwrapped foil paper from his burrito. The aroma of cumin and beans instantly permeated the room. "I see something like that video, and my reaction is, well, thank the Lord, I'm still among the living. And I become very hungry. It's an instinctive thing. It started when I was working homicide in San Francisco. We all went out at night and ate these huge meals." He took a big bite.

Sandy sat down in a chair by the door and ate daintily from a paper plate. She was wearing muddy rubber boots and a flowered jumper, her short black hair damp from the rain and her bracelets clinking on her wrists. Another afternoon thunderstorm had come up and thick drops pounded on the windowpanes from a dark May sky.

"Give me one of those, Paul," Nina said.

"Keep the paper wrapped on the bottom so you don't drip all over yourself."

"I know how to eat a burrito!"

"Life may be short, and it may be brutish, but we're still here. It's always the other guy until your time's up. Then, who cares? Not you. Or so I used to tell myself." He ate quickly, standing up, as she was.

"What a dreadful way to die."

"Shot, and left like that?"

"I don't mean that. I mean telling lies when there's no longer a point, when it's so incredible to believe she'd lie that the Evidence Code will let the lie in as evidence."

"Have a taco," Paul said. "It'll settle you down. But sit, okay? I'm just waiting for you to dump it."

Nina's hands shook. Her mind had been objective, but her body had reacted to the video.

"She lied, Paul. Kurt didn't kill her." She popped the cap on her soda and picked a taco from the bag. "You didn't believe her, did you? She hated him. He'd rejected her for the last time. Even lying there on the floor dying, she thought of nothing more than hurting him."

"The jury ain't gonna like it." Paul wiped his mouth on a napkin, burped, excused himself, and pulled a small notebook from his pocket, sitting on a chair across from her desk.

Sandy had finished eating. She bagged up some trash and went back to her own desk, leaving the door open just a crack behind her.

"You need an expert witness," Paul went on, "a lip-reader who can do better than Willie. That's your only chance. I used to know a guy from the Center for Independent Living in Berkeley who might be able to help. I'll give him a call."

"Yes! The lip-reader! Terry didn't really say those things! You've got a great idea there, Paul." But she didn't like the way he distanced himself, saying it was her only chance, not theirs.

"I hate to spout conventional cynical cop-ese."

"But?"

"Don't expect miracles. Also, you need a napkin. You're dripping, gringa. Didn't your mama teach you how to eat Mexican food?" He leaned over to hand her a stack of napkins, too late for her beige linen pants.

"You believe he killed her."

"She's bleeding rivers of blood onto the floor. She's not going to lie at this point. Sorry. And you're forgetting the really important thing."

"What might that be, O cynical ex-cop?"

"You're angry," Paul said. "It's a big blow to you personally, not just to any defense you had in mind. I understand."

"What am I forgetting?"

Paul balled up several wrappers and lobbed them deftly into the wastebasket across the room. "Somebody killed her. It's almost impossible to accept that she'd let her killer go free. You've told me yourself, she hung on to some unfinished romantic business for a dozen years. Someone like that's going to feel some little resentment toward the one who downed her for good."

"Maybe she—she blamed Kurt somehow for her getting killed. You know, indirectly. She thought everything bad that happened to her was Kurt's fault."

"Uh-oh. I'm getting lost somewhere in the highways and byways of the female mind. All I can say is, I'm lying on the floor, I'm gonna tell you who shot me. I'm not going to be planning my next moves beyond that. Look, I ought to get started if you refuse to call Hallowell right now begging for a plea bargain. How about we get into these boxes and plot where we go next. Okay, boss?"

"Don't call me that. Please. I've had the chance already to review the materials." And find herself perturbed every time she looked at the list of items recovered from the crime scene. The very long list included items from outside the studio and in Terry's house. Something was on that list that shouldn't be—something she had seen at Terry's studio that day, but no amount of looking through the list helped. "I'll get you copies of anything you need."

Paul opened the first box and scanned a list. "Crime scene, Terry London. Contents: Inventory of items removed from scene. Photographs. Lab Reports. Fingerprints. Medical examiner reports. Autopsy. Witness statements. A letter from Kurt Scott to Terry. A police statement about what Kurt Scott said when they arrested him. A video of that momentous event. The usual police reports. Looks pretty complete."

"The second box has Riesner's files. Skimpy, I'd say. And a transcript of the preliminary hearing," said Nina. "There are videotapes, here, too, that we should watch together. How's Saturday night looking for you?"

"I'll bring the popcorn." Paul rooted through the second box and pulled out a slim file folder. "There must be more than this from Riesner," he said. "Even if the prelim was a formality, he must have had notes, motions, research, investigative reports."

"He didn't feel much like cooperating under the circumstances. The prelim was brief. Maybe he had a dozen pretrial motions ready. I'll never know, because he hadn't filed them at the point I took over."

"If I were Scott, I'd demand all my money back."

"Another problem. Riesner's sitting on most of Kurt's retainer."

"Whew. What a friend Kurt's got in Nina."

"What are you saying?"

"You're financing this case, aren't you? You're risking your reputation, your security, your kid's happiness, your own. . . . He's got you good."

"You sound . . . jealous."

"Sure I am. But mostly I'm concerned. He can take you and Bob down with him. I find myself wanting to bully some sense into you before it's too late."

"Go ahead. See where it gets you." She felt her chin rising in the air, and embarrassed to find it there, moved it back where it belonged. "Anyway, it's already too late, Paul. I'm committed." She buzzed Sandy and asked her to call her son, Wish, to see if he could come to the office.

Within fifteen minutes Wish arrived. According to Sandy, Wish would be attending community college in the fall, majoring in police science. He had been after her for months to get himself involved at her office in something a little more challenging than janitorial work. Wish pushed open Nina's door. About eighteen years old, he was as tall and gaunt as his mother was short and wide. Dressed in mechanic's clothes, oil outlining his fingernails, he hesitated before entering the office. Sandy followed him in.

"Sit down," Nina said. Paul had one client chair. Sandy took another, and Wish sat on the couch, his eyes wide and unblinking.

Nina surveyed her defense team: two smart, well-intentioned but inexperienced helpers; Paul, the slick dick with a talking bear hidden up his sleeve; and herself, competence to be determined.

They would get by.

She said, "The four of us will be putting together a defense for Kurt Scott. He's charged with premeditated murder. We're going to farm out some cases, close some others, and try to do right by the ones we keep."

"Trial date's . . . when?" asked Sandy.

"July fifteenth. It's too soon," said Nina, "but I'm worried about Kurt. He hasn't adjusted to being in jail." How could she tell them that underneath the words he spoke, she sensed desperation? How she feared he would crack up in there? "He wants us to go forward as soon as possible.

"Sandy, take these boxes out to your desk and make indexed files. Start juggling my appointments so that I have some long chunks of time every day that aren't booked. Make sure you calendar all the pretrial court appearances."

"Done. Almost."

"Wish? I understand you can work flexibly, on call?"

He nodded.

"You're to work with Paul. Do whatever he tells you to do. Don't do anything you're not specifically told to do. Understand?"

"He does," Sandy said for him. Wish straightened up, nodding emphatically.

"Okay, Paul. You're in charge of the investigation. Let's talk about how to proceed."

"Other than the lip-reader, shouldn't you line up some expert witnesses soon?" Paul asked.

"That's on the list."

"I still need copies of all the witness statements and the evidence list. And the autopsy report," Paul added.

Sandy wrote.

"We'll meet twice a week from now until trial," said Nina. Wish wore a grin that showed great big perfect teeth. "What is it, Wish?"

"He's happy he gets to work on the case," his mother said, tucking her notebook into a capacious pocket on her skirt.

Wish nodded again. With his ears poking out of long, shining black hair, totally out of place in this world of ink and paper, he looked like an eager young psychotic about to do something rash.

"Okay, I've had a chance to review the reports. Let me fill you in on what we know so far. As I see it, the prosecution's case rests on five pieces of evidence. The first and probably most difficult problem we have is Jerry Kettrick's eyewitness account of that night. He says he heard two shots in close succession, then saw Kurt run out. We've got to nail down the timing of those shots he says he heard, and get anything we can that'll cast doubt on his recall of the incident.

"Second, the Remington rifle that killed Terry London was registered to Kurt and his fingerprints were found on the barrel. Kurt says Terry's had the rifle ever since he left her. Anything we can get to show that that rifle remained in Terry's possession will help. If Terry had the gun in her possession, anyone could have used it on her.

"Third, what the D.A.'s office is now referring to as the 'death video.' In that, Terry seems to be implicating Kurt in her murder. She's either lying, or the transcript of the lip-reader is flawed."

"Our fourth problem. Kurt made some statements when he was

arrested in his car the morning after that don't sound good. The arresting officer had a car that was equipped with a video camera. He taped the arrest. Paul and I will take a look at that video in the next day or two, and evaluate just how harmful Kurt's statements might be."

"What is he supposed to have said?" Paul asked.

"According to, uh—" she leafed through some papers—"Jason Joyce, the arresting officer, he had blood all over him when he was pulled over, which by the way turned out to be only his own blood. He said there had been a shooting. 'She's been shot.' "

"Not 'I shot her'?" asked Wish.

"No, but 'she's been shot' is bad enough. It puts him there."

"They fixed fast and hard on Scott. But what do they think was the motive?" Paul asked. "He's never made a statement about any of this except what you just mentioned. I realize they know by now that Scott was married to Terry, but he hasn't had any contact with her for years."

"True. That's the fifth problem. They have a note he wrote her that contains a threat. It's not dated. It could be very old. I haven't asked Kurt about it yet."

"What's it say?" asked Wish.

She picked up a photocopy and read it. " 'Terry, for the last time, get out of my life. If you continue to harass me, write to me, or attempt to communicate in any way, I will come after you and make you sorry you ever met me.' I assume it's authentic."

"Did she keep bugging him?" Wish persisted.

"She didn't find him after the last move. That was four years ago. The note was found among her effects."

"Why did she bother with him for all that time? I mean, usually you get dumped, you get over it," said Wish.

"Some people don't," Nina said.

"She hated him," Sandy said. "She did what she could to hurt him."

"Oh, yes," Nina said. Paul was shaking his head sorrowfully. She knew he was thinking about what Terry had done to her baby. "Still, from our point of view, the police have very limited motive evidence, since they can't talk to Kurt."

"Exactly," Paul said. "I know proving motive isn't essential to getting a conviction. But like I said, juries don't like convicting unless they feel they understand the why of the crime. And they're going to want to know why he would come back after all this time and kill her. Hallowell doesn't seem to have made the connection that I found Scott and told him where you were, which made him catch the next flight to warn you about Terry. If he ever does . . ."

"Riesner said I might be called as a witness," Nina said. "It would be a mess trying to sort out which of Kurt's statements to me were protected by the attorney-client privilege." Kurt's note to her, asking her to meet him at Pope Beach, for instance, certainly wasn't privileged. She looked out the window at the mountains, wondering if she would be subpoenaed. How could she defend Kurt when she might also be a major witness against him?

"Here's what we should do," she went on, putting that problem aside for the moment. "Let's concentrate on other people with other possible motives. We've got four people out there who had sued Terry. Their lawsuit was in big trouble. They wanted to stop her from distributing her film. One of them might have killed her."

"Jonathan Sweet. Jessica Sweet. Doreen Ordway. And Michael Ordway," Sandy said, reading from her notes.

"Hard to believe the film was worth murdering someone over," Paul said.

"We have to get into Terry's mind," Nina said. "From my experience with her, I would say that she enjoyed playing with people's heads, you know? What I mean is, I think the film has a subtext. It's not straightforward. She—"

Paul interrupted. "I haven't seen the film yet about the Sweet girl, but you say she hints around that she was first in a line of missing girls. We ought to run with that. What if it's more than a crackpot theory or a marketing ploy? What if whoever is responsible for Tamara and the other girls' disappearances wanted the film to disappear too? What better way than to kill the filmmaker before it gets out the door? *There*'s a guy with a motive."

Wish said, in his adolescent voice, which made it all the more chilling, "Maybe her father killed them all. Or Michael Ordway."

"Don't leave out the ladies," Paul said. "It's a brave new world of crime."

"Or it could have been somebody who isn't in the film," Nina said. "We'll have to look at her theory, though the film doesn't bring up any hard evidence of a connection between those girls."

"Which brings up the obvious question," Paul said. "You said the film doesn't even mention Scott. Scott dated this girl for a while before she disappeared. Why not hint around that he killed her? She had the perfect opportunity to cause him more grief. The film might even have brought him back into contact with her."

"I don't know," Nina said. "I agree." She ran her fingers through her hair, wondering if she would ever understand Terry. "Maybe she knew exactly what happened to Tamara. Maybe she killed Tamara herself." Sandy and Wish looked surprised at that idea, but Paul just nodded. He had already thought of it. "Or maybe she knew who did it, and it wasn't Kurt, but she only felt able to hint around for some reason."

"She must have had notes, files in connection with making the film. Where are they?" Paul said. "Either her notes are gone, or she destroyed them. Why?"

"Good questions, Paul. I hope you bring me some answers soon."

"So we have a film that oughtta point the finger at Kurt Scott, but doesn't. And we have two videos that do point the finger," Wish said.

"Interpretation is all," Paul said. "What, Nina?"

Nina put down her pen, looked at the paper she had been drawing on, crushed it into a ball in her hand, and threw it in the wastebasket. "I think we should all be very careful," she said. "Now, you all need to imprint the contents of those reports onto your brain, and Paul, I've arranged for us to go over to Terry's first thing in the morning. Any questions?"

"Yeah, one," said Wish. "Did he do it?"

"How about we go get some coffee, so Nina can work?" Paul said to him, standing up. They each picked up a box and lugged it to the conference room.

Sandy and Nina watched them go. "Our raggle-taggle gang of four," Sandy said, shutting the door firmly in the middle of Nina's next thought, a good one, that she was not alone.

21

Nina and Paul drove through the gate onto Terry's property late on Tuesday afternoon. They had borrowed keys to the studio and house from Collier Hallowell, and would be attended by a South Lake Tahoe police officer, Deputy Earl Hecker. The crime tape was gone and the place deserted, cool and shady, on one of the first of the season's warm lazy days. Nina wondered where Terry's dog had been taken.

Deputy Hecker, a buck-toothed, freckle-faced cop who looked just barely old enough to take a razor to facial stubble, stood on the porch while Paul fiddled with the studio door lock. "It's one of those where you've got to pull out the key a quarter of an inch," he offered, after Paul had lost his patience and rattled the door so hard it threatened to fall off its hinges.

The deputy waited outside, cheerfully whistling the theme song for the movie *The Bridge on the River Kwai*. They left the door open so that he could keep an eye on things.

Undisturbed since the D.A.'s investigation, the studio looked like a place abandoned for years. Some of the equipment had been taken as evidence, and what was left was blighted by fingerprint dust and rusty bloodstains, emptied of life and spirit. Nina, trying to recall the place the last time she had seen it, moved methodically around, checking the room against her notes.

"What's the story on a crime scene, Paul?" Nina asked as Paul examined the back door. "Don't they clean up after the investigation?"

"No pressing need here, and no relatives have come forward. When I called to arrange this visit, they said it was next on the list."

She had opened the locked storage closet with a third key and was studying the shelves in back. "Where's all her stuff? She had enough filmmaking equipment to stock MGM."

"Apparently, most of it was rented. She had a mortgage and money troubles. She owned almost nothing, just this property and some of the smaller pieces of equipment."

Nina looked over the list and crime photos, then looked at a spot on the floor near the doorway, where the camcorder had been found. She was trying again to understand Terry. Where were the calendars, the postcards, the pictures, the personal touches you would expect to find in a woman's home/workplace? How could Terry be so cold and single-minded as to work in this concrete box full of cables and plastic and metal?

"Anything important you saw when you were here that's not here anymore and hasn't been taken for evidence?" Paul was asking.

She turned back to her notes. "A lynx coat. It's not on the list of items removed from the scene. I've seen her in it several times."

"Borrowed, maybe," said Paul dubiously. "A fur coat was a real extravagance for a lady in such deep debt."

"I think it was her mother's. It's probably up at the house."

"Let's go."

They paraded up the path to the house, trailed by Deputy Hecker, who, perhaps unconscious of its meaning, had launched into "Pore Jud Is Daid" from the musical *Oklahoma!* He had the wonderful ability to whistle piercingly through his front teeth. He hadn't spoken at all.

The interior of the small house looked exactly as she remembered it. "Nothing," she reported. "Just a vacant house, where someone used to live." Except for the clothes in the closets and in the bureau, it was still Terry's parents' house, as if Terry had never slept, ate, or lived there. She had lived entirely in her mind, not needing to surround herself with personal items.

"No fur coat," Nina said. "It was on the bed the last time I saw it. I wonder where it is?"

"Maybe we have a simple robbery-murder," Paul said.

"Not likely."

"We can always hope. Ready, Deputy."

On the way out to the car, they ran into a sixtyish woman in a smart red suit, who came huffing up the drive.

"Hey," said the deputy. "Can't you read? Nobody on the property. Out. Out." He moved his hands as if waving off a pesky skunk.

"Who's going to be listing this place, do you know?" she asked Nina, ignoring him.

"Listing it?"

"For sale. I've had my eye on this property for years. That's going to make the cutest little guest house." She gestured toward Terry's studio. "I'd love to put in an offer before they turn it over to a realty. I'd make a very decent bid."

"Did you know the woman who lived here was murdered?" asked Paul.

"Yes. They certainly can't hope to make full price on this one. That ought to guarantee it'll go dirt cheap," she said, practically rubbing her hands together in her delight at the anticipated bargain. Hecker stopped whistling long enough to escort her to her car.

Paul started up the van and turned it around, craning his head. "Still thinking about that coat?"

"Yes." That luxurious silver coat. Terry had treated it as if it were a live thing.

Nina remembered Terry's face months before at the courthouse after the first hearing. Her face had slipped, revealing the private expression she probably didn't want seen. Her expression had been—fey, that was the word, almost teasing, sexually aware, as if she saw life as an obscene joke.

What had she said? *Women want to bury their faces in it. Men want to . . .*

What the hell was that all about?

★ ★ ★

Jasper passed him the envelope in social studies, just before noon. Bob had used Jasper's address, and Jasper had been checking the mail at home over the weekend. Jasper was his friend in the war against Taylor Nordholm. He wasn't going to tell anyone that Bob had a letter from the jail.

When the bell rang, Bob didn't go out to the tree where he usually ate lunch with his friends. He trotted as fast as his heavy backpack allowed to the damp gully on the far side of the soccer field.

From here, he could hear some of the girls scream while they played, but the sounds seemed to come from far away. Rocks lay along the edge, where they had tumbled zillions of years before. The air was cool and damp, the tops of the trees far away above him.

He picked a smooth rock with no spiders or ants and sat down, wrestling his arms out of the backpack. He pulled the envelope out of the front pocket and his lunch from the main part, squashed as usual by his books.

He held the envelope. The return address was mostly numbers. He imagined his father in striped pajamas, with "66759" on the back. Maybe they had shaved his head so he wouldn't get lice, and only fed him once a day.

Bobby had biked over to the jail after school one day, telling everyone he was staying after school to use the library. The guard wouldn't let him in without proof of who he was, and he hadn't brought his birth certificate with him. He had left the note to his father there, with the people at the jail. He hadn't copied the note he had written, but he pretty much remembered it, because it had been so hard to write. There hadn't been much time, and the guard watching him had made it hard to think. Too bad he couldn't have just gone in and visited right then and there. He would be done with feeling like he had the flu all the time. He could sleep again at night.

"Dear Kurt Scott," he had started out.

Then:

My name is Robert Brendan Reilly and I am your son. I know it because I have my birth certificate with your name on it. My mother is Nina Reilly. She doesn't know I'm writing you. Here's the story. I went over to the jail and they wouldn't let me in, so I wanted to at least let you know I'm alive. I don't believe you killed anybody. You can write me at my friend Jasper's.

He had chewed on the pencil a long time, thinking about how to sign below Jasper's address, until the guard said, "Hey, you'll get splinters in your mouth, chewing on that thing."

Finally, he wrote "BOB" in big letters, so his dad would know what to call him when he wrote back. Then a P.S.: "What do you look like? I have black hair and green eyes. I get pretty good grades. I like to swim and skateboard. This year, I won a blue ribbon during field day."

His father had written back, must have been the same day. That was good. All he had to do now was just tear open the letter and read it.

He took a few bites of his sandwich, but it felt so dry that he put it down next to him on the rock, picking up the envelope from his lap. He opened it carefully, thinking, this might be the only one he would ever get. You never could tell.

A sheet of notebook paper said "Dear Bob" in pencil, printed. His father probably wasn't sure if he could read his cursive. He ignored the stones knocking against the ham in his stomach.

I got your note. It is a wonderful surprise to find out that you're my son. I never knew. It makes me very happy.

I'm sorry you couldn't come in the day you came to visit. You probably shouldn't come to the jail again unless you have cleared it with your mother, but I'd like it if you wrote. I'd like to know all about you. You must be a brave guy, coming over on your own to see me. When this mess is all over, I promise, we'll meet face-to-face. I have black hair and green eyes too. I'm a kind of forest ranger, and sometimes I play the piano in an orchestra. Do you like music?

I'm glad you wrote me, Bob.

He had signed it, "Much love from your dad," with a P.S.: "I was on the track team in college."

Bob read the note several times, blinking. The bell rang, distantly. He would have to run but luckily he was a fast runner, fastest in the entire fifth grade. His nose was running and his eyes were probably all swollen up. He folded the note carefully back into its envelope and tucked it into his pocket. Then he rubbed his face on his gym shirt, packed up, and ran for his class.

22

"WE MET ONCE WHEN I CAME TO SEE TERRY, REMEMBER?" NINA SAID to Jerry Kettrick later in the week.

On this first clear day after three days of rain, shoots of new plants had finally broken the surface of the long frozen soil. Even at the Kettricks' unkempt house, the world looked almost perfect on the outside. On the inside, windows were blocked from the light and dust floated heavily in the air, creating an entirely different universe.

"I remember," Kettrick said.

He lounged on the musty striped couch in his living room, his legs crossed. Terry's black dog chewed on a tennis ball at his feet. Paul had sat down at a scarred pine table against the wall. The wood floor had been swept but was dark with grime, as though it had never felt a wet mop.

On the way there, Nina had listened to Paul's colorful background report. "He's half country boy, half old hippie," Paul told her. Jerry Kettrick's parents had fled the back-breaking stoop labor of the San Joaquin fields for the uncertain welcome of Tahoe. They had both found jobs cooking at a small restaurant called Mom's Kitchen in the fifties, and as soon as their five kids were old enough they, too, had gone to work at the restaurant after school and on weekends. Many thousands of griddle cakes and scrambled eggs later, they had taken over the place from its sickly owner, and Jerry spent his formative years up to his elbows in dishwater.

By the late sixties, the winds of change had hit Tahoe, and Jerry floated onward to San Francisco. He moved into a run-down Victorian near the Tenderloin with a dozen other teenagers, and learned to play guitar on a Silvertone somebody left in lieu of rent. He discovered he had fast and precise fingers. Soon, he was gigging with the Airplane and the Dead.

He and his girlfriend could afford all the speed they could shoot, and in due course they had a baby, born Rimbaud but known forever after as Ralphie.

By 1972 Jerry's personal cultural revolution was over. His girlfriend OD'd, and all the savvy docs at SF General couldn't put her together again. Jerry suffered from painful ulcerations at his favored injection sites, and nobody would hire him because he'd gotten so irritable. Ralphie was placed with a Mormon foster family. Grace Slick went into alcohol rehab and the Dead went on a permanent road trip.

Jerry moved back to Tahoe and started cooking again. By this time his father had died and his brothers and sisters had moved on from the restaurant and Tahoe. He moved in with his mother, and one day he got Ralphie back. His mother took care of the toddler, and Jerry managed Mom's Kitchen.

When she died too, he slipped back into using speed again. But it was no fun anymore. He was forty, and it kept him awake and made him paranoid instead of buoying him up. After his arrest and a diversion program, Jerry sank into a middle-aged stupor and stayed there. He worked at the restaurant, made sure Ralphie had clean socks, and watched reruns. Sometimes the old fury would still strike him, and he would go out on the porch with the scratched-up white Telecaster and his Peavey amp, and turn it up as high as it would go, with lots of distortion, and for a while he'd be back at the height of his life, fingers churning out the vicious ear-splitting notes for which he had been so briefly famed.

Then the phone would ring, and Terry London, his neighbor,

would scream that if he didn't shut the fuck up, she'd splinter the Telecaster over his head.

And that was how he'd gotten to know her, way back when.

Looking around, Nina saw why the place was so dark—threadbare blankets had been tacked up on the low windows as a substitute for curtains. Cinderblocks and boards held a large number of tattered books. A couple of sleeping bags were piled in the corner. Following her eyes, Kettrick said, "My buddies. Up from L.A. to do some fishing."

"Is your son at school?"

"Ralphie? He don't go to school no more. He's all grown up, twenty-eight. He drives a monster truck. Travels around the West to race."

"Now, there's an unusual job," Paul said.

"Dangerous," Kettrick said, rolling himself what Nina hoped was a cigarette. Wearing the same red chamois shirt Nina had seen him in before Terry was killed, over blue jeans streaked with dried brown liquid, he sported a baseball hat with a Valvoline logo. The furious, long white hair and beard, invisible eyelashes, and pink-rimmed eyes in his creased face made Nina wonder if he was albino. "But it's showbiz, Ralphie says. He's got aspirations." He reached in his pocket and handed Paul some grubby tickets from a thick roll. "Here," he said. "Ol' Ralphie's racing at the Reno Livestock Events Center on Saturday. Have a ball."

"No work today?" Paul said, leaning back in his chair. He had that wonderful easy lounge to him, relaxed anywhere, an attitude that relaxed others and encouraged them to kick back and say something they'd regret later.

"Hell, I went in at five to open at seven at the Kitchen," Ralph said. "I put in my eight hours. My niece runs the place until closing time. This is the hard-work season. I make the biscuits and gravy, play short-order cook, and run the register. Sometimes I have to hop the tables too. It ain't rock 'n' roll, but it pays the property taxes. Come on in sometime. Make you a sunnyside egg in thirty seconds, over easy in thirty-two. Best home cookin' in Tahoe."

"Oh yeah?" Paul looked interested.

"Yeah. Mom's Kitchen is second to none," Kettrick said, as if trying to convince himself. He laid down his hand-rolled cigarette, got some more Zigzag paper and tobacco from a pouch, and kept rolling.

"Lived here long?" Paul said.

"Almost twenty-five years. It's a rat hole, but it's my rat hole."

"I heard around town that you play some fine lead guitar too."

"I used to. I'm retired now. I played with the Dead, the Airplane. You name 'em, I got down with 'em. I used to be famous. A rock star. They said I was the spittin' image of Edgar Winter. See?"

He pointed to a peeling poster tacked on the wall in the kitchen, a psychedelic extravaganza announcing a 1969 concert at the Fillmore in San Francisco. Jerry Kettrick's wild white locks floated around his face, metamorphosing into one-eyed snakes. Nina and Paul nodded encouragingly.

He smiled. "You folks read the Bible? My parents used to quote Scripture at me. 'How are the mighty fallen . . . the shield of the mighty is vilely cast away.' That says it all. Now I read, watch TV, take care of Ralphie. Oh, once in a while someone who remembers me calls and I make a few bucks playing backup. But I make more cooking."

"Thanks for taking the time to talk to us today," Nina said.

"Time's what I got in abundance," Kettrick said. "I'd rather be on your side, if I could. Better witness fee, I hear. But I seen what I seen."

"I guess you'd known Terry for a long time. Her family moved here, what, about twenty years ago?"

"Except for when she was married or traveling, she always lived at that house, though we didn't really socialize. Her parents both died a long time ago, and she was a loner. Invited her to some of the neighborhood parties, but she couldn't be bothered. She called me over now and then when she needed work done, you know, toilet stopped up, so forth, and every spring Ralphie and me would climb on the roof and sweep the pine needles off, and Ralphie would do her chimney. He's skinny and he'd get right down there in it. He'd turn so black, the dog didn't know him, damn near took a bite out of him once. . . .

"Actually, Terry was a real pain in the ass," Kettrick went on. "To be honest. Complained about noise, said my dog bit her dog, didn't like the dust we raised going in and out of the driveway. She put a gate up five years ago, and I quit going over. Ralphie went instead."

"I see you took Terry's dog," Nina said.

"Hitchcock, she called him. She watched his movies over and over. He's a good pup, never does business in the house." At the mention of his name Hitchcock raised his shaggy head and the red tongue Nina remembered came lolling out in a wet grin. "He was mooning around her place, hungry, and our old dog had just passed on, so I took him in. Poor ol' Betsy. She lasted fifteen years. Ate some poison plant or something out there, keeled over and died last year." His voice lowered. "Actually, I kind of wondered if . . . Terry might've done something to our dog. She was . . . you know, deedeedeedee deedeedeedee. . . ." Kettrick fluttered his fingers and rolled his eyes, singing the old TV theme from *The Twilight Zone*. The house, surrounded by forest, stayed gloomy even though Nina could see the sun breaking through outside. She felt itchy, and hoped her chair wasn't Hitchcock's favorite.

She pulled out Kettrick's statement from the briefcase, passed it over to him, and said, "We'd like to talk to you about this."

He looked it over, said, "Yes, ma'am, that's my statement to the cops about what I seen."

"According to this, you were watching television in your living room when you heard a noise at about eleven that night," Paul said. "What kind of noise?"

"Yelling, screaming, so forth," Kettrick said, licking his cigarette paper and twisting the ends tight with a practiced motion. "Him yelling, her screaming."

"How many people were at her house?" Paul said.

"I only know about the two. Terry, and him. I stayed right there, looking out the window, 'cause it sounded bad. I thought she'd plugged him."

"Why's that?"

"Well. She was one righteous motherfucker. She had her rifle, threatened to use it on me once."

"What kind of rifle was that?" Paul said.

"A thirty ought six Remington, an oldie but a goodie."

"How many times have you seen that rifle in her possession over the last twelve years?" Nina said.

"Just that once, about five years ago. That's when I stopped goin' over. But Ralphie, he's a fool for punishment. 'Don't go over,' I'd say, but he wanted to make a few extra bucks. I tried to stop him. I knew she was a bad influence. But that boy'll hump a grizzly for a dollar cash."

Terry had been forty, so Ralph was twelve years younger. Had they been lovers?

Nina glanced at Paul, and their eyes met. They had also both registered that they now had proof that Terry had kept Kurt's rifle. This was a big break for them. Terry had the rifle, she got it out, threatened Kurt, there was a struggle, he ran. . . . Nina turned her attention back to Paul, who was asking, "Mr. Kettrick, could you understand what this man you saw and Terry were saying to each other?"

"No. But she was plenty pissed. He was soft at first, then he got into it too."

"Why don't you tell us all about what you heard and saw," Paul said. "Forget about the statement you made to the police. We'd like to hear it fresh from you."

"Well, there was the noise, arguing, for about five minutes. Then there was two shots, one right after the other. And he come running out the studio door, his shirttail to the wind. . . . In the moonlight, I could see his face plainly—"

"Could you see the studio door from your window?" Paul said.

"C'mon over here," Kettrick said. They all walked over to the window. "Stand here, in the left corner." He pushed a blanket to the side, letting in a golden shaft of sun that slashed through the dingy interior.

Nina took the opportunity to crack open the window and get some air into the room. She could see the front of the studio, the path up to it, and the porch where she had stood with Collier the day they found the body. Kettrick had a ringside view of the door, there was no doubt about it.

"He come running out—"

"Did you see any blood on his clothes?"

"Nope," Kettrick said. "Can't see colors too well by moonlight. His clothes were dark, that much I seen."

"Mr. Kettrick," Nina said. Standing right next to her, not much taller than she was, Kettrick was not looking out the window with her and Paul. He was looking at her. In a balmy summer breeze that raised and dropped the blanket over the window suddenly, she smelled him, a sour smell. His face wore an amiable smile, showing off several teeth gone over to brown, but he reeked of fear.

"Are you positive you heard two shots, not one, before Mr. Scott ran out the front door?"

"Positive," Kettrick said. "And if I'm lying may God strike me dead." She connected with his white-lashed eyes, and didn't take hers away, but looked deep, deeper, and observed his pale irises contracting to a point. Nothing else on his face moved. He edged away from her.

"Then what happened?" asked Paul. He had taken in the scene without seeming attentive, everything about him casual except those narrow hazel eyes.

"He lit out for his car and took off. That's about all. Next day, I saw the commotion over at her house and went over, and they had me go down to the station house and give a statement, and then they called me back when they busted him, and I went back over and picked him out of the lineup. There was no question," he said. "Sorry about that."

"Well, you have to tell the truth," Paul said.

"Nothing but. Anything else you want to know?"

Nina asked him a few questions about the lineup, then said, "I guess that about covers it for now."

"Them monster truck tickets go for fifteen bucks a pop," Kettrick said. "I give you two. What I mean is, I understand you can't pay me for talking to you today. But, now, if you wanted to buy those tickets off me, I mean, you know, make a donation to those hard-drivin' boys . . ."

Paul said, "Nina?"

Nina got her wallet out. "I'll even buy one more, and take my son along with us," she said, handing Kettrick the bills. "Maybe we'll have a chance to talk to your son after the show. Thanks again for your trouble."

"You're so very welcome, ma'am. I'll let Ralphie know to be lookin' out for you. Call me, if you need anything else. Sorry . . ." He stopped, looking down.

"That your testimony may convict my client of murder?" Nina said. "You're telling the truth, so you don't need to feel guilty, right?"

"I seen what I seen," Kettrick said. "You folks have a good day, now."

23

"RENO'S BIGGEST, RENO'S BADDEST MONSTER TRUCK RACES ARE SOLD out. Reno's biggest, Reno's baddest monster truck races are sold out," repeated loudspeakers positioned throughout the mobbed parking lot at the Reno Livestock Events Center that Saturday morning. Paul had to park several blocks away. Nina and Bobby trotted behind him, trying to keep up with his long legs and stride by taking twice as many quick steps, and were sweating and puffing in the high desert heat by the time they approached the entrance. So many people crammed the walkway into the arena that Nina held Bob by his sweatshirt so he wouldn't be swept away.

"Reno's biggest, Reno's baddest . . ." Paul was nervous. He did want to talk to Ralph Kettrick, but he was acutely aware that Nina's boy had come along. It was the first time the three of them had done anything together. If they got married, he'd be a stepfather, an unappealing prospect.

He had only been vaguely aware of Nina's kid before he ran away. All boys were alike to him, little numbskulls in their baggy sweatshirts and baseball hats, carrying skateboards if they were old enough, asking for the car keys if they were too old.

But he had to like Bob, and Bob had to like him. Paul watched him run on ahead, wondering what Bob thought of him. How would the kid feel about Paul taking on the dad role while his father— Why did Scott have to show up now, when Paul had just decided to marry Nina? She looked so delectable today in her slacks and red shirt, so festive, so firm, so fully-packed. . . .

They came out into the main arena under a cloudy, overcast sky and started looking for seats. The stands were almost full already, with faces he didn't see that often on the upscale streets of Carmel; ranchers with lean red faces and baseball caps that said things like "Cal Am Waste" and "Lakers"; boys in blue jeans, hair greased and combed back so perfectly you could see each individual strand; moms in black stockings and ruffled blouses, and their daughters in harsh white makeup and Raiders jackets; a sea of flannel shirts, T-shirts, pigtails, goatees, gold chains, ruffles, plastic wraparound sunglasses, pointy boots, cowboy hats, balding longhairs, black kids in heavy parkas, camouflage pants, snowcone vendors, baby strollers, Native Americans in Reno Rodeo vests, work boots, ski caps, tie-dyed sweatsuits, tattoos, and toddlers riding on shoulders.

Over the distant bleat of the parking lot speaker, which continued its proud chant, an unseen announcer said, "Let's scream out a big welcome to the Monster Truck Stomp Force!" just as they squeezed into a spot on a weathered gray bench about halfway up. The dirt straightaway beyond the crowd-control fence had been modified by the addition of three six-foot-high bumps made of hard-packed dirt, equally spaced on the track to form three massive obstacles. Looking closer, Paul could see two cars buried in each, gutted old auto bodies that were begging to be put out of their misery anyway.

Eight monster trucks revved their engines and came out on the track so the crowd could have a look-see. His neighbor on the right, a young mom with a baby in a stroller, inserted plugs in her own ears and those of her toddlers against the deafening machinery and excited crowd. Her hip pressed warmly against his from the right. With her long, scraggly black hair, long face and long nose hovering above a full-lipped, gum-chewing mouth, beer-tab shaped earrings, and the tight, short T-shirt to show off her outie navel, she made a perfect madonna of the rodeo. Nina, rubbing suntan lotion onto her pretty nose, pressed against him on the left, her breast soft against his elbow. Beside her, Bob methodically chipped paint off the metal strut holding up the bleacher below. "Bobby, stop that," Nina said, but with no force behind it. The kid ignored her.

They had a good view of the trucks. Basically a framework of gigantic tractor tires and powerful engine, each sparkle-painted body held a driver that looked as substantial as a cheap action-figure toy. The driver rode about ten feet up from the frame, revving the engine with a hot foot, like a cowboy sinking spurs into his ride.

One by one the trucks showed their stuff. Squanto roared out first. "A '93 Chevy cab, ladies and gentlemen, a 486-cubic-inch engine, sponsored by Harley-Davidson. Look out, folks, it's on the warpath today!" Then came the other contenders, Thunderthighs, Wabash Cannonball, the Mountain, Bad Dog, Venom, and, last but not least, the current champion, Satan's Hoof. Satan's Hoof, an old green cab that looked like a '49 Ford van, flashed red headlights. The windows into the cab were so small, Paul couldn't catch a glimpse of the driver. He looked again at the program.

Satan's Hoof. There it was, Ralph Kettrick's mount.

"To avoid danger to all our fans in the stands we have a new system that allows us to stop any truck with remote control from our booth," said the loudspeaker, barely registering above the clamor of machinery. "And today, we've got something really special for the young 'uns. You can win a ride in Satan's Hoof by signing up at the beer booth right beside the inflated Coke bottle. All you kids ask your dads to sign you up." A high-pitched screech went up from the Popsicle crowd.

Bob leaned toward Nina and said, "Can I, huh, Mom?"

She nodded. "Later."

An all-terrain vehicle with five fat, textured wheels flew out onto the track while the trucks moved back to the starting line. Spinning around, shooting flames, like some crazed mascot too excited to sit still, it inspired frenzy in the audience, which stomped and hooted at the sight.

"Now, we are all patriotic people here, I know, proud to be Americans at this great event, so will everybody please rise for—"

The crowd, a little surprised at the change in dynamic, obediently quieted, standing up while a scratchy tape played the national anthem, even the trucks idling respectfully in their dusty paddock.

"We'll start with single-lane qualifying to pair 'em up for side-by-side racing," the invisible announcer said, starting right up at the song's finish. Bad Dog raced first, engine revved to an angry roar, lurching forward in angry spurts like a Mad Max machine. Enormous tires launched it six feet into the air when it hit the bumps, landing it like a dump load of recycled tin cans onto the heap below. Paul heard the roofs of the buried cars crunching. "Six point twelve seconds, not a bad start," the announcer said, sounding only mildly impressed.

Next came Thunderthighs in an open cockpit, so Paul could see the wee driver frantically hanging on to the wheel to keep the whole construction upright while he jumped the hills. "He's the biggest and he's shakin' it for you." The driver hesitated at the bumps but hung on, bouncing down the track a little slower than Bad Dog. "I'm gonna bet on Venom," Bob yelled. "His fangs are flyin'."

"Bad Dog," Nina yelled back. "He won't be housebroken."

"Satan's Hoof. He's kicking in the door," Paul said, trying to sound more enthusiastic than he felt. Bob leaned over to say something and spilled his Sno-cone into Paul's lap, which set Paul to leaping up from his seat with an ungentlemanly oath, ice leaking through his fly.

Nina laughed and turned back to the trucks. Bob said, "Oops!" Paul brushed himself off and sat down again. The madonna gave him a contemptuous smile and lit up a Marlboro to make her own rank contribution to the perfume of dust and gasoline. A warm drizzle began to fall on them. He seemed to be the only person in the arena without a hat.

Venom, from Topeka, bounced across the course in five and a half seconds. "An '88 Jeep with a 484," said the invisible voice, while the titanic truck went boing! boing! boing! barely holding to the track. "No rookie jitters here. Driven by Lonnie 'Hard Case' Pace. Ladies and gentlemen, let's hear it!"

Up to the qualifying line came Satan's Hoof, spooky red headlights flashing like mad eyes. "Champion for five years running. Big cheers for Ralph Kettrick, Satan's devil driver! The demon is steamin'!"

"I have to go to the bathroom," Bob said.

"Paul, would you take him?" Nina said, her eyes on Satan's Hoof, which readied itself with mighty blasts of its 572-cubic-inch engine.

"But this is the one I need to see," Paul said. The kid had jaunted off to Monterey on his own, but needed an escort to the john?

Bob disappeared into the walkway. "Hurry, Paul," Nina said. Muttering, Paul got up again and flowed with a group of white straw cowboy hats down to the concession area, where Bob was nowhere to be found.

By the time they got back, Satan's Hoof had finished. "Wow, what a thrill," Nina said. "He hit the fence, and we thought it was all over."

"Great," Paul said.

"What took you so long?" Nina said.

"Your son wanted to stand in line to sign up to sit in Satan's Hoof even though I told him it was hopeless," Paul said.

"Kids don't know that word."

The announcer started shouting, interrupting all conversation. "If you don't like the ride, what do you stand up and yell?"

"WIMPY! WIMPY! WIMPY!" the crowd roared.

"If you want to see some action, what do you yell?"

"WE WANT AIR! WE WANT AIR!"

"Yes!" the announcer screamed. "You want them to be crazy, don't you?"

"CRAZY! CRAZY!"

While the monster trucks rested up for the next set of races, some local pickups came racing out onto the track. "Old Blue ought to be called Old Black and Blue, it's so beat up." Old Blue came off the first hill and landed with a bone-crunching thud, and didn't move anymore. "Old Blue's busted his front axle," the announcer said. A recording played a funeral march as the pickup was hauled away. "If you see this guy out front with his finger out, please give him a ride, okay?"

"Depends on which finger he uses," Paul said, trying once more for the proper spirit.

"WE WANT AIR!" More tough trucks came out. One Toyota Longbed came out low and tight and feisty, but the engine cut out halfway through. While the driver madly tried to start it up again, the announcer said, "Sounds like he's got some bad gas."

"WIMPY! WIMPY!"

"How 'bout it, Reno! Tell 'em what we want!"

"WE WANT AIR!"

The drizzle stopped, and the air turned warm and oppressive. A little yellow Mitsubishi pickup strayed uncertainly onto the dusty track. "It's Grampa driving, folks! C'mon, let's tell him what to do. 'Go, Grampa, go!' "

"GO GRAMPA, GO!" Nina and Bob yelled with the crowd. Nina drank some water from her bottle and wiped her mouth with the back of her hand. She had pulled back her hair into a ponytail and looked fifteen years younger. Paul regretted the golf shirt that made him feel like Frank Sinatra in a mosh pit.

"Aw, he's just out for a Sunday drive, look at him!"

Intermission. The Reno police appeared in uniform, nightsticks and revolvers in their holsters hanging off their belts, watching the crowd head down the walkways for beer and nachos and to use the pungent bathrooms. "Where's Bobby?" Nina said. "Oh, he must have had to use the rest room again. Paul?"

"Oh, no. I'm not going out in that crush again," Paul said. She gave him a firm push. "Okay, okay." He elbowed his way forward, thinking how he'd like to teach Bob a couple of things, like respect and obedience. When the races started up again, Paul went back to tell Nina that Bob seemed to be gone for good, but the kid was sitting there, eating another Sno-cone.

Two by two, the monster trucks matched off against each other. Venom had the track to himself when the Mountain didn't show up for the race. "I guess the Mountain blew its top."

"WIMPY!"

Paul massaged the headache in his temples. The girl on the right pulled her T-shirt up and calmly began nursing her baby, giving Paul a sideways glance that said, deal with it. Paul looked away. Babies and diapers and vomit and messy feeding . . . Nina wouldn't be thinking of having another one, would she?

"Satan's Hoof is in trouble. Folks, they're welding on a new oil pump right now!"

"SATAN! SATAN!" Convulsed, beery faces, stands shaking with

the pounding feet . . . It must have been like this years before at rock concerts, but he hadn't minded then. He seemed to have lost the ability to drown in mass hysteria, but Nina, shouting and making little horns on her head with her fingers, was gone, gone, gone.

Paul noticed that the crowd wore the same excited expression as the glittering crowd in Wiesbaden. As he pondered this thought, his reality suddenly shifted. The shouting receded into metaphysical distance and his mind floated off.

Strange bedfellows, he thought. Bach and monster trucks. Was it true that all human recreations were just re-creations of the sex act? The muscular power of the Bach fugues, played upon that enormous organ, systematically dismantling the audience's defenses with sound, teasing and pushing them toward climax, resolution, a postconcert cigarette . . . hmm.

And now, out there in the dust, the drivers in their outsize machines were gouging furrows in the earth, barely in control while the people hollered. . . .

And he himself, a peeker and pryer by trade . . . Terry London, fixated on her love-hate object for so many years . . . they were all symbolic beings, from the time they started sucking their thumbs in babyhood. Their possessions were fetishes, their pursuits vain, their pretensions laughable. A momentous thought came to Paul.

Did He smile His work to see?

Reality once again blurred and refocused. Paul slipped back into the spectacle and forgot what he'd been thinking about.

Venom and Satan's Hoof lined up against each other for the final race, their engines growling and menacing. "Let me hear you scream for your favorite!" the announcer yelled deliriously, and the crowd yelled back in an earthshaking crescendo. Both trucks shot over the first two hills. Satan's Hoof took the last hill so fast, it hit the fence on the bounce. The truck reeled to the left and the tires on the right left the ground. Breathless, they all watched as it tottered, tottered, seemed about to capsize, then fell back into a hard upright final bounce.

"It's Satan's Hoof, by a toenail!" the announcer shouted.

"No, Bobby, you cannot get in there," Nina told Bobby ten minutes later, out on the dusty track.

Ralph Kettrick stood next to Satan's Hoof, about as tall as the tires, fingering a rabbit's foot that dangled off his belt and talking to a mechanic who was down on his hands and knees looking for something.

"Hey! How did you like the way ol' Satan wiped out the competition today, l'il fan?" he said to Bobby. He shook hands with Paul and Nina, then said, "You're the lady in the fake mink collar, right? Glad you could come." His cropped blond hair, wet from sweating under the helmet, was a true blond, not the white albino hair of his father. He wore a soiled fire-retardant jumpsuit that emphasized his short, stocky body and big, vacant grin.

"It was so rad," Bobby said. "Who won the contest?"

"You mean, to sit in the truck? We're just checkin' her over, and then some kid from Elko gets to sit up there with me and have his picture taken. How's it look, Pete?"

The mechanic said from underneath somewhere, "Used two quarts of oil on that last run. I'm filling it up again."

"All right. Little oil leak, no big thing," Kettrick said.

The mechanic got to his feet, put his knuckles at his waist, and stretched backward. "It's full up. Get somebody to reweld the pump before you race again."

"Thanks, man," Kettrick said. "So, bud, you want to hop up there?"

"Not today, thanks," Nina said quickly.

"I was talking to the l'il fan," Kettrick said. He didn't seem quite as amiable.

Paul said, "Wondered if we could ask you a few questions about Terry London."

"Oh, yeah. That's who you are. I almost forgot. The lawyer for the guy that did it to Terry. You really going to do a trial? Am I gonna have to, like, show up in court?"

"I believe my client is innocent," Nina said.

"Well, you ain't gonna prove it by me. I was sound asleep when my dad looked out the window and saw the guy take off."

"The shots didn't wake you?"

"Didn't hear a thing. My dad snores so loud, I sleep with a pillow over my head. I sleep hard too."

"I was wondering why your dad didn't call the police, after hearing shots and seeing someone running," Paul said.

"He probably thought Terry had a late visitor and ran him off her property by shooting a couple into the air," Kettrick said. "See, he didn't want to mess with her. They didn't get along."

"You dad said you used to do some work for her."

"Ever since I was fifteen. Handyman stuff. Only way I had to make some money until I started driving when I was eighteen."

"Did you get to be friends?" Nina said. Bobby had walked around to the other side of the huge truck, and seemed to be climbing inside one of the wheel wells. "Bobby, come away from there!" she added sharply. Paul walked around to corral the kid. He could see and hear Kettrick perfectly well through the steel struts.

Kettrick was nodding. "She talked to me," he said. "She was lonely, didn't have no friends. She'd tell me stories, teach me things."

"Like what?"

"Just things," he said vaguely. "She said someday she would make a movie about me. She was interested in my welfare, that's what she said. My dad, though, he wanted me to stay away from her. She scared him, but she was nice to me, sometimes."

"Terry had a rifle, didn't she?"

"Old hunting rifle, a Remington," Kettrick said.

"Where did she keep it?"

"I don't know, around. But she waved it at my dad once, scared the shit out of him."

"When did you see her last?"

"About a week before. I went over and swept the needles off her roof. But we didn't really talk."

"Did she ever say she was afraid of anyone? Did she seem nervous recently?"

"You must not've known her very well. Nervous was not her style. She got mad, and then she got even."

"Did she ever mention a Doreen Benitez? or Ordway? Or Jess Sweet, Jonathan Sweet, Michael Ordway?"

"No, I never heard those names."

"How about Kurt Scott? Did she ever talk about him?"

"Wait, let me think. Sounds familiar. That's it! Her ex–old man."

"What exactly did she say about him?" Nina asked him.

"Nothing good. Nothing that's going to help your case. Kurt Scott, that's your client, right? She told me once, she was looking for him. And when she found him, she was gonna hang him upside down and flay him alive." Kettrick smiled widely, waited for the next question.

"Did she say why she wanted to do that?" Nina said.

"No. But she licked her lips like it was a sex thing."

"Was she your girlfriend?" Paul asked him from behind the truck, and for some reason Kettrick started to laugh. "She was an old lady, man!" he said. "She told me she thought the sex act was disgusting. She got off other ways, I guess."

"Like how?"

"Like I say, she was my friend, man. I mean, leave the lady her secrets." His smile and the big guileless blue eyes never varied.

"So what were you doing at her house the day I came by?" Nina said.

"Huh?" Paul was now standing so that he could see Ralph's face. A mask, Paul decided. All this cooperative pleasantry was really stressing him out. What was he hiding?

"You said to Terry, 'You promised.' What had she promised?"

"Oh, yeah. I forget." It was a big, smirking, patent lie. Paul had already decided to do an in-depth report on Ralph too.

Bobby said, from the other side of the truck, "I don't see why I can't just sit in the seat, Mom. Please, just for a minute."

Nina said, "Hush, Bobby. I already said no."

"Like I say, I wouldn't mind lettin' him up there to sit with me a minute," Kettrick said. He crawled rapidly up into the cockpit, patted the padded dashboard, leaned down, and held out his hand. "Here we go."

Bobby reached up and Paul moved to intervene, but Nina was faster. She grasped Bobby's shoulder firmly and said, "No. We don't go. But thanks for the offer."

"Party-poopin' lawyer lady," Ralph said, and now there was definitely something ugly in his voice. He started up the engine so that they all jumped back from the clouds of exhaust. "Wimpy!" he yelled, guffawing, and took off like a mountain on wheels down the track.

"God, Mom," Bobby said, brushing dust off his pants. "I may never have that chance again."

Watching Ralph Kettrick, helmetless, careen around the empty field, Paul said to Nina, "There goes one heckuva happy fella. Let's get off the track before he flattens us."

24

THE DRIVE BACK FROM RENO TOOK LONGER THAN USUAL, DUE TO THE Saturday night revelers journeying into Tahoe to make or drop some fun money at the casinos. By the time they had dinner and dropped Bobby off at home with Andrea it was nine o'clock, though the light of a long day lingered. Nina unlocked her empty office building, and, once in her office, put a pot of coffee on while Paul located the remote control for the VCR, and moved furniture around in the conference area, transforming the room into a theater for two. He didn't bother to close the blinds on the night outside, so the beams from passing cars strobed intermittently through the room.

First they watched the silent arrest video. The date and time flashed up on the screen. The camera, mounted on the police car, rode behind Kurt's rented car as he slowed and pulled over, and showed Officer Joyce approaching the car and, after a minute, motioning to Kurt to get out. The officer pressed Kurt against the side of the car and frisked him from behind. Kurt's face was turned to the camera and he was talking.

"Kurt's got blood dripping off his arm," Paul said, "and he just left the scene of a shooting. I can see why they arrested him. Best place for him was the pokey. And what happened to the sound?"

"The sound didn't record for some reason—the arresting officer said the equipment was new and he didn't know what he was doing. He must have pushed the wrong button or it was malfunctioning. Anyway, I disagree with you. They had nothing on him. All they really have is pictures of a wounded man being arrested. Everything else is open to interpretation."

"And the testimony of the arresting officer." Paul began reading from the police report. " 'I asked him, what is that? Suspect answered it was blood. I then asked if suspect was hurt and he nodded his head in the affirmative. I then asked if suspect had been in a fight. Suspect answered, she's been shot.' "

"Kurt's very clear that Terry shot at him and he ran out the door on the first shot. So he wouldn't have said that," Nina said. "The cop's lying, or mistaken. I believe Kurt."

"Maybe. I'll check out Officer Joyce. He's a rookie, so maybe he got rattled and didn't hear right. Unfortunately, it's down on paper now and he's going to be positive that's what Kurt said. If I were you, I wouldn't drink all that coffee this time of night."

"Doesn't bother me."

"I'll just have a glass of this delicious chlorinated tap water," Paul said. "So. What next?"

"Our feature presentation. *Where Is Tamara Sweet?*" Nina was already loading the tape into the VCR. She sat down next to Paul in a straightbacked conference chair and he put his arm around her. Paul clicked off the lights, saying, "Nothing like a quiet night at home watching the tube."

Nina pushed the START button.

A rainy dark road, headlights reflecting on the pavement as a pickup truck skidded into the street, turned left and drove some distance. The camera picked up the driver's point of view. Visual bumps, headlights swerving back and forth as if seen through intoxicated eyes, a country song playing mournfully from the tape deck, up a dark road lined with cabins, up a jouncy dirt road, then a swift cut to a highway turnoff, the yellow car beams illuminating dripping trees . . . WHERE IS TAMARA SWEET? superimposed on the scene, and the credits rolling . . .

"I heard the skid and looked out the window. Tamara turned left and split." A bartender smacked a mug of beer onto a bar counter, sloshing a little over the wooden surface. Behind him, bottles of colored liquid glittered and beckoned on glass shelves fronting a wall-size mirror. Small eyes peered out from his wide, friendly face. "I recognized her because her mother used to come in here all the time. Tam was only slightly whacked, not so drunk we'd be calling a cab. I remember that night because the cops came later to arrest me for serving to minors." The camera, held high so it seemed to be floating, moved backward, out the door, focusing on a yellow neon sign: MANNY'S.

"Why did she go that way? Manny's is the last business on Highway 50 heading west out of Tahoe. Tamara didn't know anyone at the private houses around the lake in that direction. It was after eleven, and she had school the next day." A robust, middle-aged woman with brilliant blue eyes traversed a ski hill, beginning in the distance, and moving in soft dips toward the camera, getting larger in the frame. Against the snow-white hill by a ski lift she stopped abruptly, her skis flinging up snow in a whoosh. She cut a fine silhouette against the harsh background, her graying hair caught in a girlish headband. A computer clicked out letters, and the screen raised them in an old typewriter typeface, one by one: J-e-s-s-i-c-a S-w-e-e-t, M-o-t-h-e-r.

The next scene, the exterior of a large cedar home, led into a living room crammed with antiques, shining hardwood floors, and to a wheelchair with a man slumped in it. "Jonathan Sweet, Father," typed the invisible computer. In a whiny voice Sweet said, "She was always asking for money that we didn't have. She wouldn't get an afterschool job, even though she didn't care about her schoolwork either. She stopped talking to us about six months before she left. We didn't approve of her lifestyle. She was supposed to be living at home, but she spent nights away. She was eighteen, a beautiful girl. I guess she had lots of boyfriends. We never met any."

* * *

A long slow fade from his complaining face merged and smoothed over into the face of a long-legged, girlish young woman squinting outside a horse corral in blinding sun, wearing a halter and shorts. "Doreen Benitez Ordway, Best Friend" typed itself onto the screen.

"We met at lunch period right after the science test. Tamara thought she had flunked it. She said she was finished with school anyway, that it had nothing to do with real life. She was laughing, and I was, like, Tamara, you better go talk to your teacher, you have to graduate from high school or you'll never get a job. But she said she didn't care. She kept talking about real life, saying real life was much more interesting."

"She came home after school," Jessica Sweet said as two skiers jumped off the lift and disappeared to the right of the frame, "and locked herself in her room, listening to that depressing stuff young people call music these days. I could smell the smoke and I yelled at her to quit. I wasn't drinking, no matter what anyone says. I just can't stand smoking. That's probably why she left that night. She wouldn't eat dinner, said she was going out with friends. I didn't know she was flunking most of her subjects."

A new face came into view, a man of about thirty, springy as a boy, touching two hands briefly to a low wooden fence and catapulting himself into focus. Though he wore rough work clothes, his face under the tan and five o'clock shadow had delicate features. Behind him a flat gray sky merged into a field dotted with low scrub. A couple of cows browsed in straw-colored grass. The bottom of the screen typed out, "Michael Ordway, First Boyfriend." He spoke in what had been an upper-class British accent, which, after years of Americanizing, retained only vestiges of its original polite air. "About six months before she went, we sneaked into the Hyatt to play some slots. A security guard kicked us out. We were drunk on the free drinks, and broke. She had a snit fit, said I bored her stiff. I was too young for her. That kind of thing. She hitched a ride home.

"I kept trying to see her again, but she avoided me. The night she disappeared, I was having pizza with Doreen at Manny's. By then

Doreen and I were together, but I was still interested in Tamara. It was a freezing cold night in the middle of winter. We were getting ready to leave. Sure, we were sloshed. We both drank all the time in those days. Then Tamara walked in at the last minute.

"So we sat back down and had another one. She was in a strange mood. She didn't want to talk about school, except to say it was boring. She said she had a late date in a little while and I asked why she was being so mysterious about it. I asked who he was. She said to stop spying on her and to stay out of her business. She threw a beer in my face so I'd get the message better. I was wiping it off when she left."

The film cut back to Doreen Ordway on horseback, her hands reining in a frisky horse. She was broad-shouldered for a woman, with the angular build that fills up fashion magazines. Her cropped top showed off a flat stomach and stretched revealingly tight over full breasts. She subdued her horse, jumped down with the grace of a dancer, and tied him to a post. Appearing coy, posing a bit, she looked directly into the camera, pushing sunglasses back on her nose.

"I said, 'Tamara, you really are going home, aren't you?' She smiled like she had a big secret. She said, 'And miss all the fun?' She made a short call at the pay phone. And she went out the door and got in her pickup. Michael was throwing up in the corner."

"That was twelve years ago. She never came home," Tamara's mother, Jessica Sweet, said, removing ski gloves to reveal chafed hands. She blew out a little cloud over them. "She never wrote, or called. I contacted the South Lake Tahoe police the next morning, and they listed her as a missing person."

Her strong tan face cut to the deeply lined face of a uniformed police sergeant, African American, old enough to retire. "Sergeant Fletcher Cheney," the typing at the bottom of the screen read. He sat at a beat-up oak desk, rustling papers. Cheney said, "The pickup, registered to her parents, had been left about a mile and a half down the highway, pulled off at a turnout. We found it the day after she disappeared. There was no sign of violence. The truck was neatly parked, locked up, no mechanical problems, with nothing inside except music tapes and some old fast-food wrappers and dog toys behind the seats. No one reported seeing the pickup or the girl after she left Manny's."

The screen blacked. Then, accompanying the voice of Jessica Sweet, lurid red letters sliced across the screen: SHE DISAPPEARED . . .

Doreen Ordway spoke, as more red letters appeared: THAT NIGHT . . .

TWELVE YEARS AGO. The voice of Jonathan Sweet finished the sentence.

Paul said, from the darkness next to Nina, "She must be dead. Twelve years . . . no word. She's dead."

A shadowy echo to his words, the soundtrack softly repeated, "She's dead, I suppose." The wide brown eyes of Doreen came back onscreen, minus her sunglasses. Silver filigree earrings twinkled in the sun as gentle breezes spun them. In the background Nina heard the unmistakable sounds of several horses whinnying, and the sound of hooves on hard-packed earth. A landscape came into view as the camera moved past Doreen to follow a horse running against the backdrop of a forest. "All her roots were here," Doreen's voice went on. "She was a local. She wouldn't just take off without a word. She wouldn't have stayed away so long."

"Until she turned eighteen, she used to go out into the backyard after school and jump around for hours on our trampoline. She never got hurt, even though she could be some daredevil. She sewed some of her own clothes. She still slept with her old doll, Melissa, every night. She was a normal, happy little girl . . ." said Tam's father. A doll with shiny chestnut tresses and pink cheeks sat on a shelf in a deserted bedroom. Her father reached over to the doll, placing it on his lap. Then: old photographs of the Sweet family, Tamara as a little girl at Disneyland, smiling gap-toothed at the camera, wearing a Mouseketeer hat . . .

Morphing out of that little face, an older face from a high school yearbook; a young girl with black-rooted, bleached blond hair parted in the middle, her face sullen, her eyes rimmed with black eyeliner, and the voice of Cheney, the policeman: "She got around."

"She treated Michael like dirt," Doreen said while the camera lingered on Tamara's face. "He's a sensitive person. His parents brought him to Tahoe from England when he was fourteen, and he had trouble adjusting at school. He really loved Tamara, and she hurt him so much."

"Funny how things turn out. Doreen and I went off to the same college, UC Davis, and got engaged. We have two little girls, twins, to keep us busy . . ." Michael Ordway said. "Tam's father was sick, you know, and he worried all the time. He was unemployed for two years and he spent the whole time hassling her. He drove her away. She told me one time he really hurt her. She showed me the scar. Of course, there was also her mother, the great overachiever who arrived on time for every appointment, who did everything faster and better than everyone else, a real control freak and secret binge boozer. She drove Tam nuts. She had to get good grades. She had to go to college. She had to keep her weight down. . . . I think Tam ran off with the guy she was seeing. Her parents didn't love her. They thought they owned her."

A jerky home video, everything in it tinged slightly blue, opened with a long pan over obscene piles of presents under a Christmas tree. Then came the close-ups of individual packages, decorated with ribbons, leaves sprayed gold, fruit sprayed gold, sleighs sprayed gold, covered in every variety of paper, from Jolly Old Saint Nick to Jesus Christ. Following several long, boring minutes of this underedited effort, Tamara Sweet herself showed up on the floor by the tree, dressed in blue velvet pants and a velvet vest, her blunt-cut hair pouring immaculately over her shoulders, about sixteen years old. She opened a present, ice skates, and proudly displayed them to the camera. "Thanks, Mom and Dad," she said in a high, feathery voice. "I love 'em to death!"

The camera had moved with Jessica Sweet into what had to be Tamara's bedroom, roaming the walls, from the doll on the ruffled bed to the violently colored punk rock posters on the walls. "I did find some marijuana in her desk, there," she said, her fingers digging through a drawer. "I told the police about it, but they didn't seem to care. I have always wondered if she smoked some of it in the truck, added to what she had been drinking, then got out and—and maybe was hit on the highway, and the driver took her . . . body and dumped it somewhere. Or maybe she stumbled out into the dark and fell into a ditch. It's wilderness here. Maybe no one could find her where she fell."

Sergeant Cheney came onto the screen, consulting a thin file. "The case remains open. I mean, you don't close a case like this even after twelve years. When a human being disappears into thin air, you don't forget. You look for evidence, because I guarantee, if a crime's been committed, there is evidence. It's just a matter of finding it. In this case, we have nothing much to go on. But girls go missing. We've had at least three other girls disappear up here since Tamara Sweet disappeared. No leads at this time. No, we don't know if they're dead or alive. Gone without warning, without a trace. Poof." A pause followed. Then, as if responding to a question, Cheney said, "Where is Tamara Sweet? I personally think she got into a car with a transient. That got her into trouble. We check on a regular basis on unidentified bodies found statewide."

"Where is my daughter?" Jonathan Sweet asked plaintively. "I pray to God she's alive, happy. Tamara, if you see this, please . . . just a note, a call . . . I . . . we need to hear from you . . ." The lighting cast long shadows across his boyish face, making him look somehow fraudulent, and Terry London's gift as a filmmaker was apparent. She let the man talk, but she interpreted what he said with the lighting; the jumpy leaps from his eyes to his hands to his mouth contaminating his sincerity.

Back to the yearbook picture. The camera traced Tamara's face in claustrophobic close-up, alighting on her eyes and pulling in tightly, until the eyes absorbed the screen, and sucked the viewer in. "You want to know my honest opinion?" Doreen's voice said coldly. "I think she was on drugs. She made that phone call, you know? I bet she was going to meet someone who was going to feed her head. She was getting a bad attitude, which hurt her family and her friends. Who cares where she is? Good riddance."

A scene followed that paralleled the beginning, starting inside a pickup truck. Now the words of a crooning country song followed the camera as the door to the truck opened and the camera moved outside into a dusky red-toned landscape.

The camera lingered on the image of a winding, ascending pathway, darkened by twilight, framed by pine branches. For a moment the image was blocked, then it became clear that the camera was behind someone. A girl whose back had filled the frame now walked away from the camera, toward the trail, getting progressively smaller as she got farther away.

"A reenactment," Paul's voice said in the darkness. "Interesting."

The slow grace of the first few moments of the scene gave way to an increasingly frantic-looking series of cuts as the girl walked up the trail, fragmenting and distorting into the night, fading as she proceeded. On a big, wide, flat granite boulder, the girl who looked so much like Tamara Sweet sat down, looking around as if she expected someone. She wore a white rabbit fur jacket, black jeans, and cowboy boots. The camera moved in close, caressing the soft fur. In the gray gloom of the evening her body lost its shape and individuality, melding into the rock.

The camera moved back. The trail recaptured its empty peacefulness, as the strains of the music played out and the camera panned down, down, down, into the grit of leaves, rock, and dirt that made the pathway, and a final caption flickered on and off: THE END.

Credits appeared over black. In the background, a simple song sung by a little girl played, a song from the nursery: "Where, oh where, is sweet little Tammy . . ." fading out before the final phrase.

BOOK THREE

Six Years Ago: Alice

For weeks before Christmas, Alice began to feel the dread wash over her, tarnishing her free time, absorbing all her waking thoughts. Was there no escape from this yearly pilgrimage into hell?

How she hated family vacations. Every year at this time, her family rented a cabin in the Bijou neighborhood of South Lake Tahoe, and her cousins and other relatives made sporadic appearances throughout the week. She was sixteen, almost seventeen. She didn't want to go anymore and be stuck in that small, hot, overstuffed place, surrounded by their eyes, their criticisms, their constant attention, like needles through her thin skin, all day long, nonstop. She had approached them like the mature person she was this year when her family began preparations for the trip, making what she thought was a pretty strong, logical case for staying home on her own.

She explained that she would not invite any friends over. She would get a head start on some term papers coming up. She would be studious and good.

Her mother looked at her like she was crazy. "But that's your problem, Alice. You don't have any fun or any friends."

She didn't talk through the long drive up into the mountains. When they arrived, Uncle Henry and Aunt Lorry were there to greet them. "Alice," they said, patting her on the head like a two-year-old, before she had even unpacked or caught a glimpse of the lake, "did you bring your boyfriend?" That was their favorite topic, her lack of a boyfriend. It would go on during the entire vacation. They would tease her and they would quiz her until she brought them an XY, stuffed and mounted.

The needling would go on during the entire vacation. She knew once she was in college, they would ask when she was going to find a husband. When she did that, they would start in on a baby. And when she died, they'd shake their heads and say what a homely girl she had been. She'd heard Aunt Lorry say that word to her mother. Homely.

"Why don't you get off my back," she heard herself say.

Her mother hustled her into the house, whispering for her to behave herself, for goodness' sake. Upstairs, Alice unpacked in the attic bedroom, took a long look at the big cold lake across the way, and flopped down on the bed, to hide and read for as long as they would leave her alone. Her sister, Ellen, came in after her, dragging a duffel, headphones glued to her head, faint tinny music surrounding her like a halo. Ellen was fourteen and popular, and remained cool under fire. She had adopted their father's way of dealing with their family. She tuned them out, but Alice didn't know how to do that.

They all had a candlelit dinner together, spaghetti with canned mushroom sauce, at a big table with a view lit by the porch light of the snow drifts lining the street. Her sister, Ellen, hummed through the din of inevitable arguments that arose when the adults all overdid the Zinfandel, while her dad kept his nose tight in the newspaper, ignoring all of them.

Her mother usually knew better, but Aunt Lorry and Uncle Henry were bad influences. She picked a hank of Alice's hair off her back and held it up for all to see. "Geez, honey," she said to Alice. "At sixteen, I knew I was born a blonde. You ought to go blond, or at least frost hell out of your hair, honey pie." Her mother had been a hostess at a supper club in Pleasanton for twenty years. Proud of her job and the big tips, she worked hard to keep a petite figure, and prided herself on what she thought were her dazzling conversational skills.

Alice stood up, shaking off her mother's touch. "Why, so I can walk around with black roots all the time, like you do?" She leaned next to her mother's deeply shocked face. "Oops, sorry," she said, looking hard at her mother. "Gray roots."

"Alice, your mother is just trying to help you," said Aunt Lorry,

steering her away from her mother's tears and firmly upstairs to her room. "We all want what's best for you. How could you be so mean?"

Lying on her bed, Alice felt deeply guilty and grieved for these things that came out of her mouth unbidden, like she had some evil devil girl speaking through her, someone cruel.

But why did they goad her like this? Nobody cared that she got good grades. Nobody saw her as a special person with a special mind, a brave and unusual person, who wanted more out of life than boyfriends and blond hair. She wanted so much more than they did. Exotic travel. Adventures beyond the books she read. Real life, outside of Pleasanton or boring old Lake Tahoe, and far, far away from the bosom of her loving, smothering family.

When she had tamped her emotions back down to the usual slow smolder, she went downstairs and did her best to make up with her mother, asking if she could take a short walk, just around the block. She wanted to get some air. Her mother, worn out with the day's arguments, loaned her her beaver coat, and let her go.

She walked straight up the street toward the casinos.

She might even stay out all night.

25

"They keep the lights on all night," Kurt said through the glass. "People talk, sing, cry. I don't sleep. I can't read anymore, either. Can't concentrate. Things aren't going well on the outside, either, are they?"

Nina had stopped by on her way to a court appearance at nine. Kurt was losing weight. His expression was despondent. It worried her. "We're doing fine," she said. "But you have to keep your spirits up. I'd like you to see a doctor friend of mine. You may be going into a depression."

"Wake me when it's over," Kurt said. "Drugs? Not my style."

"A checkup, then. I'll get an order from Judge Milne to have you seen at Boulder Hospital."

Kurt didn't agree, but at least he wasn't disagreeing.

"Okay?" Nina said.

"Okay. It's the powerlessness, not being able to help yourself. It's crazy-making."

"I know. I know. Listen, there's something you can do to help yourself. I left a video and film for you to watch. I'll be back on Wednesday and I'd like to hear your reactions."

"What are they?"

"A video of your arrest. And the film Terry made about Tamara Sweet."

"Sure." Kurt looked interested. That was good. "What do you want to know?"

"I need you to tell me exactly, word for word, what you said to that cop when you were leaning against the police car. The video may help you remember. And . . . just watch the film. You knew Tamara. You knew Terry. Why did Terry make it? What was she trying to do?" She tried to keep the frustration she felt whenever she thought about the film out of her voice.

"There's one other video," she added. She told Kurt about the death video, watching him closely. He shook his head over and over as she spoke, as if he couldn't believe it.

"Incredible," he said. "When can I see it?"

"We're getting some copies made. Soon," Nina said. She was picturing Kurt lying on the cot in his cell ruminating endlessly. She didn't want to overwhelm him, and the death video was overwhelming. Maybe after he had seen the doctor, she'd think about showing it to him.

"So how goes it with you, Nina?"

"Too much to do, not much time," she said. "The usual."

"What do you do in the evenings? You see, I think about you, your life."

"I go home. . . . I live with my brother and his wife—"

"Matt moved up here too?"

"Several years ago. I take walks, ride my bike, swim when I can. I try to keep my life quiet." She watched her words, mindful not to say anything about Bobby.

"I appreciate Paul van Wagoner's agreeing to work on the case," Kurt said. "Have you and he—that is—is there a wedding date?"

"What?"

"You know. Your marriage."

Then Nina remembered the trick Paul had played. "Kurt, Paul and I aren't engaged. We're just—"

"He lied?"

"Outright."

"Are you in love with him?" Kurt asked, his face intense and his jaw tight. It's none of your business, Nina ought to have said politely. This was her chance to draw a line, but she couldn't help responding honestly to him.

"I'm not sure," she said. At that moment she realized she had been unconsciously comparing Paul and Kurt all this time, weighing the two men. Kurt's eyes told her clearly that he was glad to hear what she had said. She felt dizzy. Usually, a mother looks at her son and sees how he resembles his father. Here, she was looking at the father and seeing Bobby in him. "He has asked me to marry him, that part's true."

"But you haven't said yes. Why is that? Oh, I know I have no right to ask you, but—"

"It's all right. I don't know if I want to get married at all."

"You ought to be married. You ought to have children," Kurt said. The way he said it, so deliberately, as if there was a hidden message behind it, scared her and intrigued her at the same time.

She said, "I have to go interview Tamara Sweet's parents now. Hang in there." She got up, knowing his eyes followed her, and rang the door buzzer to be let out into the bright world he might never see again.

On Tuesday morning, Sergeant Fletcher Cheney invited Paul into his squad car, showing off the new video camera shakily attached to a dashboard curled from many hours in the mountain sun. The schools had just let out all over the state, and traffic was heavy on Highway 50. "I'm just getting off patrol duty today. I read through my notes when you called, so I'm up on the case."

"Thanks for the ride. But aren't you a homicide detective?" Paul asked, as the car lurched once, and then eased gently forward, responding to the smoothly confident touch of a man in full control of his vehicle.

"Yes, I sure am," he said, his eyes scanning the sidewalks where the tourists were out in full regalia in various states of summer undress, lugging their vacation accoutrements: floats, beach chairs, brilliantly colored umbrellas tucked under their arms, and shopping bags drooping at their wrists. A few stunners in cutoffs and tight striped

T's ambled along, looking for trouble, but mostly moms, dads, and their perpetually grubby offspring owned the streets today. "Got two officers out with summer flu. I'm pitching in. Go ahead, ask away. I can drive and think at the same time, if I concentrate real hard."

"Tell me a little about your connection to this case. When did you get involved?"

"Well, let's see." Cheney's face, a dark bronze sheen, wore the easy smile of a man who gets along with everyone but keeps his feelings to himself. "I got going a little late in life on this business. Started off working as a bouncer in a hotel bar. Plenty of action in that business. I got a real feel for low-life scum in that job, I tell you. I always felt dirty by the end of the day. Anyway, I wanted a business where I had a little more to do than grab an angry drunk by the shoulders and haul his sorry carcass out the door, so I went to the academy and got my first job as a patrol officer twenty-two years ago, when I was thirty. Did that for nearly ten years. Made a few good arrests. Testified in a few cases. I got promoted to detective just about twelve years ago. Tamara Sweet was my first case, so I guess you could say I connected."

"In the film Terry London made about Tamara Sweet's disappearance, you said something interesting."

"Lord. Quick, call my wife. She thinks I never say anything interesting. What'd I say?"

"You said other girls besides Tamara Sweet disappeared from Tahoe."

Sergeant Cheney lost his smile and sighed. "Yes, that is so. Age range from fifteen to nineteen. Nothing else in common except being female and in that age range, that we could figure out. Different looks. Different situations. Different backgrounds. Different types."

"Would you mind if I sneaked through your files and made a few notes?"

"I'm finding it hard to figure out what the death of a middle-aged filmmaker who's most probably been killed by her ex-husband has to do with these old files, but sure. I would dearly love to have your opinion, if you form one. I keep thinking something will break, someday."

They got out of the car and walked toward the city police offices.

All roads led back here. Paul thought of Kurt Scott across the courtyard, sitting in a cell. "Let's grab coffee," Cheney said. "I'll set you up with the files while I fill out some paperwork." They spread out the paperwork in the main interrogation room.

"Before you go," said Paul, "give me your take on what happened to these girls."

"You know how many people visit South Lake Tahoe a year?"

"No."

"Three million. Now, remember, that's coming into a town with maybe thirty thousand permanent residents. And we get all kinds, all kinds. Folks who like to entertain or be entertained. Ones that like to sweat up a mountain, or ski down it. Drifters, dreamers, and telephone schemers. They all hit Tahoe at some point. That makes for a lack of predictability in matters of behavior, you see what I mean? The locals vary from sedate to downright hazardous too. Easy for a girl with a sense of adventure to get mixed up with a bad dude.

"That makes it hard, really hard, to figure out what happens when a girl ups and leaves. Did she go to San Francisco to escape an unhappy scene at home? Even a girl working in a grocery store here has unlimited opportunities to meet people. Did she run off with friends? Or someone she thought she knew well, but didn't? It's hard to be a parent in this town. You can't protect kids."

"That's true anywhere," said Paul. "So, let me see. You're saying that four girls are still missing, including Tamara Sweet. The police haven't been able to get a line on a single one? And you feel there's a connection, but you don't know what it is?"

"That's what I'm saying. Wish it wasn't so. Only one linkage I've ever been sure about. They all went in winter. January and February, the coldest months. Strange, isn't it?"

"They were all locals, like Tamara Sweet?"

"Oh, no. In one case, the girl was here vacationing with her family. Another girl lived in Cedar Flat, near Tahoe City."

"Families usually get some word from or about runaways eventually," Paul said.

"Yes, they do."

"You don't think they ran away."

"Easy to bury a body in the forest in a place it'll never be found. Or drop it in the lake. But that's just sad experience talking. The truth is, I don't know what happened to those kids. I stay in touch with their parents and study the files once in a while, just in case a clue's hiding in there that I haven't been able to find. I've got other cases. That's all I can do." He left Paul to his files and tattered notebooks.

Four girls. Paul pulled the photos first and studied them. Susana Delaware, sixteen, an olive-skinned girl with a fine aquiline nose and high cheekbones, a cleft in her chin, and round black glasses, from Cedar Flat. She had gone skiing at Kirkwood one fine morning with her brother and two other friends eight years before and never returned. One snapshot actually showed her standing beside a ski lift at Kirkwood the day before her disappearance, sunburned and smiling in her blue fur-lined parka and tight white ski pants.

Alice Grizzetti, also sixteen, had dark eyes, pasty skin, mousy brown hair, and acne dotting her nose and forehead. She had been staying at a lakeside chalet in the Bijou neighborhood with her parents and another family for Christmas. She had taken a walk after dinner six years before and never come back. Her picture was the usual high school photo showing only her face and shoulders. She looked studious, serious in her white blouse.

Deirdre Jaekelson. From Colorado. Nineteen, with her hair cut in spikes and kohl lining her eyes, she had come to town with several other friends to party and hit the ice-skating rink up at Squaw, across the lake. A trained skater, with Olympic hopes, dumped by the boy who brought her to a party at a private home, she had left the party three years before and never saw Colorado, her friends, or her contrite boyfriend again.

And Tamara Sweet. The high school picture Paul remembered from the film, with black roots and eyeliner, and several snapshots he hadn't seen in the film, presenting a different side of the girl: laughing, sitting on a towel at a lakeside beach; on horseback, wearing jeans, sweater, and cowboy boots; in front of mountains and sky. Prettier, more athletic than in the film. An alert, smart, adventurous face, regular features, big blue eyes.

She would have fought, scratched, kicked with those cowboy boots of hers, done some damage.

Paul laid out the photographs of the girls, side by side. Two pretty girls, two plain girls. Two worldly ones, and two seeming innocents.

One local, three out-of-towners. He studied interviews with friends and neighbors, typed laboriously on paper that was dog-eared from years of Sergeant Cheney's fingers traveling over and over the same ground. He found lists of shoe sizes, ring sizes, types of jewelry worn, styles of clothing preferred by the girls. He knew what perfume the ones that used perfume wore. He knew who, if anyone, each girl had dated, and when, and what they had reported after the experience to friends and family.

Among the files, Paul found that Cheney had questioned Kurt Scott twelve years before regarding the Sweet case. Kurt had claimed he hadn't seen Tamara for a month before her disappearance. He claimed he was at the University of Nevada, Reno, main library the night she left, a claim he couldn't substantiate. He had told Cheney that Tamara had ended their short relationship, the same story he had told Nina.

Many of the details of Cheney's report on Tamara matched Terry's film. They confirmed that Terry had set forth the correct sequence of events of Tamara's last night at Tahoe. But they also confirmed that Tamara wasn't the unhappy, angry little loser Terry had tried to make her out to be.

Sighing, Paul read everything twice. Time of day they disappeared: always different. Where they disappeared: always different. Character, social class, interests, all varied.

What did these four girls have in common other than vanishing from the face of the earth within a few years of each other from the Lake Tahoe area?

Quite probably, nothing. But he decided to talk to the girls' parents. See if Cheney had missed anything. See if anybody had come home.

He made notes of phone numbers of the parents and other information.

He looked at the pictures of the four girls until his eyes blurred and his head pounded, wishing for aspirin but unwilling to give up. He would check the airline flight rosters into Tahoe for a few days before each of the girls disappeared. Scott had told Nina he hadn't flown back to Tahoe for twelve years, but how could that be confirmed? To make a complete check was impossible. He could have flown in to San Francisco and used an assumed name to fly in . . .

but why fly so far to kidnap three girls nobody had linked with him? The D.A.'s investigators had already contacted the police departments in the places Scott had lived since he left Tahoe, and there was no similar group of disappearances in any of those jurisdictions. The pattern didn't seem to connect to Scott.

But if not Scott, who? Terry London, maybe? Women thrill-killers were almost nonexistent, and they almost always killed men. The London woman had been unusual, there was no doubt about that, but she, too, wasn't linked by parents or friends to any of the other three girls. Paul just plain couldn't believe that theory.

Which left two possibilities. Either the disappearances were random, the most likely scenario, or some third party was responsible, an unknown predator out there, who went hunting once every three years or so. Cheney had made a list of known sex offenders in the area, checked their whereabouts on the relevant nights, and found nothing. Everywhere his thoughts lit, Cheney had already thought it through and checked it out. The only connection Paul could find was that Terry London had made the connection in her film, and she might have done that for purely whimsical, artistic, or malicious reasons.

Cheney stuck his head in. "I'm heading out. You find anything in there? Give your brain a good workout?"

"Good, thorough police work," Paul said. "Like you said, I feel there's a connection between them, even if there's nothing specific to point to. I have this feeling that if I could just see better, there's something here. I know it. Give me five more minutes."

Cheney laughed. "Oh, boy. He's hooked. I've been there and back a dozen times, and here I sit at square one. Call me if anything pops up, okay?"

"Sure. Thanks, Cheney."

"No problem, van Wagoner. You ever consider going back to police work? Pretty little town, regular paycheck, two-buck buffet breakfasts any day of the week."

"That's mighty tempting," Paul said, smiling. "Then there's the risking your life every day to look forward to, also."

Sergeant Cheney chuckled, a big deep belly laugh that made his whole body shake. "Son, you risk your life every morning when you get out of bed. There's no getting around it." He waved and left.

Paul leaned back in his chair and closed his eyes, making a picture in his mind of them dressing to go out, leaving and fading from sight, on a street, a mountain slope. . . .

He checked the weather reports for each day. No, they hadn't all vanished in a snowstorm. No, they hadn't vanished on exceptionally clear, or foggy, or overcast days. They had disappeared during cold weather, wearing their cute little furry coats, their warm pants, and their snow boots. . . .

So what?

26

PARADISE SKI RESORT OCCUPIED THE WRONG HALF OF THE MOUNTAIN above South Lake Tahoe, the part that tourists couldn't see and had to drive farther to, the part that wasn't Heavenly. Paradise had no view of the lake, and had fewer lifts. But it had two advantages over Heavenly: with several runs at ten thousand feet, it was at a slightly higher altitude, and it was cheaper. Nina had never been there before.

The parking lot was jammed full of tour buses and vans from the big casino hotels. Paradise, with its snowmaking equipment and altitude, managed to stay open longer than almost any of the other resorts. She trudged up the cement path toward the small lodge with the die-hard spring skiers clomping along around her.

Jessica Sweet invited her into her pleasant office in back. Outside, snow piled up to the glass of a long, picturesque window wall. She sat down at her desk in a soft-looking red leather chair, two computers on a table to her left, and behind her, a full bookcase.

She looked much as she had in court and in Terry's film. Her brown face was heavily lined from years of exposure to the sun, and she had a strong skier's frame. Short silver hair and eagle eyes added to the aura of vitality. She wore a green blouse with slacks and the light hiking boots Matt called waffle stompers. Her face was calm.

"You remember my husband, Jonathan," she said.

Jonathan Sweet had changed for the worse. He was well dressed, thanks no doubt to Mrs. Sweet, but up close the boyish features were wizening without ever having turned into a man's face. He sat in an electric wheelchair by the desk. "Hello, Mr. Sweet," Nina said, but he ignored her outstretched hand, leaving his own large hand resting on his shrunken legs. Another I-hate-you-lawyer-scum greeting to brighten up her morning.

"May I?" Nina said, lowering her untouched hand to indicate her tape recorder.

"If you wish," Jess Sweet said. "I hope this won't take long. Jonathan doesn't—"

"Quit babying me, Jess," Jonathan Sweet said. "Okay, we're here. What do you want?"

"I have your statements," Nina said. "May I ask you a few questions to clarify some points?"

"Why?"

"Well, there are a few things I'd like to follow up on—"

"But why should we answer your questions?" Jonathan Sweet said. "He probably killed our daughter. He's a murderer."

"You want the law to punish the right person, don't you?" Nina said. "A fair trial means both sides have the best possible access to the facts."

"Do you deny that Kurt Scott is the man my daughter was secretly seeing twelve years ago when she disappeared?"

"He knew her. He doesn't deny that. But they were no longer seeing each other on the night she—"

"Let me ask you this," Sweet interrupted. "Are you convinced your client is innocent?"

"What I think doesn't matter. It's what twelve jurors decide after hearing all the evidence that matters."

"You'd say anything to manipulate us into giving something that might help your client. You don't care about our loss or his guilt. Hypocrite." He folded his arms, looking pleased with himself. His wife let him take the lead.

"Then why let me come?" Nina said. "Why didn't you just refuse to see me?"

"Because Mr. Riesner told us you could drag us into a deposition with court reporters and legalese. This is the only time you'll be talking to us."

"Oh, I'll be talking to you at the trial," Nina said. "We have a lot to talk about. You want to know what will happen with Terry London's film and your lawsuit, don't you? You want to know if there's a connection to Tamara, don't you? I can tell you some things, if you will answer some questions for me. I don't want to trick you or cause you any further pain. What you say may not help me at all. But if I turn around and walk out of here, you'll see me next in court, and you won't be asking me any questions then."

"Speeches," the man in the wheelchair said. His face had turned red. "Impertinence. Get out."

"Wait, Jonathan," Jessica Sweet said. She turned toward Nina. "I'd like to know anything you know about Tam. I don't care why Scott killed Terry London."

"I don't believe he killed Tamara, Mrs. Sweet," Nina said.

"You wouldn't. He's your boyfriend now as well as your client, isn't he? Mr. Riesner told us—"

"Your daughter cared about Kurt Scott at one time, Mr. Sweet. Stop one moment and try to imagine that he is suffering and being persecuted, not that he is guilty. You sued Terry London because she had distorted the memory of your daughter, made her something she wasn't. Have you ever stopped to think why she did that?"

"Sleaze makes money." But he seemed to be thinking about it.

"She knew your daughter, Mr. Sweet. She had a romantic interest in Kurt Scott. As you know, Terry London was both single-minded and unscrupulous. If your daughter has come to harm, one theory would have to be that Terry London caused the harm."

"She knew my daughter? How do you know that?"

"From Mr. Scott."

"I don't believe anything Scott says, considering the jam he's in."

Mrs. Sweet said to her husband, "If Terry knew Tam—it's unbelievable! And she never once told us. Jonathan, listen to her."

"How was the decision made to have Terry London make this film?" Nina went on when Jessica Sweet nodded for her to go ahead.

"I was talking to some television people about making an unsolved case files show. You've seen them," Mrs. Sweet said. "They reenact a crime, or a disappearance, then put up a phone number to call after the show in case anyone who sees it recognizes something or has information to offer. And she called me to offer to produce it and take care of everything. That way the film could be more widely publicized."

"How did she hear about it?"

"Well, for once the *Mirror* had some news to report. They saw it as a chance to resurrect the old story about Tam disappearing, because I was in the talking stages with a producer. She said she wanted to make the film, had some money lined up and the whole bit, and suggested that I cooperate with her. She was a local girl and seemed truly interested in my little project. Well, of course I wanted to see something happen that might bring our daughter back, so I . . . convinced Jonathan. We agreed and pitched in what money we could. She expected to make much more back when the film went into distribution, so she asked for most of the profits. That seemed like a good deal to me. We didn't care about the money and we didn't know if this TV thing would pan out or not. Those people are hard to pin down. So she made her film. And you know how that turned out."

"You didn't agree, Mr. Sweet?"

No response. Mr. Sweet breathed heavily. Finally he said, "I thought it was a waste of money. And boy, was I right. But my wife was dead set on it." Was it her imagination, or did he grip the sides of his armchair hard when he said that?

"Jonathan was quite right, as it turned out," Mrs. Sweet said, moving around to touch his shoulder. He shrugged her off and scowled at Nina.

"Let's get this over with. You have three more minutes."

"What was Terry doing before she contacted you?"

"She said she was out of work and looking for a project. My impression was, it had been some time since she had done anything at all substantial, work-wise. She was glad to see this project come her way," Mrs. Sweet continued, as if her husband wasn't acting hostile. The trick apparently was to ignore his little displays of temper. Sweet was an angry man. He and his wife hadn't adapted well to his handicap.

"Yes. Very glad. Much too glad," Nina said. "She makes the film so no one else will, controlling the viewpoint and the information that goes into it. She gets to blacken your daughter's reputation, since she is connected to Kurt Scott, the man she still feels great animosity for. She even makes money. She does a good job and kills three birds with one stone."

"I don't believe it," Mr. Sweet said. "If she was such a manipulator, why not kill four birds and make your client into the bad guy? If she . . . hurt Tamara, why not blame it on him? She didn't even mention his name!"

"I don't know the answer to that question yet, Mr. Sweet. But I do owe you and your wife an apology. When I agreed to represent Ms. London, I didn't investigate the situation thoroughly enough. I was taken in by her, and I found myself on the wrong side when I realized the film was in fact malicious."

"It's too little and too late," Sweet said, his voice hostile.

"The film is part of her estate, and as far as I know, she has no heirs. I will cooperate with Mr. Riesner to ensure the film is never shown except in court, if that becomes necessary."

They looked at each other. Nina let it sink in.

"It's a strange way to win the case," Mrs. Sweet said with a nervous laugh. "So your theory is that Terry London was responsible for our loss . . . and she manipulated us, cheated us, took our money twelve years later. . . . It's almost too dreadful to think about."

Nina said, "She was capable of it."

"What do you want to know, Ms. Reilly?"

"I'd like to know if you were ever in Terry London's house or studio."

"Jonathan?" He shook his head, tight-lipped.

"No," his wife said. "Oh, except that she filmed one of our interviews there. She made coffee, and smiled and laughed and told us the film would help us find our daughter."

"I'd like to know where you were the night Tamara disappeared."

"Like it says in the statement, we were at a meeting of the Zephyr Cove Property Owners' Association until ten-thirty. We waited up for Tamara until two, then we got concerned and called the police," Mrs. Sweet said.

"You both waited up for her?"

"We tried to keep a close watch on her."

"Why?"

"We had had . . . a bit of an argument before she left. About her staying out so late. She was eighteen, but young for her age. Also, we had been bothered by a Peeping Tom for a couple of weeks before that."

"Someone was looking through your windows?"

"Into Tamara's bedroom. She had seen him twice."

"Was she sure it was a male?"

"Women don't do that," Jonathan Sweet said. "It's a male sexual perversion. Read up on your psychology."

"Was she sure?"

"She hadn't gone up to the window to see, no." Mrs. Sweet had taken up the thread again.

"Was the peeper ever caught?"

"No. We called the police both times, and we told Sergeant Cheney about it. They never found anything."

"Did you ever see the peeper again? After Tamara disappeared?"

"No." Mr. Sweet broke his silence and leaned forward in the wheelchair. "It was probably Scott. She dropped him, and he wouldn't give up."

Undeterred, Nina said, "It says here in the statement that you were in San Francisco the night Terry London was shot, Mrs. Sweet. What were you doing there?"

"I was at a conference. The Northern California Ski Resorts yearly meeting. I stayed at the Hyatt and I returned the next day."

"Did you have a single room?"

"Yes."

"I see what you're trying to do, don't think I don't," Jonathan Sweet said.

"And you, Mr. Sweet—"

"I was at home alone. But you don't believe that, do you? Okay.

I got so mad at Terry about that film that I ignored my paralysis, jumped up from my wheelchair temporarily cured—and went there and shot her. Heh, heh, heh. Happens all the time on TV."

"The studio was on level ground, Mr. Sweet. You wouldn't have to walk."

"Oh, what do you know about being in a wheelchair? My wife and Terry London both had to help me up that path to her studio—it's too narrow to be entirely safe for me. Also, there's one step up to the porch, you probably didn't notice. And the doorway's tight, with a ledge I had to be pushed over to get inside. I'm not saying it's impossible, just that it's ridiculous. Plus, one thing being in a wheelchair takes away is your ability to be anonymous. Everyone notices me, and pretends not to. I guarantee, I'm not instantly forgotten. And the witness saw your client come out of there, not me. How are you going to fool the jury about that?"

"I'm not suggesting you killed Terry London."

"Come on! What else do questions like that mean?" Nina followed the progress of his blood pressure as it pinked his skin and mottled his nose.

"You have to pardon my husband. He took Tam's disappearance very hard. We haven't forgotten her, not for a minute. And then he's had his own problems."

"I am sorry."

"No, you aren't," Jonathan Sweet said, wheeling himself away from Nina, toward the window, catching a ray of sun that sparkled off the metal of his chair. Outside, a girl skied by and waved through the window at them, vigorous and happy, full of grace, blessed with all the gifts they had wanted to give their daughter.

In the parking lot, through her sunglasses, Nina watched the colorful dots whizzing down the white hill. She felt afraid for the skiers, as if there might be an avalanche any minute.

The case was like a damn avalanche, too full of people and facts to get a handle on it, and she felt buried in an airless tomb of snow, unable to dig her way out, suffocating on too many billowy suppositions.

She brought an odious thought from the interview to consciousness. Why didn't Jonathan Sweet want the film made? What was he hiding? The statistics on murders of women consistently showed that many knew their killers. . . . How far would Mrs. Sweet go to protect him?

Had Sweet killed his own daughter?

27

"HEY, MAN. YOU DRIVE LIKE A CRAZED BRONCO," WISH SAID, HANGing on to the ceiling strap with both hands as Paul sped down the steep Kingsbury Grade in the gathering dusk.

"Thanks," he said. "But this is a gen-u-wine Dodge Ram. Nina has the crazed Bronco." He flicked on the headlights to reveal two deer directly in his path.

"Look out!" Wish shouted. Paul twisted his driving arm hard to the left and sped on along the shoulder, leaving the deer to look after them in amazement.

"Reflexes," he said peacefully. "I notice you're much more talkative when your mother's not around."

"Wouldn't you be?"

"I get your point."

"You oughta get back in the right lane." They were already there, doing sixty-five on a silvery stretch of mountain road, bounded on both sides by the silhouettes of the forest.

Paul opened the window and breathed deeply. "Ahhh. Look at

that big yellow moon, rising out there over the Carson Valley like a shiny Krugerrand."

"You're makin' me cold, man."

"Put on your sweatshirt. So. Getting back to Michael Ordway. You were saying you know him."

"I know him. He raises cattle and sheep out here, about a mile past Gardnerville. He has about a hundred fifty acres of desert, good water supply. Some kids. Flirty wife."

"Doreen Ordway, born Doreen Benitez. How long have they been married?"

Wish shrugged. "I don't know that kind of stuff."

"Well, what do you know?"

"The pay is good. He treats his workers right."

"Okay, that's something. You can tell everything about a man from the way he treats his employees."

"He's all right, for a foreigner."

"A foreigner? Oh, you mean because he's English."

"Yeah. But he doesn't act English. You know."

"No, I don't know," Paul said. "I'd be very curious to hear what that means."

"Well, he doesn't mind getting dirty, even though he's the owner. He doesn't sit around playing lord of the manor," Wish said.

"I see." They slowed down as they passed through the lonely hamlet of Minden. The big, bright town casino was the only business open. As soon as they came down the eastern side of the Sierra on the Grade, they had entered high-altitude scrub desert. The trees disappeared, and the sky took over. The night was still.

"Gardnerville," Wish said a minute later. "Now you see it, now you don't. Nice hotel there. That's where the shepherds eat. Good food."

"The shepherds."

"Yeah, the Basques. They live all over here. Take a left at the dirt road there."

They bumped down the road in second gear, between barbed wire fences. The moon rode serenely above, staying right with them. Paul said, "We could eat at that hotel afterward. On the expense account."

"Oh, man, I love this job."

"You haven't done anything yet. Let's review your private eye lesson."

"Listen and observe," Wish said. "Keep my mouth shut while you talk. Go to the bathroom and check the medicine cabinet for pills. Try to have a look at the bedroom, see if there's a desk and what's on it. Snoop around but always have an innocent explanation. Leave the tape recorder playing in my bag right next to you the whole time. Steal the glass or can he uses if possible."

"Do all that, I'll see you get a big bowl of mutton stew," Paul said.

They drove into a big dirt lot with several broken-down trucks and a tractor. Two small brown terriers came running out, barking, tails wagging. Behind them came a man in overalls and muddy boots.

"Michael Ordway," he said, shaking hands.

A good-looking woman with long legs in a pair of faded cutoffs came out behind him. "My wife, Doreen. Marley, Watson, down! Get down, boys!" At the door, Ordway took off the boots, and they followed his socks into the house, the dogs trotting alongside.

"Sit down," Doreen Ordway said. They sat at the cherry dining table, looking around at the hutch full of flowered china, the Persian rug, the landscapes on the walls. "Very nice," Paul said. "Not what you'd expect at the end of this road." He looked right at Doreen as he spoke, and she looked back.

Doreen gave him a smile bigger than the compliment deserved.

"I wasn't sure we should talk to you," Michael Ordway said. "But we are both very curious about all this."

"I appreciate it," Paul said. "It shows you are open-minded people."

Doreen liked the answer. She said, "Can I get you anything? A cup of tea or some coffee?"

"Coffee sounds good," Paul said.

"Where's the loo?" Wish said. Paul kicked him under the table, first for jumping the gun before the pleasantries had been exchanged, second for using the word *loo*.

"Oh. I don't have to go after all," Wish said quickly.

Paul kept himself from rolling his eyes and said, "I hear you're a transplanted Englishman."

"Born in the shadow of the Tower of London," Ordway said.

"But I've been here many years. We took a trip to England for our honeymoon. Ghastly weather. Drizzled the whole time. But, of course, the British Museum made up for it."

Doreen said, "Can you imagine? We spent the entire time looking at mummies and dusty old manuscripts."

"How did you folks end up in the desert, ranching?"

"My father, actually," Ordway said. "He moved the family out of Tahoe not long after Tamara disappeared. He grew up watching cowboy movies back in jolly old, and he finally decided to try it himself. Turned into a fine calf-roper. Rest his soul."

"Been married long?"

"Ten years," Doreen said, pouring him his coffee. She had an enticing low-slung set of knockers under her T-shirt. Paul tried not to look. She noticed him not looking, and casually brushed against him with her hip. "We have four-year-old twins. Annie and Sarah. They've gone to bed. So you're a private detective. Like Sam Spade and Lew Archer. I've never met one of you before. Do you like your work?"

"It beats police work," Paul said. "Do you help Mike with the ranching?"

"Michael. My hands are full with the girls. He runs the ranch."

Paul drank some coffee, asked a few more questions, nudged Wish's big foot under the table again. Wish jumped up.

"It's right through that door, first door on the left," Doreen said. "You know, I want you to tell Ms. Reilly something," she said, turning back to Paul. "About the invasion of privacy case. Jessica called me this morning and told me it's all over. Tell her thanks. It wasn't so much what the film made us look like, it was what was done to Tam. Tam was my friend. That film Terry London made was just sick. We had to do something."

"The film," Ordway said, shaking his head. "She was good. She got us to say things we really regretted later. Like my crack about poor Mrs. Sweet being a boozer. It infuriated me to see myself on the screen with my words taken out of context and twisted into nasty insinuations. We felt like right fools to have agreed to be filmed without some sort of power to veto the finished product. I suppose I should be grateful the Sweets didn't sue us." He had a friendly, open face, long and narrow, carefully shaven. His nails were clean and his thick brown hair recently cut. The very picture of a gentleman farmer, thought Paul.

Doreen said, "Jessica Sweet called me today and told me that Terry knew Tam before she disappeared. Did Terry have something against her? Do you know, Mr. van Wagoner?"

"Call me Paul."

"Okay," she said, smoothing her hair behind her ear with an arm that just brushed a nipple sticking up through her shirt. Wavy blond-streaked brown, her hair made a sexy contrast to her shapely black eyebrows. Paul mentally ripped off the shirt, enjoyed the sight, and dressed her again. She went into the kitchen, moving her hips in a most unwifely manner.

"I'm afraid I can't get into that," Paul said. "So you're saying the girl in the film was nothing like the real girl."

"Well, the film accentuated the negative. Tam was a smart girl, very pretty," Ordway said. "She loved horses, and she wanted to become a vet."

"But she did throw a drink into your face the night she disappeared."

"I deserved it," Ordway said. "I . . . you might say I had been pressing my attentions on her. She really wasn't interested, but I was too self-absorbed to see that. She had rather suddenly stopped seeing Kurt Scott, or so she said. By the way, I saw his picture in the paper, and I recognized him. I'd met him once with her. He was just out of college then, I remember she told me that, and he was a few years older."

"Her father never liked her boyfriends," Doreen called from the kitchen.

"Her father was trying to keep his little girl at home," Ordway said. "She had all these rules to follow. I've always thought she just left. She wanted to see the world. She was bored with school and angry at her parents. It happens all the time. She's probably a typist in Melbourne, and we'll hear from her one of these days."

"Maybe," Paul said. "On the other hand, it's unusual that she would make no attempt to call home in all these years, if she's still alive. Something else I was wondering. Had you ever met Terry before she contacted you about the film?"

"No. We never saw the woman before last year. We talked to her at the studio once, and then she came out to the ranch to film Doreen. We were just high school kids twelve years ago, you see, and she apparently lived at Tahoe, but she was quite a bit older, late twenties back then, I'd say. Anyway, Jessica asked us to cooperate with her and the filming, so when Terry called we said fine, we'll come up and talk to you. She seemed so pleasant at first, but after a while I did start feeling a bit uncomfortable around her," Ordway said.

A crash came from the bathroom. "It's nothing, don't come in," they heard Wish call in a muffled voice.

"Is your, uh, associate ill?" Ordway said.

"No, no, he just drank a quart of Gatorade on the trip down the hill," Paul said.

Ordway cocked an eyebrow, but didn't get up. "What else did you want to know?"

"Tamara made a phone call from the pay phone that night, just before she left. Who would she have been calling?" Paul said.

"The police asked us that too," Doreen said. She had turned off the light in the kitchen, and returned wearing a green frilly apron over her clothes. The curtains were drawn across the main window, and the house felt warm and cozy. Ordway fit his house, but Doreen Ordway didn't. She looked all wrong in that apron, like a scorpion hiding behind a pile of laundry. "It had to be a boy," she was saying. "I mean, who else would she be calling? I suppose she could have picked up with Kurt again, but if it was Kurt, why wouldn't she talk about it with me? We stayed at Manny's for a couple of hours after that, but no one else showed up there."

"The bartender at Manny's said you left a few minutes after she did."

"What did he know?" Ordway said. "I never understood why he lied like that." Wish was taking a long time, and Paul could see Ordway was about to go check on him.

Quickly, he said, "Have the police contacted you regarding Terry London's death?"

"This morning. They came out to the house. They wanted to know where we were on the night Terry was shot. They can't really think we'd hate the film so much we'd shoot her, can they? I told them we were home in bed, where we belong."

"Right," his wife said, nodding her head like a good wife, but nevertheless oozing sexiness out of every pore.

"I'd sure like to get a copy of your statements, when you receive them for signing," Paul said.

"Sure, I'll send them along." Ordway got up, looking toward the hall.

Two identical small girls with glorious blond ringlets, in identical Princess Jasmine nighties, came running in from the hall. "Mommy! Daddy! There's an Indian in our bedroom!"

"Wish must have gotten lost," Paul said.

"I'll just go and see what's up," Ordway said, but then Wish appeared, his head scraping the low ceiling. "Sorry to scare the kids. I got disoriented coming back out."

"In a two-bedroom house?" Ordway asked.

"Yeah, well, just got lost, I guess."

Doreen took the little girls back to bed, giving Wish a wide berth.

"I'm terribly sorry not to be able to invite you to dinner," Ordway said in a final tone. Paul had no choice but to take the hint. He offered his hand again, but Ordway's whole manner had changed, Paul and Wish found themselves outside the warm house and back under the moonlight, Wish saying, "Sorry, man."

On the drive back up into the mountains, Wish said, "You want me to drive?"

"Nobody but me drives my van," Paul said. "Okay. What was all the crashing in the bathroom?"

"Oh. I was trying to weigh myself on the scale, and I lost my balance and grabbed the shower curtain, and the rod fell into the tub. I almost got hurt."

"Fine," Paul said. "Just fine. Anything at all connected to the case?"

"A tin can from the trash for her, and a used shot glass from the sink for him," Wish said, bringing the items, wrapped in a red bandanna, out from somewhere inside his denim jacket.

"Maybe he opened the can, and she tossed back the shot."

"Women don't drink straight Scotch," said Wish firmly, "and men don't open cans of spinach."

"Aren't you forgetting Popeye?" To say nothing of the few dozen serious female drinkers he'd met in a lifetime.

"Who's that?"

"Never mind. They were in the studio last year, so the prints aren't going to help much. Anything else?"

"There was a set of handcuffs and keys in her bottom drawer. Very suspicious. And a little switch, like for a pony," Wish said. "Do you think that means anything for the case?"

And then he reached inside the denim jacket and pulled out the items. The handcuffs fell clanking onto the gear shift between them.

"I took them for Nina," Wish announced. "They could be important." He flicked the toy whip at the dashboard. "What's the matter? Why are you making those funny noises?"

28

"NINA. IT'S GOOD TO SEE YOU," KURT SAID INTO HIS PHONE. HE directed a short smile at her, catching her eyes once, then letting them out of his hold.

He looked worse, very tired, unshaven. Outside the jail, the world was summery and warm, and after seeing Kurt, Nina would stop by her favorite doughnut shop and eat a cinnamon roll. He would return to the permanent twilight where time was inconsequential, and the future held no promise.

She smiled back, and tried to pass on a silent message. She would try to get him out of this. She would try to save him. Sometimes he seemed to hear her. Other times she knew he did not.

She couldn't help reacting to him, the sight and sound of him. She couldn't help remembering his touch and the scent of his skin. When he smiled, she wanted to smile. When he despaired, she felt a wave of the same feeling. A new relationship was growing as they discussed his case and pointedly ignored the currents that passed through the glass between them, each protecting the other. There was no time for love or sex or any feelings at all between them. They bowed to the mutual understanding that there was only time to try to save his life.

"I watched the copies of the arrest video and the Tamara Sweet film and the death video with the transcript you sent over," he said. "The death video was horrible stuff. She was faithful to the end, I see. Saying I pulled the trigger. Talking about the Angel of Death. After everything, I shouldn't be surprised. But I just keep thinking, how could she? How could she lie like that? It's an incredible piece of work, just like she was. Maybe she thought everyone would enjoy watching her death as much as she would have enjoyed it."

"I wasn't going to show you the death video at first. Did you notice anything in the video that might help us?"

"What can I say? If the transcript's right, she lied, or she was out of her head."

"Okay. What did you think of the Tamara Sweet film?" She saw the answer in the way he grimaced and shook his head. "You think Tam's dead."

"Yes, I do."

"Why?"

"I saw it the first time through. At the end. She found some actress to play Tam walking into the woods in the twilight. The resemblance from the back was creepy. She even had Tam's walk. Terry coached her well. Then Terry had the girl walking up the path. Did you see where she goes?"

"Off in the woods somewhere."

"Didn't you recognize the area?"

Nina thought back. "No."

"The girl goes up a wide trail. That's the path that winds around up toward Angora Ridge. I know that trail."

"Okay. So she takes the path up to the ridge."

"She sits down on a rock. It's getting dark and she's looking around. Remember how the camera panned up from her on that flat piece of granite, leaving her behind? I think Terry knew Tam was dead when she made this film. And I think there's something up there . . . something that will tell us where Tam is, maybe even her body. I think Terry intended to reveal something with that scene. It would amuse her to actually film the place Tamara died, if she—if she killed her. Very few people would be able to identify it from the shot."

"Kurt. Talk about wild guesses. You see a rock on a path in twilight, and you think you know the rock?"

"I'm a naturalist. I work . . . worked in a forest. I notice things about nature. I recognized several landmarks. Somebody has to go up there."

"Don't you see, Kurt? All the people who have seen the film, and you're the only one who says he knows where that rock is and wants to go looking around there? What if the girl is up there? Is anybody going to believe you didn't know she was there all along? I'll pass on your thought—after the trial."

"She must have killed that poor kid," Kurt said as if to himself. "Tam never had a life. Tam would have straightened out. Then she—killed my baby. She got me to go to her, and shot me. You were next, Nina. She set out to destroy every human being I cared about." His face twisted into that intent, inward, suffering look she had noticed before.

"She was very sick," Nina said.

"No! She chose it. She didn't fall ill. She made herself that way. I suppose that's why I ran and didn't try to stay and confront her. She had turned into something beyond my . . . She had made me afraid."

"We've all been there, Kurt."

"I'm back there now." His words reminded her of her talk with Collier about Bumpass Hell. Kurt had fallen into it, and he was burning.

"Trust me, Kurt. And gather your courage. Hell is the place where people go when they're afraid."

"Yes. Let me ask you an old question that I've been asking myself. Do you believe in evil, Nina? Not just as a metaphor. As a real thing." Though she was surprised at the turn their conversation had taken, she tried to answer.

"I try not to. I try to think it's only ignorance or anger. I try to translate what I see in my law practice into those two human failings. But every once in a while I meet someone like Terry, who does seem to have literally gone to the devil. All those old folk phrases come back. Possessed by a demon. Sold her soul.

"I've seen people in the middle of divorces become possessed for weeks or months by a vindictiveness I could barely call human. And I've handled criminal appeals for people in which I was happy they were in a penitentiary and not in my office. Lost souls. But I think they are rare, people like that."

"You're in a difficult business," Kurt said, and she felt he really did understand how sometimes it became too much and all she wanted to do was quit and do anything else. "You will meet more of those rare people," he went on. "But here's what I'm trying to say. If you're possessed by evil, against your will, you're not responsible. You're insane. You couldn't help it. Terry loved her demon, allowed herself to be possessed by hate. She wasn't insane."

"You mean, it didn't happen against her will."

"Right. I knew her as well as anyone. I've had years to think about Terry, and that's how I see her. Well, she's dead. You and— You're safe."

Nina didn't respond to that. Kurt wasn't thinking straight. Whoever had killed Terry was still out there, unless Kurt had done it. And she wasn't as sure as he was that Terry had killed Tamara.

Now was a good time to say something she had to say sometime. "You know, if you did shoot Terry, I could make a good case for self-defense. I think we could make people understand what happened," she said.

"Dammit!" Kurt said. He got up and turned his back to her. She was left holding a dead phone. She rapped on the glass, and he finally picked up the only physical link they had.

"I wish you could trust me again, Nina. The worst thing is knowing you don't," Kurt was saying, echoing her thoughts. She didn't answer, because she had nothing to say. She couldn't trust him enough to tell him about Bob. Period. Time to move on.

"How's your arm?" she said.

He rolled up his sleeve to show her the ugly pink crease across his forearm. "All healed up. No permanent damage. How's your chest?"

So he knew. "Guns," Nina said. "I don't like them."

For a moment neither spoke, but they were still communicating. It was this unspoken linkage that had made her sure, twelve years ago, that she loved him. The only way she could keep going and keep up the pretense that nothing was happening was to avoid his eyes. She looked down, bit her lip.

"You are so lovely," Kurt said softly into the phone. "I'm so sorry about everything."

"Forget it," Nina said. "Concentrate on your defense. Back to Terry. Did you ever meet her parents? What do you know about her past?"

"Her past," Kurt repeated, lingering on the words. "She spoke of her parents with the same contempt she had for everyone. I think her father was in banking. They were much older than she was. He retired early. They both died early. Nothing suspicious. They were both dead by the time I met her."

"Where did she go to school?"

"South Lake Tahoe High, and Sacramento State. English major, I think. She took some photography courses, but she didn't really get into film until she took that film course the summer I met you."

Nina wrote it down. Keeping her head down, she said, "There's something else I have to ask you. You know, Kurt, as far as we can tell, she had no relationships with men after you. No boyfriends, or girlfriends, for that matter. Are we missing something? She did have normal sex drives, didn't she?"

"Let me put it this way," Kurt said. "It took me a long time to figure this out. She only made love for a reason. The sex act was a performance, like so many other times when she performed correctly to look normal. I don't know what turned her on, unless maybe it was looking. She told me once she liked to go to these private clubs during college and watch people going at it."

"But what about companionship? She did look for love with you—"

"And look how that turned out," Kurt said. "It doesn't surprise me, what you say about her recent life. She was terribly lonely, but she never could connect. She was perverted. I mean that in a bigger sense than just sexual perversion. She took pride in going beyond the bounds. She always said she was an artist, a genius, and someday everyone would know it."

The guard had opened the door to her cubicle.

"He can take a shower now," he said.

"Time to be going, I guess."

"Nina . . ."

She was putting her papers away.

"They need to get people and dogs up there searching! Can't you understand? I can't leave Tam lost in the woods, if I know how to find her!"

"Do yourself a favor, Kurt. Try not to think about it for now. You were right to tell me your suspicions. Now I'll figure out what to do. That's my job, to figure out how to handle your case. Take care of yourself. Your doctor's appointment is coming up in a few days. I'm worried about you. Please?"

"Yes, sure. Bye, Nina," he said. He sat behind the glass, watching her, until the door closed behind her. That wasn't a good sign.

Other cases claimed her attention for the rest of the week. Paul was working exclusively on the London case. He sent a steady stream of reports, which she read at night, lying on her bed, when she should have been sleeping.

On Friday afternoon Nina appeared in court in her new black suit for a long-postponed divorce trial. Her client, the wife, wanted to keep the family house until the youngest child had turned eighteen. She knew she could never buy another one, and she didn't want to take away the little remaining stability the kids had. The husband wanted to sell the house so that he could rent an apartment and free up some cash to pay the heavy load of bills. They had no savings accounts or assets except their old cars. Nina had talked to her opposing counsel, a young woman lawyer from Sacramento, where the husband now lived, several times, but they had not been able to resolve the issue.

After the testimony had been taken, Milne said, "This is a very hard call. I sometimes think decisions such as these are among the hardest I have to make, where both sides are right and one party is going to have to take on more of the burden than the other. The Court rules that the wife will have possession of the family home for five years, until the youngest child is twelve. At that time, there will be another hearing to determine if the house may be sold. It is the Court's finding that the needs of the children outweigh the advantages to the father of being able to pay joint debts and have additional funds for living expenses."

In the hall, Nina's client hugged her and said, "Five years is enough time. Thank you."

"It's a tough situation for all of you. I wish you luck," Nina said.

"Ms. Reilly?" Barbet Cain, the *Mirror* reporter, called to her as Nina's client went down the hall to her children. "I'd like to talk to you about the Scott case. Are you going to resign from the case due to a conflict of interest?"

"Not at all," Nina said. "There is no conflict of interest. I haven't done anything wrong, and neither has my client."

"Some people are saying that you yourself may have had something to do with the murder of Terry London."

"That's a crock," Nina said. "I'm not getting out of this case. It's that simple."

"What has been the effect on your son of having his father arrested? Does he know about it?"

Nina wanted to say, don't you dare go near him, but instead she said, "He believes, as I do, that Mr. Scott is innocent."

"Don't you agree that it's unusual for a lawyer to take a murder case in which she's so closely involved with both the defendant and the victim?"

"That's how it worked out. It won't hamper my performance."

"Well, I have to say I'm surprised. I thought I wouldn't get anything but 'no comment' out of you. Thanks," the reporter said.

"No sense trying to hide behind a wall made of paper," Nina said. "I'm beginning to see that. But do me a favor. Next time, call me during my office hours when you want a comment."

The reporter nodded. "Sorry."

Nina went outside and drank water from a drinking fountain attached to the courthouse, then organized her files on a concrete bench nearby. In the early afternoon, few people remained to lounge around the grounds. Most court work occurred during the morning hours. Yellow pollen drifted through the air and the June sun beat warmly down.

Her mind drifted, as it had several times over the past few days, to Kurt's idea that the dirt trail that led to Angora Ridge held the final ending to Tamara's story. Her lawyerly side said, do nothing, try to keep the whole idea under wraps. But a story begun and not finished nagged at her. The best endings offered justice, sometimes interpreted in a new way, didn't they? Could finding Tamara possibly help Kurt?

While she thought it over again, Collier Hallowell sat down beside her. She took in his expression and the brows that were knit so tightly they made a 3D star between his eyes.

"Uh-oh," she said. "You've got bad news for me, don't you?"

"Your murder client just knocked out a deputy, kicked out the window of the police van taking him to the doctor, unlocked his handcuffs with the deputy's key, and never looked back. Where is he, Nina?"

Silent alarms shrieked in her head.

"How long ago?" She moved away from him. This was no friendly interaction.

"About an hour. The van stopped for the traffic light on Al Tahoe at the corner of Highway 50. We're searching the area, but he may have hitchhiked. Or an accomplice picked him up."

"I was in court. I don't know anything about it. He's not violent, Collier. Please don't go looking for him with guns out."

"I don't believe you," Collier said. "You know where he's headed. If you don't tell me right now, that makes you an accessory. Talk to me. Don't make me arrest you."

She pushed her files into the briefcase, thinking fast.

"You're in love with him," Collier said, a slight vulnerability sneaking into his voice, sounding a little more forlorn than a prosecutor out to track down a killer ought to sound.

She didn't have an answer ready.

"Are you helping him escape because of your son? Help me now, and I'll try to help you."

"No! I had no idea he was planning this."

"You set up the doctor's appointment," Collier said. "You told Milne he needed to be seen. Either you helped him deliberately, or he used you."

"Unless you're going to arrest me, I'm going now."

"I should," he said. "For your own good."

"Haven't you noticed yet, I get to decide what's good for me?" She picked up her papers and turned her back on him, heading for the parking lot.

"Nina!" he called sternly after her.

She ignored him. Her power walk to the Bronco took forever. She hustled the car into gear and took off before he had time to develop further plans for her.

Driving home, she looked back now and then to see if she was being followed. She found Bob in the backyard with Andrea, clipping dead heads off the white-flowered marguerite bush. Taking Andrea aside, she said, "Kurt's escaped."

Andrea gasped and looked over at Bob, who clipped energetically away, felling a low branch full of dead leaves. "Timber!" he called out.

"What do you want me to do?"

"If he comes here, he might see Bob. They look so much alike—Kurt would know. I'm not ready for this."

"Does he know where we live?"

"He knows Matt's name, and Matt's listed in the phone book. Andrea, the police will be after him with guns. You've got to get out of here."

Andrea said, "Here's what we'll do. I'll call Matt and then the shelter. I'll take the kids over there and spend the night there with them. It'll be safer than staying here."

"Perfect. Thank you, Andrea. I'll make it up to you."

"Let's go pack some bags," Andrea said. "So now the director of the shelter for battered women is taking shelter there. My clients might find that pretty funny."

"I don't. C'mon. Let's get busy," Nina said.

Fifteen minutes later Andrea left with the kids. Nina got on the phone to Sandy. "I need Paul," she said.

"He's working with Wish. They check in at five."

"Doesn't he have a cellular phone?"

"Won't use one. Says they cause brain tumors and absorb the last remaining solitude on earth. What are you going to do about Kurt? Do you know where he is?"

"I have an idea," Nina said. "Tell Paul, when he calls, to drive up to Fallen Leaf Lake and take the road around the south side of the lake. When he gets to where the cabins are, tell him to locate the dirt trail up to Angora Ridge. Tell him I've gone there."

"Kurt's up there?"

"I sincerely hope not," Nina said. "Just tell Paul to find me there."

"Wait for Paul," Sandy said.

"Kurt's my client," Nina said. "He's not dangerous, and I can bring him back with me safely if I can get to him. But I have to hurry." She hung up, ran into her bedroom, and undressed quickly, pulling on jeans, a T-shirt, and hiking boots. Surprising herself with the impulse, she threw a shovel into the trunk of the Bronco before taking off.

29

"She's where?" paul said to sandy over the phone.

"No need to holler." Sandy gave him the directions. "Take Wish," she said.

"Why didn't you stop her?"

"She ran over me like a V10 pickup," Sandy said.

Benignly neglected to discourage the weekend tourist, the green-fringed road around Fallen Leaf Lake narrowed to one lane soon after the turnoff from the highway. As she bumped over the potholes, Nina wondered how Kurt could have gotten to this area, which was several miles from the main road.

How could she second-guess him? Had she in her wildest dreams thought he would initiate something that would compromise them both so utterly?

If she had any luck at all, at this very moment he sat high in the cab of a semi, a hard-driving trucker at the wheel, heading east on Highway 50, across Nevada toward Utah. A runner from way back,

Kurt would run straight out of her and Bobby's life, and they could go back to the old life without him.

No. They would never be the same.

And she knew him well enough to know how he thought, and where he would go first. He would probably need some tools.

Rounding a bend in the road beyond the country store, she spotted the metallic roof of the cabin in dense woods up an overgrown dirt road.

The Bronco kicked up a storm of dirt as she pulled over into a wide area and parked. The trail to Angora Ridge was nearby. By standing in an open field off the road, she could just see the tip of the fire-tracking station that sat near the top of the trail. She could follow parts of the ridge trail, straining with her eyes.

She saw no movement up there.

Wind through trees. An airplane far off. Quiet. Many of these lonely cabins were unoccupied except on weekends.

Climbing onto the sagging porch, she tried the knob. Something broke and she pushed the door open. Inside, undisturbed dust on the floor told her right away the place was empty.

"Kurt," she whispered. She felt his presence. Fallen Leaf Lake, the cabin with the stone fireplace . . .

Memory mixed with fear. She remembered him as he had been, so beautiful in his youth and strength, his kisses, his hands. . . . She didn't know. She just didn't know. Was she running after him to bring him back? Or was it the promise of him free again, without the glass wall to keep them apart?

Out back, the toolshed had been recently disturbed. The rusting lock had been knocked open.

Brushing aside cobwebs, she examined the assortment of old tools that lay scattered on the floor. A rake. A plastic snow scoop. A hoe hanging loose on its screw. A trowel without a handle. And a relatively clean spot on the floor suggesting that he had found the tool he needed.

She did her best to replace the lock on the shed, and hefted the shovel she'd brought from home in her right hand, walking the few hundred yards to the trailhead that led up to Angora Ridge.

The sun glanced through the pines. The air filled with peeps and flutters, as unseen birds, small ground animals, and insects burrowed and buzzed their way through the forest. Ahead of her in the path, she saw several kinds of shoe prints, and the prints of a dog far apart. She could picture the dog off his leash bounding ahead of its slow-poke two-legged owner. She stopped. From far away, down in the more settled area near the lake below, she heard a whistle.

Unaccustomed to such a steep climb, she felt her knees begin to quiver about a quarter of a mile up. Soon she saw areas of brush flattened regularly, every fifty feet or so, and small dirt piles. "Kurt?" she called, but there was no reply. She rested her knees and continued.

The trail became rockier. She came to a place of granite boulders, the kind of place she usually stayed away from because bears liked the caves they made. Kurt had called it "beartown." . . . The memory was so sharp she could see it descend like a transparent veil over the present, turning the scene before her into one layered with the emotion of the past.

She heard a shovel clang against rock.

"Kurt!"

Nothing.

"Kurt! It's me. I'm alone."

Shuffling feet. Kurt came around the corner, holding a shovel.

He dropped it, throwing off some gloves, and held his arms out to her. She saw again the livid scar from the bullet that had nicked him.

She went. Their bodies met. They held on, Nina holding her arms around his neck and her head pressed against his chest, feeling his heart beat, and smelling dust and sweat. He stroked her hair.

"Kurt," she said. And "Kurt," again.

"Don't let go," he said.

"No."

"I love you."

She didn't answer. Like ivy vines that had rooted and tangled together, they supported each other. Then he put his arms around her and squeezed her, lifting her from the ground, swaying her back and forth, back and forth.

After a long time, he set her down carefully, saying, "Now I have everything I want. I've held you. But . . ."

"You've found something, haven't you?"

"Yes."

"Show me."

He led her across a grassy space behind the flat boulder Nina could now recognize from Terry's film. A small black opening about eighteen inches high and two feet wide formed where the boulder met other, smaller rocks. He replaced the gloves he had taken off.

He reached in. "Don't be afraid," he said. He pulled out a long bone.

Leg bones, bones of a big animal. And . . . shreds of faded cloth, tattered, musty, begrimed. More bones, many more.

A skull, blond hair still clinging to it in tufts and patches.

Tamara?

His body half propped against rock, half falling toward the dark hole he had exposed, Kurt dug with increasing frenzy, as if afraid a bit of Tamara might remain forever lost in the cave. He continued a heap he had already begun in the dry ditch, made of dirt, rock, pieces of a girl, determined to complete what he had started, intent on his task, as if he'd forgotten that her eyes were taking in the macabre scene.

The shock of seeing the bones restored Nina to herself. "Kurt, stop!" she said. "The medical examiner has to see this intact. Don't disturb the scene any more!"

"I can't leave her like this," Kurt said.

"Sit down here with me for a minute. Please let me talk to you."

He looked irresolutely at the bones, then seemed to fall down beside her. She realized he was exhausted, near collapse.

"How did you get here?"

"I got a ride to the lake road," he said. "And then I ran. Do the police know I'm here?"

"No. I wish I didn't. And I wish you hadn't touched anything."

"Poor Tam. She never deserved this kind of ending. I didn't plan to dig her up all the way. Just . . . once I saw her, I couldn't leave her like this."

"We don't know it's her yet, do we? I mean, until there's some record checking."

"Are you kidding? I bought her the damn belt."

For the first time, Nina saw a silver buckle, shaped like an eagle's head, that he clutched in one gloved hand. He took the gloves off again, laying them beside his shovel, and set the buckle on a flat part of the rock.

"I don't think I'm going to make it," he said. "I'm cracking up. Those are her bones, Nina."

"You did what you set out to do. We have to go back now."

"Better if they shoot me and get it over with. Better for you too. Let me rest for another minute with you." They rested against each other. She felt disoriented by all the pieces of herself that wanted to come forward, mother, lawyer, lover, abandoned one.

"We'll get you back. Quickly. Salvage the situation," she whispered.

"I'm not going back. Please try to understand. I can't."

"Then you'll stay afraid for the rest of your life. In hell."

"Better than a stinking prison!"

"Just don't throw away all hope. Please—I have to tell you something—" She realized he was going to leave, and instinctively pulled his head toward her. He began to kiss her, her cheeks and nose and forehead, her wet eyes. His lips on her mouth were warm and soft, pressing harder as she let her body relax against him. She opened her eyes and looked into his. Time fell away. They were kissing at Fallen Leaf Lake, and they would be married soon. . . .

"I have to go now," he said, drawing his head away. In a moment he would stand up and take the first step that would lead him forever out of her life. . . .

Paul sprang from the bushes and pushed Kurt off her. For a moment Nina just sat there, unable to take it in.

They rolled into the side of a boulder and Kurt's head hit it with a crack, but he managed to push Paul away. Before he could stagger up, Paul had grabbed his legs and brought him down again. His expression was distorted with anger.

"Stop it! Stop it! Stop it!" Nina shouted. Kurt forced Paul's head into a crevice between two rocks and she heard herself screaming, and saw for the first time that Wish stood behind the pile of bones waving Paul's revolver and yelling at them to cut it out.

Kurt raised a rock above Paul's pinned body and Nina shouted, "No!" and he heard her, turning to look at her, startled. Paul rolled away and jumped up.

This time Kurt had no chance. Paul moved toward him, light on his feet, and they grappled again. Paul wrestled him down and smashed him in the face.

Wish seemed paralyzed, the gun dangling from his hand. A trickle of blood ran down Kurt's face.

Nina picked up a good-size rock, jumped on Paul's broad back as he drew his arm back to pummel him some more, and hit him on the back of the head. He let out a grunt, toppled over, and lay on his back, his eyes closed.

"Did you kill him?" Wish said, running up. Kurt sat up slowly, unbuttoned his torn shirt and held it to his face.

"Shit," Paul said weakly from the ground. "It feels like she did." He tried to raise his head and Nina helped him sit up.

"What are all these bones?" Wish asked.

She moved toward them, but Paul said, "Stay away from him," never taking his eyes off Kurt.

"We'll talk later," Nina said. "Did you come in the van? Help me get these two down there." Paul groaned. "We're going to Boulder Hospital. Wish, help Kurt up. Give me the gun—you're going to shoot someone by accident. Come on, help him up! Go on in front with him, and I'll help Paul."

They would take him back now. He had almost escaped, and they had prevented it, reshaped his future. The responsibility was staggering. Should she have followed him here? Had she just condemned him?

Kurt leaned on Wish as he limped back down the trail. He didn't look at Nina, and he didn't try to take off into the forest. If he had, she might have let him go. She would never know. He went quietly, wiping his face on his shirt.

30

"You almost broke Kurt's nose," Nina said, settling herself beside Paul's hospital bed the next afternoon. Paul looked fine except for the bandage in the back of his head, which he was showing her now.

"You almost bashed my brains in," Paul said. "But you missed. I'll be released this afternoon."

"There are brains in there?" Nina said. "I hadn't noticed."

Paul saw the expression on her face, and adopted a less jaunty tone. "Look at it from my point of view. He escaped from jail. Flight tends to make people think you're guilty. The police were after him. Fugitives, and the people they're with, tend to get shot. He put you in danger. You didn't wait for me. I saw him grabbing you, and—"

"You didn't have to jump him. You had your gun. You wanted to beat him up. You were angry, so you taught him a lesson. He's your employer. What's the matter with you?"

"If it comes to that, you're my employer. Has he started paying any of the bills yet?"

"I don't want you hovering over me, jumping my clients, acting like a gorilla! I hired you to investigate the case!"

"Come on, Nina! I love you! I'm trying to take care of you!"

"Love," Nina said. "You jerk. You're both jerks." She reached out and smoothed his forehead.

"You have this . . . bad habit . . . of being the eye of the cyclone," Paul said, wincing in pain as he tried to get up on his elbow.

"What do you want? Shall I call the nurse?"

"I want you to bend down here and kiss me and say 'my hero.' Please." His eyes fastened on hers with a little-boy expression that was laughably incongruent with his big hairy male body. She bent down to give him a chaste peck on the cheek, but he turned his head fast and his lips found hers, startling, warm, and full of wanting.

"Mmm," he said. "Cavewoman hit man on head, take him into lair, do nasty things to him."

"Shut up, Paul. You really are a caveman. You go too far."

"Okay, okay. I'm sorry I got carried away. Maybe I should have let him run," Paul said. "That's one way to finish up a case, except that you'd probably be in jail as an accessory to his escape."

"I wish I'd never gone up there. I didn't have time to think it through."

"Not to change the subject, but what now? Am I fired?"

"I need you even more now. But I suppose you're going to quit if you don't get fired."

"I'll stick around if you want me to, now that he's back where he belongs, until all this gets sorted out. Someone has to watch out for you, and I'm the best. What does he say?"

"He's leaving it up to me."

"He asked for it," Paul said. Nina thought to herself, they don't have to like each other. She needed Paul. Kurt needed Paul. She didn't push it.

She said, "He's in bad shape psychologically, Paul. He's in maximum security now down in Placerville. It's as if he had to find Tamara, to see if his worst fear would be realized. And it was. He doesn't seem to care what happens to him anymore. I'm very worried about him."

"I told you before, and I'll say it again," Paul said. "You're much too close to this case. Don't tie your emotional well-being to this joker."

"I'm trying to stay cool. I have to."

"Are they going to charge Scott with Tamara Sweet's murder?"

"Well, I called the D.A.'s office this morning and talked to Collier Hallowell. It's too early to say, but I don't think Hallowell has enough evidence to charge him at this point. It's a twelve-year-old murder. I talked to him this morning. If I guess right, he's not going to seek an indictment and file formal charges against Kurt for Tamara Sweet's murder."

"That's good, right? So why do you look so gloomy?" Paul said.

"Because I think he's going to pull a legal maneuver that's much smarter. He's going to get the evidence in that implicates Kurt in Tamara's murder indirectly."

"I thought you couldn't do that. I mean, show the guy might have murdered somebody before, so he's a bad guy who probably did the current murder."

"That's generally true. You can't bring in evidence of a prior crime to show bad character or a predisposition to commit another crime. But that general rule is riddled with exceptions. One of the exceptions is that you can bring in evidence of a previous crime to show the motive for a subsequent crime."

"So?"

"The prosecution theory now seems to be that Kurt killed Tamara. Terry made a film that delved too deeply, and he killed her to stop the film from being released. So Tamara's murder would be the motive for Terry's murder."

"But the film doesn't nail Scott as the killer!"

"It's probably suggestive enough, with the talk about the mystery boyfriend, to get the Tamara Sweet evidence in. By the way, Hallowell says Doc Clauson, the medical examiner, did a quick autopsy. He says the remains are consistent with death occurring years ago, though he can't date the time of death precisely. He says Tamara was shot twice in the pelvis right there, near the rock. They even found a .30-06 rifle casing."

"Don't tell me," Paul said. "Remington?"

"Yes. Which could point to Terry as well as Kurt. The problem is, I can't let Collier talk to Kurt. He has to be thinking that only the killer could have marched up there and dug up the remains. Anyway, he'd never believe Kurt went up there to the ridge just because a rock in the film looked similar."

"Do you believe it?"

"I watched the film again last night. It did look like the same turn in the trail, the same square white rock. I couldn't have made the connection, but Kurt—a forest to him is like a city. The rock was like a traffic light at the corner of a road."

"Which would bring us back to Terry London," Paul said. "And nobody knows where she was the night Tamara Sweet died. I've checked. She wasn't even questioned. She only knew Tamara because it's a small town if you're a local, and they both liked to go to poetry readings and that artsy-fartsy stuff. They didn't go around together, and no one would think she would know anything."

"Of course, we know from Kurt that Terry made her move on him not long after Tamara disappeared. The police are at a disadvantage. Twelve years have gone by, and the only one of the three of them still alive isn't talking to them."

"The good old Fifth Amendment," Paul said. "The defendant zips his mouth, and nobody can hold it against him."

"Don't be knocking the Constitution," Nina said. "The good old Fifth Amendment is an important protection against the state."

"And sometimes the guilty go free."

"You still think like a cop, Paul."

"Yes. That's why I'm so good as a defense investigator," Paul said. "Speaking of being good, my old friends the cops arrived this morning to take a statement about the events of yesterday. I carefully explained how you had this wild idea about where he might be and didn't want to bother them with it, and how you just happened to be in the neighborhood and took a look-see, and how you were trying everything in your power to persuade Kurt to come back in, and how you left a message for me to come armed, just in case, et cetera et cetera. You're off the hook. I even gave Kurt a break, said I didn't realize he'd agreed to turn himself in. I taped the statement. It's right here under the covers."

"Thanks," Nina said absently.

"Aren't you going to reach under the covers and find it?" Paul said in a silky voice, pulling the covers down to his waist.

"Give me the doggone tape. I have to go."

"Well. There will be plenty of time to explore under the covers later."

"Paul."

He gave her the tape. "Don't fret so much. If Scott is innocent, we'll find a way to raise the ol' reasonable doubt. Justice tends to be done."

"I've heard that unwritten rule. I'm . . . uh, sorry I hit you, Paul."

"I forgive you. I'm sorry I beat up on your boyfriend."

"I don't appreciate that statement."

"You were kissing him back."

She had no answer for that one. Paul's tone was joking, but he was hurt, and he was letting her know it.

Paul pushed up on his arm to watch her go. She had already stepped toward the open door when a uniformed cop blocked her way, papers in his hand, saying, "Excuse me, ma'am! Excuse me!" So she waited irritably, thinking, like Dorothy Parker, what fresh hell is this? He brandished a paper, and when she didn't take it immediately, pushed it into her unwilling hand. "You've been served, ma'am," he said swiftly. "Contact Collier Hallowell if you have any questions. Witness in the Scott trial."

Paul laughed at the look on her face. The cop smiled too, passing Nina and walking up to his bedside. "Mr. van Wagoner, I presume," he said, offering a second page, which Paul, still laughing, took.

"Hey!" said Paul.

"You folks have a delightful day," said the officer.

After leaving the hospital, Nina drove Bob and his cousins down to the beach at Ski Run Boulevard, where Matt ran his parasailing business during the summer months.

Daylight savings meant no sunset until eight. Four tourists from Japan were receiving instructions from him on how to wear the harness hooked to the parachute and a long boat line. One by one, they ran down the beach while Matt took off in the boat, to be borne aloft, several hundred feet above Lake Tahoe, flying into the orange sunset.

While Matt huddled with his tourists, Nina waded out into the cold, calm water and had her first swim of the summer, gliding through ripples of pink and orange light until she was tired, then rolling onto her back and looking back at the beach. She was the only swimmer. From this far out, the people on the beach became silhouettes. A trick of the sunset erased the line between lake and sky, so she seemed to be floating in air. For a few minutes she forgot her worries and rested quietly in the arms of the water.

Then the sun slipped below the mountains, and the lake turned indigo. She swam quickly back, wrapped up in a thick towel, and stretched out on the sandy blanket. She and the kids ate their sandwiches, enjoying the warm summery evening. Bob seemed back to normal, and she hoped he was over the latest troubling news.

Relaxed, she watched Matt check the harness of the only young woman in the group, then get into the boat. The boat moved out into the lake, and the woman half-ran, half-dragged toward the water, hanging on to the harness with all her might. With a whoosh, the parachute lifted behind her. Just at the edge of the water her feet left the ground as if by magic, and the tricolored chute rose gracefully into the air, the legs of the little figure underneath still chugging energetically. Matt looked back as he steered the boat to make sure she was all right.

Good old younger brother, Nina thought, remembering how he had taken her in the year before and given Bob a father figure and both of them a home. He had done a lot with a little. Matt had never made it to college and never had a cent handed to him. He made his way by combining an inventive mind with hard work. His fierce love for his wife and children had put an end to the aimlessness and negativity that afflicted him in his early twenties, before he moved to Tahoe.

They watched the boat with its flyer tethered overhead, the parachute high enough to again pick up bright rays from the invisible sun. Then the boat turned and came back toward shore. Slowly, slowly, as Matt carefully slowed the motor, the parasailor fell from the sky into the sea, and Matt pulled her into the boat and brought her back. He started folding the parachutes in the deepening twilight, and Nina gathered up the kids' stuff and helped them pack up the trash. Her rest was over. She was on duty. Matt would finish up and pick

Andrea up at the shelter. He and Andrea had planned a late dinner out together.

Later, wandering around the warm house in her old silk robe, she closed the windows and curtains, locking up tight. Her uneasiness was returning little by little. She had the feeling of something prowling outside, though when she looked out she saw only the stars and the black outlines of trees.

When everything was as physically secure as she could make it, she walked down the hall toward the kids' bedrooms. Checking on the boys, she saw in the orange illumination of the Flintstone night-light that Bob was still awake, talking softly to his seal. Troy snoozed in the other bed.

"Night, honey," she said, about to close the door.

"Mom? I got a problem," he whispered. "It's about your case."

She started to tell him to go to sleep. It was late, she had too much on her mind already. . . .

"Could we talk about my father?"

So gently he asked. . . . "Okay," she said.

"When can I see him?"

Nina said slowly, "Not right now. Maybe after the trial. We'll see."

"Are you afraid of him?"

"No."

Troy turned over and kicked his sheets off, smacking his lips in his sleep.

"That's good. Are we gonna win?"

"I don't know, honey."

"I don't understand about that Terry lady. How did she get killed, Mom?"

Letting him lead, she answered his questions. As she told him about the neighbor saying he saw Kurt the night Terry was shot, Bob interrupted, "She came to the school, Mom. The week before that. She had this big black dog. I think she came especially to talk to me, and she asked a bunch of questions about when I went looking for my father."

"She did? You talked to her at school? You're not supposed to talk to—"

"But she wasn't a stranger! I met her at your office, and she said she was your friend." Before Nina could launch into a battery of questions about this event, Bob reached his hand up and put it over her mouth. He had never done anything like that before. The motion had its intended effect—she was speechless.

"Wait, Mom. I have to know exactly what night she was . . . you know . . ." He took his hand away to let her answer, his expression tormented.

"It was on March thirtieth. Not long after Paul found you and I brought you back from Carmel."

Bobby wailed, "Oh, no."

"What? What is it, Bobby?"

"The phone rang that night after dinner, remember? I answered it and told you it was nobody."

"She called the house?" She could not keep a little of the alarm she felt out of her voice. "Why didn't you tell me?"

"She called about my father. That's one of the things I couldn't talk to you about. I felt like I was on my own."

His voice was thin, as though he was about to start crying. Nina said, "Shhh, it's all right. Go ahead and tell me, honey. I promise I won't be mad."

"She said, 'Bobby?' and she was really happy it was me and not somebody else, and she said"—he clutched at her now, as if he realized what he'd done in not telling her earlier, stammering in his haste—"she said, 'Your father's here visiting me, and he wants so much to meet you'. . . ."

"What did you do?"

"I snuck out and went there on my bike after everyone was in bed, like before. I had to, Mom! My father!"

"It's all right, I'm listening. . . ."

"I got to her house on Coyote. The light was on in the little building down the trail and the gate was open. I put my bike down and I was just about to go in, when I felt this hand on my shoulder! If I had been on my bike I would've fallen off! It was Uncle Matt, Mom. He took the bike and took my hand. He didn't even yell, he was so mad. Then we went around the corner and down the block to his truck and he made me get in there. He locked it up and told me if I got out, he'd beat my butt!

"Then he left for a few minutes. He wasn't gone very long. Then he unlocked the driver door on the truck and we took off fast and came home."

"So you never went through the gate? Look at me! You never went through the gate?"

"No, trust me, Mom, I didn't get that far."

Oh, thank you, thank you, Matt, you saved my silly boy from I don't know what—

But why hadn't Matt told her? And what had he been doing there?

"Uncle Matt brought my bike back. We talked about how stupid I was. He said that woman was a liar and she might have hurt me. My father wasn't there at all. Is that true, Mom?"

She took him by the shoulders and shook him. "Why didn't you tell me! Why!"

"I wanted to, but Uncle Matt said he wanted to tell you! Ow, you're hurting me!" She let go and he fell back on the bed.

It took her a minute to find herself again. In the steadiest tone she could muster, she said, "Listen, Bob. I'm glad you told me all this. I wish you had told me earlier. I'm going to talk to Uncle Matt when he gets home, and we'll get this all straightened out."

"Go ahead, ground me again. I deserve it," Bob said. She released him and stood up. Tears glistened in his eyes. He rubbed the squeaky seal against his cheek as if it were a soft hand.

He was just a child, with a stuffed toy.

"We'll straighten this out," she repeated. "Don't worry, honey."

He pulled up his blanket, comforted, and she checked the window one more time before she left the room, her heart pounding.

31

WHEN MATT AND ANDREA CAME HOME, NINA'S FILES COVERED THE kitchen table. They breezed in on a drift of cold night air, arm in arm, full of thanks, Andrea laughing, Matt tilting slightly to one side as she leaned her full weight on him.

Matt took one look at Nina and said, "Go on to bed, Andrea, okay?"

"How about a nightcap?" she said teasingly, sneaking an arm around him, trying to tickle his waist. "Not that we need one more thing."

He extricated himself from her, saying, "I'll be up in a bit."

She looked from Matt to Nina and back. "What's up?" she asked.

"Nina and I need to talk."

"Can't I listen?"

Nina said, "Why not? No more secrets, right, Matt?"

"Why don't we sit on the porch? It's stuffy in here," Matt said.

"Let's talk here. I'm not going outside," Nina said.

"Goblins? The Jabberwock?"

"I'm staying right here. And now, the truth, little brother. I talked to Bobby."

"That's obvious," Matt said. "I think I'll have that nightcap." He went to the cabinet above the stove and came out with a shot glass full of whiskey, which he downed in one gulp.

"It must be bad," Andrea said. "The last time I saw you do that, you thought one of your parasailing clients had passed out before landing." She pulled out a chair and sat down.

"I meant to tell you right away, Nina, but you were in such a goddamn hurry. You took the case before I could explain," Matt said, standing at the cabinet.

"You don't like to talk about bad things, Matt. Remember when Mom and Dad separated? None of us talked at all. We pretended everything was normal, when really it was awful. That's when you got into drugs for a while, remember?"

"And you started sleeping with everything that moved," Matt said. He went back to the cabinet again, this time returning with the bottle. He wore plaid shorts and a white hooded sweatshirt, his tan thin face fine of feature, with Harlan's shock of hair and their mother's blue eyes.

"Nina, sweetie, you look like you've lost your best friend," Andrea said.

"You've got a lot of nerve, acting like I'm the problem around here," Matt said. He put the bottle on the table, sat down again, and crossed his legs. Nina knew his expression. Defiant. She thought about a time when their parents had decided to give their dog away, and Matt had run down the block with the dog and hid in Mrs. Fielding's garage. He had been eleven, and she had been thirteen. She had known where to find the runaways. His expression had been the same. She'd told him to come home, and he'd said he'd rather run to Albuquerque.

"Tell me what happened that night, Matt. I need to know."

"Yeah. You do." He began to talk, hesitatingly at first.

Bobby had told Matt about Terry the day she came to the school. He told him about the dog, and everything that was said, and Matt decided to handle it, not to go crying to Nina, but to protect her from needless worry because the situation seemed harmless enough.

He had also scolded Bob and warned him to stay away from Terry. And he had started watching out for him.

A few days after the incident at the school, Matt overheard Bob on the telephone. "I guess we've learned Bob doesn't let bedtime stop him," he said. "So I was still watching that night. And damn if the little sucker didn't hop out of bed and slip out the kitchen door. He jumped on his bike and took off. I was astounded, but I pulled my pants on and went out to the truck and followed him with the lights off."

"Nothing he does could astound me anymore," Andrea said. "I believe I'll have a drink myself." She poured a shot into the glass Matt had set on the table and drank it down. "Okay, I'm fortified," she said.

"Go ahead, Matt," Nina said.

His first instinct had been to stop Bob before he hit the porch, but then he decided to find out the tale in its entirety, so as Bob rode down the hill in the full moonlight, Matt followed a long way behind, following Pioneer Trail toward Meyers for several miles.

"Bobby loves maps," Nina said. "He probably knows more than we do about getting around Tahoe at this point."

"He turned off on Coyote and walked his bike up the hill. I went on around the corner and down the street. I parked and ran around to see what he was doing. I almost didn't catch him. He'd parked his bike in the trees, like he didn't want anyone to see he was there. He opened the gate and a dog came running out, but it didn't give him any trouble. Then he started up the path toward this little detached building I could see past the gate. I moved up fast on him and I grabbed him.

"I marched him and the bike back to my truck. I put him in there and I said to him, 'It's all over, whatever you thought you were doing. You stay right here. I'll be right back.' I locked him in the car. He wasn't moving. He knew how much trouble he was in. I was boiling mad. I went back to check it out."

"Oh, really?" Nina said, and Matt gave her a puzzled look.

"What, do you think I'm lying?"

"You parked Bob safe and sound in the truck?"

"Yes! That's what I'm telling you! Do you want to hear this, or not?"

"Don't let me stop you," Nina said.

"But you didn't go in the gate. You got in the truck and went home," Andrea suggested.

"I wish to God I had," Matt said. "I went up to the studio, but she had dark curtains or something on the windows, too thick for me to see anything. I went around back through the trees and saw a back door. I didn't know who she was at the time, but I knew the black dog, so I knew she was the woman who had been talking to Bobby at the school grounds. Some watchdog. He wanted to lick me into submission.

"I didn't understand, Nina. A woman letting a kid play with her dog—what's the harm? But I couldn't imagine what story she had concocted to lure him to that place in the woods, or what she wanted with him. I was getting more pissed off by the second. I decided to tell her to lay off my nephew.

"I tried the knob on the back door, and it was open, so I went in."

Andrea, who finally realized the direction this story was heading, shook her head. "Stop, Matt. Stop right now! This is going too far! They'll make you testify against Scott." When Matt said nothing, just shook his head, she turned to Nina. "Nina, don't do this to him. Don't make him send Bob's dad away!"

Nina said, "Let's hear his story." She put her elbows on the kitchen table and cupped her chin in the palm of her hand. Matt was pouring himself another shot. His face was flushed.

"The porch light in front was on, but inside, all the lights were out," he said. "She was burning incense. I could hear noises, like electronic equipment operating, and I could see a bank of red lights on the right. Then I heard her voice out of the gloom, harsh, saying, 'Who the hell are you?'

"And I said, 'Turn on some lights, I want to talk to you. I'm Bob's uncle.'

" 'The hell you are,' " she said, and she didn't seem to move to turn on the light. I felt as though she could see me but I couldn't see her, her eyes were used to the light, and I felt menaced, you know, Nina?"

"Go on," Nina said. "Finish your story."

"Bob was safe in the car," Matt said. "I decided to get the hell out of there. But she said, 'What do you want to talk about?' So I said, 'I want you to leave Bob alone. Stay away from him, or I'll see to you personally.'

"And she said, very coolly, 'He's outside, isn't he? He's here to see his father. You can't stop him.'

"So I asked her why. She said, 'Because I'm staging a little family reunion here today. His father will be here any minute to join in the fun. Is Bobby outside? Move slowly, now. Let's go get him.' She came toward me, and that's when I saw she had a rifle trained on me.

"It's funny, I didn't even feel scared. I was still feeling I could get out of there, that she'd get over whatever was bugging her and let me go. She motioned for me to go out front. And then I saw her eyes. I have never seen a look like that in any woman's eyes, Nina, drunk or sober. She had murder in there. Uncontrolled, rampant, out-of-her-mind blind bloodlust."

Andrea, silent, pale, and shocked, listened intently to Matt's voice, staring at Nina.

"I turned and started to move back toward the back door instead, but I heard a click, like she'd released the safety on the rifle. She said, 'C'mon. Let's get him.' But then there was a knock on the front door. I felt her behind me, and the rifle poking in my back. Right at that moment, I think she wanted to shoot me, but she was afraid she would be heard by whoever was outside. She pushed me into a storage closet on one side of the room, near the back door, and closed the closet door very softly. I heard her jingling some keys and fiddling with the lock, and another knock came on the door. She got it locked and said, 'One word, and I kill you both.'

"What the hell could I do? I checked the closet, but the only way out was through the door. I got my Swiss Army knife out and started picking the lock, listening. She was talking to a man, someone I didn't know then. But I knew this had to be the guy she called Bob's father."

He stopped. Nina nudged him with her hand. "Come on," she said. "Finish."

"They had this . . . surreal conversation. She said she needed to tell him a few things, and then she would introduce him to his son. She wanted to give it all 'the proper context.'

"She started ranting about a baby, saying everything was his fault.

He had lied to her and made her have this baby and he had never loved her. He kept trying to interrupt her, saying things like, so it was all just a story, he didn't have another child, that she was a cruel bitch and he'd had enough of her and she'd better stay away from you and him. I was pretty shocked to hear your name come up in this nasty argument, Nina."

Andrea said mournfully, "Oh, Matt."

"She was losing it, and he started trying to calm her down. 'I'm going now,' he said to her. Her voice changed then, like she knew he meant it. She said, 'I don't think so,' and there was this horrible silence for a minute. I thought he was a goner. I huddled in my closet, cringing like a kitten while I worked on the lock."

"What else could you do, Matt?" Andrea said. She took his hand.

"He said, 'This is the end for us, Terry. But if you do anything, anything at all to hurt Nina Reilly, you can see me one last time when I come back to kill you.'

"I was going to bust out and make a run for the back door as soon as she blew him away. That was my entire plan. I couldn't get heroic. She'd go get Bob.

"That's when I heard the shot. The front door banged. She was screaming."

"He came back," said Andrea. "He came back and shot her."

"I thought of Bobby out there in the car. The lock clicked open, and I pushed open the storage closet door. She was standing there by the closet not two feet from me with the rifle in both hands, staring into space, just holding it, so I tried to get by her. She raised it and pointed it at me, finger on the trigger, getting ready to kill me dead right at that moment. I got a good look in her eyes, Nina. I saw it. My own death. You know, Nina. You've been there."

Nina said nothing. She was conscious only of waiting.

"She said, 'You're not going anywhere,' but I had my hands on the rifle by then. We fought for it, moving toward the front again. The rifle went off. We both staggered back; I saw my chance and took off through the back door."

"Matt," Andrea cried, her anguished voice so different from Matt's matter-of-fact tone. He held his finger to his lips, and kept on, looking down at the table.

"I ran along the fence in the woods to the corner of the property.

That stupid dog ran alongside me, not barking, just out there having a frolic. I climbed the fence out to the road, and I got out of there with Bob. I told him I would talk to you about it, and he looked relieved. I think he fell asleep. It was way past his bedtime and he'd been out pedaling halfway across town. He was out of it.

"I drove the rest of the way home, going as fast as I could without creaming the car. I ran in the kitchen door. I didn't turn on the light, and I sent Bob off to bed."

Matt leaned toward Andrea wearily. She stroked his cheek, murmured to him.

Then she turned to Nina, and Nina saw the same defiant expression Matt had worn earlier. "He did it to protect Bobby," she said.

"Yes, he did," Nina said. "And he still is protecting Bobby."

She got up painfully as an invalid, splashing cold water on her face at the sink, unable to look at her brother, thinking of Kurt and Matt and Bobby, and the darkness Terry had brought into all their lives.

"What exactly do you mean by that?" Andrea said.

Nina walked back to the table and picked up the evidence list she had been examining before they arrived. She pushed it in front of Matt, saying, "It's a good story. You've got the Irish gift for embellishment and credibility in spite of facts to the contrary. But the black corduroy baseball cap's there on the list of items collected by the police in the studio. I turned the house upside down hunting for Bob's hat, Matt. It isn't here. That's because Bob left his No Fear hat in the studio that night, didn't he, Matt? He told you that story, didn't he?

"So tell me the whole truth this time. Did Bobby see Kurt kill her? Or . . . did Bobby kill her?"

32

"BOB WAS IN THE TRUCK. HE NEVER CAME INTO THE STUDIO. I'M telling you what happened!" Matt paced around the kitchen. Nina stood with her back to the sink, leaning against it for support. Andrea still sat at the table, watching them, her eyes stricken.

"His hat just floated off his head and into Terry's studio," Nina said. "He never goes anywhere without that hat. How can I believe you?"

"He took mine in the dark. I put his on because it was cold and I wasn't going out without a hat."

"I'm sorry," Nina said. "I just don't believe you. You're protecting him. You're both lying."

"How could he lie about something like this? Didn't he tell you he barely made it past the gate before I got him?"

Nina thought back. Bobby had spoken quickly, pouring it out, blurting, trying to explain. She allowed herself a small, frail hope. She hoped Matt left the hat in Terry's studio. She hoped Matt killed Terry, because Matt was a man and Bobby was still a boy. Matt might survive this. Bobby wouldn't.

"I'm going to get Bob up," Nina said. "Ask him. This can't wait."

"Hang on," Andrea said. "You can't just drag him in here and start cross-examining him."

Nina said. "I have to know, Andrea. How can we do this?"

"Let me get him," Andrea said, moving toward the door. "And both of you keep your mouths shut when I get back."

"I'm not lying," Matt said to Nina. "You'll see."

But Nina had nothing to say to him. She pulled out a chair and put her head in her hands.

A moment later Andrea came out gently guiding Bob, who blinked and rubbed his eyes. Andrea said, in a voice so soft it would fit right into his dream, "Now let's get that glass of water." She went to the sink and got him some water, while Bob sat down on the chair next to Nina, half awake, half asleep, in a state of unreality, a child in pajamas in the alien light of a late-night kitchen.

"I'll take you right back to bed," Andrea said, her voice soothing as a lullaby. "Oh, sweetie, where's your hat? Did you forget your black hat?"

He yawned and half closed his eyes, reaching a hand up to his head. "I lost it," he said.

"Do you remember where you lost it?"

"I put it on the hat rack. Then it was gone," he said, and took a sip of water. "I need a new hat," he added. The water was reviving him.

"We'll get you one," said Andrea. "What kind do you want?" She took his arm, easing him out of the chair.

"Another No Fear. Mom knows the store that sells it." He leaned over his mother, falling groggily into her arms. "G'night, Mom." He kissed her on the cheek and Andrea led him back to bed.

"Satisfied?" Matt said.

Andrea came back. The clock in the living room chimed one o'clock. She said, "Tomorrow's another day. We'll decide what to do then."

"I've got a trial starting up in one week, and now I know my client didn't do it," Nina said. "Ethically, I have to talk to the district attorney's office right away. They'll dismiss the case—"

"And arrest Matt," Andrea said, as if Matt wasn't sitting there, listening.

"It was self-defense! Matt can explain—"

"He doesn't have any corroboration," Andrea said. "He didn't come forward. They won't believe him. They'll arrest him. He'll go to jail."

"I can get him out on bail—"

"Like Kurt, right? What if he's convicted of manslaughter? Sent off to some penitentiary?"

"We can't leave Kurt in prison either. You have no idea what it's like for him!"

"You'd rather Matt was in there than him?" Nina had never seen Andrea like this. She was still wearing the soft flowery dress she had worn to dinner, but there was nothing soft about her now. She was standing behind Matt, her hand on his shoulder. Nina had the feeling that she wouldn't hesitate to do anything necessary to defend Matt.

"Of course not! Jesus, Andrea!" she said.

"They'll call Bob as a witness. Maybe they'll look at the hat thing too. Maybe they won't believe him. You didn't. And you're his own mother." Her voice rose. "Don't you dare hurt Matt!" she cried.

"Stop," Matt said, squeezing her arm, his eyes on Nina. "No more," he said. "Nina is going to have to decide what to do."

Andrea put her head down close to Matt's. She began to sob.

"I'll help you, Matt, defend you. . . ." Nina said, ready to break down herself.

He reached over and stroked his wife's head. "I never meant to keep it from anybody. It's just that—I feel like the same person. The one from before I killed someone. Every day that went by with Scott in jail in my place—believe me, Nina, I've suffered too. I planned to tell you before he took a plea or went down. You believe that much, don't you?"

"Of course."

"I'm ready to face whatever has to happen next."

"What do we do, Matt? Help me. Don't give me this responsibility."

"I don't know," he said. "I thought of packing up Andrea and the kids and going away to some new place. But they'd probably find me, and we'd be afraid all the time. I thought about killing myself. I don't want to do that to my kids. I'm in your hands. I know I can trust you, Nina."

"Let's go to bed, Matt," Andrea said, tugging a little at his sleeve. Nina thought, she wants to get away from me. I don't blame her. He got up without another word and went to the door. Nina saw the look of melancholy resignation on his face before he turned away.

As soon as Matt had left, Andrea went over to Nina and whispered, her face white, "It's your fault. You got him into this, by not telling Bob about his father in the first place. You made Bob vulnerable, and Matt was only trying to help you when he followed him. Now you take care of it. Whatever it takes, do you understand?"

"What am I supposed to do?" Nina said again.

"You're the big-shot lawyer. You figure it out," Andrea said. "Family comes first. You hear me? Protect your family, like Matt protected Bob."

By one A.M., "Hollywood Hijinks," the midnight show at Caesars, had hit its stride. Paul had slept so much at the hospital that he couldn't lie down in his room, so he'd come down to see what was shaking in the main ballroom.

About thirty girls were shakin' right now, all flounce and feathers and sequins, most of the costume on their heads. They were all young, thin, and enthusiastic, with small, naked breasts. A lounge lizard fronting the dancers sang "At the Copa . . . Copacabana . . ." Paul was fairly sure the Copacabana was far from Hollywood, but it was a fine song for the girls to strut their stuff, and he had a table close to the scenery.

The third girl from the left was giving him a special smile—he was sure of it—and she was a knockout, with legs like long, tan carrots—no, not carrots, that didn't do them justice—like the slender glass vases that held a single rose—that was better, but still not very good, he was lousy at similes . . . She definitely was trying to catch his eye. He held his hand on his heart, then pointed to his watch, gesturing the message that he'd wait for her after the show.

Another blinding smile, while she made a kind of hula move with the other girls. The loud music, the shifting lights, the dancing girls, and the Jack Daniel's made him feel almost like his old self. He rubbed his head gingerly where Nina had beaned him with that rock.

Lately he had been feeling somewhat insecure, wondering if Nina was in love with her killer client. He'd seen Scott kissing her, and her willing welcome of it up there on the trail; Nina's head fallen back with the satiny hair almost touching the ground, her eyes closed, her white throat offered, her full soft lips murmuring sweet nothings, or case citations, who the hell knew. . . .

The show ended. Paul made his way backstage, thinking the last time he went backstage he'd gotten into a lot of trouble. The bouncer at the dressing room door gave him the evil eye, but he said, "I'm expected," and the guy let him peek inside so he could wave at her.

Thirty sumptuous women chattered and laughed, getting dressed, combing their hair, flesh, flesh, divine female flesh . . . without the blue headdress he would never find her—

"Hello, Paul," Doreen Ordway said, back in her miniskirt, with a delicious smile that thrust her rosebud lips his way. "Remember me?"

"Uma Thurman," Paul said. "Nicole Kidman." Streaked hair, low-slung . . . oh, yes, he remembered her well . . . "Great show."

"Silly," she said, patting her hair, pleased. "I'm dying for a drink. Shall we go?"

"I'll have a double kamikaze," Doreen said when they were settled at the small glass-topped table in the bar next to the casino area. "No time to waste."

"A margarita," Paul told the waiter. "No salt."

"Marnagrita," Doreen said, and giggled. "That's what they're called after midnight."

"Ha, ha. So . . . your husband around?"

"Of course not!" she said. "He disapproves of my dancing. But the money's good, and we need it. My friend Ginny lives in Minden, not far from the ranch. She's driving tonight. She's over at the black-jack tables. She loses as much as she makes. Anyway, we go home at two-thirty. Are you staying at Caesars?"

"Right upstairs," Paul said. She looked up at him, flapping her lashes, flirting like any woman with an hour left to get drunk and laid before she had to get home. "Hard work, dancing."

"It is hard. Try kicking your leg higher than your head while wearing a pair of high heels. I take ballet lessons and lift weights twice a week."

"Does your husband mind, you know, the costume?"

"He's never seen a show," Doreen said. "He doesn't know I go topless. He'd never leave the ranch if he didn't have to go to the cattle shows."

Their drinks arrived. Doreen's glass was a black-and-red volcano. His glass looked big enough to dive into. She drank as if straight off a parched desert, and said, "So you liked the show, darlin'?"

"You were great. To be honest, I couldn't take my eyes off you."

"I noticed." A little late, Paul held up his glass and said, "To beautiful dancers," winning another melting smile. "So you don't mind having to earn a second paycheck for the family?"

"Oh, I love it. I get out of the house, away from the little ones, come up here three times a week where it's so exciting, and I get to dance—I don't mind it at all."

"It's kind of surprising, the ranch not being all that profitable. Mike has a fine reputation as a rancher, I've heard—"

"Michael. We're damn near bankrupt, Paul. He overpays the hands and refuses to take any risks. He's got us so deep in debt we'll never climb out." Her foxy little face turned sullen. She upended her volcano again.

"Could he sell out, do something else?"

"Are you kidding? It's the only thing he's ever wanted to do, and he's lousy at it. Paul, there's a question I've been meaning to ask you. Did your associate take anything with him when you left our house?"

"Why, that would be theft," Paul said.

"I'm just curious," Doreen said. "Some of my little things are missing."

"The handcuffs?" Paul said. "Do you like cuffing, or getting cuffed?"

"Would you like to find out, darlin'?" Paul considered this proposition. She finished off the drink and ordered another one.

"It's a thought," he said at last. "My associate shouldn't have taken anything. I have them up in my room. Perhaps I should just run up and get them. But on the other hand, I like having them. I can picture them on you, and you're not wearing as much as you do in the show, either. Or maybe I should give them to your husband," he said. "I mean, if he doesn't already, maybe he ought to know just how naughty you are."

"Don't tease me, Paul. What is it you want? To go upstairs?" She lowered her voice, leaned forward to give him a good look down her shirt, and said, "Let's go, then. I still have an hour."

"In a minute," Paul said. "I want to know about the night Tam disappeared."

"God, you're starting to bore me. I'm sick of talking about her. She's been gone forever. It doesn't change anything, that they found her."

"What's the harm in telling me what really happened?" he said. "Then we can move on to other things." He put his hand on her leg under the table and moved it upward, until she giggled.

"Well, hurry up," she said. "What do you want to know?"

"You were with Mike and Tamara at Manny's. It was cold and snowy outside. She threw a drink in Mike's face—"

"Michael," she said. "He deserved it, in a way. He called her a nasty name, knowing she was already in a bad mood. She'd already had a fight with her parents. We were all pretty drunk. Like we are now." She looked at her empty glass. "He was"—a hiccup—"jealous. He still wanted her, and she knew it. It was disgusting, how she played with him. She said she was gonna go get high, and he didn't want her to go. She got up to make her phone call, and he grabbed her arm and wouldn't let her go. She had her drink in her hand an' she let him have it."

"Who'd she call?" Paul said as casually as he could.

"Her connection. The new dude. She said he gave her all she wanted. I mean, I didn't hear her, but who else could it have been? She called and then she whiffed. Michael was cryin', so I took him out to his car and made it up to him. It was our first time. He wasn't very good. I got out and got in my old bomber of a car and went home."

"So you didn't stay after for two hours? Like you said in the film and in your statement?"

"Two hours! It was more like two minutes. Are we gonna go upstairs or not, baby?"

"She never mentioned who her new friend was?"

"No. Michael might have called the cops on him. She was poppin' pills, uppers and Quaaludes to mellow out after, she told us."

Paul said, "If it was me, I wouldn't have been able to resist going along sometime. Just to experiment."

"I never did. And neither did Michael. We weren't invited, and we weren't interested. We were potheads, that's all."

"So many loose ends," Paul mused. "Another?"

"Just a single this time," Doreen said. She put her small white hand with its sharp little nails on his arm, and said, "Then take me upstairs." She hiccuped again. "Don' you want me, Paul?" She took his hand and put it back on her thigh. She was hot as an oven down there.

"Of course I do," Paul said.

Her drink came quickly. "They know me," Doreen said. "Say, you're not tapin' this?"

"Heavens, no."

"Good. 'Cuz jus' 'cuz I say it now don't—doesn't—mean I'm gonna say it again."

Doreen was entering the stage of drunkenness in which the mind gave up and the body took over. She was giggling again, though Paul hadn't said anything.

Maybe Michael Ordway could have followed Tam. She might never have made it to her appointment.

Or maybe Doreen had killed her. She had a voracious quality. She had strong hungers, and she had wanted Ordway, but he had wanted Tamara.

"I'm ready. Poop or get off the pot," Doreen said.

"What an attractive thought," Paul said. "Unfortunately, I can't take you up with me."

"Huh? What's wrong, darlin'?"

"I'm afraid I've got a terrible headache," Paul said. Thank Nina for that.

"Then get out of my way," Doreen said, soused and definite, her eyes narrowing.

Paul stood up as she walked away from their table.

She was already scoping out the Texan at the next table. As he walked to the elevators, Paul wondered disinterestedly if she would make her two-thirty deadline.

33

ALTHOUGH SOUTH LAKE TAHOE WAS BY FAR THE LARGEST TOWN IN EL Dorado County, itself one of the largest counties in California, Placerville had once been the bigger town, back when the rushing streams nearby yielded gold nuggets by the pound. The citizens had changed the name from its original appellation of Hangtown. No one knew just how many miners had dangled from the tree at the center of town. Tourists came up from the smoggy valleys on Sunday mornings to eat "Hangtown Fry," a concoction of oysters, eggs, and bacon, and to check out the old mine shafts and the Pony Express memorabilia at the town museum.

But today Nina wasn't on a pleasure trip. The June air grew progressively hotter as she descended the four thousand feet and seventy miles, her windows open to the smells of the Sierra.

She had awakened before dawn, slipped on her glasses and robe, and sat with her coffee out on the porch, dimly aware of her surroundings, her mind traveling through its own landscape. As the sun came up it evaporated the dew from the fenceposts Matt had made, making a fine mist that blurred the air. The forest seemed to stir and shake itself as the warm yellow rays cast themselves through the branches.

Dawn, the moment in the day when hope should be at its highest. Dawn, the time for firing squads and duels.

She had to decide immediately. Kurt or Matt . . . Matt or Kurt. How could she let an innocent man endure another day in prison? Kurt had entrusted her with his liberty. If being a lawyer meant anything at all, it meant that she could not withhold information that would exonerate him.

She would be committing a felony if she withheld Matt's information from the police. She couldn't talk to Paul or Sandy about it, because that would make them equally culpable. She should go straight to Collier Hallowell and beg for mercy.

But . . . Matt would be arrested. She didn't see how he could avoid being charged with manslaughter. She, the big sister, had always protected him when they were kids. He might not make it through the process. He might even . . . do something rash. He didn't trust the system that was her life. And if she turned him in, he might try, but he would never, never be able to forgive her. And Bob, a reluctant witness, maybe a suspect—her family would be ruined.

She loved them all. How could this be happening?

She thought back to each conflict, each problem, each challenge that had been presented to her since Bob asked her about his father a few months before, during their picnic at the snowy beach. Her choices had been difficult at every turn. But she had tried her best. She had tried to help. What had she done wrong? What could she do?

The thought came, as she sat on the porch in her wobbly chair, at her wit's end, that she had to go see Kurt. She had to tell him about Matt. She had to tell him about Bob. He had a right.

She turned down Main Street at nine-fifteen and was buzzed into the holding area right away. The atmosphere at this jail made her uncomfortable. She wasn't known here. Kurt's legal position had become even more precarious—he was an escapee. He had assaulted a guard in a prison van, even if the guard hadn't been hurt beyond a bruise or two. The other guards would make sure he paid for that one way or the other, no matter what the law said.

When the guard brought him in, Kurt sat down but wouldn't look at her. This time there was no glass, but a chain-link grille. Another guard read the paper behind his desk not twenty feet away.

His nose was still bandaged. Paul had given him shiners on both eyes and a cut on the cheek.

"Kurt?"

He sighed and looked up. "Hello, Nina."

She opened her mouth to tell him everything.

And lost her courage. Maybe if they talked about something else for a few minutes. . . .

"The medical report says you'll be fine in a few days," she began. "How are you feeling?"

"I'm feeling . . . glad you'll still come see me, after I took off like that."

"The bones have been identified as Tamara Sweet's remains. She was shot twice. The D.A.'s office is investigating."

"I suppose they think I killed her."

She didn't know much more yet, so she stopped and let him direct the conversation.

"How's Paul?" Kurt said.

Surprised, Nina said, "Paul? Oh, he's back on the case. He feels terrible about losing his temper like that. He's fine."

"That's good."

"You don't have to be so nice about it."

"I started it," Kurt said, repeating Paul's words. "Are you . . . and Paul . . . ?"

Nina turned her head away, embarrassed.

"None of my business, of course."

"No. It's not that. Let's just say, all that's on hold."

"He doesn't believe me, does he?"

For no reason at all, her mind swung wildly into a new suspicion. Maybe he hadn't killed Terry, but what about Tamara? He saw her eyes change, and said, "What is it?"

Her stomach hurt. The decision to tell him might be wrong. He might tell others. She must be crazy to trust Matt's future to this man. "It's a problem, you finding Tamara," she said abruptly. "I watched the film again. Now I do notice the rock. You were right, it's the same rock. But it's such a feat of memory for you to have remembered it."

"I told you, I'm a forest ranger. It's like the trees and rocks and streams are furniture in my house. I notice."

She wanted to believe him, she really did.

"Poor Nina," Kurt said. "I'm so sorry."

She didn't know what to say. She was being torn apart. She was being so unfair to him, and he was trying to comfort her. He could be out today, free . . .

"I have to go," she said. "I'll drive back down day after tomorrow to talk about the mechanics of the trial."

"Only a few more days," Kurt said. "I know you're doing your best."

"There's something I want to tell you before I go, Kurt."

He waited.

"I want you to know, I do believe you. I believe you didn't kill Terry."

Kurt said, "Thanks. I don't know what made you decide to trust me, but it means a lot to me."

His voice broke a little when he said *trust.*

Just like that, Nina made up her mind to tell him.

"That's not all," she said, her voice not faltering any longer.

"What's happened? It must be bad, judging from the way you're looking at me."

"I hardly know where to start," she said. "I—I know you didn't kill Terry, because I know who did, and why. I came here to tell you—"

"Oh, thank God!" Kurt cried. "You mean I'll be free? Who killed her? How did you find out? When can you get me out of here?" He stood up, his eyes squeezed together and his mouth drawn tightly, as if delivering himself of a great pain. He turned away from her and faced the wall.

She watched his shoulders heaving, her own eyes wet.

When he finally came back to the window, he said, "It's such a shock. Such a relief. I've been holding so much in . . ."

"I understand." Registering her own miserable expression, his ecstatic expression turned to bewilderment. "I have some things to tell you. Things that are hard to say. So I'm going to start by telling you something I've withheld from you, something very important."

She took a deep breath and plunged in.

"You do have a son, Kurt. Our son. He's eleven, going into sixth grade, big for his age. I was pregnant when you left, and I was so angry that I wouldn't tell Bob about you. I was wrong. I'm not angry anymore. I understand—"

To her amazement, Kurt said calmly, "I know about my son, Nina. I can't wait to meet him. He's written me twice. I couldn't tell you. I was afraid you'd prevent him from writing."

They had put their heads close to the grille. They spoke confidentially, like old friends or old lovers.

"That little . . . dickens!" Nina said.

"I can't ever explain how it felt when I opened his first letter. He's someone to live for," Kurt said. "I asked him not to come to the jail. I couldn't let him meet me this way. If I was convicted, I planned to bow out. But now—do you have a picture of him?"

Nina held Bob's fifth-grade school photo against the grille so that he could see it. Bob smiled, his lips in a tight smile, his chin and eyes the biggest features, the eyes clear and bright and healthy. Kurt studied it for a long time, not saying anything.

She put the picture back in her case. "I'll leave it with the guard for you, Kurt. You should have it. Right now, I have much more to tell you."

"He looks like me," Kurt said. "He looks a lot like me. How about that! Tell me about him." So she told Kurt about Bob, about his skateboard and his school and how much he liked hot dogs, small stuff, while Kurt's eyes lit up in a way she'd forgotten. For five minutes they both forgot about where they were.

Finally, Nina said, "Let me go on."

"Go ahead. Tell me whatever you want."

Nina talked for a long time. She wanted him to know everything, so she started from the picnic, through Bob's trip to Monterey, Terry, Paul, and finally she told him with great difficulty about Matt's confession from the night before. During that part she couldn't face him. Her feelings were too complicated.

When she finally looked up, Kurt was staring at the ground with the same bleak look she'd seen in her mirror that morning, the mask of a human being faced with a problem too big to understand or deal with.

"So I came to you. I've told you everything I know. I'm your lawyer and it was my duty to tell you," she finished, but she didn't feel the relief she had hoped for from laying it all at his feet. She felt inchoate rage, and she wanted to find a way out, but there was no way out.

"Thank you," was all he said, and she knew he understood her, at least.

"It's terrible," she said.

"I don't understand," he said, "why my freedom is so costly. Because my freedom can only come from your family's anguish. We couldn't be happy after that, either one of us."

"Yes." She couldn't believe it. He wasn't thinking about how he could walk away, go back to Germany and forget her and Bobby and Matt; he was thinking only about her happiness and Bobby's.

"I'm glad Bob never met me and got attached to me," Kurt said suddenly. "Nina, here's what I want you to do. I want you to walk out of here and forget Matt ever said a word."

"You don't have to sacrifice yourself. That's not going to happen."

"I'm expendable," he said. "I have no family, except Bobby, Nina, and he hardly knows me. He loves Matt and you. You and your family have much more at stake."

"Wait! Kurt, wait. Talk to me."

He wavered for a moment, then turned back.

"I'm going to tell the D.A. I have to."

"Don't." Kurt was shaking his head. "I'll tell him you're all lying to save me, to confuse the case. He knows about us, doesn't he, Nina? He knows you might lie to save me. I'll confess."

"Listen. Maybe there's another way." She had thought the case through from the beginning, and although she never once expected this reaction from him, she was who she was. And what she was, was prepared. "What about if we don't believe a word Matt said? How about we go to trial? It's only a week away. Could you possibly hold on through the trial?"

"Sure," he said, and there was the smile she had loved so much, or had she just fallen back in love with him this minute? "Give you a chance to pull the rabbit from the hat? I can handle it if you can handle it."

Nina said, "You're very generous to do this. You make me feel brave again."

"How about your brother? Can he hang in there?"

"He's expecting to be arrested today. Anything short of that, he can handle. I should have gone to Terry's that night, not Matt. He tried to help me with Bobby, in spite of having his own family to tend to, because I didn't have time to watch over my own son. He was trying to protect Bobby when it happened. He's always been so tenderhearted and gentle. He's really shaken."

"Tell him I'm glad she didn't blow him away," Kurt said. "Thank him for saving Bob's life. I think he did. We were all lucky."

She had a hard time leaving. She had taken a huge step with Kurt. And she knew when she left she would have to get into the Bronco and say to herself, it's a felony. You'll be disbarred. You'll lose Kurt and Matt, your job, your reputation. The police will find out. They always do.

BOOK
FOUR

Three Years Ago: Deirdre

After a day ice-skating up at the rink at Squaw, they had moved on to this big house hanging over a cliff near Tahoe City, owned by Ray's parents, with a spectacular view of the lake and the twinkling lights of the lake towns. Where Ray's parents were, Deirdre didn't know or care. He had invited a bunch of people, and they all came, throwing their sweaters off and turning up the music.

The first thing Ray wanted to do once they got everyone inside was kiss Deirdre, which was fine by her. She'd felt his eyes caressing her while she skated this afternoon, and it was a feeling she loved. She basked in his admiration. After two months going together, she was still semi-crazy for Ray, with his bushy black hair and permanent five o'clock shadow. Her parents didn't think much of him, but at nineteen, she felt she had joined them on the adult plane, and took care of their concerns by lying through her teeth whenever his name came up.

He kissed her for a long time, rubbing her cheeks with his whiskers until they hurt. She let his hands wander; she swayed with him, and met him skin for skin, but after a while he went off to attend to his guests, promising to return.

She stayed in the kitchen waiting for him to come back, experimenting with a new kind of corkscrew, opening every bottle in sight, taking a few sips here and there. When he didn't return for a long time she discovered him panting over Hanna in the living room, his tongue hanging out like a goddamned dog all over the place.

She went to work on her revenge. All the rooms in the house were dark, except for light from the fire and a few candles, and dark shapes thumped the hardwood floors to the music booming out of speakers on both sides of the long living room. She let Tony drag her into the next room, where he kissed her until she made an excuse and tore herself away. Within minutes Jordan had pressed her against a wall in the hallway, and was moving his tongue down her throat. She even got Leo the Loser out on the freezing cold balcony. Everyone knew Leo had the hots for Hanna, and she found it especially satisfying to draw him into her web of sex, pulling her sweater down over her shoulder just slightly and asking him to smell her new perfume, pouncing at just the right moment.

She made a little game with herself about how many boys she could get physical with in one night, selecting her prey carefully so that no one would get too heavy on her. Ray finally spotted her making out in the corner and seemed to remember she was supposed to be with him.

"Get your dirty hands off of her, Evan," Ray said, directing his words one way, and his hard eyes directly at her. "I'm not kidding."

"Fuck off, Ray," she said, before Evan had a chance to reply, enjoying herself, blitzed on the vodka. "Mind your own business."

Which led to a delicious fight that almost stopped the party.

Ray finished the evening off by throwing her out, pulling her by her short hair out onto the steps in the front of the house, and giving the front door a hearty slam.

Whoa. It was freezing, no moon. To hell with him, she thought, feeling the icy blow of wind, pulling the fur hat he had tossed after her down over her ears.

She knew a couple of the guys would be delighted to give her a ride home, but she was in no mood to go back inside and ask someone and possibly run into Ray again. She was awfully drunk, she realized, stumbling up the slippery walk, but she knew she wasn't far from the highway. She could thumb a lift.

Serve him right if some butcher picked her up.

34

The treetops yellowed under a blistering high mountain sun as the one-week-to-trial countdown began. Midsummer was a bad time for a trial. Court reporters, clerks, witnesses, all wanted to be somewhere else. No one returned phone calls. Paul wanted to be out on a boat or turning over a king and an ace at Caesars.

Instead, he wrote up reports on Doreen Benitez Ordway, mildly censored, and Sergeant Cheney, and the parents of the girls, and wrote a note about Terry London's fur coat, which was gone and uninsured, and passed them all on to Sandy by the middle of the week. He didn't see Nina. She was at a pretrial conference that Sandy told him would last all day.

The missing coat was interesting. Murders had been committed for less: the lynx was worth over ten thousand dollars, even though, as it turned out, Terry had inherited it from her mother. But why not take the lipstick-size camera, the Steenbeck editing equipment, the video recorders, all now repossessed? Those items would be easy to hawk, easier maybe than the lynx.

Sandy gave him copies of the experts' reports. Their fingerprint expert hadn't been able to I.D. any of the partial prints, quite a disappointment, though he was sure some of the partials were not the prints of either Scott or London. Win a little, lose a little. The expert lip-reader hadn't helped much, either, but his time might come if Willie Evans's testimony left any loopholes.

The independent lab tests were also uninspiring—London's blood splattered all over the wall and pooled on the floor; Kurt's blood trailed from the studio floor outside. No sign of a third party nicking his finger. No third-party evidence under Terry's nails.

No third-party physical evidence at all, in fact, except prints all over the studio of about two dozen people. Smeared and useless prints on Terry's camcorder. Smeared prints on the rifle along with clear prints from Terry and Scott.

He pored over his copies of the autopsy reports on both women, the ballistics results, the witness statements. Nothing. What kind of defense was Nina going to put on?

He called on Thursday, and Sandy said Nina was a mess. They had a last meeting of the Gang of Four at her office on the Friday before the trial. Wish, who Paul had kept busy running around to the experts and tracking down the small stuff, lay down on her couch immediately. "Your second home," Paul said.

"I think better lying down," Wish said.

Nina had temporarily abandoned her contacts for horn-rims that she must have kept since college. They made her look smarter and distracted his attention from the full lips and womanly curves crying out for his attention. She started right up. She thought Jerry Kettrick's eyewitness testimony could be attacked. She had formed a plan to attack Willie Evans's lip-reading. Other than that, she seemed to be spinning her wheels.

They talked once more about the problems: Kurt's statements when he was arrested, the death video, Jerry Kettrick, and the registration and prints on the Remington. They talked about the new problem: Scott's escape from custody and beeline for Tamara Sweet's remains.

"Their main problem is still motive, even if it's not a required element of proof," Paul said. "It's important to the jury."

"The jury may not need that much motive, Paul," Nina said. "A boyfriend and girlfriend, Tamara a drug user, late at night in the woods. Milne's going to let in the rifle registration, the rifle casing, the finding of the bones, the relationship. It's not much, but if they think it's enough, covering up Tam's murder would provide enough of a motive for killing Terry. And there's the note Kurt sent her, telling her to leave him alone."

"And we know he was worried about you," Sandy said.

"So he says," Paul said.

"How could that come into evidence?" Sandy said. "Since he won't testify."

"Collier will ask me about any contacts I had with Kurt before the shooting," Nina said. "There's no attorney-client privilege for events occurring before Kurt retained me."

"I keep coming back to the fact that the film doesn't specifically implicate him," Paul said.

"That's right, Paul. It's a weakness in the prosecution's case, and I'm going to exploit it all I can."

"It's pretty weird that you have to testify," Wish said from the couch. "Who's gonna be your lawyer in case you do something wrong?"

"I'm up on the law, Wish. I don't need a lawyer. I know I don't have to go into some things that are privileged. But some events aren't. I fought the good fight at one of the pretrial hearings, and I lost. I'll be a witness."

"Aren't you supposed to, you know, spring some big surprises for them? Something brilliant, so someone stands up in the audience to confess?" Wish said.

"Unfortunately, though it looks good in the movies, it's not something that's going to happen. We're waiting for them to make a mistake," Nina said. "They will. Every case has weaknesses."

"Oh."

"I'm a lousy substitute for Perry Mason," Nina said. "Sorry, Wish."

"And I'm no Paul Drake," Paul said, getting into the spirit. "In spite of the similarly unflawed talent."

"And I'm not good ol' Della," Sandy said, smoothing her fringed cowgirl skirt.

"Who are these guys?" Wish asked. "O.J.'s lawyers?"

On his way out, Paul said, "Nina, let's get together Saturday night. Don't shake your head, you can't work all the time. You need to relax."

"I can't, Paul. When I'm not working, I sleep and try to take care of Bob. It's all I can do right now. I'm sorry."

"If that's how it has to be. Have you got anything for me to do over the weekend?"

"I don't think so. I'm working up witness questions and preliminary jury instructions."

"Then I'll just head down the hill to my neglected life in Carmel." And have a bourbon and soda at the Hog's Breath, and maybe pick up a nice blond tourist from Sweden, and good luck to you, lady, he thought, exasperated. Competing with both Scott and her workload was getting irksome. "See you Monday."

Back at Tahoe on Monday morning at nine-thirty, Paul ducked reluctantly from the glorious outdoors into the stuffy Superior Court courtroom. He sat next to Nina at the defense table, while she shuffled papers and psyched herself up, ignoring Collier Hallowell and his consorts, ignoring even Paul after a brisk greeting.

Even before the jury selection began, the day slid downhill like a spring avalanche. Kurt dragged in, the deputies helping him shuffle his chained feet. Nina exploded at the sight. Collier Hallowell refused to stipulate that Scott's shackles could be removed while he was in court, although he had no problem with allowing him to wear his own clothes.

The two lawyers argued heatedly for some time in front of Milne. Nina, who had definitely had a rough weekend, used phrases like "chain him like a wild animal" and "just a ploy to prejudice the jury."

"He's charged with murder. His home is in Europe, and he's already engineered one escape from custody," Hallowell practically shouted. "He knocked over a deputy, stealing the key for the handcuffs. I don't intend to give him a chance to pull another stunt like that one."

"He turned himself in! He didn't hurt anyone!"

"He was trying to hide the evidence of his wrongdoing," Hallowell said. "He only came back because Mr. van Wagoner, here, managed to talk him into it, and he's got the bruises to prove it. I'm not going to stipulate to removing those shackles. If she hates them so much, maybe we can cover them up with a blanket or something."

"Sure, make it even more obvious. Humiliate him. Make him look like a dangerous fiend who can't wait to jump up and rip the throats out of the jurors'—"

"It's awfully early in the morning for oratory," Judge Milne said. "It's the policy of the El Dorado Superior Court to shackle defendants in all court appearances after an escape attempt or any violent act. I realize this leads to some prejudice on the part of the jury, Ms. Reilly. If you want, I will caution them that in their deliberations they are not to consider the fact that the defendant is shackled."

"That sort of admonition is just a verbal blanket over his feet, Your Honor. The jurors won't be able to think about anything else."

"Can you suggest some alternate method of mitigating the prejudice?"

"Well, he could just plead guilty right now," Nina said hotly. "He looks guilty and dangerous sitting there in chains. The jury can see the court considers him dangerous. Please, Your Honor. Don't shackle him."

Milne said, "Once in a while, couldn't we just have a trial start on time? All those people are standing around outside, wondering why they had to report so early. Why didn't you raise this earlier?"

"I didn't know they were going to chain him up until they brought him in!"

"I'm afraid Ms. Reilly wasn't aware of the court rules, Judge," Hallowell said. "She isn't in here day in and day out, familiarizing herself with the processes of this court. She's off in the mountains running around with escapees."

"Why, Mr. Hallowell, Ms. Reilly here brings out a sarcastic streak in you," Milne said. "Let's calm down. I don't want to hand you an issue for appeal this early in the game, Ms. Reilly. I'll give both of you until noon to bring me some case law. Just attach complete copies of the cases to a sheet with the case heading. Don't bother to write up an argument. I've already heard your points. I'll read it over the lunch hour, and at one-thirty we will start jury selection, is that understood?"

"Thank you, Your Honor," the two lawyers said in perfect unison, ignoring each other while the audience tittered. Nina came back to the defense table, overtly squeezing Kurt's shoulder as he was hauled to his feet and herded out. She packed up all the files she had just unpacked, and marched smartly out into the hall, which was full of curious eyes, then made her way toward the law library, with Paul ambling beside her.

"I won't let Collier get away with this," she said, not slowing her step.

"I thought you were on pretty good terms with him," Paul said.

"That was then. We're in trial now."

"You started off with fireworks. Why not save them for a grand finale?"

"Listen, I'm sorry. I've got to run, Paul. Collier's going to be back in his office, handing out assignments to a bright paralegal or two. They'll sit at a computer and access some computerized legal research service. That's the fast way to go. And people assume with that kind of access they're getting everything. But you can miss a case, especially if you're trying to beat the obvious precedents. I'm counting on that. And I'm going to have to dig deeper, over a wider area."

"So split, Paul," he said, sorry for her at that moment. She looked immobilized by the weight of her responsibility, as if the gravity around her pulled harder than it did on other people. "Okay. I wish I could help you."

"You've helped enough."

"Is that a crack? You still mad at me?"

"There's no room for anything inside me right now except to hang on. Try to understand, Paul."

"I've got something I left in my car for you. I'll meet you over there in a few minutes," he said as she tapped off toward the law library. She left without smiling. He'd seen a moment there when she looked like she might, before the old iron wall clanked down.

Shackles. She looked it up in Witkin under *S,* knowing it wouldn't be there. Those unworldly scholars who indexed legal books and computerized legal research didn't think like she did. She was going to have to find every case Collier might come up with in support of his position, as well as offer countervailing authority.

Local court rules, exceptions to . . . inherent powers of the judiciary . . . escape . . . prisoners, physical restraints on . . .

Paul came back and dropped into a chair beside her.

"Not right now, Paul."

"I'll just leave these with you, then, and go and have a big breakfast at Heidi's before I head off to serve subpoenas."

"What are they?"

"Last-minute supplemental reports on the witnesses."

"Anything new?"

"Yeah. Four items. First, I finally lined up the police report from 1984 where Jonathan Sweet supposedly pushed Tamara down the stairs. Jess Sweet signed the statement. She tried to withdraw it the next day, but they wouldn't let her. He went into some kind of diversion program and the assault charge eventually was dropped. You ought to be able to raise some hell with the report."

"Good work. I can use it to impeach him. It ought to be easy to set him up."

"It could have been Sweet. He doesn't live up to his name."

"Even if he killed his daughter, I doubt anyone would believe he could kill Terry from a wheelchair."

"One murder at a time," Paul said. "Okay. Second, the prosecution's lip-reader, Willie Evans, has an estimable reputation. His testimony is really damaging, and our expert's not helping. Maybe you can get Evans to change his mind."

"Well, I can try. What else?"

"The third thing is that the patrol officer, Jason Joyce, who stopped Kurt the morning after has as bad a reputation for honesty as Willie's is good. I told you all about it in the reports."

"Thanks, Paul. It's a big help." Shackles. Fetters, bonds, chains, leg cuffs, irons, manacles . . .

"One more fun item, and I'll go. Jerry Kettrick checks Ralph into the local psychiatric ward once a year, whether he needs to or not."

"Go on," Nina said, keeping her finger in the book to hold the page.

"But that isn't the most fascinating thing."

"What is?"

"Don't let me keep you from your books. I'll just go off and eat my eggs and—"

"Don't play with me! What?"

"You lawyers can be so humorless," Paul said. "Now, why is that? Ralph is having the occasional psychotic episode. He starts thinking rats are climbing out of the walls and floors and coming to get him. He's terrified of rats. They think his mother's drug use during her pregnancy screwed him up."

"God. And I almost let Bobby get up in the cab with him. Where did you find this out?"

"The Filipina nurse on the graveyard shift at the hospital," Paul said. "Of course, if you want the psych records, we'll have to come up with a reason for a subpoena."

"Okay," Nina said. "I'll put a subpoena and declaration together tonight. Milne will have to issue it. The hospital will fight." Maybe some smoke and mirrors would appear to obscure the case. "Rats!" she repeated thoughtfully.

"They fought the dogs and killed the cats," Paul said, yawning. "Ralph's alibi boils down to his dad saying he slept through the shooting. Doesn't cut it, if you ask me."

"The big smile, the rats, the monster trucks . . ." she said.

"He's a fine young American," Paul said.

"Thanks for all the ammo," Nina said. "Maybe I can use Ralph to raise a glimmer of doubt about Terry's murder at least."

"How many glimmers does it take to add up to a flaming reasonable doubt?" Paul asked.

"Only the jury knows."

"Well, I'll let you get back to your labors, unless there's something I can do to help. There are a few other tidbits about other witnesses you'll want to read over tonight."

"Okay." Paul lingered for a moment, as if he had more to say. She noted it, then chose to pretend she hadn't. She kept her nose to the table.

"Bye," she said lightly.

"Wish you could come along." She didn't react. Shuffling his feet for the briefest moment more, he left.

Nina pulled out her yellow pad and started writing down case citations.

★ ★ ★

"I've read your cases," Milne said after lunch. "I'm going to allow the shackles, though I will admonish the jury to disregard them."

Nina felt the flush of anger coming back up her neck. She said, "Your Honor—"

"Let's get the pool of jurors in here," Milne said to Kimura.

Put on a happy face, Nina told herself. As the rather resentful-looking people filed in to take up almost all the seats behind her, Nina tried to connect with each of them, adding to her silent hail-fellows an expression of buoyant confidence. "Kurt," she whispered. "Remember what we talked about. Sit up straight and keep your face impassive."

She glanced at Collier. He smiled slightly at the incoming jurors, a practiced smile that gave away nothing. However, she could see from the way he was stroking his tie that he, too, was nervous. She had gotten to know his moods and his moves.

Milne's brusque demeanor underwent its own transformation, to bland and agreeable. They were all acting for the benefit of the prospective jurors, trying to make a good first impression. From now on, what the jurors thought was the only thing that counted.

The laborious process of selecting the jury began. They broke off at five, and were back at it at nine on Tuesday. All week long prospective jurors had a final opportunity to speak, answering sometimes lengthy questions with lengthy replies. After this, those who were chosen would have to play dumb to the end, at which time the punch line belonged to them.

By Friday night, when the whole process was over, she wasn't satisfied. She told Paul, as they waited in her office for the pizza man, that there were too many middle-aged women, and that she thought they would tend to support the prosecution.

She thumbed through the piles of paper on her desk and said in a voice that let the fatigue leak through, "I'll be here until midnight. The trial has hardly started, and I'm already in sleep-deprivation mode."

She wanted some emotional support. But Paul's blond eyebrows were drawn close together, and his face had a peevish look she hadn't seen before. She didn't let herself consider too closely that, after a long, wearing day, Paul might be waiting for a gesture of warmth from her too.

"No problemo," Paul said shortly. "Turn those ladies to your side. Make them feel sorry for him. Use that boyish charm he seems to have for you women. Make him the victim. Make them feel motherly toward him."

"Very good," she said, tapping her pen against her lip and nodding. "I like that. He is a victim."

Her tone seemed to anger Paul.

"That's how you feel about him, isn't it? Motherly? You better step up to save him, because he is one sorry S.O.B.," he said, with a hardness she did not like.

"Believe me, I don't feel like his mother. Maybe you'd like that?"

"You've convinced yourself he's innocent, haven't you? You actually believe it."

"He didn't kill Terry London, Paul."

"You're sure? How are you so sure? Are you keeping something from me? And how about Tamara Sweet? Are you sure he didn't kill her?"

"I have to believe—I think Terry London killed her, or someone else. Not Kurt."

"I've seen many criminals in my time," Paul said, standing up, leaning over the desk, his lips curled into a sneer. "And the women hanging off them. They're expert manipulators. This guy's doing fine with the ladies already. He's got you jumping through hoops, doesn't he?" He straightened up and kicked at the desk angrily.

"Get off it, Paul. Am I not supposed to have warm feelings toward anyone but you?"

"He's using you," Paul said savagely. "And I'm getting tired of it. Because of him, your reputation around here is in the dumper. Hallowell's half convinced that you engineered the escape and the whole town sees you as just another fool in love, soap opera trash. Meanwhile, you're bankrupting yourself. I know Riesner hasn't turned over that retainer to you. Sandy says she sends him a letter a week."

The hotter he got, the cooler she felt. It had struck her that she had to sacrifice Paul, get him out of the case. He was too sharp. He was going to figure it out sooner or later. He had to go, and this was the perfect way to make it happen.

She stood up, facing him across her desk. "Keep your voice down. This is my case, and don't you forget it. I make the decisions. By the way, who's being motherly here today? I don't get to toddle two steps without you hovering over me in case I might bump my knee. In between bouts with the jealous-gorilla lover routine, you treat me like a child."

Paul flushed darkly at her counterattack. The veins stood out on his throat, and his eyes bulged slightly. He was tired and spoiling for a fight anyway. He was locked in battle now, and he had forgotten everything else.

She folded her arms, glowering at him.

"Well, make your plans now. After he's convicted, you'll be wanting to hijack a helicopter and break him out of the prison yard. You want to go down with your lover, show him you're loyal wife material for when they let you both out of the pen in twenty years."

"As opposed to being your submissive little playmate, with never a serious thought in my head?"

"Beats pretending to be a man," Paul said loudly, "in sleazy high heels."

"Dammit, Paul, I've got more on my mind than sex, unlike some others in this room."

"I had more to offer than that," Paul said. "I'm going. Back to Carmel. You obviously don't need me." He stomped out to the outer office.

For some time now the clacking had stopped, and Nina suddenly realized Sandy had been listening, because as Paul threw open the outer door, she heard her say to him, "Get some attitude surgery before you come back."

"Who said I'd be back?" The door slammed behind him, and the thin walls of her office shook.

Sandy came into Nina's office, hands on hips. "Late for the party, as usual," she said. "Nothing left but cleanup."

"Sandy, I want to ask you something."

Sandy came over to Nina's desk. "Shoot," she said.

Nina pushed dark blue heels out from under her desk with her stockinged toe. "Is there anything wrong with these shoes that you can see?"

"Well, they're a little high for my taste," said Sandy, shifting her weight from one tennis shoe to the other.

"No, I mean, are they too dressy for court? It's not like they're black patent or something. I paid eighty bucks for these shoes." Nina slipped them on her feet and immediately felt sleazy. "Trust a man to make you feel insecure right down to your most cherished accessory," she said.

Okay, she had played a dirty trick on Paul, and now she felt—

"Very sleazy," Sandy announced. "And I'm not talking about shoes."

She was giving Nina that inscrutable stare that always unnerved her. Nina remembered a short phone conversation with Andrea the day before. Had Sandy been listening?

"You can always go on the stage, if you get disbarred," Sandy went on, and Nina realized she knew about Matt. She understood what Nina had just done.

"If you keep eavesdropping on me, you'll get yourself into trouble. Just so you know," she said, "that makes you an accessory." Nina's mind swirled with the ethical and criminal implications, around and around, complexity upon complexity. . . .

"Fancy words like that don't mean anything to me," Sandy said. "Somebody has to try to sort this out, and you got elected. People are depending on you. Somebody has to keep you going. That's me. It's simple. So let's get on with it."

Her words were as pure and bracing as icebergs cutting through a frigid sea. Nina actually jerked in her chair as the doubt and confusion abruptly gave way. "Damn, Sandy," she said.

Sandy said, "You don't have any choice but to be brave. That's good, because fear bored a hole into you, and this could heal it up." She winked.

A knock came on the outer door and a voice said, "Pizza man."

"They better not have forgotten the extra cheese," Sandy said.

35

On the following Monday morning, Milne finally said, "We now have a jury of twelve with five alternates."

The jurors, including nine women, a critical mass that meant women would run the deliberations, sighed and shifted in their seats, with Mrs. Bourgogne, stately and stern, solidly in control of the front row middle position. One of those highly paid jury experts should do a study of how often the front row middle seat occupier became jury foreperson. Mrs. Bourgogne had a sharp, impatient eye, the kind of eye that went in after the room cleaning was finished and spotted the tissue still under the bed and the cobweb not swept from the ceiling corner.

Maybe she would think Jerry Kettrick's eye wasn't equally sharp.

Kurt sat to Nina's left, in the shackles, at least wearing his suit. He had hardly spoken to her. His face had a gray cast to it, and his eyes showed hollow from weight loss. Again she remembered what she was doing to him. He didn't have to go through this. He could be back at his piano, playing Bach, while she spent the next year preparing a defense for her jailbird brother. As the remaining members of the jury pool walked out, she squeezed his hand and whispered, "It's a good jury. We'll do fine."

The audience filled the seats, whispering as the people who had not been selected filed out. Barbet Cain of the *Mirror* was there, and a couple of other reporters. The Sweets sat quietly at the end of a row, Jonathan Sweet parked in his wheelchair in the aisle beside his wife. Doreen Ordway had dressed up, in a pale yellow miniskirted suit, her streaked hair glamorous in a French braid. Michael Ordway wore his usual jeans, his dark tanned face looking out of place.

The police witnesses had been excused and would be back the next morning, except for Frank Fontaine, the criminologist, who would be up first, and who was probably out in the hall reading his notes for the fiftieth time.

No relatives or friends showed up for Terry, unless you included the Kettricks, who seemed to be enjoying Jerry's privileged position as an eyewitness. Her parents were dead, and Nina hadn't been able to find anyone who knew her well. Even her associates in the film business could tell little about her. She had faxed her proposals and correspondence from Tahoe, and stayed shadowy as a person.

Kurt's parents were also dead, but his sister, Becky, had come from Idaho for the duration of the trial. Becky was ten years older than Kurt and had already married and moved to Boise when Tam disappeared. She had heard occasionally from Kurt, and was trying to show support for him, but his years away had attenuated their relationship.

The courthouse cronies had claimed their places in the back, three women and a very old man who tended to fall asleep and snore.

And that was it. No hordes of curiosity seekers, no aisles full of aggrieved family members.

And of course, no Paul. He had called Sandy to say he couldn't get up there. But she wasn't going to think about Paul's withdrawal from her and the case. Sandy was sitting up there at the counsel table with her and Kurt, dressed in black flats and a khaki skirt and a large, ill-fitting black jacket. Nina needed her to keep track of the volumes of paperwork that might be needed for reference at any moment. She would take notes and keep the files straight. Back at the office, Wish would take phone calls and keep the office going.

Collier stood up and moved around the table to the podium that had been set up in front of the jury box. Laying his papers gently down, he then walked to the side of the podium and began speaking. He looked at home in his old gray flannel suit, easy, like he had a story to tell his pals on a park bench.

"This is a homicide case. A woman named Terry London was shot with a Remington rifle at her home studio at about eleven forty-five P.M. on March thirtieth of this year. I'm here to present those facts to you in the clearest, simplest way I can.

"The facts you hear will slowly come together into a story about a man—this man here, Kurt Scott, defendant. You'll learn that Mr. Scott has a way with women, a way that has led to at least two deaths. You'll hear how this man seduced a young girl named Tamara Sweet twelve years ago, and carried on a clandestine affair with her. Then, on a mountain trail, he shot her twice and buried her body. You'll hear how he then, a few months ago, used the same gun to shoot and kill his ex-wife, to cover up the previous crime."

The jury listened with interest as Collier, hardly ever walking back to glance at his notes, detailed in a simple, logical way what he expected to prove. He was at his best, perfectly prepared, workmanlike, showing the jury—by not overstating anything and by not indulging in emotion—that they could trust him and follow him. There were no surprises for Nina in what he said; California had developed an extensive pretrial procedure designed to ensure surprises would be kept to a minimum at trial.

Still, as he summarized the testimony he expected to present, Nina was shocked at how strong the prosecution case sounded. She objected when she should, took notes, watched Mrs. Bourgogne and the other jurors, got to know their expressions, and tried to keep her confidence up.

Collier finished at four-fifteen, and Judge Milne adjourned for the day. Kurt was led away.

Nina and Sandy drove back to the office in a long line of traffic. Once they were inside, Nina pushed aside the phone messages and paperwork, looking for a clean legal pad. "Sandy, you type up the notes of the day, and then go home."

"What are you going to do?" Sandy said from the doorway.

"I'm going to water the plants and think."

"If you go eat dinner, then come back, the typed notes will be finished, and you can think better." Sandy booted up the computer. Nina came out in her flat shoes, brushing her hair.

"Uh, Sandy."

She turned and raised a bushy eyebrow. "Well?" she said.

"Any word from Paul?" Nina said. "I heard you running back to listen to the voicemail messages."

"No word. But Wish wants to know what you want him to do next."

"Oh. Nothing right now."

"Can I give him a few errands to run for the office, then, while you're in court?"

"Sure. Say, Sandy, is Wish your only son?"

"The only one," Sandy said. "But I have three daughters."

"Where's his father?"

"Long gone," Sandy said, with a glint in her eye that made Nina decide not to ask any more.

"It's an incredible thing, having a child," Nina said. "If I'd had to plan to have a child, I don't think I would have done it, but I'm glad every day he's in my life. You know, I'm just going to go home. I can stop by the office early and run through my opening statement. I feel like helping Bob with his homework, talking to him a little about court today. He's pretty anxious."

She stopped at the store to buy spaghetti fixings, made a big supper, spent time with Bob, had a long bath, and slept for nine hours. When the alarm went off at six, she was ready.

Court. Kurt beside her, impassive. A gray dress today, with a white collar. "Ms. Reilly, you may proceed," Milne said.

She started slowly and kept her words plain, using the phrase, "reasonable doubt" over and over again so it would be branded into the jurors' brain circuits. "The prosecution will try to convince you that these are cold-blooded murders planned and executed by the defendant. The fact that the Remington rifle used in both murders was purchased by the defendant will be used as a support for that idea.

"But the testimony will show that Terry London had access to this rifle twelve years ago, when Tamara Sweet was killed. Jerry and Ralph Kettrick will both testify that Ms. London kept the rifle in her studio, and it was there not long before she was shot. The defendant is supposed to have shot her on his first visit to the studio where she worked. It won't add up, ladies and gentlemen.

"We will show you that Kurt Scott is guilty of neither murder, and we will present evidence to indicate that Terry London was an unbalanced and violent person, who may herself have killed Tamara Sweet because she was in love with the defendant and he was dating Miss Sweet. We will show you that the defendant, far from being a cold-blooded killer, is a victim of Terry London as surely as Miss Sweet was.

"We will show you that every bit of the so-called evidence linking the defendant to these murders has an alternate, innocent explanation. We will show you that others had the motive, means, and opportunity to kill Ms. London. And we will show you that Mr. Kettrick's so-called eyewitness identification is questionable, so questionable you should not accept it.

"As to the video made by Ms. London as she lay dying, there are two questions that we hope you will ask yourselves as you watch it. First, could anyone, even the most highly trained lip-reader, really know what she was saying? And second, did her vindictiveness toward the defendant extend so far that in her last words she may have thought only of him, and damned him, instead of the real killer?

"That may seem unlikely to you now, ladies and gentlemen, because you have not yet met Terry London through the testimony. But as you grow to understand her, and the sickness in her soul that made her want to destroy the defendant if he would not love her, which grew stronger rather than weaker with the passing of years, you will understand that Terry London, whatever her exact words, lied as she lay there dying.

"And I ask you to examine the evidence sharply and with the proper measure of skepticism. Don't accept things at their face value. Look deep, and I am confident you will find doubt in your minds as to whether the scenario the prosecution would have you believe is true."

She wound her way through the points in the prosecution case she felt were weakest. Mrs. Bourgogne's eyes never left her. What was she thinking?

Nina paused. She was about to begin the conclusion she had

prepared, when someone coughed. Behind her, she heard the steel chain on Kurt's feet clanking as he shifted his weight.

She put her notes down, came rapidly around from the podium, and held her hand toward Kurt. "You've probably been looking at Kurt Scott's feet," she said, holding her hand out toward the shackles. "I know I would. Maybe you've been trying not to look. But I'd like to suggest that you think about these shackles. Look at this man. He is brought to you humble and degraded, in chains. He's been made to look like some kind of savage—"

"Your Honor!" Collier said.

"Please remember, no matter what they've done to make him look bad—"

"Ms. Reilly," Milne boomed. "Step up here . . ."

"He's an innocent man, until proven guilty. An innocent man!"

"Ms. Reilly! Step up here!"

She went. But she knew the jury had heard the conviction in her voice.

He was an innocent man. She ought to know.

36

THE COURTROOM BECAME NINA'S WORLD AGAIN. THE EYES OF SOME of the woman jurors seemed permanently stuck on Kurt.

On Tuesday, Terry's letter to Kurt, found in his Wiesbaden apartment and dated 1990, was introduced. As it circulated, Nina reread her own copy:

> Dear Cowardly Lion, A little elf told me you were in London and I came to visit. But you had run away again, and I have to go home. So maybe you will get this, maybe you won't.
>
> I'm going to find you someday. It's not right for you to be enjoying your life while I suffer. You made me this way. I think about you every day. I remember your lies about loving me, and what you made me do. You have to be punished, if there is any justice in this world.
>
> Do you really think I can stop now? Or ever? I'm the kind of woman who only loves once.
>
> Kurt—how long can you run? I am steadfast. I am stronger

than you. I am your Wife, Kurt. I have my rights, do you understand?

The note was signed "Terry."

Collier followed that letter with Kurt's response, which Terry had kept, in which he told Terry he would make her sorry if she kept up the harassment—and she knew exactly what he meant.

On Wednesday, Collier brought in Jason Joyce, the South Lake Tahoe patrolman who had pulled Kurt over at dawn. Officer Joyce wore his bristly brown hair very short. He sat at attention like an army recruit.

"He was weaving back and forth across the center line on Pioneer Trail," he said in answer to Collier's question, consulting his notes. "This was at five-forty in the morning. I drove up alongside him. His head was hanging like he was very tired or sick. When he saw me, he looked scared. He wasn't wearing a seatbelt, either.

"I pulled him over on the shoulder just past Jicarillo. I asked him to get out his driver's license, and there was blood on his hand, running down from his sleeve. I held my flashlight on him and had him get out and lean against the car. There was a lot of what looked like dried blood on his clothes, down the left side. I said, 'What is that?' He answered, 'Blood.' I said, 'You hurt?' He nodded, so I said, 'You been in a fight?' And he answered, 'A shooting. She's been shot.' "

"He said those words? 'She's been shot?' " Collier said, raising his eyebrows at the jury to register the importance of this statement.

"Yes, that's the note I made here."

"What happened at that point?"

"I called for backup and an ambulance, and he was checked into Boulder Hospital at six-twelve. He'd been shot in the left arm, a soft-tissue wound. He told me on the way in where this woman lived. He said he'd been driving around for the whole night, parked somewhere and went to sleep for a while, and had decided to go to the police station and report it and get some medical attention, when I pulled him over."

"What did you do next?" Collier said.

"Officer Booth and I went to the address and we went directly to the studio next to the main house."

"Why did you do that?

"Two reasons. There were dark-colored droplets on the path to the studio. And the door was wide open. The temperature was in the forties. If anyone was in there she was in trouble. So we announced ourselves at the doorway. It was dark inside but I could see a lot of equipment. Then I saw what looked like the butt of a rifle. We pulled our weapons and went in."

"What did you find inside?"

"Female lying on the floor about ten feet in from the entrance. She wasn't breathing. The body was covered with blood that had partially dried and was stiff and cold. I called for another ambulance, but it was clear to me she was dead."

Joyce continued with the long story outlined in detail in the police reports: the Remington on the floor beside Terry, the signs of struggle, the video camera propped between her legs. A homicide investigation team, which consisted of a photographer, two criminalists, and a detective, Lieutenant Julian Oskel, had arrived within an hour and started their work.

"What did you do at that point?"

"I returned to the station and worked on my report."

"Thank you, Officer Joyce. Your witness."

Nina took the patrolman back over his conversation with Kurt.

"No tape was made of these statements?" she asked.

"No. I filmed the stop from the recorder in my vehicle. That's standard procedure. The sound was out."

"Let's see that film," Nina said. Once again the courtroom lights went down. They watched the film, Joyce pulling Kurt over, walking over to the car with his flashlight, Kurt opening the car door and leaning over the hood. On a crystal clear Tahoe morning, with the camera carefully set to capture anyone in the car in front, Kurt's unmistakable face turned toward the camera, talking earnestly.

"Stop right there," Nina said. "What exactly did he say at that point?"

"Okay," Joyce said patiently. "This is according to my notes. I said, 'What is that?' He answered, 'Blood.' I said, 'You hurt?' He nodded, so I said, 'You been in a fight?' And he answered, 'A shooting. She's been shot.' "

"Do you have any independent recollection of what he said? Without your notes?"

"Vague. It was several months ago. I rely on my notes."

"And what is the precise time that these notes were made?"

"It says right here, at the top, 0730 hours. Seven-thirty A.M."

"And what time, again, did the defendant actually say these words?"

"That would have been—you can see the time on the film tape on the frame where you've stopped it. 0544 hours."

"Did you discuss the defendant's exact words with anyone prior to making those notes?"

"The exact words? No."

"So between the time the statements were made and the time you made your notes one hour and forty-six minutes intervened?"

"Yes."

"And during this time you were involved in the grisly discovery of a body covered with blood, with all that entailed."

"Yes."

"Isn't it possible you forgot the exact words the defendant said during that intervening period?"

"No. I'm trained to retain things like that."

"Your memory has been trained to recall the exact words of statements that have been made to you."

"Yes." The young patrolman looked at her with a self-satisfied smile. He knew all he had to do was hold the line. "She's been shot." It was almost as good as a confession.

"Well, then, let's just test your short-term memory, shall we?" Nina said. Officer Joyce's smile faded fast. "Here's the test: What is the question I asked you three questions ago?" Nina said.

"Objection. Not a proper test, Your Honor."

Up to the sidebar they went. In the witness box, Officer Joyce's face was screwed up in concentration, using the extra minutes Collier had gotten for him. "So what's the problem with it?" Milne asked Collier. Collier repeated that it was unfair and made his argument, while Joyce thought. Milne noticed Collier looking at the witness, and, observing his expression, said brusquely, "Overruled."

Back at the counsel table, Nina said, "Your response, Officer?"

"I don't know what you mean. Three questions ago, what does that mean?"

"I'll even start out the question for you. 'And during this time . . .' "

"And during this time . . . you were involved with discovering the body and all that . . ." Officer Joyce said tentatively.

"That's what you remember?"

"It's hard to remember exactly. I mean, it's very stressful, being here in court."

"And it's not stressful pulling a man over who's got blood all over his clothes and finding a shooting victim?"

Officer Joyce had no answer for that one.

"Request that the question beginning 'And during this time . . .' be read back, Your Honor."

The court stenographer took a moment, then read: "And during this time you were involved in the grisly discovery of a body covered with blood, with all that entailed."

"Right," Officer Joyce said. "I had most of it."

"I submit that you weren't even close to the exact words, Officer. How much time elapsed between my asking that question and your attempt to repeat it?"

"Three or four minutes," the young patrolman said, slouching in his seat.

"That's all. Thank you," Nina said. She looked over at the jury. They were sitting up as straight as Officer Joyce had, starting out. Good. Wake 'em up. Down with predictable endings.

"State your full name," Collier said from his counsel table. It was Thursday morning, and the case against Kurt was in full swing. It would be a hot day, and the air-conditioning had quit.

"Willie Gershwin Evans. Call me Willie, please."

The lip-reader who had made the transcript of the death video had taken the stand. In his seventies, an upright, healthy-looking man who obviously took his vitamins, he wore rimless glasses and a starched white shirt and striped tie.

"Where are you employed?"

"I'm retired now, but until then, I was a benefits worker for the health department out of Placerville." He spoke clearly, though his voice had a hollow tone, as though produced from an unusual place.

"Have you served as a lip-reading expert on behalf of the county on any other occasions?"

"Oh, many times, over forty years. I helped hearing-impaired people fill out applications for benefits. In court, I spoke for witnesses who use American Sign Language. I'm good at that, and lip-reading helps with sign language. I helped the police, too, when they were watching people through windows and needed to know what they were saying."

"Are you yourself hearing-impaired?"

"I used to be. Back in the days when they called people like me just plain 'deaf.' Diphtheria when I was a child. I couldn't hear again until I was thirty-eight. And then my wife got me tested at Stanford, and lo and behold, they thought they could operate and fix my hearing. They got me up to seventy-eight percent. My hearing aid fixed the rest. But they couldn't help my wife, so I stayed up on American Sign Language and the lip-reading."

"And do you consider yourself an expert in the area of reading lips?"

"I do it better than anyone I've met," the old man said confidently.

Collier said, "Request that this witness be qualified as an expert in the area of lip-reading."

"Ms. Reilly?"

Nina thought. She could make a big deal out of Evans's competence, or she could try to turn his testimony to her own ends. She decided not to quibble. "No objection, Your Honor," she said.

Collier said, "I'd like you to demonstrate for us how you read lips. I'm going to write down a sentence and read it without sound to you, and you tell me what I've said, if you will. I will represent to the court and counsel that I have not rehearsed any of this with the witness. That's true, isn't it?"

"All you said was, you might give me a little test," the witness said, nodding. Collier thought a moment, wrote something down, and handed the paper to Milne. Then he stepped up close to the witness and said, "Ready?"

"Go ahead."

Collier mouthed some words at the witness.

"Do it again," the witness said.

As soon as Collier's mouth closed, the witness said, "Got it now. You said, 'The price of eggs has gone up to forty-nine cents a dozen.' When's the last time you shopped for eggs, sir?"

The spectators laughed, and Collier smiled and retrieved his paper from the judge. He gave it to Nina to read at her seat, then said, "May I show the jury?"

"No objection," Nina said. The paper went around. The witness had it word for word. Collier walked over to the clerk and picked up some exhibits.

"Now, on March thirty-first of this year were you asked to perform lip-reading services for the South Lake Tahoe Police Department in connection with an ongoing investigation into the death of Theresa London?"

"I was."

"Describe the services you were asked to perform."

"They had a videotape of the, uh, deceased lady. She'd been shot, and couldn't speak, but she was moving her mouth like she was talking. So they wanted me to see if she was saying anything."

"And did you review the tape, which has been previously admitted as People's Exhibit 45?" The witness looked at the tape offered by Collier and said, "Sure did. When I was done, I put my name on it, right here on the label. And the date."

"Where were you at the time you viewed the tape?"

"In the conference room at your office. An officer ran the tape and when we were done he rewound it and put it back in the box."

"Were you at any time left alone with it?"

"Nope."

"What happened then?"

"I wrote down what she said, leaving blanks where I wasn't sure. Your secretary typed it up and I made sure the typed statement was exactly the same as mine. Then I signed it."

"And is this document, marked as People's Exhibit 46, the original handwritten notes you made?"

The witness bent his head down, examined the paper closely. "That's it."

"And is this typewritten document, marked as People's Exhibit 47, the document the secretary typed up, which you signed?"

He made the same close examination. "That's right."

"Request that People's 46 and 47 be admitted into evidence," Collier said.

"No objection," Nina said.

"The exhibits are admitted into evidence as numbered," Milne said, writing his own notes.

Collier said, "Now tell me, Mr. Evans—"

"Willie."

"Please read those notes to the jury."

"Objection. Best evidence rule," Nina said.

"Come on up," Milne said.

When she, Collier, and Milne had their heads together, Nina whispered, so the jury couldn't hear, "The witness's recollection is the best evidence, even if he uses the notes to refresh his recollection, so he should be testifying from memory to the extent he can do so."

Milne said to Collier, "She's right, but she's wrong. The best evidence is the videotape. The witness is the interpreter. Why aren't you starting with that?"

"I thought we needed more of a foundation. Show the chain of custody is intact. Unless, of course, counsel is willing to stipulate—"

"That you haven't tampered with the tape? So long as it's the same tape I saw that day in your office, I'm not going to object," Nina said. "Let's show it. I'll reserve any objection."

"It will save a lot of time. Thanks," Collier said, casting her a puzzled look. She knew he was wondering why she didn't use every technical tool to keep it out.

They went back to the counsel tables, and Collier had a whispered conference with a deputy. In a few moments a screen had been set up and the deputy had set up a projector in the aisle.

"The objection is sustained," Milne announced.

"At this time, the People would like to show the witness Exhibit 45, a videotape apparently made by Terry London after she was shot."

"No objection."

"Just a moment," Milne said as the lights dimmed. "Ladies and gentlemen of the jury, I am going to advise you that this tape is quite graphic and shows the physical effects on a human being of being shot. You are going to see quite a bit of blood. If at any time you feel unable to continue, please raise your hand and you will be escorted from the courtroom."

The jurors lifted a collective eyebrow. Mrs. Bourgogne took a deep breath and folded her hands in her lap, and several of the others followed suit.

"Proceed."

Collier motioned with his hand. Suddenly they were all in Terry's lurid studio, with all the shocking sounds pouring out of the speaker. The stricken courtroom watched and listened to her gagging on her own blood, mouthing words with hideous resolve.

The tape ended. The jurors appeared to be in shock. Kurt said in a low voice, "God, it's horrible, horrible!" He seemed to be in the grip of a great upheaval, as if he would jump up in a moment and say something he'd regret. Nina laid a restraining hand on his.

The video had yanked Nina from the game of trial strategy back into the reality of a human being whose life had ended in front of her. And yet—and yet—Terry London had died hating. She had to remember that.

"Is that the tape you saw?" Collier was saying to Evans, in a matter-of-fact voice.

"The same."

"And you watched it several times?"

"I did."

"Your notes, Exhibit 46, are a result of lip-reading the words of the victim?"

"Yes."

"Can you remember her exact words without reading your notes?"

"No."

"All right. Read your notes," Collier said.

Evans hesitated, looked over at Nina as if she intended to stop him.

"Go ahead, Willie," Collier said again.

"All right. This is according to my notes, which I took while I was watching the video over and over. She said, uh, 'It doesn't hurt pause I'm dying pause It's your fault Kurt pause oh oh I'm dying pause You blanky blanky pulled the trigger pause what a surprise pause The Angel of Death pause I'll see you in hell.' Then she trails off, saying 'oh oh oh.' "

The courtroom had fallen silent. The words, read in the elderly man's hollow voice, were so powerful, so chilling. One of the young woman jurors pressed her hand over her mouth.

Collier let the silence die away. Then he said, "When you say 'pause,' what does that mean?"

"Oh, she didn't say that. It's just to make it clear that she paused between those words."

"And when you say 'blank'?"

" 'Blank' means there's a syllable I couldn't catch. 'Blanky' is two syllables."

"So, to make it a little easier, without the pauses and blanks, she said, 'It doesn't hurt. I'm dying. It's your fault, Kurt. Oh, oh. I'm dying. You pulled the trigger. What a surprise—the Angel of Death. Oh, oh, oh."

"Yes. Those are the words I saw."

"Thank you. Your witness."

"Good morning," Nina said.

"Good morning," Willie Evans said, flashing a sparkling pair of dentures.

"Your hearing is normal with the hearing aid?"

"Yes."

"How's your eyesight?"

"My eyesight? About what you'd expect. Fine, so long as I wear my specs."

"That conference room you were sitting in—about how far were you from the TV monitor?"

"Oh, about as far away as you are from me."

"Good," Nina said. "Because I'd like to give you a little test like Mr. Hallowell did, only from the distance that you observed the TV monitor."

"Okay," Willie said. "Let me wipe my glasses." While he wiped them, Nina wrote something down on a card and passed it to Collier, then to the judge.

She mouthed some words, and Willie strained toward her.

"Again," he said. She did it again, and he said, "It'd be better if you came up close."

"Oh, but that would ruin my test," Nina said. "Tell the jury what I just said."

"Well, I missed a couple of words. You slurred them."

"Did the woman on the tape slur words too, Willie?"

"Sure. In her condition, I would too. That's why I had the blanky blanks."

"Okay, use blanky blanks if you need to," Nina said. "Want to see me say it one more time?"

"Sure."

She mouthed the words once more.

"The best I could tell," Willie said slowly, "you said, 'You might's well of pulled the trigger.' Say it again."

Nina sat there, made words with her lips.

" 'You might's well of pulled the trigger,' " Willie Evans said hesitantly. "That's what I see."

Nina said, "Thank you," then got up and took the paper to the jury. As they passed it around, she said, looking at Mrs. Bourgogne, "Let the record show that I wrote on the paper, 'You might as well have pulled the trigger.' "

"Like I said, you slurred it a little bit."

"And could the lady in the video have said 'might as well have' where you wrote 'blanky blanky' in your notes?" Nina said.

Evans picked his notes up again, adjusting his glasses as if they could help him divine what the blanks said. "I can't tell right now," he said.

"As you sit here right now, is it possible that the lady said that sentence in the video? 'You might as well have pulled the trigger'?"

"Objection! Calls for speculation!" Collier said quickly.

"Withdrawn," Nina said. "I'll tell you what, Willie. I need you to look at that bit of the tape one more time. Can you do that?"

"If you insist," Evans said.

The tape rolled again. This time Nina motioned for the deputy to stop it in the middle. Terry's agonized face filled the screen. Evans craned his neck to see better.

"What did she say right there?" Nina asked.

"She said, 'You blanky blanky pulled the trigger.' "

"Can you fill in the blanks, based on this viewing?"

" 'You might's well've pulled the trigger,' " Evans said. "Yes, it would fit right."

"I'm not asking you if it would fit, Willie. I'm asking you, is that what she said?"

"I don't know. It's an art, you see."

"Is that what she said?"

"Objection! Asked and answered! Calls for speculation."

"Overruled," Milne said unexpectedly.

"That could be what she said, all right. It could be. But you want to know for sure, is that it? I can't tell you. I sure can't. She said some words in between 'you' and 'pulled.' Four syllables. She was coughing. I can't tell you."

"But it could have been, couldn't it, Willie? 'You might as well have pulled the trigger'?"

"Objection! Argumentative! Request a sidebar conference! Your Honor . . ."

Willie was nodding his head, saying, "It could be. Yep, it could."

"The answer will stand. Move on, counsel."

"All right," Nina said. "Was any portion of the video blown up or refined for you using computerized techniques, Willie?"

"No. But I watched the video at least ten times. I don't think I would have—"

"Thank you. Did you see any still pictures from the video?"

"No. It wouldn't have helped."

Nina went on to the other words in the video, especially the "Kurt." But Evans wouldn't budge on that one, and stood up to her very well for the remainder of the morning. The lunch recess was coming up. Nina thought she had gotten everything she could, but she felt reluctant to let Evans go. She felt that Willie had another treasure for her, if she could just dive deep enough for it.

Finally, she said, "That sentence, 'I'll see you in hell.' The *H* is an aspirant that you can hear but not see, isn't that right?"

"Right. But I got it easily from the context."

"What you actually saw was 'I'll see you in *L,*' isn't that right?"

"Sure, but there is no *L.* Some say there's no hell, either, of course." Some of the jurors smiled.

"How do you know there's no *L*?" Nina said. "It could be an initial for a certain place, couldn't it?"

"No. I don't think so," Evans said. "She said 'hell.' It was in her eyes, her expression, the context. She said 'hell.' "

She wasn't getting anywhere. And Mrs. Bourgogne yawned, a discreet little yawn, but a yawn. She gave up. "Thank you," she said. Sandy elbowed her.

"Just a moment, Your Honor," she said.

Sandy whispered, "Put him on the film the cop took when he pulled Kurt over."

Nina thought, said under her breath, "Wow!"

"Are you finished, counsel?"

"Just a few more questions, Your Honor. Willie, you say lip-reading is an art—"

"And I'm an artist," Willie said, grinning. "I see a lot of speech you wouldn't believe. You want to know what the lady sitting next to you said just now?"

"No! But I guess you know what I want you to read for us now."

"That I do."

"With the court's permission, I'd like to have Mr. Evans read the defendant's lips on the tape made by Officer Joyce at the time the defendant was stopped on Pioneer Trail. People's Exhibit 14."

"That's completely improper, your Honor," Collier said. "It's beyond the scope of direct examination. It's cumulative. The witness has already demonstrated his competence. She's using our expert as a defense expert."

Milne had followed the last interchange with the witness keenly. Now he said, "Your objections are technically correct, counsel. However, the request to show the witness that portion of the tape in which the defendant's lips are moving is granted in the interests of justice, in the Court's discretion."

Collier sat down, whispering in agitation to his paralegal. The deputy had already located the film.

Once more, the soundless film Officer Joyce had made was shown. Kurt's cheek pressed against the window of the Pathfinder he had been driving. He was saying something.

"Again," Evans said. He had leaned forward toward the screen. The film appeared again.

"Okay," he said. "Those boys don't take any chances. They got a good shot of his face. It's nice and clear." The lights came up again.

Nina said, "What did the defendant say as he leaned against the car, Willie?"

"He said, 'Blood.' Then he nodded, and he said, 'A shooting. I've been shot.' "

Collier slammed his file down on the table. Nina had never seen him look so angry. "Objection!" he said. "The prosecution has been unfairly surprised—"

"To the sidebar, both counsel." Nina stood there and didn't say a word, while Collier raised every argument he could to have the line of testimony stricken. Milne listened carefully, then said, "You should have had him do it yourself. He's uncovered some shoddy police work you should have uncovered. Live with it."

"Anything further?" Milne said to Nina as Collier returned, shaking with anger, to his place.

"Nothing further, Your Honor."

"Mr. Hallowell? Rebuttal?"

Collier shook his head.

"The witness is excused. Thank you, sir."

"A pleasure." The bright-eyed retiree hopped nimbly from the stand.

"The court will recess until one-thirty," Milne said, and the jury filed down the center aisle.

The deputy was already approaching to take him away, when Kurt leaned toward Nina and Sandy and said, "I don't know how you thought of that."

"Thank Sandy," Nina said. She smiled encouragingly. He clanked off.

37

"Call frank fontaine."

The criminalist shuffled up and sat in the witness box. Still in his twenties, with sleek, straight black hair and tufted eyebrows, even in street clothes he had the disinfected air of one who wears a lab coat most of his life.

Collier asked a number of preliminary questions establishing that Fontaine was employed by the county sheriff's office and was loaned out on a regular basis to help local police with homicide investigations.

"And it is correct that your services have been employed in collecting and examining physical evidence in connection with the deaths of both Theresa London and Tamara Sweet?"

"I'm going to interrupt right here," Judge Milne said, turning to the jury and putting his glasses down on his bench. "You have probably noticed that, although the defendant has been charged with only one homicide, that of Terry London, from time to time there is evidence coming in about another homicide, that of Tamara Sweet. I want to make it clear that the defendant is not charged with the murder of Tamara Sweet. The evidence concerning her death is to be considered by you only in regard to the question of motive for the murder of Terry London. I will instruct you further on this matter at a later time."

Nina watched Mrs. Bourgogne. As she had expected, it looked like the forewoman had not heard one word of Milne's advisement. She was examining the short skirt of the juror next to her. The rest of the jurors looked lost too. She could only hope they would figure it out from the jury instructions, which they unfortunately wouldn't hear until the close of evidence.

"Go ahead," Milne said, looking satisfied with himself.

"Yes, sir. I was called out on both cases. The London case first."

"State the circumstances of your assignment to the London case."

"South Lake Tahoe police contacted the sheriff's office in Placerville requesting a criminalist be sent out to a crime scene located at 8 Coyote Road at nine-fifteen A.M. on March thirty-first. I was already working at the sheriff's substation at Tahoe, so I went directly to the crime scene."

"Does this report, marked as People's Exhibit 12, summarize your activities at that date and time?" Nina thought about objecting to the report, which was hearsay, coming in, decided it might help, and said nothing.

"Yes. I remained there for several hours. I collected blood samples from the walls and floor and from the body of the decedent. I also collected fingerprints from a number of surfaces, including a Remington .30-06 rifle found at the scene, and took into custody two bullets and bullet casings."

"All right," Collier said. "Please summarize your findings with regard to each blood sample which has been marked as an exhibit and summarized in this chart."

Fontaine patiently and exhaustively detailed his findings. His lab methods were irreproachable. He used gloves for everything. He had kept orderly and legible notes. "Blood spatters here, and here," he said, pointing with his marker to the chart. "Found five feet one inch up on the wall near bullet one, are intermixed with tissue—"

"Human tissue?"

"Correct. Indicating that the tissue and blood spattered against the wall at the same time as the bullet."

"Did you compare the blood samples from the wall with the blood of the decedent?"

"The DNA tests indicate that all samples were from the decedent."

"You are aware of the coroner's finding that the decedent was shot through the neck and that a large rear entry wound was present in the posterior portion of the neck?"

"Yes."

"What if anything can you conclude about the position of the decedent at the time the bullet was fired?"

Fontaine established that Terry London had been standing, close to and facing the rifle at the time she was shot, and that the rifle had been at an angle pointing upward.

"Indicating that the assailant was kneeling on the floor?"

"I'd have to defer to the coroner on that. Dr. Clauson."

"What about bullet two?"

"That bullet was taken from a different wall, facing the outer door. There was also blood and human tissue beside the bullet in the wall."

"Were you able to match the blood and tissue samples taken near bullet two with any other samples available to you?"

"The samples matched the defendant's DNA sample provided to our office."

"Indicating what to you?"

"That bullet one struck Theresa London, and bullet two struck the defendant."

"Did you compare the striations and other evidence from firing the bullets with the Remington rifle you also took into custody?" The rifle was brought up.

Kurt wrote on his notepad, "If only I hadn't left it with her."

"Yes. Both bullets were definitely fired from the Remington," Fontaine said, and proceeded to show the jury another chart with blowups of the bullets and test bullets he had fired for comparison. Even Nina could see the striations were almost exactly the same.

"Now, with regard to the fingerprints you took," Collier said, and almost three hours went by while Fontaine explained in mind-numbing detail how each fingerprint had been taken, labeled, and analyzed. Nina's own fingerprint expert had spent hours going over the expected testimony with her. She checked off the testimony on her notes, point by point.

Finally Fontaine stated his conclusions. On the barrel of the rifle he had found complete prints from both Kurt and Terry, along with several unidentified partial prints, though the prints on the trigger had been smeared into unidentifiability. On the camera he had found only smeared and partial prints. The front doorknob was too smeared to make any identifications. All around the studio, Terry's prints showed up as ghostly markers from the chemicals used to locate them. And there were other, unidentified prints. But no full prints on the rifle, except for Terry's and Kurt's.

"Okay, let's talk now about the homicide investigation of remains found in a small cave near Fallen Leaf Lake."

"Right."

"Your Honor, at this time we intend to offer the evidence discussed last week," Collier said, cuing the judge.

"Very well," Milne said. He turned to the jury and read from his notes, "At this time I am going to instruct you regarding certain evidence to be introduced in this trial. The evidence is all statements and physical evidence that may be introduced regarding the death of another person, named Tamara Sweet. I am instructing you that the defendant is not charged with the death of Tamara Sweet. You will not be asked to decide whether he should be convicted of any crime in connection to her death. However, you may consider evidence that the defendant caused the death of Tamara Sweet in considering what if any motive the defendant may have had to murder Terry London."

Mrs. Bourgogne listened politely. She could have been following Milne perfectly, or she could have been thinking about buying a new car. There was no way to tell.

"You may proceed, counsel."

Collier said, "Were you called to assist in the investigation of bones found near Fallen Leaf Lake on June twenty-fourth?"

"Correct. Remains eventually identified as those of Tamara Sweet." Fontaine was pulling out a new set of notes. He detailed how he had been called to the scene, and listed the evidence he had found. Photographs were passed around. One human skeleton makes a large pile of bones. Nina would never forget the sight.

"There was still some rotted blue cloth, probably clothing, under the body. Her . . . wrist"—he intentionally chose the common word over the scientific one—"still, ah, carried a watch on it." He drew out the watch carefully from the evidence bag. "A Timex," he said. "But it hadn't kept on tickin'." He smiled at his little joke, but no one else did. "The mother, Mrs. Sweet, recognized the Timex," he added. "Dental records confirmed the tentative I.D."

"And did you assist in a search of the surrounding area to try to ascertain where the death actually occurred?"

"Yes, and I received and read supplemental reports filed by the deputies. But it had been too many years. The cave was close to the trail that leads down from the ranger station at Angora Ridge to Fallen Leaf Lake, so I would think she was perhaps killed on the path—"

"Objection. Speculation."

"Sustained. The jury will disregard the last sentence of the answer to the last question."

"Mr. Fontaine, were you able to ascertain the source of the bullet found in Tamara Sweet's body?"

"Yes, we were. Your office suggested that we compare that bullet to the ones we recovered in the other homicide. Our tests showed it to be from the same Remington rifle that killed Teresa London. Registered, as I previously testified, to the defendant."

Collier kept Fontaine on the stand until the mid-afternoon break. When she finally had her chance, Nina said, "Just a few points, Mr. Fontaine." Keep it simple, she thought to herself. Hit hard and run.

"Regarding the two bullets found at the London studio . . ."

"Uh-huh."

"You labeled them bullet one and bullet two. Do those labels indicate your opinion as to which bullet was fired first?"

"No, just the order in which they were discovered."

"So the defendant could have been shot first, and then the victim?"

"Well, I am sure the coroner will tell you the victim was not able to shoot after being shot in the neck. The wound was too grievous."

"Based on the evidence you have, could the victim have shot the defendant first, and then someone besides the defendant have shot the victim?" Nina said.

"No," Fontaine said. "There were only the two sets of prints on the gun."

"That's not quite true, is it? Don't you want to be precise here? Isn't it true that there were several indistinct prints you could not identify on the gun?"

"Yes, but they were most likely made by the same people who left the full prints we did identify," Fontaine said.

"Isn't that just a sloppy assumption, Mr. Fontaine? Isn't it also possible that one or more of the partial prints was made by a third person? Or that the shooter wore gloves?"

"We'll never know," Fontaine said.

"So you are guessing?"

"I'm stating my opinion."

"But your opinion is baseless, isn't it? You're clutching that microphone right now. Your prints are on it, along with many other people's prints, right?"

"I suppose. I don't know when they clean it."

"Suppose they haven't cleaned it in twelve years," Nina said. "Or let me put it this way. Suppose they don't clean it for twelve years—it gets put in a closet after today and not used again. Tell me, would your prints still be on the microphone?"

"If they weren't overlaid by the janitor," Fontaine said.

"Okay. Now let's suppose the defendant here touched that rifle twelve years ago, and didn't touch it since, and no other prints were overlaid on it. Couldn't his print still be there?"

Fontaine stroked his chin. He didn't want to answer.

"Well?"

"With our current advanced methods, a print could show up that was that old," he said. "It would be very faint, but faintness also can occur when the grip of the fingers is very light."

"Do you have any way of dating exactly when the fingerprints you found on the gun barrel were made?"

"I suppose not. One could overlay the other, and that would give you the fact that the overlying print came second, but it wouldn't tell you when the first print was made."

"So let's be very clear about this. Based on all your observations, Mr. Fontaine, regarding the fingerprints as shown on your chart, could Mr. Scott's prints have been made as long as twelve years ago?"

"Objection. Vague. Calls for speculation."

"Rephrase the question, counsel," Milne said.

"Mr. Fontaine," Nina said doggedly. "Based on all your observations at the crime scene and analyzing all the evidence you obtained, and based on your advanced training in forensic science and your experience in law enforcement and criminology, is it inconsistent with any of the evidence that the defendant's fingerprints on the gun were placed there some months or years prior to the death of Ms. London?"

"Same objection."

"Overruled."

"Not inconsistent," Mr. Fontaine said.

"Did you, or anyone in your office, perform a fluorescein test—which would have indicated whether or not he had recently used a firearm—on the hands of the defendant, Kurt Scott?"

She already knew the answer, of course, just as she had known he would ask the question. As expected, he frowned, then squirmed, a perfectionist caught in a glaring oversight. He read through his notes, looking for a way out, and finally had to answer. "Unfortunately, my understanding is that the fluorescein test was not performed on the defendant."

"Wouldn't it be standard operating procedure to perform such a test on a shooting suspect?"

"Yes. But we're a small department up here. We do our best. Somehow it was overlooked."

"Isn't it true that if the test was performed early enough after the arrest, the police department would have known if Kurt Scott had fired a weapon within the previous twenty-four hours?"

"Maybe even longer."

"So he could have been completely vindicated, if the fluorescein test had been negative?"

"I'd say it's lucky for the defendant we didn't perform the test. It would have nailed him, if it was positive."

"I see. We're left with our doubts," Nina said, as if to herself.

"Objection!"

Nina said hastily, "Withdrawn, Your Honor. So . . . you have no evidence that Kurt Scott handled or shot the rifle on the night of Terry London's death?"

"No, but—"

"Thank you," Nina said. She sat down.

Jerry Kettrick stepped up to the stand, dressed in baggy jeans and a wide tie, his rubbery lips spread wide as if to say, "Let me entertain you."

Jerry was a very important witness. He was getting an uncalled-for extra fifteen minutes of fame. He understood that. Today he looked like Pete Townsend giving good interview, or Alice Cooper, dignified and polite in a black-eyeliner, ravaged-albino kind of way. His tufty beard had been trimmed for his legal debut and a rubber band held most of his scraggly white hair back, but the burnt-out look in his eyes and the length of the white hair flowing down his back told on him. He was the quintessential aging hippie, Nina thought, the kind who doesn't move on to politics or the Sierra Club or Buddhism, but just gets older, wondering where the revolution went.

Nina ran her eyes down the transcript of the interview with Jerry and glanced again at Paul's background report.

Collier asked a few preliminary questions, then said, "Where is your house located in relationship to hers?" A diagram had been prepared, and Jerry pointed out his front porch, about a hundred fifty feet from Terry's gate.

"Did she have any neighbors on the other side?"

"No, that was one of the lots the TRPA wouldn't let anyone build on," Jerry said. "And behind her was still forest. She had fenced her property. We were her only real neighbors."

"Did you or your son ever go onto her premises?"

"I went over there to sweep the roof, fix the plumbing, whatever. That was a long time ago, when her parents were still alive. She went away for a few years after her parents died and rented the place. When she came back, she didn't want me around."

"Why was that?"

"We had a falling out, you might say. Neighbor problems. I liked to play my guitar cranked up high. I'm a night person. She was a good-looking woman and I was lonesome, but she wasn't interested. One time, she got mad at me for no reason and told me to get off her property. But then she started calling on my boy, and he done the same kind of chores for her."

"Did you remain on a social basis with her?"

"Not hardly. At one time I thought we were gonna, you know, get together. But she wasn't ready for a real man. She had a shrine thing set up in her bedroom for some dude she used to know. Anyway, she got hostile with me a few times. She locked up the gate and you had to ring a buzzer, and then her intercom would come on. She wouldn't let me in. I can take a hint. Her loss." Kettrick swept his hand over his white hair.

"All right. I direct your attention to the night of March thirtieth."

An expression that said grandly, I am at your service.

"During that evening, did you hear anything unusual?"

"I sure did. I heard gunshots."

"What time was this?"

"About eleven-thirty. I had dozed off in my living room chair, and I heard the shots."

"How many shots did you hear?"

"Two."

"How far apart were the shots?"

"Mmm. Only about a minute apart. I jumped out of my chair, man, I'm telling you, flew to the window and pulled up the blinds. They came from Terry's house. I'm leaning out, eyes wide open, you know, looking toward the gate. It was pushed aside, like she was expecting a visitor. And I saw the man run like hell through there, jump in his car and make tracks."

"Did you on the following day identify that running man in a lineup?"

"I did. And I can identify him again today."

"You see that man present here in the courtroom?"

"Of course I do," Kettrick said. "I wouldn't be here otherwise. It was the defendant over there."

"Pointing to Kurt Scott, the defendant," Collier said. "Was Mr. Scott carrying a gun?"

"No, he was bare-handed. But he was holding his arm like he had been hurt."

"How soon after you heard the shots did you see Mr. Scott?"

"Right away. Very soon. I went in the bedroom and got my own rifle and I stood there at the window and tried to figure out what to do. Ralph had a long, hard day, and he sleeps with a pillow over his head because I snore, so he was still sound asleep. And Terry was capable of firing off a warning shot if she wanted somebody to leave. And she had kept telling me, mind your own business, talking about her privacy and leave her the heck alone type stuff . . ." Kettrick's voice trailed off, and he said, "What was the question again?"

"Let me ask a new one," Collier said. "What did you do after you heard the shots?"

"I thought about calling the cops. I really did," Kettrick said.

"But you didn't?"

"I didn't. I didn't want to be involved in Terry's stuff. I thought she had scared this guy off, her own way. Good fences make good neighbors, you know? Or vice versa, I forget. So I got my gun and sat there by the window a long time, but nothing else happened. And I guess I got sleepy. Next thing I knew, it was seven-thirty and the cops were pounding on my door."

"At that time the body had already been discovered?"

"Yeah. They wanted to know why I didn't call when I heard the shots. How was I to know, man?" Kettrick's eyes blinked angrily.

"Did you then proceed to the South Lake Tahoe Police Department and provide a statement and identify the defendant in the lineup?"

"Exactly. I proceeded. I provided. I identified."

"Thank you. Nothing further."

Milne took a short break. Nina drank down her caffeine dose, thinking hard. Kettrick was a key to the case. Two shots, and he had gone to get his gun, but he hadn't gone over to Terry's or called the police.

Odd behavior, even for an old hippie. A brave man would have investigated himself. A scared man would have called the cops. Why had Kettrick done nothing?

Besides, she knew he was lying or mistaken. Kurt had come running out the front, and then Matt and Terry had struggled, and the second shot had killed her. Matt had jumped the fence after leaving through the back door, the one Kettrick couldn't see.

She couldn't think of any reason he'd lie, so he must be mistaken. There had not been two shots, followed by Kurt running out the door.

How could she fix this?

She lowered her head, praying to something she wasn't sure existed for a sharp, concentrated mind, shamelessly scrabbling for anything that might give her an edge.

38

"MR. KETTRICK," NINA SAID WHEN COURT RESUMED.

"Ma'am," Kettrick said, inclining his head gravely.

"Let's go over that sequence again, from the time you heard the first shot."

"Okay."

"You were dozing, and you heard a shot."

"Right."

"Where were you sitting?"

"My recliner, right by the TV."

"The window was open?"

"No, it was freezing out. I had a fire going in the stove, the windows shut. Cold day, parka weather."

"Then how could you hear the shot?"

"It was a blast that shook the windows. I woke up and tore over there to the window."

"Was the TV on?"

"Sure. I sleep through everything these days."

"Had you had anything alcoholic to drink?"

"A few beers, nothing really."

"How many beers?"

Kettrick thought a minute. "Oh, I guess a six-pack," he said. "Bottles. Bought it at the Seven-'leven. Henry Weinhard's Pale Ale. Guess I was on the last bottle when I fell asleep."

"Six bottles of beer," Nina said. "A closed window. A fire going. The TV on. You were asleep. But the shot was so loud, you jumped right up?"

"That's how loud it was, ma'am. What are you getting at?"

"Oh, nothing," Nina said. "I was just wondering how Ralph slept through it."

"I told you, he sleeps with a pillow over his head. I told him, he's gonna suffocate."

"Did you go in and check on him?"

"It wasn't him I was worried about."

"Did you go in and check on him?"

"No! Didn't need to!"

"When did he get home that night?" Nina said.

"Before ten," Kettrick said.

"Were you already dozing at that point?"

"Well, I—"

"Did you see him come in? Did you actually see him, Mr. Kettrick?"

Kettrick's pale face blushed. The blush started at the neck, roseate, moved swiftly up his cheeks, and enveloped his face all the way to the forehead.

Nina had been looking for an opening. The blush told her something was up—what, she didn't know.

"You never saw Ralph that night, did you, Mr. Kettrick?" she said.

"You've got a nerve," Kettrick said. "What do you think you're—"

"Answer my question," Nina said. She was breathing hard, every muscle tense. Sandy had moved slightly away from her as if to give her space. Kurt watched her, his lips slightly open.

The jury watched Kettrick. They watched the blush he couldn't control. On his white skin, it was like a pink lightbulb going off underneath. The blush worked like a polygraph.

"Answer the question," Milne said. His voice had the masculine gravity she would never muster. He was the voice of the village chief over a hundred centuries, telling the villager that to lie was death.

"Sometimes he comes in late. He's a grown man," Kettrick said. He looked out into the audience for Ralph Kettrick, who sat in the corner in the back.

"And you were asleep when he came in that night?"

"Dozing."

"Did you see him?"

"Objection. No foundation. Third-party culpability foundation problem," Collier said.

"I'll allow it," Milne said, sounding just like Judge Ito.

"Not when he came in," Kettrick said. "Next morning when the cops came, he was there in his bed."

"How did you know he was there when you heard the shots?"

"He usually is home—"

"He might not have been there, isn't that right? You heard a loud shot. Did you call Ralphie? Did you, Mr. Kettrick?"

"It was the pillow, must of been. He just didn't hear a thing."

"He wasn't there, was he?"

"I wouldn't know."

"You don't know if he was there or not."

"I wouldn't know."

"Thank you for telling the truth, Mr. Kettrick."

"Your Honor . . ." Collier said.

"Move along, counselor," Milne said.

"After the first shot, you jumped up from your chair?"

"Yeah. Went to the window."

"You knew the direction the shot came from?"

"Yeah. Knew it was Terry's house." Kettrick's mind was still back on the questions about Ralph. He was trying to remember what he had just said.

"You went to the window, and listened, and then you went to get your own gun?"

"Uh, yeah." His face had reddened again, this time with anger as he decided Nina had tricked him.

"After the first shot?"

"Wait, you're confusing me."

"You heard the shot, you ran to the window and opened it, you listened, you went for your gun?"

"There were two shots."

"You went for your gun, and you saw a man running."

"Yeah. Okay. That sounds right."

"Is it right?"

"Yeah, I had him in my sights—"

"And then? And then? What happened?"

"I heard another shot," Jerry Kettrick said. "Yeah. I was at the window, watching."

"The second shot?"

"Yeah! He ran. He got in his car and drove away. Another shot came."

"Where was he when you heard the second shot?"

"Driving off. But how could that be?"

"That's right. Not shooting at Terry London. He was running," Nina said. "Right, Mr. Kettrick?"

"You're getting me all confused," Kettrick said, then said again, "How could that be?"

"No more questions," Nina said.

"You trying to hurt my Ralphie?"

"No more questions!"

And Collier brought Jerry Kettrick back into his own scenario, in which two shots were fired before Jerry went for his gun, in which Ralphie was safely home in bed, but Nina could tell it didn't wash with Mrs. Bourgogne. She had seen dust and trash all over the testimony, and it just wouldn't do.

Sandy finished her notes, leaned over, and said, "That guy dropped too much acid for his own good. He's got fried eggs for brains."

Milne called a short recess and Barbet Cain and the rest of the reporters crowded around her.

"Dr. Clauson, when were you called to the scene at Coyote Road?" Collier asked his next witness.

"Eight thirty-five A.M." Dr. Clauson was just as Nina remembered him: a slight, pale, almost bloodless man with a receding hairline, thick glasses, and a package of cigarettes tucked into his shirt pocket, the same age as and the complete antithesis of Jerry Kettrick. Nina also remembered he was an excellent witness for the prosecution. "I was picked up in a patrol car from my home and met my assistant with the equipment at the crime scene. Fontaine was taking samples from the wall."

Charts and pictures appeared, and Clauson went through the preliminaries, establishing the position of Terry's body, the standing blood under it, and the direction of flow from the neck wound in front and in back. "After examining the body on scene we transported it by ambulance to the mortuary on Emerald Bay Road. That was much later, in the afternoon, after photographs had been taken and all the evidence had been collected. I performed a complete autopsy the next day."

"Was an inquest held?"

"No. No inquests for years up here. I ruled out suicide. It's very difficult to shoot yourself in the neck with a rifle. Length of the barrel, trigger placement. With a rifle, you have to use a string or stick of some kind to pull the trigger usually, though I've heard of a yoga teacher who used his toes, and you usually have a contact wound. She couldn't have shot herself, from what we can tell, though it was close. Besides, she had bruises on her arms, consistent with a struggle."

"How do you determine the distance from which the rifle was shot?"

"Diameter of entry wound, powder residues around the wound, what we call the 'tattoo marks' at the point of entrance."

"What was your finding regarding cause of death?"

"Single rifle bullet through the neck. Nicked the carotid artery, smashed the hyoid bone, injured the vocal cords, and exited through the rear of the neck. Just missed the spinal cord. Took a while. She stayed conscious until she finally suffocated. Some blood in the windpipe. She managed to get a pillow under her head, soaked through by the time we got there. Plus managed to operate the video camera."

Collier waited to let the jury absorb that unpleasant information.

"Odd thing," Clauson said. "Phone was two feet away. Easy to pull on the cord, get it down, call 911. Serious wound, but I think she would have lived. But she didn't call."

Nina thought, one more twist from Terry. She could have lived.

She remembered Matt's description of Terry after Kurt escaped. Matt came out of the storage closet and she was holding the gun loosely, staring into space. She had lain down on a pillow, started the camera, but not saved herself. She hadn't wanted to live.

Nina was sure she had never spared one moment of those last minutes regretting what she was doing to Matt. She was still too busy hating, living in the hell she'd created long before she died.

Collier was saying, "All right, I'd like to ask you about the time of death."

"Ready," Clauson said. He took out the pack of cigarettes, playing with it like a toy, obviously dying for a smoke.

"Were you able to establish an exact time of death based on your medical findings?"

"Nope. Not on the medical evidence. But if you put it together with your witness who saw the defendant, you can establish it."

"Objection! Lack of foundation, goes beyond the qualifications of the witness—"

"The last sentence is stricken. The jury will disregard it," Milne said. Clauson gave Nina a mischievous look. He was up to his old tricks, and she would have to be sharp.

"What conclusions if any did you reach as to the time of death based solely on your medical findings, Doctor?" Collier had hit his stride, establishing a smooth rapport with his witness, just laying it all out, damning fact by fact.

"Well, based on the rigor mortis, blood loss compared to the wound, stomach contents, pooling of blood under body, lividity, I found the time of death to be about nine to ten hours prior to my arrival at the crime scene."

"And what time would that be, Doctor?"

"Time of death? Between ten-thirty and eleven-thirty the previous night."

"Can you be any more exact than that?"

"Not me," Clauson said. "But you can." Nina let it pass.

"All right. You also, on June 25th, went to the scene of the discovery of other apparently human remains, is that correct?"

Milne interjected, "I remind the jury of my previous instruction." The jury looked mystified.

"Yes. That was a whole different ball of wax," Clauson said.

Something about the way he said it made Nina shiver. He looked down at his report. "Arrived with my assistant twelve-fifteen, fifteen minutes past noon. Sheriff's deputies had secured the scene. Remains had been shoveled into a cave originally, although some were piled nearby by the defendant, I understand."

"Objection!" said Nina. "No foundation. Hearsay."

"Sustained," said Milne. "The jury must disregard the last comment."

"Human bones, hair. Bits of rotten cloth. Metal belt buckle and remains of leather belt. Timex. Like Mr. Fontaine said."

"From your observation, could the decedent have crawled into the cave and died?" Collier asked.

"Oh, no. Really more of a hole in the ground, under a good-size boulder. Too small to crawl into. Would have to be a contortionist. Shoved in there after death."

"How long had the body been there?"

"After death, insect and animal life tend to destroy body tissue in a short time, during summer at least. There were no soft tissues remaining when this body was moved. The ligaments holding the spinal column were entirely gone. Each vertebra could be picked up without attachment to those adjoining, totally out of order. Left fibula was missing, so animals had probably gotten to the body at some point. We never found it. Taken by a coyote after the remains were moved to the cave is my guess. We used trained dogs to sniff around for it, but no luck. Make a long story short, body had been there some years."

"And did you subsequently perform an autopsy on the remains?"

"Yep, same mortuary. No rush, but we don't get that many murders. I worked on it right away."

"Were you able to determine cause of death?"

"Well, can't be positive. You can't check for most poisons, drugs, and so on at that late date. But pelvis had been shattered by two rifle bullets. They were still embedded in there, right upper quadrant. We passed them on to Mr. Fontaine. That type of injury is going to cause death quickly if not attended to right away. So my opinion as stated here is bullet wounds. Mr. Fontaine identified the rifle that shot it, as you know. Same one killed Terry London."

Before Nina could get up, Milne said, "Doc Clauson, you know better. No more of that, please. The jury will disregard the last two sentences of the witness."

"Sorry, Judge, have a hard time resisting sometimes."

"Dr. Clauson," Collier said. "Let's get back to your work—"

"Your Honor, could the witness be instructed to use complete sentences?" Nina said.

"Always use complete sentences," Clauson interrupted.

"I regret to state, counsel, that Doc Clauson can't talk any other way. He's been testifying for twenty years in my court and we'll just have to live with it," said Milne. The audience snickered.

"Based on your findings, could you establish a time of death?"

"We studied the bones to determine how long she'd been dead. Still can't say with much certainty. Ten years. Possibly more. That's just an educated guess."

"Did you subsequently make an identification of the remains?" Collier said.

"Analyzed the bones and teeth for the age of decedent. Check of missing persons reports turned up old one from South Lake Tahoe, which would be about fifteen miles from location of remains near Angora Ridge. Dental records and fingerprints confirmed remains were those of Tamara Sweet. Found a belt buckle tucked in there that her folks recognized as one of hers. Also her watch had an inscription, 'Tamara.' "

After Milne recessed for the day, and the expressionless jurors filed out, Nina followed Collier back to his cubicle in the D.A.'s office.

The bare walls and piles of files seemed just the same. Nina could never have tolerated the drab efficiency of the place. They needed Sandy over here, with her baskets and decorating schemes, to spark the place up. Collier hung his jacket on the doorknob and sank into his chair, comfy as if he was falling into bed, scanning the paperwork his secretary handed him on the way in.

"No matter what happens in the trial, I'm buying you a potted plant afterward," Nina said.

"What? Oh, don't bother. I've been given flowers, ferns, succulents, and cacti. They all die. No direct sun, and I forget to water." He laid the papers down, pushed back in his chair, put his arms behind his head, and sighed. "It's a sad thing," he said. "A key witness in my Mexican Mafia case. One of the defense attorneys found out she was an illegal alien and told the Immigration people about her. I doubt if I can keep her here for the trial. She'll be deported back to Guatemala with her kids. God only knows what it took her to get here. She's going to think the lawyers ruined her life, and in a way, she's right."

"Too bad," Nina said, feeling slightly hypocritical. A hostile prosecution witness had been disposed of, quite legally. It was a reprehensible, acceptable defense tactic.

Collier looked so weary, so resigned. His shirt had spent a cramped night in the dryer. He closed his eyes, his hands still folded behind his head, as though he had momentarily fallen asleep. Trial work had a way of retiring its practitioners by the age of forty-five or so. The body reacted to the stress with a heart attack, or an addiction in many cases. How old was Collier? Forty? Fifty? If he became the district attorney for El Dorado County, his trial days would be over, in a natural and wise progression.

Strange. They were antagonists, and here she was, worrying about his health.

Sitting across from him on her metal folding chair, she studied him. He had more resources, more experience, more colleagues to share his problems with. But she had more freedom, more chance of financial success, and no burden of proof to speak of.

"You need someone to take care of you," she said, and he jumped.

"I was just thinking the same thing about you," he said. "You were shot last year, you work in this despised profession, you're a young woman with a child—you need someone to rub your feet at night and put you to bed."

"Nobody would put up with my schedule," Nina said. "Oh, well."

"Oh, well," Collier said. Neither of them spoke for a moment.

Collier said, "Cup of coffee?"

"Not the stuff they make here."

"I bet you're going to grab a pizza or a burger on the way back to work at your office until eight or nine. That's why we die young."

"I bet that's your plan too," Nina said.

"Let's go grab some dinner at a casino," Collier said.

"I don't know. That would be, er . . ."

"Fraternizing? Look, we have to eat, and we have to talk about this case. So let's put on our best Type-A personalities and combine the two. I promise you won't have any fun."

"Fun? What's that?" Nina said. "Okay. Let's go." They left, ignoring the pointed stares of the secretaries.

Prize's Club was jumping. The line for the buffet stretched back to a line of slot machines. "Excuse me," Nina said, feeling around in the bottom of her purse for quarters, her fingers itching to hit the machines.

Two cherries popped up, and she made her money back, plus two. "Quit while you're ahead," Collier advised, but she kept going until she'd emptied her pockets of coins.

"I've lived up here long enough for all the glamor to fade. So why do I still throw my money away?" Nina said.

"You never want to miss a bet, even a bad bet," Collier said. They argued at the cashier over who would pay. Nina won, saying she'd bill it to her client as a business dinner, with a passing thought about whether Kurt could ever pay her, and how to stick Riesner for holding back the retainer money.

Inside the huge ballroom, they took a table in the middle and went down to the front where buffet tables flaunted mounds of colorful food. When they returned, the waiter had brought a carafe of red wine.

"To Justice with a capital *J*," Collier said, raising his glass. "May it prevail over all the bullshit."

"I'll drink to that," Nina said. She let the wine warm her. Over the buzz of hundreds of diners, she said, "We're totally anonymous here. Tourists from all over the world meet here to lose their money. It gives you such a warm, fuzzy feeling." Three of her salads had gotten mixed up on her plate. The result was delicious.

"You are about to say, why don't I drop the premeditated murder charge in the London shooting, since she kept the gun at her house for years and no other evidence of premeditation showed up?" Collier took a bite.

"How about it?"

"I'll do it if you'll sleep with me tonight." Collier hit his head with his palm, said, "Oh, sorry. Forgot. I'm not supposed to require that anymore."

"Ha, ha. Will you? Drop the first-degree charge?"

"Might as well. Milne will grant your motion. We're both tired. Let's save ourselves the trouble of arguing it."

"That's great."

"Your good work. I had no idea the Kettricks knew London well enough to know the gun was at her house all along. Now it's your turn. Want to talk to your client about one count of second-degree murder? Fifteen years with credits if Milne's in a good mood."

"And you would agree not to bring any charges regarding Tamara Sweet?"

"I couldn't promise that. Something new may come in."

"Forget it. I don't think he did either of the shootings. I'm getting some ideas about some of the witnesses—"

"Raising those reasonable doubts—"

"I'm trying to say something sincere. This is not a trial tactic."

"Everything we do in this situation is a trial tactic," Collier said. "Even sincerity."

"I'm not going to plead Scott out," Nina said. "Let my actions speak for themselves."

"You just don't have a good enough offer yet. Really, you're playing the usual defense game. Look what you did, bringing in Ralph Kettrick and serving him up to the jury to distract attention—"

"He doesn't have an alibi. He was as close to Terry London as anyone got. His dad lied for him—"

"Or maybe you just confused his dad. Or are you saying they're both in it together?"

"I'm not saying anything. I'm just catching flaws in your case when they leap out at me. It doesn't help that you've managed to mix the Tamara Sweet shooting up in it."

"You ought to quit while you're ahead."

"Oh, let's just give it a rest, Collier. I'm too tired to spar with you right now."

"Good enough," Collier said. They finished the meal in companionable silence. He drove them back to the courthouse parking lot, saying, "I'll be calling you to the stand after Mrs. Sweet. Tomorrow's a Friday and Milne's going to recess early, so I suppose it will be Monday morning. Nervous?"

"No." She was lying. She had had a classic dream before the trial started, when noises were first made about her being a witness. Naked except for her briefcase, which she tried to cover herself with, mightily aware of her physical imperfections, the mental imagery of her audience spilling into her mind as they criticized and judged her, she was marched to the witness box and turned to face her accuser.

"Are you ready to confess?" said the judge, who was gradually assuming the hard-planed, malicious face of Terry London. The court, the audience, and the prosecution merged into a faceless crowd of accusatory looks.

"Confess what?" she had asked. A big laugh. Everyone knew what she was supposed to confess, everyone but her. Her confusion and growing consternation made them laugh harder. They saw inside her, everything, even the secrets she kept from herself. The judge whipped out a video camera and began filming her as she tried to cover up her private parts. . . .

" 'No fear,' " she said, quoting the logo from her son's hat, which presently reposed in the police evidence locker. If Collier only knew . . .

"Well, good. And good luck on your work tonight."

"Bye. Same to you." And with that half-ironic good-bye, Nina drove off.

39

"CALL JESSICA SWEET."

Tamara's mother took the stand on Friday, eleven days into the trial. Outside was another one of the 307 days of sunlight Tahoe enjoyed each year, a clear and perfect late July day. The jury had divided into the alert and the inert, but Nina thought she knew what one thing they all agreed on. Anywhere but here, in this airless closet of emotion and death.

Everyone connected to the case seemed to have showed up today to see Terry's film.

Mrs. Sweet's tan had deepened since Nina last saw her, if that was possible. Her blinding health had to remind the jury that her daughter should have had a lot of good years ahead of her. She wore her silver hair shorter than ever and turquoise studs in her ears that brought out the blueness of her eyes. She looked competent and respectable. The women on the jury would find her stalwart and believable.

Her unhappiness could be seen only close up, in the way her mouth habitually turned down at the corners. Her destiny had been a missing child, years in limbo while she tried to find out what had happened, and her husband's crippling accident. Then she had suffered a final blow, finding her child was dead, had been dead the whole time. But she was strong, and she hid her unhappiness as well as she could.

Collier took Mrs. Sweet through the story she had already told Nina, how she and her husband had gone to a property owners' meeting the night of Tamara's disappearance, how they had worried when she didn't come home, how they had reported her missing the next morning. She gestured gracefully with her hands as she talked about the investigation that followed, the false leads, the hope slowly evaporating as days became months and years. It was a sad story, and at times her reserve failed her, and her chin trembled.

"Had your relationship with your daughter changed in the year prior to her disappearance?" Collier asked.

"Uh-huh. She used to share her life with me. I thought we'd gotten through her adolescence very well, with a minimum of the misery you're told to expect. But during her senior year in high school, she turned away from us. We tried to talk to her many times, but . . . she was angry. It seemed as though we disagreed about everything. She stopped communicating with us. Then, one night about three weeks before she disappeared I found a piece of paper in her dresser drawer. Some pills fell out when I unwrapped it. We had a heated argument. She was hostile, resentful. She said to quit snooping; she was over eighteen and she'd move out if I didn't respect her privacy.

"She stopped talking to me. I lectured her, I admit it, and I tried to get her to talk to our family doctor. I told Jonathan what I had found and he was sick about it. We talked about having her leave the house, because we didn't know what to do. I knew she was seeing a lot of Doreen and Michael. I thought it was strange. She and Michael had broken up, and now he was with Doreen.

"She came home late and left early. I thought, it couldn't just be the three of them. Tamara was so lovely. There had to be a young man she was seeing too." Mrs. Sweet turned to the jury and said, "If we could have just got her past this one bad spot, she would have been all right. She fell off the edge. So many children do at the point of adulthood."

"Did you learn who this young man was?"

Her hands wrung themselves. "I had seen a young man pick her up in front of the house a month or so before I found the pills. I described him to the police, but my understanding is they didn't have enough evidence—"

"Objection," Nina said. "Calls for hearsay. Nonresponsive."

"The jury will disregard the last sentence of the testimony," Milne said.

"And is the young man who you saw twelve years go, a few weeks before your daughter disappeared, in the courtroom today?"

The jury's eyes followed her finger to Kurt. "The record will show the witness has indicated the defendant in answer to the question," Milne said.

Kurt scribbled a note to Nina. He had become agitated. Nina wrote back, "Don't worry. Several weeks before. No big deal."

"Last year, did you and your husband meet with Terry London for any purpose?" Collier went on.

"Yes. About two years ago we contacted an old friend at UC Davis who had made some documentary films, and asked her if she knew of anyone who might be willing to make a short film about Tamara's disappearance. We would pitch in financially. She got one of the real-life mystery shows interested in doing their own story on Tam.

"Then the Tahoe paper, the *Mirror,* did a story about the renewed interest in the case, and that's when we got a call from Terry London. She offered her services for a very reasonable price, if we would help with expenses. She seemed to think she could make a profit. By then, the television people seemed to be stalling, so we talked to her several times, and decided to go ahead."

"Did Terry London then make this film?"

"Yes."

"Titled *Where Is Tamara Sweet?*"

"Yes."

"Your Honor, if I may," Hallowell said, waving to the projector that had been set up.

Nina didn't object. The lights went down, and this time the jury saw not Terry but her work, the film Nina still didn't fully understand. As she watched, all the old questions came back: Why had

Terry made the film? Because she killed Tamara, and couldn't take the chance someone else might discover that fact in the course of the filming? It sounded like a good theory, but it just didn't work. If Terry had to make the film to protect herself, she would never have suggested Tam had been murdered. She would have suggested Tam was alive, living a new life, to deflect attention.

If Terry hadn't shot the girl, then why not make Kurt the killer in her film? With Terry's obsession to find him, why hadn't she accused him? Then the police might have started looking for him, have located him, even charged him with the murder and brought him back, as she seemed to desire.

The film was nearly over, and now Nina saw again the actress playing Tam walking slowly, on that freezing day, toward that familiar trail. . . . Kurt's note, passed down the counsel table and hard to read, said, "I'd swear that was Tam."

Put it together. If neither Terry nor Kurt killed Tamara, who else could have gotten at the rifle? The young girl sitting down on the white rock while sad music played, snowflakes falling on her long hair, wearing her boots and black pants and that ratty rabbit jacket . . . Where was that jacket?

She remembered Terry's amusement, her knowing attitude, her grandiosity. Terry thought she was above ordinary morality, ordinary life.

The thought came to Nina that the film was Terry's macabre joke. She'd known who killed Tamara. She had told the truth for once, obliquely, "artistically." Terry couldn't resist revealing what she knew, that it wasn't her, and it wasn't Kurt.

It was someone else. The eyes watching from afar. The secret watcher, deeply hidden in elemental darkness. Who?

The thought came, like a door opening into that chaotic darkness, what about the three other girls who disappeared into the snow? Why include them in a tight film that probably involved a lot of cutting?

Why not just take the film at face value? The film suggested Tam was murdered, before her body was found. So Terry had known for twelve years that Tamara was dead.

She looked at the girl on the screen, beginning to fade into darkness. She covered her mouth with her hand, sickened, watching, watching, thinking, oh, no, it can't be, she wouldn't. . . .

But of course Terry would. She had been there that night, on the trail up to Angora Ridge. She had filmed Tamara, the real Tamara, her camera whirring quietly behind one of the boulders. And she had seen who came to meet Tamara.

Tamara's slight figure slowly faded out, and the music and credits began to cross the screen.

There was no credit for the girl in the reenactment. Terry's audacious hint just made Nina feel sicker.

Terry had known all along, had seen the murder, had filmed at least this part. And one day, she had learned a film was to be made. Of course she had approached the Sweets. She couldn't resist the joke on everyone, going as far as she dared. And inserting the real footage of the real girl . . . How Terry must have hugged herself and laughed!

Nina felt the eyes, in the dusk of the courtroom, looking at her. She was sitting there, and the dark person could hurt her there, just as she had been hurt before. She began to shiver uncontrollably right there at the counsel table. Someone watched from a seat behind her. She felt once again the shot that had knocked her into the witness box. Run, before it's too late! She jumped up. Kurt's shackles clattered. He was turning to her in surprise. She opened the gate to run the gauntlet of the crowded aisles, to get out of there. . . .

The film ended. The lights came up. Deputy Kimura watched the crowd alertly. There was no gun trained on her.

She surveyed the audience. Barbet Cain and the other reporters. Doreen and Michael Ordway whispering at each other in their usual chairs. The Kettricks, father and son, seated together, on the left. Monty Glasser, the producer of *Real-Life Riddles,* who had come up from L.A., probably thinking about what a great episode this trial would make. Jonathan Sweet, pugnacious and resentful in his wheelchair; detectives and criminalists courthouse cronies in the back. Milne and Collier—and Kurt beside her, saying "What's wrong?" in a low tone.

"A lot," she whispered back. But court was still in session, and she didn't have time to think. As soon as the day was over, she would go to the office, lock the door, think it through . . .

"Is this the film that Terry London made and thereafter showed to you?" Collier asked Mrs. Sweet.

"Yes." The film went in as evidence.

"Now, were you asked in June of this year to provide the South Lake Tahoe police with the name of Tamara's dentist?"

"Yes. I knew they'd found . . . remains. I went to see them. I'd seen the belt before. She told me it was a present, but she wouldn't say from who. And that watch. I certainly didn't recognize anything else as my daughter." Her chin was trembling again.

"Thank you, Mrs. Sweet. No further questions," Collier said.

Nina gathered her thoughts, driving the panic of the moment before from her mind. She looked up at Tamara's mother. A composed Jessica Sweet waited, hands in her lap. "How long have you been married, Mrs. Sweet?" she asked.

"Thirty-five years next fall."

"How did your husband get along with Tamara in the year before she disappeared?"

"If you mean that stupid police report—"

"You did call the police?"

"Yes, but—"

"Your husband did knock Tamara down the stairs, resulting in a trip to the hospital and permanent scarring?"

"The paramedics called the police, not me. It was an accident, but by the time the police had given the report to me to sign, it looked like my husband had . . ."

"Assaulted her? You did sign the police report?"

"Yes. I was angry at Jonathan. No charges were ever brought. It was an accident, I tell you. I was there." She made a washing gesture with her hands, then clenched them firmly together under her chin, as if to stop them from talking.

"Did your husband have a number of arguments with Tamara during that time?"

"Several. Naturally. He was concerned at the way she'd been behaving."

"When Tamara disappeared, you were quite adamant when you talked with the police that she had not just run away, is that correct?"

"Uh-huh. I knew she didn't."

"Why were you so sure? She had developed a problem with drugs. She had threatened to leave. She didn't get along with her father. She didn't talk to you . . . Why were you so sure?"

"I just knew she wouldn't take off like that."

"Did Mr. Sweet go out again that night, after you returned from your meeting?"

"No!"

"You were concerned about her. He didn't go out to look for her?"

"I said he didn't."

"Was he suffering from the disability that requires him to use a wheelchair at that time?"

"No. The car wreck happened the following year."

"Your husband also gave a statement, Mrs. Sweet. Twelve years ago. You evidently haven't reread it recently in preparation for your testimony." Nina brought up her copy.

Mrs. Sweet said, "Oh, yes. He ran out for half an hour, but he didn't see her."

"How do you know that?"

"It says so right here—"

"Do you have any personal knowledge that he never found her?"

"Your Honor, is this attack on my husband allowable?" Mrs. Sweet said, shifting in her seat.

"You'll have to answer the question," Milne said.

"I can't believe she's doing this!"

"Answer the question."

"How could I have personal knowledge?" Mrs. Sweet shouted. "I wasn't with him! But I know he didn't do it!"

"And how do you know that?"

"Because she did it!"

"Who?"

"Terry London!" Mrs. Sweet said defiantly.

"Did she tell you she killed your daughter?"

"She didn't have to. It was there, in her attitude, the night she showed us the film. I couldn't prove it. I just knew, when I saw the film, that Tam was dead, and that Terry London knew all about it." She hid her face in her hands.

"Let's give the witness a moment, Your Honor," Nina said.

Milne nodded, and Nina sat down. The courtroom filled with whispers.

Nina's hand sketched a funny animal picture: a rabbit and a catlike lynx. She looked down. What was her unconscious mind trying to tell her? The secret was there, but it was so extraordinary, so perverse, that none of them were bold enough or smart enough to perceive it.

Terry had known it was beyond their experience, and she had enjoyed the mystery.

Damn her! Terry had been a part of the darkness. At that moment, Nina felt no sadness that she had been swallowed up in it. Matt was her victim, not the other way around.

Mrs. Sweet was quiet again. Nina said, "You don't have any proof that Terry London killed your daughter, do you?"

"No," she said in a subdued tone.

"Her manner at the time of the screening indicated to you that she knew who killed your daughter?"

"To me, yes. Other people might not have been so aware as I am. My husband doesn't agree with me."

"What did she say that caused you to think she had something to do with your daughter's death?"

"Well, when Doreen was watching the film for the first time, for instance, she asked Terry, 'How did you know Tam tripped on the way out and was limping a little? I'd forgotten it myself!' How could she know that? And Terry just laughed. She wasn't there, how would she know!"

"Perhaps it was just her artist's vision," Nina said dryly.

"And the jacket," Mrs. Sweet said.

"What?"

"The jacket. Tamara's rabbit jacket. We had forgotten to mention to the police that Tamara had worn that jacket that night. And Terry put the girl in the reenactment into a rabbit jacket exactly like Tamara's. How did she know to do that?"

"I believe you're supposed to be asking the questions, not the witness," Milne said to Nina.

"So Terry seemed to know more about the disappearance than she should?" Nina said.

Mrs. Sweet said, "Where is that jacket?" almost to herself. It was eerie. Nina had asked herself that question only a few minutes before.

"Answer the question," Milne said to Mrs. Sweet.

"Oh. She knew. I could see it in those yellow eyes of hers," Mrs. Sweet said.

Nina brought her back to the pills she had found in Tamara's drawer and made the other point she had prepared for this witness, that Tamara might have been killed as part of a drug deal. She had fought to bring in this theory over Hallowell's objection. Milne had allowed it. She had high hopes that the jury might find reasonable doubt from this alternate theory for Tamara's murder.

Several times during the course of the rest of the long day of cross-examination, Nina lost her concentration. The drug theory, Mr. Sweet, Mrs. Sweet's theory that Terry was the shooter, the invasion of privacy lawsuit—she covered all these points, the preludes to her defense case, thoroughly and methodically. But she could hardly wait for the court day to be over. She felt close to the secret of Tamara's death.

As soon as the recess for the day was called and the jury had filed out, she and Sandy gathered their papers and left. On the drive back to the office in the Bronco, Sandy kept glancing at her curiously. Finally, she said, "I've seen that look before. Like you're wrestling with the devil." But Nina kept silent throughout the drive to the office.

When they arrived, Sandy and Wish left their boxes of files and went home, leaving Nina alone.

She called Andrea and said she'd be late. She closed the blinds, locked the door to the outer office, and ate a yogurt from the minifridge in the conference room. No matter what she did, she couldn't shake the feeling of foreboding afflicting her, or get her thoughts together. She was too tired. She just couldn't concentrate.

Maybe a short nap would help. She put her head down on the desk and fell asleep.

When she woke, sunset filled the lakeside window of her office. It was eight-thirty on a summer night, warm—as Tahoe got on deep summer nights—balmy, perfect, the moon just rising. Her shoulder muscles had frozen and her eyes felt like the Gobi after a sandstorm.

She got up, yawning, and raised the blind on the window that framed her view of the lake.

Across the terra-cotta marshland, Lake Tahoe burned into the windless sky, rose and orange and magenta. Behind the lake, the western mountain ridge sawed black against the colors, splitting the sky and water. Gulls danced a slow dance on the currents. No one walked the trail down to the water.

The sun had set on this majestic scene for many millions of years. Nature was at her grandest.

But it had no human scale or function. She was alone in a small outpost in the middle of mountains, with her cares and conflicts, and the sunset breathed loneliness.

She touched the scar on her chest. It had become a habit in these moments. What had Sandy said? Something about fear boring a hole through her.

She took her notes from the day and began flipping through them, stopping at the animal picture again. Animals with human heads. . . . winter, fur coats . . .

The phone rang. She turned from the window and picked up the receiver.

"Nina? Get over here," Matt said. "Bob's missing again."

40

"He rode his bike down the block. He was supposed to be back in ten minutes, way before dark. That was an hour ago. I cruised up and down the streets. I looked everywhere," Matt said, his voice rigid with apprehension. "He swore he wouldn't do this again. He swore it to me."

"His backpack. Did he take it?" Nina said. They stood together in the doorway, looking out at the street.

"No. It's in the kids' room. No note, nothing like that." Andrea, behind Matt, folded her arms around Troy and Brianna, trying to look calm.

"Troy. Brianna. Did Bob say anything to you about running away? Did you see anything at all?" Brianna sucked her thumb vigorously, her eyes wide, shaking her head. Troy said he hadn't.

"Nina, let's call the police," Andrea said. She held out the cordless phone.

"You shouldn't have waited this long to call me!" Nina shouted. "You shouldn't have let him go out alone!" She took the phone. Her hand shook. "It has something to do with the trial," she cried. The abyss opened beneath her feet and she fell. Somewhere down in the chaos Bobby, too, was falling.

She dialed 911. They told her to look around some more. He hadn't been gone for long enough. She should call back in another hour if there was still no sign of him. Matt left again to search.

She called Collier at his office. He said, "Someone will be out to your house as quick as I can get them there."

She called the jail. They hadn't seen him. She called Paul at home in Carmel, across the state.

"Paul, Bob's gone. I don't think he ran away. It's something else."

"Jesus. How long ago?"

"An hour and a half. It's dark out now, and he knows what being late will do to Matt and me. He only took a short bike ride!"

"What do the two kids say?"

"They don't know anything. He didn't take anything with him. He didn't run away this time, I know it. Collier's sending some patrol officers to help search. Matt's out there riding around. Paul, I—I've been stirring up such ugly feeling in the trial . . ."

"Check every house on the block. Call the hospitals, the bus depot. Check every restaurant around. Search his room. Look for notes, maps, anything unusual. Check your messages at the office every ten minutes. Keep the phone line at the house free in case you get a call." Paul paused.

"I need you, Paul."

"Listen. Don't break down now, you can't afford to. I'm already on my way. It's ten P.M., too late to get a flight out of the airport or arrange a quickie charter on a Cessna. I'll drive. I'll be there by two A.M."

"I knew you'd come."

"I never should have let you chase me away. You had a bad case of pretrial jitters and I took it personally. Get Sandy over to the office. I'll stop by on the highway to check in on my way up without tying up your home line," Paul said grimly. "Keep your chin up. He needs you. Don't leave that phone!"

* * *

The minutes crawled by. Andrea went next door with the kids to make the calls. The police still hadn't arrived. She was alone in the house.

She couldn't stand sitting there by the phone. She went upstairs to his room to search for some clue, anything. There was nothing. She picked his pajamas off the floor, folded them carefully, set them on his bed. They smelled like him.

She picked up his seal, tucked lovingly under the covers by Bobby, and put it in her pocket. He would want it right away, wouldn't he? His favorite thing.

The phone rang, and she dove for the upstairs extension, picked up the receiver, and said breathlessly, "Bobby?"

"Is this the lawyer lady?" said a jovial man's voice, a little slurred and slow. She knew immediately who it was.

"What do you want?"

"I want to talk to you. Your kid is visiting me and I know you'll want to see him."

"Please. Don't hurt him!"

"You call the police?"

"No," Nina said. "He hasn't been gone that long."

"That's good. Very sensible. Don't call them. Come on over. You and me, we have to talk."

"Sure," Nina said. "Okay. Just don't—"

"You bring any police, then the l'il fan might have an accident before they can get close."

"No police. Don't hurt him. Do you want money?"

"Money? I don't need your money. Like I say, just bring yourself."

"All right. Where?"

Ralph Kettrick didn't answer immediately, and she heard wheezy breathing, a stifled cry—Bobby—oh God!

"The Angora Ridge Fire Lookout," Ralph said. "Be there, or be square." With a grotesque laugh, he hung up.

Paul started calling as soon as he hit 101 at Salinas, but no one answered at the house. He was at Pacheco Pass—stopped for gas, promising himself a cellular phone by tomorrow—when he finally got through, but it was Andrea who answered. "They're both out looking, Paul. Nina's in the Bronco and Matt's knocking on doors. Nina really thinks he's been kidnapped, I could see it in her eyes."

"Okay. You stay right there by that phone. Someone might call you, understand? I've got her car phone number here somewhere. If I don't reach Nina for some reason, when she gets back, make her stay there. They might refuse to talk to you. Next time I'll call Sandy at the office."

"She should be there by now. There's a policeman coming up the walk," Andrea said.

"Good. Make him take it seriously." He hung up and jumped back in. For the next fifteen minutes he screeched around the sharp curves of the pass into the San Joaquin Valley in the van.

He was furious with himself. He could have been there, prevented it. He had been taking a good hard look at himself over the past few days anyway, and he had been about ready to come back up and apologize for being a prize asshole. She had needed him. This might not have happened. . . . Where could the kid be? The first few hours were the most important. Murders occurred much more often than kidnappings. There was a good chance the kid was already dead.

Bob woke up slowly. He opened his eyes to utter darkness. He was lying on a wood floor in a small dark room that stank, really stank. He'd never smelled anything like that before, a rank-out putrid smell that wafted up through the floor. Something was in his mouth, and he couldn't spit it out, wadded-up fabric that got into his throat and made him gag. His wrists and ankles hurt sharply—he was tied up! He struggled wildly.

The flashlight blinded him. "So you ain't dead," Ralph said. "It's hard to judge how hard to hit with a l'il dude your size. Bet your head hurts bad. No use squirming, boy, you're tied tight while I decide what to do with you. Hell, it was your mom I was looking for, but don't worry. She'll be along soon. She was sitting right there by the phone, and I told her she could visit you, long as she left the police out of it. I got to go outside for a minute, but I'll return directly."

Bob's eyes were adjusting to the darkness. He seemed to be in a shack, a chicken coop or something, his pants sticking to a dirty wooden floor. Too spooked to cry, he tried to hear something in the stillness.

Ralph clomped back in and sat down in the corner with his legs drawn up. "Thought that might be her," he said. "We want to be ready for her visit."

He didn't talk for a while. Bob strained as quietly as he could to pull his hands out of what tied them.

"You know, death is all around us," Ralph said in a ragged voice. "That's what Terry told me. Back when I was just a little older than you, fifteen. She told me, Ralphie, half of us don't deserve to live anyway. Lyin' sacks of shit, that's what the girls are."

"Now your mom, she's got my dad thinking bad things about me. That ain't right, is it? Is it?" His hard foot kicked out, and Bob yelped from the pain in his leg. "Oh, I forgot," he said with a laugh. "So, like I say. If I let her keep goin' like she is, my dad's going to have to put me away. Why'd she have to pick on me? I never did her any harm. All I wanted was to be left alone. Shhh. I think I hear your mom. Let's listen."

No sound at all. Then . . . the crackle of dry pine needles. Bob pressed fiercely against his bindings.

"Be right back," Ralph whispered. "Don't go 'way."

Ralph had said he'd kill Bob if she didn't come alone and unarmed, in a voice dripping jocular menace. Nina believed him. She knew exactly what she should do. Call the police immediately, and leave everything in their hands. If a client had called her in this desperate situation, that's exactly what she would have said.

But she sat at the kitchen table under the stained-glass globe that lit the kitchen table, rocking slightly, biting her knuckles.

Bob was all that mattered. Ralph could probably kill him before the police could get to him.

He was holed up at the fire-tracking station on Angora Ridge. A boarded-up building perched uneasily where the ridge road widened slightly, on the steepest portion of the ridge, it sat at the top of the trail where Tamara had died. She remembered the view from the station. To the north, Fallen Leaf Lake and Lake Tahoe stretched into the sky and snow-topped mountains, and to the south, the expansive green valley that fringed the city of South Lake Tahoe spread out below, as finely detailed as a Turkish carpet, magical, flying between mountains.

Sneaking up on Ralph would be very difficult.

She rocked. Bob was her connection to life, the only one she had, really.

She had to do something. Think!

Paul wouldn't be there in time. She couldn't involve Matt and Andrea in such danger. The cops . . . loudspeakers, a hostage situation . . . and Ralph, obviously sick in the head. Deadly.

But what could she do alone? Offer herself as a sacrifice? Apparently Ralph wanted to kill her. Could she talk him out of it? But why would he let Bob go?

He wouldn't. So . . . go alone, appear to surrender, get a gun on him, and shoot him if she had to. . . . Matt had a gun, which he kept locked up in a wooden case in his closet. He had told her where the key was hidden, in case of emergency.

Nina rushed into the bedroom. Yes, the key was there, taped behind the dresser mirror. And the old Colt .45 was still in the case, with six bullets. Her fingers clumsy, she loaded it, thinking about how she hated touching it.

In her bedroom she laid it carefully on the bed, throwing a sweatshirt over her slacks, pulling on heavy socks and her hiking boots. In the kitchen she found a paring knife, which she wrapped and inserted into her boot. Her flashlight was in the Bronco. She had to hurry. Ralph might not wait, and she had to get out before anyone came back. She picked up the loaded Colt and checked the safety, then stuck it in her big pants pocket. The heavy sweatshirt covered the bulge.

She passed Matt on the corner, talking to a neighbor. He tried to flag her but she pretended not to see.

Pioneer Trail to Upper Truckee Road. Moonlight sifted into the black forest. She passed the last house and the Bronco labored up the steep road to the turnoff, which wasn't marked. The road became washboard gravel and asphalt, and she passed a meadow, the tall grass and trees rejoicing under the moon.

Such a beautiful night. She drank it in, the perfection and harmony of it, as if it were some treasure she was throwing away. Really, it was simple. She didn't care if she lived, if Bob died.

She stopped a half-mile away from the lookout, hoping Ralph wouldn't hear the Bronco. She was high on the ridge, and there was nowhere to hide, only barely room for the road. The heights of the mountains shone whitely down their thousands of feet. On her right, illuminated into stark black and white, the U-shaped glaciated valley of Desolation Wilderness fell to Fallen Leaf Lake. Behind, to the right, Lake Tahoe stretched away endlessly. To her left, thick forest obscured the houses where vacationers and locals watched their TVs and slid under the covers, safe in a life she seemed to be climbing away from forever. Quietly, very quietly, she crept forward, along the spruces and pines that shadowed the sides of the road from the treacherous moon.

Paul called Andrea once more from a gas station on Interstate 5 somewhere north of Stockton, knowing he shouldn't call the house, but unable to help himself. "Nina hasn't come back," she reported. "Two officers came and I told them everything I knew. They're patrolling town and have alerted all the other police on patrol in El Dorado County and Douglas County on the Nevada side."

Paul said, "How long has she been gone?"

"That's just it, we're not sure. We were both out looking and she was getting ready to go out in the Bronco—Matt saw her go by in the car, alone, some time ago."

"She stayed home, while you went out?"

"I suppose, for a short time. Then I came back to watch the phone while she went out, and she was gone."

Nina would have left the phone for only two reasons. First, and more likely, she got a call. Second, she had been kidnapped. If she was alone in the car, theory number one looked most probable.

"Any sign of a break-in?"

"Oh, no. She locked the front door. It's been an hour and twenty minutes. We called the South Lake Tahoe police and told them. Paul, what else can we do?"

"Stay by the phone. Stay there with Matt and keep the doors locked, just in case. Be careful. Do you have a weapon at the house?"

"Matt has a gun."

"Go get it."

A few seconds later, Matt got on the line. "It's gone!" he said in a high voice. "What's going on? My wife and kids are here! Are they in some danger?"

"I don't think there's any danger at your house," Paul said. Eighteen-wheelers roaring by the station at eighty miles an hour made it tough to hear. "My guess is Nina's got the gun. She got a call, and she's gone to try to take care of it herself."

"If she took my gun, it wasn't Bob on the phone," Matt said. He sounded far away, on another planet. "Jesus," he said. "Why didn't she tell us, call the cops?"

"She was told to come alone, I'm sure. Who's been sitting in at the trial with her?"

"Sandy's been sitting in. Since you . . . weren't around."

"Believe me, I wish I hadn't left," Paul said. "I'm kicking myself all over this highway."

"You're not the only one," Matt said.

"Anyway. Call Sandy and get a list of all the nonpolice witnesses she's cross-examined. Ask her how far Nina's been getting, if there's something new coming out regarding the killer. Have her stay at the office."

"Okay."

Paul replaced the phone in its holder, jumped into his van, and rocketed out of there. Outside, he was passing through farm country, a sea of darkness to bypass as quickly as possible. Far off to the right the town of Lodi twinkled under the moon. He banged the flat of his hand against the steering wheel. Damn the woman!

In the empty darkness of the shack, Bob needed to pee. He had heard nothing for some time from the outside, not even a bird. Ralph was out there somewhere, looking for his mom. He yawned, amazed that he could feel so tired, but it was late. Way past his bedtime.

He worked his hands harder. Ralph had twisted the leather thong around his hands several times, but leather stretched. Stupid guy! Little by little he inched it over the big part of his right hand. Squirming there on the floor, he worked it harder and harder, tears starting out of his eyes at the pain.

It snapped off. For a second he just lay there, getting his breath back, not believing it. Then he ripped it off his other hand. Bound much more tightly at the feet, he couldn't get the knots undone even with his hands free. He worked the gag in his mouth, pushing the kerchief that held it in place over his head.

The table in the corner might have something he could cut with. Don't make a sound. . . . He wriggled through the awful muck on the floor until he bumped up against the leg, and tried for long minutes to pull himself up. At last he was standing, his hands groping. He touched something long and metallic. A big, sharp knife.

For the first time since that freak had hit him and knocked him off his bike, he felt a twinge of hope. Hurry, hurry! He fell to the floor as quietly as he could and began cutting the leather. In no time he was free, standing there holding the knife up. He wanted to scream and dance up and down. He would cut Ralph's head off with it! He sneaked to the door.

It was padlocked from the outside. He could hear the chain when he pushed.

Around the shack he roamed, pushing at the boarded-up window, searching the walls with his fingers. Nothing. He couldn't get out.

Then he remembered feeling a square where the floorboards didn't come together while he was wiggling around on the floor. He scrambled to find it in the disgusting muck.

His hands found a ring, and he raised a trap door. Dank, cool air rushed up at him. He dropped three or four feet into a dirt-floored, polluted-smelling cellar in pitch blackness. He reached around him for the walls.

He was in a sticky, fur-lined nest full of smooth, hard, sticklike things, loosely connected to each other and covered with some substance that smelled like nothing he'd ever smelled. Oh, man! Bones!

He crawled jerkily as far away as he could, searching the walls for a way out. Concrete, a couple of steps—push, push hard, into the welcome creaking sound of a short cellar door opening.

He slipped into the night, knife clutched between tremulous fingers, running straight across the road and down the mountain, just far enough away to feel safe. He saw headlights in the far distance, but they went out before reaching the summit. Who?

41

NINA CROUCHED ON THE NARROW RIDGE ROAD FOR ONLY A MOMENT. The Bronco sat well back in the trees on the last turnout before the road became too narrow for turns. The only direction she could go was down.

About twenty feet below the road, she began scrambling sideways along the steep hill, belly close to the ground, slithering like a snake, aware of every leaf she crushed. She had left the road before she could see the lookout and before Ralph could spot her. Now closer, she saw no signs of human beings. Either Ralph and Bob weren't there, or Ralph had parked farther up the road. Or he had lied.

It could have been a lie. Ralph could have summoned her to an intermediate place where he would meet her and take her to some other hidden place. That would be smart.

But Ralph wasn't smart, or even cunning. He was unpredictable, though, and he had Bob.

She moved along, almost flat on the steep ground, from bush to tree to bush. Occasionally she dislodged a rock, or lay on a crackling branch, sounds that discharged like firecrackers into the still night. The stars and moon lit the scene like a dreamscape.

She rested behind a boulder, panting as quietly as she could. Over the top she could just make out the green top of the station roof and the roof of the old storage shed beside it.

Raising herself on her hands, she lifted her head to see better.

And a hand grabbed her ankle, squeezing hard. She was being yanked down the hill too fast to wriggle around and get the gun trained that way.

A big body landed full on her, squeezing the breath out of her. Hands held her hands down. Her head was shoved into the dirt so that she breathed it in, coughing and choking, and the gun was roughly pulled from her pocket. Pinned, immobilized under the heavy weight, she thought she might suffocate. A hand pulled her head up by the hair and she gasped in some air. Matt's Colt flew off to the side, scuttling into the brush.

"You ain't following the rules," Ralph said very softly in her ear, his breath coming out in hot gusts, her body cringing at the feel of it. "But I got you now. Easy to do you now. But I got a plan for you and the l'il guy."

"Let . . . go."

"You come alone?"

"Can't . . . talk."

He let go, and she tasted dirt again. His knee pressed into her back. He pulled her to her knees, so that her back remained to him. A hand moved down her back, to her rear, fondling her roughly. Wrenching one arm behind her, and keeping her head up, he pulled her sweatshirt off her, to her confusion, leaving her T-shirt intact, and maneuvered her left arm through the arm of a long jacket, then the right arm: silky, incredibly plush on the outside.

Fur. Terry's lynx coat.

"Little different from court, hey? Now who's on top? I get to be judge." He pushed her face down again, and spread himself over her, rubbing against her, working himself up, while she frantically tried to breathe, to kick. . . .

A scream cut through the darkness, echoing on both sides of the drop-away ridge, all the way to Tallac, hovering over the Tahoe valley, long, wailing, endless. Ralph's body jerked, then fell away from her, and she clawed upward, clutching at the hillside.

Bobby had appeared beside her out of nowhere. He half ran, half crawled to her. She took his arm and turned her back to the man writhing on the ground, his right arm reaching back to his left shoulder where Bob had sunk a knife in him. . . .

And Ralph screamed, "Stay right there or I shoot you both, I shoot the kid, don't move now, careful . . ." Nina turned back, still holding Bobby, and saw Ralph holding another handgun in his left hand, pointing at them from six feet away.

"We won't move," she said, her voice gentle, soothing. In the moonlight Ralph's eyes seemed to be starting out of his head. His right hand pulled at the haft of the knife, and he screamed again as he slowly pulled the blade out of his left shoulder. You didn't pull knives out of wounds, Nina knew. They kept the blood inside. . . . She prayed that he would pass out and give them one chance to make it to the road. His eyes rolled back into his head for an instant, but the gun only wavered for a second.

"Unh!" Ralph said. His face convulsed. The bloody knife in his right hand dripped onto the hillside. His gun steadied itself, aimed at them.

He wiped his hand, the bloody one, on his cheek. He looked like a statue she had seen of the Hindu goddess Kali, black and terrible, weapons in all her hands, blood dripping from her jaws. . . . She tried to think of something to say. She knew if she or Bobby moved they would be killed instantly.

They watched him, horror-struck, as he pulled himself up and leaned against the rock, breathing hard. He looked at the knife, at them, then flipped it down the hill toward the lake far, far below.

He shifted the gun into his right hand, said, "Naughty, naughty." Then he gestured up the hill with the gun. They climbed up slowly, Ralph grunting behind them.

At the road he staggered up behind them before they could make a break. "Get in the shed," he said. Still holding the gun on them, he painfully pulled the key chain on his pocket and opened the padlock, forcing them inside.

Bob clung to her, hanging back. "Get that boy inside or you're both dead right now," Ralph managed, nudging her with the gun barrel. She wondered if she should shove him past Ralph to freedom, felt terrified by the risk, and finally couldn't take it. She half dragged Bob inside, and Ralph followed. The door slammed shut behind the three of them, and Ralph turned on a light.

They were in what must have been the storage shed for the station, a single room cobwebbed and empty, abandoned of its original purpose for years. A filthy sleeping bag covered with an even filthier long piece of fur lay in a corner on a floor practically papered with torn and tattered magazines, empty bottles, and decaying rags of clothing.

The violent light from the swinging bulb exposed them to each other: the man, tearing a rag with his teeth while he stared fixedly at them, his bloodshot eyes and hideous face, the red smears all over his shirt; the frightened boy's eyes that moved back and forth, captive, hunting for freedom, and Nina, vigilant, as potentially lethal, as amoral, mind casting about for weapons to kill the bloody oaf who wanted to hurt them. She still had the knife in her boot. . . .

He stuffed the rag under the shirt against his back and slumped down onto the floor in a sitting position. "Stabbed me with my own knife," he said in wonder. "How the hell did you get out?" His eyes fell on the bare floor of the trapdoor, and he pointed to it with the gun, saying, "Oh. Went down through the toy bin. Saw my playthings. Well, you two done caused me a lot more trouble than you're worth. Get over here, both of you. Don't try anything."

He made them crawl over to him, lie down prone, and put their hands behind their backs. He removed the coat from Nina, gently laying it beside him, and he tied them both up, his hands twisting the leather so tightly, Nina's feet and hands began to numb almost immediately.

"That's more like it," Ralph said in a calmer tone, and, lurching to his feet, he padlocked the door from the inside this time, then turned off the light. Nina heard him slide down the wall again a few feet away.

Silence. No, not silence, three sets of breaths in the room, each with a distinct rhythm. Bobby lay beside her, not moving. Over the next long quiet moments his breaths became deep and regular. He had fallen asleep! Was it possible? Had he passed out? Had Ralph hurt him? She began moving slowly, cautiously, thinking maybe somehow she could get at the knife in her boot.

"Don't do that," Ralph barked. "I'm thinking."

"We'll never say a word," Nina said, her voice low and cajoling. "Let us go."

"Like hell. Shut up." They sat there in the dark. "Last warning."

She wanted to say, kill me, please, just let my boy live, but she was afraid if she spoke one more syllable he would shoot them both. They had sunk into the darkness where the horror lived.

"You smashed up my whole life," Ralph said out of the darkness. His breathing had slowed. His voice barely disturbed the air. "They fired me offa Satan's Hoof yesterday 'cause of what you said in court. The mechanic was ridin' me, and I got upset and decked him. The owner comes runnin' up and says get off the track or he'd have me arrested. I ain't never gonna be famous now. Ain't never gonna get myself fixed up."

"I'll help you find another job."

"Too late."

"Ralph, you've got problems. I can get you help."

"You tell anybody else to come?" Ralph said, his voice raspy and menacing. "You tryin' to get me talkin' so I can't think?"

"I think you wanted to talk to me, Ralph. Things just got out of hand. I'm sorry if I upset you."

"That don't do me no good now."

"I'm worried about my son," Nina said as ingratiatingly as she could. "He's sick. Could you—"

"The li'l dude knifed me. He ain't goin' nowhere."

"I'm a lawyer," Nina said. "Think of all the good I could do you—" She stopped. Ralph was laughing over there in the darkness.

"Yeah, a lawyer," Ralph said. "A lawyer doin' something good. That's rich. I ought to shoot you right now. But I'm thinkin' up a better plan, so shut up." She heard a curious soft rubbing sound, and realized he was kneading Terry's fur, lying on the sleeping bag, like a baby kneads his blanket.

"Tell me about the fur, Ralph," she said in a breathy little voice. "It seems so exciting."

"You like it?"

"I like fur," she said, hoping for the right words.

"I need it for my satisfaction," Ralph said, and Nina felt nausea coming up, she was going to throw up for sure, but even this she managed somehow to suppress.

A fur fetishist. Ralph was a fur fetishist. She had read about a case of fur fetishism years ago, in Krafft-Ebing.

"Girls wearing fur. All I need is to stroke my face on the fur and rub against it a little. That's all she has to do, just wear the fur for me. It's not much to ask," Ralph said in a voice heavy with self-pity. "Thick, smooth, long, stand-up hair. I heard once they're called bearded furs. Not coarse and bushy. That turns me off."

"Like rabbit? Is that the kind you like?"

"Not the cheap hides," Ralph said. "Too thin. But the best ever is the lynx. I love my sweet lynx." He was rubbing it now, she could hear it. "She had the coat, and she would watch me touching it. When I was fifteen, Terry wore the coat for me," Ralph said. "She got me so excited, I thought I was gonna die. God, it was so good."

"The lynx coat," Nina said. "The one you've got there."

"Usually I keep it down the trapdoor in the toy bin. What do you care? Shut up." His voice had that odd, raspy, frightening tone to it again.

"It's all right to talk about it, Ralph," Nina said very softly. "I enjoy listening."

"You could take another minute or two," Ralph mumbled to himself. "No, you stupid fool! She's buttering you up. She doesn't care. Do 'em like you planned." He was still muttering, but she couldn't catch the words anymore.

"Did Tamara wear her rabbit jacket for you, Ralph?" she said desperately, breaking into the stream of broken words, and at the same time working on her bindings, the knife useless in her boot.

"What? Oh. Tamara. That was a long long time ago. Tamara was the first."

Placerville, still an hour away from the lake. Paul stopped again at a phone off the highway, his fears for Nina at fever pitch.

"Sandy's here," Matt said.

"Put her on."

Sandy said, "She's been putting a few noses out of joint." She sounded just like usual, her voice matter-of-fact.

"It has to be something to do with the trial," Paul said. "Does she know anything more about the murders?"

"Nothing that's going to help."

"Who's she made nervous?"

"Today it was Jessica Sweet on the stand. Nina talked about Mr. Sweet hitting Tamara."

"Yeah. I gave her the police report."

"He's in a wheelchair. Hard to believe he could kill Terry London. But I guess she could."

"Where's Wish?" Paul said.

"Right here."

"Send him to the Sweet house. Have him pound on the door, do whatever he needs to do to make sure the Sweets are home and Nina and Bobby aren't in there."

"He's on his way."

"Tell him to watch his behind. What else have we got?"

"The day before that, Jerry Kettrick was testifying, and she got him upset about his boy. Made him admit he didn't know if the son was home the night Terry was shot. Ralph, his son's name was."

"Has anyone been to Kettrick's?"

"I don't think the police are looking at it that way. Anyway, nobody but you has asked me my opinion."

"I'm going to stop there on my way in," Paul said. "Roust them both. I know where they live. What else?"

"The Ordways called the office today. Mrs. Ordway wants out of the subpoena."

"They may have killed Tamara. They were right there. I served their subpoenas last week. Tell Matt to get out there."

"He's a nervous wreck," Sandy said. "I'll go myself."

"It could be dangerous, Sandy."

"I'll bring some friends. Relax."

"I feel like—if I'd only stayed up there—"

"It's her job, turning over stones and looking at the bugs. You know that. You can't protect her from everything."

"I walked out on her."

"Get a grip," Sandy said. "Are you gonna turn to mush? I thought you were some hot ex-cop."

"Yes, ma'am."

"I'm leaving now. Don't be crashing the van on the road, now, Wish wants to buy it off you someday."

Paul hung up, and, influenced by her zany sanity in the face of all distress, allowed himself to breathe a little deeper.

"Terry told me about Tamara. She took me to peek in her window. Terry hated her, I don't know why. I started watching her. She wore that rabbit jacket, not as nice as Terry's coat, but she was pretty, and the rabbit was so soft . . . white, real pure looking."

"You wanted to touch it. . . ."

"Oh, yes. So I got to know her. She liked to party: pot, pills, any kind of drug crap I could get ahold of, she'd try. She'd get high and let me play with the coat she wore . . . she thought it was funny. But then . . ."

"What happened?"

"She was the first," Ralph mumbled. "Terry wanted to come and film me and her that night. Who knows why? She had her reasons, I guess. She got to the trail first and went and hid behind a rock. Tam was waiting when I got there, and I knew Terry was somewhere around. We got high and then Tam wanted to leave.

"She wouldn't let me fondle her jacket. She made fun of me. We were down the trail in the dark where nobody came. She called me crazy. I'm not crazy! I could be fixed. I had Terry's rifle in the truck—Terry said I could take it hunting—and I ran back and got it. I tried to make her pay up. Boom, boom, she got in the way and she fell down. I was scared. I called Terry but she didn't come. She said later she left before any of that."

"It was an accident," Nina said. She had loosened one hand, but couldn't quite work it free.

"I didn't touch her after. That would be perverted. I pushed her into the little cave because the ground was frozen and wiped my hands in the snow. I kept her soft little rabbit fur," Ralph said, spinning the word *fur* out as though it gave him pleasure just to hear it, almost rolling the *r.* "It's mine now. I keep it down in the toy bin."

"What else is down there, Ralph?" Nina said, trying to keep her teeth from chattering, trying to keep up the soft, interested, little-girl voice.

"The other girls. Alice, and Dee, and whatshername. I forget. Goddamn, he stuck me good. I'm still bleeding. Shit."

"The [illegible] other girls?"

"Oh. Yeah. They all wore furs. One of 'em had a mink collar, so beautiful, stiff on the tips and velvety, feathery soft farther in. It's down there now. I was nice to them, but they'd all get disgusted with me sooner or later."

"And you'd have to keep them quiet."

"Yeah. I was merciful. I gave 'em lots of pills, some decent booze, and they just went to sleep and never woke up. I came up here by myself after Tam and started the toy house. Always meant to move her up here, but didn't get around to it somehow. But I got me three more. Girls are always passing through this town alone, at the casinos, walking to the beach, hiking, at the rallies. One of 'em, Dee, she'd seen me at a rally . . .

"And now I have to put my toys away for good." Ralph sighed deeply. "No job. No toy bin. No nuthin'. Because of you."

"What did Terry say? About what you did to Tamara?"

"She said 'Good riddance.' " Ralph grunted, or maybe it was a laugh. "And she said I'd get away with it. A long time after, she told me she got away with it too. She killed someone with a pillow."

"Her baby," Nina said in a choked voice. The darkness and the stench were suffocating her. She gave up on her left hand and went to work on her right.

"Really?" Ralph said. "Terry was cruel. She was very cruel to me sometimes, but she had the coat, so I had to do what she said. Not sex stuff. She just didn't care about it. It was like her sex drive got turned into something else."

"Did you know Terry made a film about Tamara?" Try to keep him talking, because she didn't know what else to do. Bob was breathing, but he wasn't conscious.

"Not till I saw it in court. My dad told me there was a film, but I didn't know what was in it. All that fur. Tam's coat there, and the trail. Terry shouldn't have hinted about me. I couldn't believe she kept the video from that night with Tamara all these years. She told me once, she was gonna make a film about me, but I thought she meant Ralph the driver of Satan's Hoof, not Ralph the—" He stopped, as if unable to describe the other Ralph. "Nobody got it, so

I thought it would be okay. But then at the court recess today, I saw your doodle."

"What?"

"You know, the picture you drew. The rabbit and the cat with the long fur. I was watching you anyway. You were mean to my dad. And now he's suspicious. Now he keeps asking me questions. Why couldn't you just leave us alone? You stuck your nose in my private business. I never did nothing to you."

"I'm sorry. I'm sorry I caused you so much trouble. Did you . . . did you see what happened to Terry, Ralph?"

"No! I know it wasn't me like you made out, though! I was asleep, just like my dad said! I had took some heavy downers and I never heard a friggin' thing! How do ya like them apples!" His rasping chuckle filled the shed. "Only thing I did was sneak over and get the coat when the cops left the next day. It was layin' on the bed in the bedroom like always. She wouldn't have wanted me to have it. She always said I was a low-class boy and her coat was too friggin' good for me!" He laughed and moaned, and Bobby never moved, and Nina thought, we're going to die soon, and she felt like Terry must have when she saw the angel of death. . . .

42

A NEW NOTE HAD ENTERED RALPH'S VOICE. "YOU COULD WEAR IT again," he said, "with nothing under it this time. That's the best way. Like I say, we'll do it right, this time, go down in the toy bin so he wouldn't have to watch. I know you wouldn't want that. Before I do you and the kid. Looky here, up on the table? I got tequila, 'ludes, grass, even a little coke. It's more fun that way. If you wear the coat for me, I'll make sure you two go out real easy, relaxed, smiling even."

Bob groaned.

"Better not mention the plan to her," Ralphie was muttering to himself. She could hear him shifting around in the darkness. "Forget the toy bin. Bad shoulder. Time to go," he said.

Nina could hardly think, she was so scared, and her feet were burning with pain from the bindings, but she managed to gasp, "Ralph . . . we can talk about it . . . in a minute. But first, let me ask you one little question. Would you . . . like to be famous?"

"Now how'm I gonna do that? You ruined me for driving."

"I was just thinking," Nina said. "You could be famous now.

The Tahoe serial killer. I could represent you at the trial. You'd be as famous as O.J."

"I did kill four," Ralph said. "Over twelve years. But I don't want to be famous that way."

"Girls would want to know you. You know how many people proposed to Ted Bundy?"

"He fried though."

"We should talk about this," Nina said. "It won't hurt you to let me explain for a minute or two, would it? But I can't think, my hands are tied so tight." She nudged Bobby with her foot. She thought he stirred. Was he injured or had he passed out?

Paul had never driven to Tahoe that fast, or crossed so many double yellow lines passing slow cars. He squealed to a stop around the corner from Terry's place and approached the dusty drive of the Kettrick place cautiously, not knowing what to expect. He had his gun, taken from a locked case in the van. He moved quickly to the porch, and pounded on the front door.

Hysterical barking. After a minute or two a blinding floodlight came on, and Jerry Kettrick's voice came through the door, yelling, "Ralphie? Where's your damn key!"

"Where's Ralph, Mr. Kettrick?" Paul said through the door.

"What th'? Who's that?"

"Paul van Wagoner. Nina Reilly's investigator. Ralphie's in trouble."

"Go 'way. Come back tomorrow."

"Let me in, Mr. Kettrick."

"Get lost, or I blast you with my rifle."

"Okay," Paul said. "Give me ten minutes to get back to you with a couple of uniforms in tow. Or talk now. It's about Ralph." He let Kettrick think it over. Slowly and reluctantly, the door swung open, and Terry's black dog rushed out and ran around in circles, barking.

Jerry Kettrick slept in his briefs. His skinny legs poked out of a pair of slippers, and he held his old rifle on Paul. "Shut the door," he said. "What's this all about?"

"Ralph isn't here?" Paul said.

"Answer me."

"If he is, I'll go away and not bother you anymore," Paul said. "Let's check the bedroom."

"Not until you tell me what—"

"He's kidnapped Nina Reilly and her son," Paul said. "He's holding them somewhere."

"What? How do you know that?" The rifle shook a little.

"Has he ever done anything like this before?" Paul said, and his heart stopped beating, because Kettrick was blushing there in the dim, dirty hall; he could see it and it told him the answer. "He has," Paul said. "He's got mental problems. I know about them. Are you going to help me with this?"

Kettrick let the rifle fall. "Come on in," he said. "Let's go see if he's come in."

They walked together through a sea of newspapers and garbage, the dog following behind, to a small bedroom off the kitchen. Kettrick pushed the door open.

A mattress on the floor, heavy metal and monster truck posters, an old TV set. On the floor, automotive tools, cereal packages, dishes and milk cartons, clothes strewn everywhere. The air smelled sour.

Coat hangers hanging off hooks in the ceiling, a dozen at least, and hanging queerly from the coat hangers, bits and pieces of fur, raccoon tails mostly, some swatches from clothing. They hung low enough to walk through.

No sign of Ralph. "He won't eat nothing but cereal," Kettrick said as if in apology, ignoring the evidence of stark raving insanity hanging from the ceiling.

Paul turned to Kettrick, took him by the throat and pushed the rifle onto the floor, all at once.

"Where is he?" Paul said in a quiet voice.

"How—how do I know?"

Paul's grip tightened. "Tell me or I'll kill you."

"Then you'll"—Kettrick was choking, and Paul loosened his grip a little—"never find out."

"So you do know. Speak up, Jerry." Kettrick's eyes bugged out with terror. Paul raised his free hand. Something in his eyes must have made Kettrick decide enough was enough. He nodded. Paul dropped him, kicked the rifle away. Kettrick choked and gasped.

"Goddamn. You don't have to be so rough. I want to stop him, too, before he goes too far. My poor boy. He gets upset, he can't take it no more, a storm comes up in his brain and he has an attack. We gotta find him."

"Where is he?"

"He's got a place up in the mountains, somewhere around Fallen Leaf Lake. Some abandoned old building. He told me about it. He goes there to be alone. I don't know why. He's got no friends down here."

"What else did he say?" Paul's fury had built to the point that he had to smash something. He walked over to the TV, picked it up and threw it into the closet door. The door splintered with a satisfying crack.

"Hey! That was a twenty-inch with remote control!" Seeing the look in Paul's eye, Kettrick said, "Jus' let me think. I never paid much attention."

"Yeah. You think. In two minutes I'm going to make it so you can't think." Paul prowled around the room, knocking everything over, kicking at the comic books. He kneeled down and reached under the bed, pulled out some sex aids. Disgusted, he went to the bureau and threw open the drawers. They were empty, except for more swatches of fur.

"I do remember one time he said he was going up to the lookout," Kettrick said from behind him. "Then he gave me a funny look and told me to forget what he said."

"You got a good Tahoe map?"

"In the kitchen." They tore the map opening it up together. "The Angora Fire Lookout Station. On Angora Ridge," Paul said.

"It's the right area," Kettrick said. "Hey, wait, lemme get some clothes on. I'm coming too. Ralphie'll listen to his dad. Don't call the cops. He'll think I'm going to put him in the hospital again. He'd rather die, I swear. He'll do something bad, and he's very fast."

Paul hesitated.

"Please. He always listens to me. I'll get him to come out peaceably. He's my boy. He loves me."

Paul nodded and went out to the van. Kettrick jumped in a minute later with the dog and his rifle. They sped down Pioneer Trail toward the Angora Ridge road.

* * *

As Ralph talked to Nina and swigged from the bottle of tequila, his voice grew more strange, as if telling her his story told him for the first time how far he'd gone. Progressing beyond her initial terrified paralysis to teeth rattling, she could hardly keep the questions coming. She worked the thick knots in the bindings around her hands, fingers bleeding, nails broken as he talked, her knife so close by, but beyond her reach. Bob was definitely conscious now, but seemed to know enough to stay silent.

"And then I—I could get a ghostwriter, you know, pay somebody, and tell all about myself. Surefire bestseller, but wait a minute, I'd be stuck in jail, I couldn't get out, with a bunch of criminals and bad food—I heard about that. Worse than the hospital. They might even give me the needle, execute me, even though I'm fixable. I been sick a long time, makes it so hard to think, but first and foremost her and sonny boy seen too much, now I gotta do them—"

Nina said recklessly, "No problem. I'll get you off. And you could write anything you wanted."

"They won't let me drive no more. I could still drive for Bad Boy, I'll go over to Reno and talk to them boys tomorrow. . . ." He had stopped listening to Nina, seemed to have forgotten she was there.

"Except for them two," he said then in an ugly voice. "Them spyin' and pryin'. But the little guy ain't done nothin', ain't done nothin'! Sure he ain't, Ralphie! Nothing but knifed you. You forget that already?"

"Ralphie. Ralph!"

"Shut up," Ralph said. "Party's over. I'm done listenin' to you. You're history." He got up. A rush of fear incapacitated Nina's vocal cords. She struggled hard. Bob kept silent somehow, but she knew he sensed her fear.

"Think I got some bad gas," Ralph said, chuckling to himself. He opened the lock, went outside. A moment later they heard a sloshing sound, working around the shed.

"Mom," Bobby whispered, "what's going on?"

Nina didn't answer. She applied her frenzy to the knots, but it was hopeless.

She knew what that sloshing meant. She could even sniff out the fumes drifting through the fetid air.

Gasoline.

"He can't help it," Jerry Kettrick said, holding on to the oh-shit strap above his head as they careened around a corner. "I always told him how beautiful his mom was. She was twenty-three when she died, and Ralphie was two. While she was pregnant, some dude at Golden Gate Park gave her some pills and told her it was mescaline. Turned out to be some squirrelly mix of speed and PCP, and she almost lost the baby. We didn't know anything back then about the pills causing a problem. By the time Ralphie was born she was bouncing back and forth between uppers and downers. Ralphie, he bounced too. Then we lost him once when he just started to walk. He stayed overnight in an alley downtown and the cops found him in the morning with rat bites all over him. After that I didn't leave him alone with her. She was an addict by then. She just couldn't handle the whole scene."

"How long did you think you could cover up for him?" Paul said, hitting a straightaway and giving it the gas.

"I swear to God, I didn't know how bad it was. He told me once, a couple of years ago, he took girls up to the lookout. He didn't tell me no more. It was hard to believe a girl would go with him on her own, but I didn't ask about it. What the hell could I do? I made him go to the hospital once in a while, 'cause he was in bad shape. The medicine helped, when he took it. I kept after him, I tried to take care of him. Take a left. Sharp left. Yeah. Next right."

"What did he say about Nina Reilly?" Paul said.

"He heard her raggin' on me in court day before yesterday. He stopped eating, stayed up all night, and then went up to Reno to run a race. Something happened. They fired him, and he came back mumbling about the lawyer lady. Monster trucks was just about the only thing he loved. He locked himself in his room today. I could hear him carryin' on in there. He was really upset. I was thinking I'd have to take him back to the hospital."

Paul assumed he was talking about Nina. He didn't interrupt.

"She made it seem like Ralphie killed Terry—he wouldn't take kindly to that. Terry was like his guru, I'm not kidding. She had an evil hold on that boy. She treated him like a dog, but he didn't mind. Ralphie thought Kurt Scott did it, and the lawyer lady was accusing him just to get her client off. A reporter tried to talk to him. He hates attention like that."

"Of course he does!" Paul shouted, losing his temper as they climbed the hill toward the ridge, "He was lying to you! He did kill her!"

"Gah-damn! Ain't you listening! I told you and that Miss Reilly, he was sound asleep! I was there! As God is my witness! I ain't goin' any farther. You can find the goddamn lookout yourself." Kettrick pulled the door handle and the door on the van swung open in the dark, catching against some bushes.

Paul wanted to let him jump out, but he still needed him. He took a firm hold on Kettrick's arm and said, "Take it easy. You want to help him, stick with me."

Kettrick allowed himself to be drawn back in, muttering, "I oughtta know . . . I was there. . . ." Gradually he calmed down and resumed giving directions, at the same time resuming the tale of Ralph's babyhood. "Anyhow, his mom, Meredith her name was, got out of bed one night and went outside onto Haight Street. She was barefoot, wearing her nightgown, a shawl, so forth. All the girls wore those clothes anyway back then. She didn't bring any money, but somebody was tryin' to be nice and gave her some tabs of windowpane. Acid. And a speed chaser."

"Where's the turnoff? Goddammit, I can't see it!"

"About two hundred feet farther. There you go. The dirt road there. Her poor little heart gave out. Ralphie, he lost his mother. How I loved that little girl. I wrote a song about her. Made it into the top 100 during May 1972. I buried her in the mink coat I bought her on my last tour with the Dead, and—"

They turned onto Angora Ridge Road. Paul slammed on the brakes as he passed Nina's Bronco, shadowy off the side of the road. He pulled over in front, and the two men jumped out, Paul praying she was sitting safely in there, waiting.

No such luck. She must have tried to sneak up on Ralph. The Bronco was empty.

"Come on," Paul said, climbing back in and starting up again.

"I came back here to take care of him. I love him," Kettrick said next to him. "Every parent loves his kid, you know? You think I don't know it's my fault?"

Ahead, Paul saw a light.

Ralph Kettrick held a flaming torch above his head, his grotesquely twisted features lit from above, a horror show in real life. When he saw the van, Kettrick tossed the flaming torch toward a small shed next to the fire-spotting station.

Jerry Kettrick jumped out of the van, stomping at the fire. Paul joined him, tossing dirt on the flames.

Somehow they managed to stop the fire before the gas ignited. Ralph had run back inside, still holding the can.

Silence. The air itself crackled with ghastly possibilities.

In his years as a homicide detective, Paul had never had to deal with death personally. The bodies were already there, anonymous, cases to close, evidence. He had never known a victim. Sometimes there had been danger, but it was only to himself, and he could handle that.

Never in that time had he felt the gut-wrenching fear he felt now.

He had no idea what to do. Kettrick was in there with Nina and Bobby, and he could shoot them or set them all on fire any second.

Jerry Kettrick put his hand on his arm, said in a low voice, "Keep your mouth shut." Then he called over to the shed, "Ralphie! Hey, Ralphie! I come to take you home!"

"Dad?" Ralph Kettrick's voice said.

Another voice yelled, "Help! He's going to kill us!"

"Dad? You hear that?"

"No, boy, I didn't hear anything, just some crickets down the hill. It's late. I'm going to take you back home now."

"I have to finish my game."

"Come on out, boy, or I'll have to take you back to the hospital in the morning."

"You're gonna do that anyway, Dad, quit lyin' to me."

"Ralphie. I love you, boy. Let me help you with this trouble."

"Dad? I ain't never going to be famous now. I've been killing girls. Did you hear what I said, Dad?"

"I couldn't hear that, Ralphie. The breeze is out. But I bet you're hungry. Come on home with me."

Silence.

In the pitch blackness of the shed, Ralph said, "This is it." Nina sensed the Colt moving through the air as he listened for their breathing. They lay sightless in the corner of the dark room. Suddenly a small flare of light turned the dark into dimness. She realized Ralph had dug a cigarette lighter out of his pocket so he could see to shoot. . . .

Her pocket! She twisted and plunged both her hands, still bound together, into her pocket. And found nothing but Bobby's squeaky seal. Ralph clicked the lighter several times, but it kept going out.

Something about rats. They fought the dogs and killed the—

"Squeee-ak!"

Ralph twitched. She heard the lighter clatter to the floor, and watched fearfully for a spark that didn't come. "Omigod, Ralph! There's a rat in here!" Nina cried. "Right behind you!"

"Squeak! Squeak!"

"Oh no, no . . ."

"A bunch of them, don't you hear them? Rats! Everywhere! Huge!"

"Squeak!"

"Ugh!" Ralph wheeled around and shot the wall behind him.

"Red eyes! Up in the ceiling!" Nina wailed. "They're everywhere!"

Ralph shot the ceiling, tottering back as if he expected a rat body to land on him.

"Squee-eeek!" Screaming, Ralph ran outside.

To where Paul waited, gun drawn. "Put it down!" Paul yelled.

"Please," Jerry Kettrick said. "Please, boy. Put it down. . . ."

Ralph turned toward the shed, raising the gun again to shoot into it, and Paul aimed, released the safety . . .

But it was Jerry Kettrick who shot Ralph, the loud, stinging report echoing down the hills on both sides. Ralph looked down at his chest, then at his father, fell to his knees, and said, "Dad, you shot me," in a bewildered, childish voice.

He fell heavily to the ground and lay still.

Jerry Kettrick dropped his rifle. "It's my fault, boy," he said, "that I didn't kill her a long time ago."

He rushed to his son and Paul rushed inside.

She was babbling about rabbits and Krafft-Ebing and rats, tied up like a human sacrifice, huddling with Bobby in the corner of the stinking shed, but they were both alive.

43

AT COLLIER'S REQUEST, MILNE POSTPONED THE TRIAL FOR A WEEK. Bob was resting at home. The doctor had insisted that he stay in bed. He had a black eye and bruises on his wrists and ankles, but no other physical trauma.

He talked about Ralph a lot. The worst and yet somehow the best part of it had been the moment when he knifed him there on the hillside, defending his mother against her attacker. He called Harlan in Monterey and Nina heard him describing how he had saved her, pride bursting in his voice. He boasted about it to Troy, who sat by his bed and wanted to hear the story over and over. It seemed to compensate for the terror of the experience. He had been brave, had fought back.

At the same time, Nina knew how relieved he was that he hadn't killed Ralph. The doctor couldn't tell her whether Bob had fallen asleep or fainted during the last hour in the shed. "Babies and children often just switch off when they are very frightened for a long period of time," he said. "I had a baby in the hospital this morning who choked on a pebble. His mother called 911. By the time the medics arrived she'd knocked it out of him. He fell into a deep sleep in the ambulance and we were afraid of brain damage, but the baby had just used up all his adrenaline and fallen asleep. Bob went to sleep, I think."

Andrea had recommended a child therapist. Nina had decided to wait and see.

On Sunday, two days after Ralph's death, Paul called her at home. "I know this is the last thing you want to be thinking about now. But you'll be back in court on Friday and I can't stop thinking about it. Ralph didn't know about the film, but his dad did," Paul said. "When we interviewed Jerry, he said so."

"Mmm-hmm." Paul was right about one thing. She'd spent two days talking to many people and staying close to Bob. She didn't want to talk anymore.

"Listen to this. Jerry Kettrick hears the shot, sees Kurt run out. Doesn't call the cops. He walks over and blows Terry away."

"What brings all this on?"

"I can't stop thinking about what he said right after he shot Ralph. He said, "It's my fault. I should have killed her a long time ago."

"That's not a confession. Besides, how—"

Then she thought, Jerry Kettrick loved his son. He hated Terry. What if . . .

What if Jerry walked over after Matt shot Terry and ran out the back, and what if she wasn't dead, she was wounded and she was making the tape when Jerry came in . . .

"A pfennig for your thoughts," Paul was saying. She was remembering Terry in the death video, mouthing the words Angel of Death, looking up as though—as though someone else had just come in! And then the video went black. . . .

But . . .

But Terry hadn't reached up to turn it off after Matt left. The video would have shown her reaching up.

Someone else turned it off.

But how do you kill someone without leaving a mark? All that blood, Terry lying on the floor, the bloody pillow under her head . . .

"Oh, Paul," Nina said.

You put the pillow over Terry's face, just like she had done to her own daughter. . . .

Justice with a capital *J*. "It's possible," she said. "I wonder if Jerry did kill her. But he saved me and Bob. He helped you find us, even though it would be the end for Ralph. And he—he shot Ralph."

"No way to prove it," Paul said. "Kurt's going to be all right. No jury would convict him now, with Ralph right next door with no alibi and his dad the eyewitness."

"Why don't we ask him, Paul?"

"I like that. Simple and direct. I'm on my way out of town. I'll stop by."

When no one answered Paul's knock at the Kettrick place, he tried the door, which was unlocked, and went inside. On the living room floor, empty bottles, pills, and a plastic bag with a couple of pills remaining inside ringed the recliner. So Kettrick had gone on a bender. He had loved his son, in spite of everything, the lunacy, the murders, that room. . . . He called out, but the cabin was silent and cool, the windows blanketed against the summer sun outside.

Down the hall, he could see the door to Ralph's room, closed. He went the other way, and found a bed, neatly made with a light cotton spread, unwrinkled, untouched. The bathroom door stood agape, and the peeling vinyl floor was bare. He walked down the hall, back toward Ralph's room, calling Jerry, but getting no reply. At the closed door he stopped to think. A draft blew up from under the door, chilling his brow, which he realized was sweating. Ralph—or Jerry—must have left a window open in there. One part of him put his hand on the knob. Another part held back. Here he stood at the gate to hell and the abyss, a madman's city of woe. All hope abandon . . .

He opened the door. He stepped inside.

Late that night, Paul called Nina again. Sounding subdued and unusually shaken, he simply said that Jerry Kettrick had hanged himself in his son's room, leaving a short note in which he confessed to killing Terry London.

He didn't describe the scene in detail. He didn't have to. He had told her about Ralph's room before. She could imagine it.

"But why?" she said.

"Ralphie had told him she was going to make a movie about him. Jerry thought he knew what about. He thought she'd corrupted him and now was going to profit from exposing him. Ralph had told him about Tamara."

Nina was quiet, thinking about how Matt would feel when he heard about it. Paul, all of them, would think Jerry had fired the second shot.

"Terry spread all that death," Nina said finally. "So many who came into contact with her didn't survive."

"You, for instance. You went to hell and back. How are you feeling?"

"Relieved."

"I'll be there for the court appearance," Paul said. "Take care."

"Paul."

"Yeah?"

"Thank you again for everything."

"I was doing it for you."

On Friday morning, Milne entered a directed verdict of acquittal and dismissed the jury.

Pandemonium. Amid the noise, Kurt hugged Nina, holding her for a long time, while Paul stood impatiently by. When he had finished, Paul shook his hand. Well-wishers came up, patting her on the back, full of praise and compliments. Collier managed to work his way through the throng. "Here you've gone and done it again," he said, telling her he'd call her with his congratulations after he had fully licked his wounds and disappearing into the mob.

They led Kurt back to the jail to be processed out. She said nothing to him, nor he to her, about what would happen next.

Outside in the corridor, flashbulbs popped, questions were lobbed, and people jostled to shake her hand. Smiling, she said only that she was pleased that justice had been done. The jurors waited for her, and she went over to talk to them and thank them. Mrs. Bourgogne told her she liked her style, but she should keep her hair out of her face and wear longer skirts. Then Paul helped clear a path so they could get out to the parking lot.

44

Bob took a shower the following morning, Saturday, without any reminders. He wore his favorite baggy T-shirt and shorts and the new black hat that Nina had given him. His new hat looked just like the old hat that sat anonymously in a police locker, with "No Fear" embroidered in white just above the brim.

At noon exactly, the doorbell rang. Matt was making punch in the kitchen, and Andrea had run out for some more charcoal for the grill.

Looking through the spyhole in the door, Nina saw Kurt, standing with a huge bouquet of flowers in one hand and balloons in the other.

"Bob," she called softly. He came running and stretched up on his toes to peer through the spyhole with a kind of strained anticipation.

"What do you think?" She put her arm around him, whispering, "Ready?" Then she opened the door.

Twelve years, Nina thought, as if she'd never seen Kurt in jail, never gone through the trial—twelve years, and he's come back.

Kurt handed her the flowers and Bob the balloons. He cleared his throat and said, "Hi," and Bob said, "Hi," to him.

"You must be Bob," said Kurt.

"And you must be . . ." words failed Bob. Nina gave him a little nudge.

"I'm your dad."

Bob put out a hand to shake, which Kurt solemnly took. They shook hands for a long time, looking at each other. And then they laughed.

Then they rushed together, knocking Bob's hat to the ground. Bob's arms reached around his father, one hand still clutching the balloons.

After a long time, they both turned to her.

Two pairs of identical green eyes smiled at her.

After dinner, Kurt and Bob went for a walk. They hadn't touched the hot dogs Matt had grilled. Nina watched them go, sitting on the grass of the front lawn with her arms around her legs.

"It's unbelievable. They look so alike," Matt said. "It's like seeing Bob grown up. Say, Nina . . ." he began.

"What?"

"Is it true what they said about Jerry Kettrick? I mean, you wouldn't rig something like that just to save me. Would you?"

"He killed her, Matt. She was lying there making this video. She didn't resist. I think she wanted to die, Matt. It was over with her and Kurt. Her hatred for him consumed her life, and she used her dying moments to condemn him."

"I wish to God it never happened. But I can live with this," Matt said. "If you can."

Nina said, "I think of what she might have done if you hadn't been there. . . ."

"Let's forget it happened. That's my plan."

She didn't believe a word of it, but she appreciated the forceful words from her brother. He didn't want her to worry about him, so she would try to respect that. He would deal with what he had done in his own way, in his own time. "Have some more wine," Matt said. "It's good for your heart—I heard it on a talk show.

"Oh," he added, "and I have a present for you."

"What might that be?"

"You're going to fly like a hawk tomorrow night, lady. The breeze calms at five or so. The lake goes flat. I'm taking you for a ride."

High in the sky, looking down at the mountains and the blue water . . . "I could handle that," Nina said.

Andrea came out in white shorts and a straw hat, carrying a crystalline glass of white wine.

"So who's it going to be?" she said. "Paul? Or Kurt?"

When Kurt and Bob came back, Kurt said, "Can I borrow your mother for a minute?"

"Okay, but don't forget. I have to show you my computer later."

"I won't forget."

Nina and Kurt went across the street to sit on a stone wall over a brook, dangling their bare feet in the water. Kurt, so handsome beside her, so different from the desperate man behind bars, made her feel shy. He seemed thoroughly relaxed. His life had changed completely. He had a son, and he was freer than he'd ever been since she first met him. Gradually, in fits and starts, wetting their toes in the sunshine, they began to talk, just chatting, not trying to cover everything, just touching bases. A tacit understanding between them said, there will be time now for everything.

"I never will get over losing Lianna," he said after they had talked a long while. "But finding Bob makes life worth living again."

"I'm glad you came back."

"In spite of everything? Terry? The trial? Matt?"

"In spite of everything. You were always part of our lives, or rather, your absence was. Oh, it's hard to explain. But Bobby needed you, and now he has you. I know how much that's going to mean."

"And you? Do you need me, Nina?"

Nina took her time answering. "This morning I had a happy fantasy of the three of us together, a family at last. And—God, this is hard to say—I love that fantasy. It's very satisfying. But real life isn't that tidy—do you know what I mean?" She felt deep joy mingled with deep sadness, as if they were survivors of a small war, picking over the rubble of their home, rejoicing at finding an old letter, crying in the next moment over a broken pot. "I don't know where we go from here."

Kurt took her hand. "I know. Germany is my home now. I have to go back, at least for a while—to work out the music, and my work, and Bob and you. Let me be your good friend for now."

"I expect you'll be a big part of our lives from now on. I expect now that you know about Bobby, we won't be able to get rid of you." She smiled, trying to keep things light. "That's good. That's what I need."

"We've lost a lot of time. I intend to make it all up to you."

"Now, that sounds promising."

They got up to go back to the house. "Once, you would have followed me anywhere," he said, a little sorrowfully. "My passionate Nina. We have changed so much."

"I don't agree," she said.

"You're right. Some things never change," he said, smiling.

At the office on Monday morning, Paul's phone message sat at the top of the pile.

"How's the weather in Carmel?" she said when she had him on the line.

"Foggy. The weather gets hot, and the fog moves in off the ocean. Foggy, misty, and cool," he said, sounding far away. "Good beach bonfire weather."

"It's ninety in the shade here. The lake's swimmable. I've been going in every evening, when the water is warmest."

"So. How are and Bob doing? How was Kurt's visit?"

"Fine."

"Fine as in you're packing your bags and moving to Wiesbaden?"

"Fine as in Bob's in heaven."

"So I suppose you and Kurt had a chance to talk? What's he going to do?"

"I think he realizes his home is in Germany now," said Nina.

"What about your home?"

"Bob's already talking about spending Christmas with Kurt. It's a whole new world for him. As for me, I'm going to be moving from Matt's myself."

"Oh?" he said, his voice tight.

"I've made some decisions."

"What kind of decisions?"

"So will you come up this weekend and do some cabin hunting with me?" She could almost see Paul's ears pricking up. She grinned into the phone.

"You're looking for a place in Tahoe?"

"Yep. For Bobby and me. And we're going to get a dog. And if you want, you can come see us—a lot."

"I can?"

"As for that marriage proposal of yours . . ."

"Waiting," said Paul. "I'll just be over here waiting."

"You don't really want to marry me. You don't want to be a stepfather. You don't want a wife who's gone all the time. You know it, but you're too much of a gentleman to say it."

For once, Paul didn't have a snappy comeback. "All right," he said. "I've always married the ones I loved before. I just don't know any other way to be. Have you got a suggestion?"

"Why don't we just stay the way we are?"

"You mean, coworkers and friends? What about romance?"

"I'm sure we could fit some of that in too."

"I'm not sure about this," Paul said. "But I'm willing to discuss it further in the spa at Caesars Friday night."

"Can't wait to feel those bubbles."

"There's something new about you. I can't quite put my finger on it. You're more confident, confident from deep down, if you know what I mean."

"There's not much left to be afraid of."

"Okay. Let's give close friends a try. Which doesn't mean I don't love you," Paul said.

"See you Friday?"

"Next time, boss," Paul said. He hung up.

Sandy came on the line. "Excellent footwork," she said.

"Dammit, Sandy, quit listening in on my business," Nina said.

"I can't help it," Sandy said. "Your new risk-free life nets me nothing but these boring wills to work on. Wish called me. He's raring to go on the next exciting case—"

"There will be no more exciting cases," Nina said. She began sorting her phone messages. Sandy buzzed again.

"He's here," she said. "He" was Jeffrey Riesner, whose name Sandy had trouble saying. The lawyer already loomed in the doorway to the inner office. Without a word he went to Nina's desk and dropped a check on it.

"Twenty-two thousand," he said. "Scott's retainer less expenses." Behind him, Sandy was clapping her hands soundlessly.

"Well," Nina said. "What made you decide to pay up?"

"I got a call from Judge Milne at my house yesterday. He suggested that I stop by." Sandy was vigorously mimicking Milne kicking Riesner in the rear end.

"I see," Nina said.

"It was merely an oversight."

"Of course."

"You never should have taken the case in that underhanded fashion. If you had cooperated with me, we could have worked it out. What's so funny?" Sandy had grabbed her nose and—her eyes bulging in mock terror—pulled her fingers back as though her nose was growing, longer and longer. . . .

"Funny?" Nina said, her right eyebrow raised.

"Well, aren't you going to thank me?"

"Thank you, Mr. Riesner," Nina said gravely. "Sandy, will you see Mr. Riesner out? Oh, and Mr. Riesner . . ."

"What?"

"Better luck next time." The door shut behind them, and she held the check up to make sure Riesner had actually signed it.

The outer door slammed. From the outer office Nina heard a strange, dry sound, like bark being stripped off trees.

Sandy was laughing.

She looked out her window. Mount Tallac loomed above the lake. "Get Collier Hallowell on the line for me," Nina said, when the sounds finally died out.

When Collier came on, Nina said, "Want to go on an adventure?"

"Any man who said yes to an adventure with you without knowing what you had planned would have to be dumber than poor Ralph Kettrick."

"Just a little hike," she said. "I was thinking about this weekend."

"A hike?"

"Let's live a little. Everyone else does. I've never made it to the top of Tallac. Let's get up there late, and look at the stars from up close."

When he didn't say anything immediately, she added, "Or we could get started really early, if you have other plans."

"The Perseid meteor shower is this weekend, Nina," Collier said.

"It is? Oh, Collier, I'm sorry . . . your wife . . . I forgot . . . Forget I said anything. . . ."

"It's an all-night show," he said mildly. "Don't forget your sleeping bag."